# Love in the
# Headlines

# Love in the Headlines

## PENNY ZELLER

Maplebrook

# ALSO BY PENNY ZELLER

## Maplebrook Publishing

**Standalone Books**
Love in Disguise
Love in the Headlines
Freedom's Flight

**Wyoming Sunrise**
Love's New Beginnings
Forgotten Memories
Dreams of the Heart
When Love Comes
Love's Promise

**Love Letters from Ellis Creek**
Love from Afar
Love Unforeseen
Love Most Certain

**Chokecherry Heights**
Henry and Evaline (Prequel)
Love Under Construction

**Horizon Series**
Over the Horizon

## Whitaker House Publishing

**Montana Skies**
McKenzie
Kaydie
Hailee

## Barbour Publishing

Love from Afar
*(The Secret Admirer*
*Romance Collection)*

Freedom's Flight
*(The Underground Railroad*
*Brides Collection)*

## Beacon Hill Press
(Nonfiction)

77 Ways Your Family Can
Make a Difference

Dedicated to my favorite niece, Ally,
and her dog, Sulley Jaxx, the inspiration
behind Sullivan Theodore IV's character.

*This is the day that the Lord has made;*
*let us rejoice and be glad in it.*

- Psalm 118:24

# Chapter One

IT HAD BEEN AN exhausting day, and Carleigh Adams figured a hot bubble bath followed by snuggling up with a good book and a cup of tea was the perfect agenda for a Tuesday evening. The article she penned from last night's long-winded and interminable city council meeting had taken its toll.

She unlocked the front door of her house, stepped inside, and slipped off her shoes.

Finally. Time for some rest and relaxation.

An over-exuberant Sullivan Theodore IV bounded toward her, his white fur blowing away from his face with the breeze he caused with his rapid rate of speed. He slid on the wood floor, reminding Carleigh of a race car driver struggling to maintain control on a slick track.

She set her purse on the counter and gave Sullivan Theodore a pat. "Hey there, boy."

Sullivan Theodore lasted about three seconds before impatiently wiggling away from her. He ran toward the door, his little yips loud in the otherwise quiet house.

"All right," she said, traipsing toward the back door to allow him outside. But Sullivan Theodore would have none of it. He dodged past her in a quick one-eighty degree turn and sprinted as fast as his short legs could carry him back toward the front door. He barked, his fluffy tail wagging so fast it rivaled a high-powered fan. "You know I am not going to let you out front, Sullivan Theodore."

He ceased barking for a split second and cocked his head first to one side, then the other, as if to say, "And why not?"

"Come on, let's go out the back door." At least in the backyard, Sullivan Theodore was corralled by a fence.

Instead of obeying, the dog edged closer to the front door, resuming his series of yips.

Carleigh sighed. What harm could it do to allow him into the front yard to do his business just this once?

"All right, all right. But you have to stay by the porch."

Sullivan Theodore's suspicious lack of eye contact concerned her, but giving her pooch the benefit of the doubt, Carleigh opened the front door and stepped outside. She closed her eyes for a second, longing to feel any warmth from the soon-to-be-setting sun. It was a welcome change from that morning's snow, which still lined parts of the lawn and sidewalk. Forget April showers bringing May flowers. More like early May snow showers bringing June flowers.

She opened her eyes just in time to see Sullivan Theodore escaping down the sidewalk at an excessive rate of speed, determined to catch a squirrel that was equally determined not to get caught.

"Sullivan Theodore IV, come back here!"

The shih tzu paid her no mind and continued bounding away from her house.

A car full of teenagers whizzed by and Carleigh prayed they wouldn't run over her pet. Eyeing her flip flops, she slipped them on over her socks and took off down the sidewalk, trying to keep her pet in sight. In doing so, she nearly slid on a random clump of snow. *The things I do for you, Sullivan Theodore.*

Pausing to adjust her feet more securely into her turquoise flip flops, Carleigh marveled that she still had the "gift" of wearing such shoes with thick socks. Perfected in childhood, she hadn't realized just how handy her "talent" would be later in life.

Heart racing, Carleigh continued down the sidewalk as fast as she could, but lost sight of Sullivan Theodore a few seconds later. Stopping less than a block from her house, she looked first to the left, then to the right and called his name at least a gazillion more times. *Where is he?*

He couldn't just disappear. Carleigh strained her eyes in hopes of seeing where Sullivan Theodore may have ventured to. Did he make a turn she hadn't noticed? Was he hiding in someone's backyard? Was he in plain sight?

"Excuse me." Her wheezing breath drew the attention of a couple walking nearby. "Have you seen a Maltese shih tzu? He's white with a navy collar."

"Sorry, we haven't," answered the woman.

Desperation consumed Carleigh. What would she do if something befell her precious pet?

If only Sullivan Theodore was a Siberian husky or Saint Bernard. Such an enormous dog would be harder to lose than one weighing a mere seven pounds.

Panting for breath, she trudged up one side of the street, turned around, then repeated her route. He couldn't have gotten far. But then again, according to the people who gave her Sullivan Theodore, he descended from a long line of runners. If that was the case, he could be to the next town by now.

She offered her sixteenth prayer heavenward and did her best not to lose hope. The row of quaint older craftsman-style homes with picket fences and manicured lawns offered no sign of her dog. At least with the tag on his collar, someone would turn him in and she could retrieve him from the pound.

As Carleigh trudged home, she saw something causing her to take a double, then a triple, glance. She jolted. A familiar dog in the window of a house about a block from her own stared at her. Could it be?

*Sullivan Theodore IV, so help me if that is you...*

A white pooch very closely resembling her own naughty pet peered at her through the window of an unknown tan house. Perched on the back of a couch, his gaze seemed to mock her.

But how could Sullivan Theodore make his way inside another home? And that fast?

Perhaps it was a dog that only looked like her dog. But the white fur, suspicious expression, and navy collar...

Better to be safe than sorry, so just in case, Carleigh trotted toward the porch of the home. She'd just ring the doorbell and ask about the dog. Simple as that.

Either she would be successful in locating Sullivan Theodore or it would give someone a reason to call the police and report her as a suspicious person. She

4

adjusted her striped socks once more in her flip flops and rang the bell. As she did so, Carleigh noticed a doggy door. That could have easily been the way Sullivan Theodore—if indeed it was Sullivan Theodore—entered the stranger's home.

She rang the doorbell again and waited. A booming bark of what sounded like a much-larger dog sounded from the backyard.

Carleigh backed up off the porch and meandered her way around a few patches of snow. She faced the front window and peered directly at Sullivan Theodore.

Yes, it was him.

She was ninety-nine, point nine-nine percent sure of it.

"Sullivan Theodore IV, you come out here this instant."

The dog looked at her, an ornery gleam in his brown eyes. "Who, me?" his expression seemed to say.

"I mean it, Sullivan Theodore IV. You are in a lot of trouble."

He merely looked in the other direction, as if she wasn't standing in the front yard of a stranger's house waving her arms like a lunatic.

Carleigh stepped forward and tapped on the window. What if the person really was home? Or a neighbor called the police? Imagine those headlines.

And tomorrow was her day to cover the police blotter.

Her boss wouldn't take it lightly that she was an active participant in the local crimes listing.

Finally, a light-bulb moment entered her mind. Carleigh strolled back over to the porch and up the three steps. Crouching onto her hands and knees, she shoved aside the doggy door covering. "Sullivan Theodore, come here, boy."

Maybe some gentle coaxing would work better than the tough love tactic.

She could hope, anyway.

"Come on, Sullivan Theodore." Carleigh made some kissy noises like she did at home when she called him to dinner.

Feeling pain in her kneecaps, she leaned back on her heels and took a deep breath. This was not going well.

Her mind went into its usual overthinking mode. Was this really Sullivan Theodore? Or was it an imposter and her dog was running free along the streets of some town, far, far from home?

She was so not cut out for this parenting gig.

All right. She'd try one last time, and then wait patiently on the porch until the owner came home. But what if the owner was on a cruise, only to return in two weeks?

Ugh. What a pickle.

Carleigh balanced again on all fours, this time poking her head as far as she could inside the doggy door. "Sullivan Theodore, you come here this instant!"

No response from her dog, but the barking of the dog presumably in the backyard increased.

If she didn't get more authoritarian in her parenting approach, Carleigh feared Sullivan Theodore would be unmanageable and rebellious as a teen. "Right now, Sullivan Theodore IV!"

At some conscious level, she supposed she heard a nearby vehicle. If anyone confronted her, surely they would understand her plight after she explained about Sullivan Theodore's shenanigans.

A car door slammed and she thought she heard footsteps close by.

But given the gravity of the matter, Carleigh chose to ignore them. She called to Sullivan Theodore again, made more kissy noises, and promised him unlimited doggy treats.

All a big mistake.

"Can I help you?" a male voice asked.

Carleigh jumped, causing her head to hit the top of the doggy door. Reaching up to soothe her now-pounding head, she slowly turned on all fours to the direction of the voice. Wincing at the pain, a thought struck her that it couldn't compare to the trauma she experienced at seeing the owner of the voice.

*Oh, no.*

"Umm, hello, Trey."

"I thought that looked like you. What are you doing here?"

"Here?"

Trey stuck in hands in his pockets and looked down at her. Such a high-and-mighty arrogant man. As if he was the neighborhood watch patrol. What was he doing in her neighborhood anyway?

Hopefully not covering a story.

Carleigh gulped. She'd not even entertain that idea, although her imagination began to weave together an article that he was possibly covering at this very house about an intruder. The intruder being her.

Had the neighbors called the police after all?

Finally, getting some gumption, Carleigh grasped the porch railing and pulled herself up on shaky legs. Her left leg foot had fallen asleep, and she shook it, causing the flip flop to fling into the air and past Trey into the yard. His gaze followed it.

"Well, Trey, I could ask you the same thing. What are *you* doing here?"

"What?"

"You asked me what I'm doing here, and I'm asking you what you're doing here. Covering a story?"

"Hardly."

"Then, what?" Carleigh imagined Sullivan Theodore still perched on the back of the couch watching the entire scene.

There would be no more doggy treats for him until he was twenty-two.

"This is my house."

The air left her lungs. "Your..."

"Yes, Carleigh, *my* house. You're in *my* front yard on *my* porch. As a matter of fact, when I drove up, you were perched here on all fours, talking to yourself, and trying to break into my house through the doggy door. Are you feeling okay?"

The question wasn't so much filled with concern as sarcasm. Typical Trey. "For the record, I had no idea this was *your* house or porch."

"Why are you here?"

"Because my dog is in your house."

Trey squinted at her. Did her statement sound as ludicrous to him as it did to her the second she uttered it? "Your dog is in my house? Why?"

8

"He's perched on the back of your couch, watching this all unfold."

Trey glanced in the direction of the couch through the window. Carleigh stood on one leg to give her un-flip-flopped foot a reprieve from the cold cement porch.

She probably looked like a flamingo or something. Just grand.

"Let me get this straight," said Trey, holding up a finger. "Your dog is sitting on the back of my couch, watching us through the window."

"Yes."

Trey peered in the direction of the window, which was to her back. "And are you sure about this?"

"Yes."

One hundred percent sure?"

"Look, Trey, I'm sure. Are you trying to kidnap my dog or something?"

"Kidnap? No. But he *and* you are trespassing."

Carleigh sucked in a breath. He spoke it like she was some sort of common criminal. If it wasn't so awful, she'd write it in her notebook to save for a scene in her novel.

"You need to go home, Carleigh. There's no dog on my couch peering at us through the window."

"Oh, yes there is. Can you please just get him for me and I'll be on my way."

"Your imaginary friend isn't here."

"Imaginary friend?" Carleigh emitted a shocked inhalation of breath. A perusal in the direction of the window indicated Sullivan Theodore was nowhere to be seen. Gone. Poof. Vanished. "Where did he go?"

Trey shrugged. "No idea. A better question would be whether he was ever really here."

"Oh, he was here all right. He took off down the street after a squirrel. Please. Can I just see if he's inside? I promise I'll grab him and go home and be out of your life."

"Until tomorrow when I see you at work."

That was true. But why add that depressing note?

Trey moved past her and unlocked his door. She followed him inside, feeling odd in doing so. "Sullivan Theodore IV," she called.

"Sullivan Theodore IV? Who names their dog that?"

"It's after my favorite author, Sullivan Theodore."

Trey tossed her a look that intimated that if he didn't think she was crazy before, this confirmed it. "Feel free to look around." He tossed his keys on the counter and walked toward a glass door on the other side of the room. Unlocking it, he opened it and a large German shepherd bounded through.

Again, she called Sullivan Theodore's name. Finally, he came springing around the corner from the hallway. She scooped him up. "You are in such trouble."

The German shepherd wandered over to see about the fuss. Sullivan Theodore waved his tail and tried to escape Carleigh's grasp. "Oh, no you don't. I am not letting you down again until we are at home."

She took a moment to observe the appearance of Trey's house. Typical bachelor pad, but cleaner than she expected given the way he kept his desk at work. When she looked up, she caught his gaze. "I'll be going now."

"Guess you were right about your dog. But you need to do a better job of keeping him out of people's houses. There is a leash law here, you know."

"Perhaps you need to get rid of the doggy door. It's not like your German shepherd can fit through it."

"True. Jaxx can't use it anymore."

"Jaxx? Who names a dog that?" Not such an uncommon name, but after what Trey said about *her* choice of dog names...

"Ever heard of the famous hockey player, Jaxx Morgansen? He's named after him."

"Oh." Figured. Trey was a huge hockey fan. "Well, it's been nice visiting, but I better go."

Slipping out the door, she retrieved her flip-flop from the yard before heading home. How had she not known Trey lived in her neighborhood?

What a dismal discovery.

But she would relent from thinking at this moment because thinking would only add to the painful throbbing in her cranium due to the headache she received when she bonked her head on the doggy door. She probably had a concussion, or at the very least, a lump the size of an Easter egg.

Three things were certain: Sullivan Theodore would never again be allowed in the front yard, her adversary lived a mere block away, and Trey Montgomery would never let her live this down.

Perhaps she could call in sick tomorrow.

"You're such an easy child compared to that brat," Trey told Jaxx.

Jaxx bobbed his head, as if he understood he was nowhere as bratty as the oversized fluffy rat-dog that had illegally broken into his home.

Trey opened the cupboard where he stored the container of Jaxx's kibble. Unfortunately, he had to see Carleigh tomorrow at work, as he did every day. He dreaded it. Maybe he would call in sick. Today's episode had been totally embarrassing. To come home, park in his own driveway, and see a woman on her hands and knees peering into the doggy door of his house had been nothing short of what a corny chick-flick movie was made of.

Only this had been reality, and the woman in the doggy door was none other than his own coworker.

He shrugged. They'd never gotten along. Their relationship, such as it was, consisted of always being in competition for the best story at *The Oakville Daily*. "Sure, she's cute and all, but..." Jaxx wagged his tail and expectantly awaited his kibble. "And don't you tell anyone I said that because I will deny it one-hundred percent."

Instead of making a devout promise, Jaxx leaned back on his hind legs and raised his forepaws, as if to beg for his food.

"Oh, yeah. Sorry, buddy. Got a little sidetracked there." Trey poured the dog food into Jaxx's dog dish.

When he did see her tomorrow, how should he react? Like nothing had happened? Look at her with suspicion? Ask if she got home okay with her criminal breaking-and-entering fluffy rat-dog?

Trey microwaved his dinner and sat down to eat. After praying, he opened the page of the newspaper. One of the perks of being a reporter and photographer at *The Oakville Daily* was that he got a free subscription.

Pride welled within him when he read "Trey's Sports Corner," the two paragraphs of commentary on local and national sports. It was his favorite piece to write because it was more of an opinion piece.

He then flipped through the rest of the few pages and came across "Carleigh's Creative Corner." Carleigh wrote the three-paragraph section each Wednesday about something she deemed "creative." She was creative all right, in a peculiar sort of way.

In this week's edition of "Carleigh's Creative Corner," she had written an article about how to make a tie-dyed t-shirt for a dog. "And you don't even need a crafty bone in your body!" the second sentence exclaimed.

Jaxx would no more wear a tie-dyed t-shirt with optional jewels on it than Trey would make it for him.

The woman was an oddity, that was for sure.

He took another bite of his meal. The only thing worse than finding Carleigh on his front porch looking through the doggy door would be teaming up to write a story with her.

And not just any story, but a sensational one.

13

No worries there. For one, Howard, their boss, would never dream of putting the two of them together as a team to write an article. And two? Nothing sensational or exciting ever happened in Oakville.

# Chapter Two

THE FOLLOWING DAY, TREY passed Carleigh's desk at work. "Good morning," he said. "Look through any doggy doors lately?"

She didn't answer, but instead gave him the stink eye.

It was at that moment Chip, the man in charge of marketing, subscriptions, and classified ads, walked toward them. "Hey, Carleigh and Trey," he said, huffing and puffing as if he'd run a marathon.

"What's up, Chip?" Trey asked. Chip was at least six-four, about one-hundred, thirty-five pounds, and full of boundless energy.

Chip pushed his thick glasses up his nose. "So, look. I found out Mrs. Velasquez's son is back from Afghanistan. He's the one who saved a fellow soldier and lost his leg while doing it. I already told Howard and he agreed it's one of the hottest stories to hit *The Oakville Daily* since the drug bust two years ago."

Trey watched as Carleigh sat up straight in her chair and leaned forward. She likely wanted the story as badly as he did. "Did Howard say who would get the story?"

"Dunno. Although I can say each of you has a thirty-three-point three percent chance of getting it." Chip half-laughed, half-snorted.

"Do you think he'll give it to Margie?" Carleigh asked.

Chip shrugged his narrow shoulders. "He could. She could use a break from obituaries."

"Chip, my man, you're slacking. You usually have the inside scoop."

"Not this time, Trey. I'm just the messenger. But man, Howard's ears perked up when I told him about the story. He likes those human-interest angles, you know."

Carleigh tapped her fingers on the desk. She seemed to do that when she was anxious about something. "I knew Zander in school. He was a year behind me."

Great. She had an "in."

"My dad served in Operation Iraqi Freedom." Trey smirked at Carleigh's renewed glare. How was that for an "in?"

"I'm not the boss, so who knows who will get the story. I like both of you, so I'm glad it's not up to me. If I were Howard, I'd give it to Margie. She's motherly and articulate and about the age of Zander's mom. They would probably connect well. Besides," said Chip, again pushing his glasses up on his nose, "Howard should do whatever he can to avoid causing more competition between you two."

"We don't compete," Carleigh said, a little too quickly.

"Uh. Yeah. Okay." Chip looked down at his feet, his eyes darting. "You sure about that?"

"All right. Maybe we do. Just a little."

"We do a lot, Carleigh, and you know it," said Trey. "We compete for every story. We always have. It keeps Howard on his toes."

"What keeps me on my toes?" Howard emerged from his corner office, his arms crossed against his considerable girth.

Carleigh's eyes grew behind her glasses. Chip shifted from one foot to the other. Trey would have to be the brave one to answer their boss's question. "Just having to decide who gets what article."

"On that note, Trey and Carleigh, I need you in my office, pronto."

This couldn't be good.

The day already hadn't started off well, and getting called into the boss's office was the proverbial icing on the cake. Carleigh hadn't slept well after nearly losing Sullivan Theodore. And then the whole incident at Trey's house.

Embarrassing.

Horrifying.

Cringeworthy.

Need she gather her favorite book, her used, gently loved paperback thesaurus from 2003, and look up more words to describe the latest episode of her life?

She was only twenty-three. Surely things would get easier.

It didn't help that Trey had sarcastically asked her about the doggy door when he passed by her desk. And then Chip mentioned that fantastic article idea.

Perfect for her resume.

Excellent for honing her skills.

Top-notch experience for securing a book contract when she finally finished her manuscript.

Instead, Trey the Irritating had a thirty-three-point three percent chance of winning. That's if she included Margie. Which she shouldn't because Margie wouldn't be given the assignment. So that upped Trey's chances to fifty percent.

Just grand.

She needed this assignment. Perhaps she should have grabbed an "emergency" chocolate candy bar from her desk drawer.

Except Howard would look down on bribery. It wasn't his style.

Carleigh followed Howard into his office and took a seat at his desk. Trey sat beside her in the chair, looking cool, calm, collected, and confident.

Howard shut the door and pulled down the blinds to the window peering into the rest of *The Oakville Daily*.

Not a good sign.

He traipsed across the floor behind his desk. Back and forth. Forth and back. Shuffling across the already-threadbare carpet that once upon a time was green indoor-outdoor carpet and now had a brownish hue to it. Howard laced his fingers behind his back and focused his attention to the floor.

Carleigh swallowed hard and averted her gaze out the window to Howard's view of Oakville Farm Supply. Mr. Jones climbed out of his 1960s pickup truck, thumbs looped through the straps of his overalls, and sauntered into the store.

She reluctantly returned her gaze to Howard. He continued his pacing, his rotund belly slouched over his navy slacks and a pencil protector was stuffed in the pocket of his button-up plaid shirt. Tufts of grayish-orange hair stuck at random angles from the sides of his glasses—glasses far too small for his large eyes. His puffy cheeks gave proof of one too many donuts his wife, Karen, prepared each day for the staff from her local donut shop. Howard had long ago lost the hair on the top of his head. Carleigh recalled when she was in junior high and he was balding even back then.

A thought struck her. Howard would be the perfect character to play Rufus in her novel. Why hadn't she thought of that before? She'd only worked for *The Oakville Daily* for two years and had known who Howard was for over a decade. Astonishing how ideas hit writers upside the head at the most unexpected moments.

While Rufus may not resemble Howard in personality, their appearances were that of twins. Rufus had the same plump stature, wore similar outdated clothes for the time period, and was always frazzled. He even held the same crabby resting face as Howard.

Carleigh needed her idea notebook to jot down these ideas. She closed her eyes and committed them to memory, as her mind tumbled forward with numerous ideas to advance the plot of her story.

"Now then," Howard, aka Rufus, said. He squished his wide frame into the too-narrow office chair, rested his freckled arms on the armrests, and stared at Carleigh and Trey.

Back when Carleigh first started at *The Oakville Daily*, the entire staff went in on a new chair for Howard as a Christmas gift. It was the same chair in which he now sat and it had clearly seen better days.

Carleigh held her breath, wondering what Howard would say. Would he give them a promotion? A demotion? Relegate them both to delivering newspapers door-to-door?

"Now then," he repeated, ramping up the suspense.

Just like Rufus would do.

His phone rang and Carleigh jumped.

"Howard, it's Kevin from Buy it All," Lindy, the receptionist, administrative assistant, and payroll clerk said.

"Put him through." Howard looked from Carleigh to Trey. "I need to take this call."

Carleigh hesitantly glanced over at Trey, and he returned her glance and shrugged. Was Trey nervous about this whole meeting too? If he was, he sure wasn't showing it.

"Yes, Kevin. What can I do you for?" Howard chuckled at his own play on words. "Yes, of course. Sure. Not a problem. When is the customer appreciation day?" Howard jotted down some notes with his mechanical pencil. "Sounds good. We'll have someone cover it. You bet. Have a good day." Howard hung up the phone. "Kevin over at Buy It All is having a customer appreciation day next week. There will be free hot dogs and pop.

20

I think we could really put a unique spin on the story. Folks like customer appreciation days."

Nothing noteworthy ever happened in Oakville. Well, if you didn't count the time Mr. Schwartz tried to pawn the items he'd stolen at the pawn shop owned by the man he'd robbed or the tourist drug bust from two years ago.

That was all right with her. Carleigh appreciated the calm and peaceful life in her native town. As long as there were enough articles to write to keep her job, she was fine with the slow-moving pace of Oakville.

Howard sighed and thrummed his fingers on his desk. "Now then. Do you know the reason I called you both into my office?"

"No, sir," answered Trey.

"Is it because you are going to assign the story about Zander Velasquez?" The words popped out before Carleigh could stop them.

Howard narrowed his gaze at her. "How did you know?" he asked, as if she'd somehow discovered information privy only to him.

"Uh..."

"A good reporter never reveals her source, eh?"

"Exactly."

Howard nodded. "Now then. I did call you both into my office to discuss the story of Zander's return from the Afghanistan. He is a decorated hero who saved the life of another man in his unit. In doing so, he lost his leg."

"My dad served in Operation Iraqi Freedom," Trey piped up.

Howard spun in his chair and crossed his ankle over the opposite knee. "Very patriotic. Tell him thank you for his service."

"I will, sir."

"Now then..."

"I went to school with Zander." Again, the words flew from her mouth before Carleigh had any power to stop them.

Howard pinched the bridge of his nose. "That's nice. Now let's stop delaying the inevitable, shall we?"

The inevitable? Carleigh bit her lip.

"It has come to my attention that the two of you are most often at odds with each other. You see this job as a competition." He eyed them both, his round eyes seeming to peer right through them. "You both have written articles and have both taken photos. Carleigh, you've written a lot of our human-interest pieces and have, at times, covered the police blotter and community and school sports."

Carleigh smiled. "Yes, sir." This was going well. Howard recognized her experience with the human-interest articles. Could the assignment for Zander's story be forthcoming?

"And you, Trey, have mainly written sports articles, but also some of the court articles."

"Yes, sir, but I can write human-interest stories too."

"Not really. Your human-interest stories leave a lot to be desired." Howard took a drink of his coffee.

Carleigh felt a twinge of pity for Trey, but it passed quickly.

"And just as you can't really write a good human-interest story, Carleigh has failed miserably at writing the school sports articles."

Her eyes widened. How could one "fail miserably" at writing about sports? The person kicked the ball, threw the ball, hit the ball, caught the ball. It was all so simplistic.

"So, here is what I am going to do. From now on, no more working separately. You two are a team. Carleigh writes all human-interest articles, handles the police blotter, writes the court articles, and takes some pictures at the sporting events. Trey, you take pictures for the human-interest articles and write all the sports articles and take most of the pictures for those articles. You two will share the faith-related articles and the late-breaking crime stories if there are any, with Trey doing a majority of the photography for both. My goal is to have an entire cache of outstanding photos and well-written articles that will cause parents, grandparents, aunts, uncles, and everyone twice removed to purchase copies of *The Oakville Daily*."

"Did you say work as a team, sir?" Trey asked. A frown wrinkled his brow.

"Yes. A team. You go to every event and every story together, with a rare exception."

Carleigh's headache was returning. "With all due respect, what if there are two events going on at once?" Not like that would happen in Oakville, but one could hope...

"Then we'll figure it out at that time. Perhaps Margie can pitch in if there aren't as many obituaries that week."

"I don't know if this is a good idea," Trey said.

"Are you criticizing my idea?"

"No, sir, not at all. Well, not really. It's just Carleigh and I don't like each other."

"That is evident. But we are streamlining some things here at *The Oakville Daily*, and if you want to keep your jobs, you'll need to be open to change." Howard cleared his throat. "Whenever there's a story, you both take *The Oakville Daily* minivan and cover it *together*. Am I clear?"

"Yes, sir."

"Now then, since that is settled, on to the Zander Velasquez story. You'll need to call Mrs. Velasquez and Zander and arrange for an interview time that works into both of their schedules. To reiterate: Carleigh will write the story, which I might add is front page and very important to *The Oakville Daily* and its subscribers; and, Trey, you get some good photos. Understood?"

When Howard opened the door so Carleigh and Trey could return to their desks, an interesting sight met them. By the window with the dropped blinds, Lindy, Chip, Margie, and Bubba all stood, their heads pressed against the slim window, likely in an effort to hear the private conversation in Howard's office.

But instead of glowering at his nosy employees, Howard puffed out his chest. "I pronounce Carleigh and Trey our new journalism team. Notice the emphasis on 'team.' From here on out, Carleigh and Trey handle all stories together. Please keep that in mind, Lindy and Margie, if you help make interview appointments. This newest development in *The Oakville Daily's* history will allow us to streamline our operations and make us the number one paper in Oakville."

The only paper in Oakville, but Carleigh didn't mention that fact.

Carleigh definitely needed to relieve the serious stress stemming from Howard's announcement. She plopped down on her blue-and-white cottage-style wingback chair after work and propped her feet on the matching round footstool. Every article? Howard's disturbing voice rang through her ears, as if he stood directly in front of her in her living room. *From now on, no more working separately. You two are a team.*

She groaned.

Unacceptable, unsatisfactory, and completely objectionable. Oh, and repugnant.

Working with Trey the Irritating on every article. Never a break from his annoying antics. Never a hiatus from seeing and arguing with him. At least, to Howard's credit, the change would lessen the competition for articles.

Still...

Sullivan Theodore took a flying leap into her lap for a snuggle. Her pet reminded her of a stuffed animal, and his fleecy fur tickled her nose when he placed a doggy kiss on her cheek. For a moment, her mind was relieved of the tension of Howard's news.

"It was a difficult day at the office, Sullivan Theodore. Howard assigned Trey and me to work together on all articles, with a rare exception. Mainly with me doing the writing and him handling the photography. What a predicament."

Sullivan Theodore tilted his head to one side, then gave her another doggy kiss, as if to reassure her this wasn't the end of the world, even though it seemed like it at the moment. And probably for a gazillion moments after this one.

"We need something to take our minds off this appalling turn of events. Would you like to go for a walk?"

Her pet practically bounced on the pads of his paws on the arm rest, as if understanding exactly what she said. "I thought so. Let's get your leash."

A short jaunt around the block was just what she needed to relieve her mind of today's developments.

She changed into some striped exercise leggings, grabbed her favorite yellow jacket, and wrapped Sullivan Theodore in his plaid knitted sweater, a gift from the ladies in her Bible study.

A chill was in the air, reminding Carleigh the volatile spring weather was delaying its turn to summer. The thermometer reflected a chilly forty-six degrees and confirmed her suspicions of a brisk evening. Still, she needed this walk, and for sure wouldn't let Sullivan Theodore down by changing her mind. "Just a sec. I'm going to grab my earmuffs."

Sullivan Theodore yanked on the leash, his excitement far from contained. Carleigh put on her earmuffs, adjusted her glasses, and tied her sneakers. "All right, let's go."

When Carleigh was little, she had recurrent ear infections. After the tubes were placed in her ears, she still had sensitivities to wind and water, so wisdom dictated donning her colorful purple earmuffs. She hoped they never went out of fashion.

She turned toward the east to begin their walk down the quiet street of Maple Avenue. But Sullivan Theodore would have none of it. He angled himself and did a one-eighty to walk in the opposite direction. "No, Sullivan Theodore. Let's go this way."

But her pet wouldn't listen. He tugged on the leash until Carleigh acquiesced. "All right, I guess we can go this way for a short distance. But just for a block or so."

Sullivan Theodore held his head high in a prideful stance, likely proud of himself for getting his own way. Again.

The leaves were starting to bud on the trees. Spring was Carleigh's favorite time of year, especially in Oakville. Everything was green and plush from the recent rains and the smell of promise filled the air. Soon lilacs would be blooming and the days would be longer and sunnier.

She couldn't wait.

This was just the remedy for the lousy news at work. Nothing could dampen her spirits when she was wandering through God's Creation with her favorite pet.

Well, her only pet.

Soon, her problems took a seat in the past and Carleigh's mind wandered to the novel she was writing. Her dream was to become a novelist and to be published by one of the bigger Christian publishing houses. Most days, her mind roared at full capacity between writing articles for work and dreaming up new characters for her novel. She'd read a meme on the internet the other day reminding her of herself—"So many characters to write about, so little time in which to do it."

Indeed.

She smiled at the blue sky and breathed in the crisp air. One of her favorite Bible verses—the one from Psalm 117:24—floated through her mind. *"This is the day that the Lord has made; let us rejoice and be glad in it."* Such a glorious evening and she'd not let the events of earlier ruin the present. Instead, she would allow the jaunt to remove all of the day's stress and fuel creativity for her novel.

Oblivious to how far they had walked, Carleigh only realized the distance when Sullivan Theodore decided to stop suddenly. Real life popped her out of her imaginary world where her main characters were just getting ready to embark on their journey on the Oregon Trail. They didn't yet know each other, the hardships they would face, or the fact that they would fall in love. The wagon master, Rufus, modeled after Howard, had begun to give instructions.

Her mind snapped to the present where she and her pet stood directly in front of Trey's house. How had this happened?

"Well, hello there. Fancy seeing you here."

Carleigh turned her gaze toward the familiar voice and lifted an earmuff. Trey sat on the steps of his porch crunching on what appeared to be chips, with Jaxx sitting beside him, chewing on a doggy toy.

"Come on, Sullivan Theodore. Time to turn around."

"Looking for a house to break into?" Trey asked.

"Very funny."

"I thought so. Look, we can move out of the way of the doggy door if Theodore wants to add another breaking-and-entering charge to his record."

"It's *Sullivan* Theodore, and he doesn't want to go in your house again."

But her dog had other plans. Sullivan Theodore yipped and tugged on the leash toward Trey and Jaxx.

"Looks like Sullivan has other ideas."

Carleigh crouched beside her dog. "Sullivan Theodore, we have talked about this numerous times. We have to be careful who we hang around. There are many bad influences in the world. I cannot allow you to be friends with that Jaxx character. It's highly unacceptable, displeasing, and ill-favored. You have other friends. We'll visit them soon."

Trey laughed. "You think Jaxx is a bad influence on Theodore? That's funny *and* ironic." He chuckled again, throwing his blond head back in jest.

He would make an ideal antagonist in Carleigh's book. She made a mental note to model Reginald after Trey. Blond hair, green eyes, athletic build, and a no-good shyster who was disloyal and stole from the other members of the wagon train.

Perfect.

During her moment from the present, Jaxx had wandered toward Sullivan Theodore and they greeted each other like best buds.

"Well, we better go. Come on, Sullivan Theodore."

"Sure you don't want Sullivan to test his burglary skills again?"

"I'm quite sure."

"What's with the earmuffs? Part of your disguise in case your dog trespasses again?"

She rolled her eyes. The man was relentless. "No, not part of a disguise."

"Just asking. You never know these days."

The sooner they ended this asinine conversation, the better. She was about to whisk Sullivan Theodore into her arms and haul him home when Trey interrupted her plans with a smirk.

"Rough day?"

He most certainly had the voice of an antagonist.

"I don't think you can fathom the magnitude of horror I experienced today."

"Bummer about the whole working together as a team thing, huh? I mean, what was Howard thinking?"

"He wasn't."

Trey laughed again. "That's true." He joined Jaxx and now stood next to Carleigh.

She needed to analyze him from this close distance to get his full features memorized so she could do a characterization of Reginald, the villain, tonight after dinner.

"Are you staring at me?"

"What? Absolutely not." Her face burned with embarrassment. "I'm just pondering why I got a demotion. I've given it my all for *The Oakville Daily* and for Howard. It just doesn't seem fair."

"A demotion? I hear you on that one. Well, if you want, I can pass along the book I checked out from the library after I finish reading it."

"Which one is that?"

"Mrs. Hopkins saw my misery and suggested I read the bestseller, *Working with Your Enemy and Surviving.* She's quite knowledgeable about books."

"Yes, well, it helps that she's been there for one hundred and four years."

"I thought it was one hundred and five." He offered a lopsided smile.

The man was incorrigible. "As much as I would like to stand here wasting time debating Mrs. Hopkins's tenure at the library, I really must go."

"All right, see you tomorrow at work then, Quirky Carleigh."

*Quirky Carleigh?*

She gave him the stink eye and lifted Sullivan Theodore, who did his best to squirm from her grasp.

Yes, Trey was the perfect person to model her book's antagonist after.

# Chapter Three

HOWARD CALLED TREY, CARLEIGH, and Chip into his office first thing the next day. "Now then, have a seat," he said, pulling along an additional chair for Chip. The chair bumped along on the worn carpet and Trey wondered how there would be enough room in the closet-sized office to fit all four chairs and Chip's boundless energy. Howard then sat in his own office chair and steepled his fingers.

Never a good thing when their boss steepled his fingers. Meant things were going to get serious in a hurry.

But how could anything be worse than yesterday's news? With the exception of a demotion or outright firing, of course.

"Chip, would you like to explain your idea?"

"Sure." Chip stood, unfolding his tall lanky self. "So, writers aren't the only ones with fantastic ideas in the middle of the night." He half-laughed, half-snorted. "Last night, at precisely 2:42 a.m., I had a brilliant idea."

"Yes, and a text came through from you at that time." Howard tossed a glower Chip's way.

"Sorry, sir. It was just that I was so excited I could no longer sleep."

Likely Chip also drank too much coffee, but Trey didn't mention that possibility.

A corner of Howard's mouth lifted into a slight smile indicating all was forgiven. "Proceed."

"Yeah, so like I was saying, I had this idea of magnificent proportions. As marketer extraordinaire, classified ads supervisor, subscription administrator, and all-around highly-competent idea guy, I decided that one of the ways to increase our readership is to create a brand for Carleigh and Trey."

"A brand?" Carleigh shifted in her seat. She had to be as disturbed by this as he was. Only difference was that he hid his dismay much better than she did.

Chip's nervous energy took off and the man was nearly jogging in place while constantly adjusting his glasses. A multi-tasker at his finest.

"Get on it with, Chip. We don't have all day," Howard growled.

"Yeah, okay. Sorry, sir. So, we create a brand for Carleigh and Trey and call them...wait for it..." Chip pressed his hands out, palms facing them. "We call you two 'The Oakville Daily Duo.' Your tagline will be, 'Keeping you updated on the daily news of Oakville.'"

When no one responded, Chip's shoulders slumped. "Come on, people. This is the marketing marvel of the year! When people realize you're both on the same team, rather than competitors, they'll rush out and buy—or subscribe to—the latest issue."

"I seriously doubt anyone realizes we're competitors," said Trey. "That's something we all know in this office, but it's not public knowledge."

Chip shuffled from side to side. "It might be known to more than just this office."

Trey groaned.

Chip paused and peered at his audience over his glasses. "I may have mentioned it to Debbie, the produce manager, over at Buy it All, and we all know what a gossip she is. If we didn't have *The Oakville Daily*, Oakville would be fine because Debbie would be the news source."

"We get it, we get it," grumbled Howard.

"Well, competition is healthy," suggested Carleigh. Was she as concerned about the gossip debacle Chip mentioned? The horrified expression that remained on her cute face did likely mirror his own.

*Cute face? Nah. Chip just has you all riled up with his crazy idea and you're not thinking straight.*

Howard tapped his mechanical pencil on the desk. "Competition *is* healthy and in many arenas of life, we promote it. However, here at *The Oakville Daily*, we pride ourselves on being a prodigious team of professionals comprised of you three, Margie, Lindy, Bubba, Justin, our three newspaper delivery folks, and myself. People in Oakville have come to depend on forthright news delivered at a reasonable price by conscientious and honest journalists."

"Wow, sir, can I quote you on that in my marketing campaign?" Chip asked.

"Sure, whatever." Howard rested his thick forearms on his cluttered desk. "So, henceforth, you'll be known as *The Oakville Daily* Duo.' Chip will prepare promotional material, and we'll have Margie interview you for a front-page article. Understood?"

"Yes, sir." Carleigh looked as though she might faint.

"Look at it this way," said Chip with another of his half-snorts, half-laughs. "You'll no longer have to worry about the possibility of a thirty-three-point-three percent chance of getting the article you want to write. From here on out, it's all laid out in print." At his play on words, he snort-laughed again.

If he didn't love his job at *The Oakville Daily* so much, Trey might have to search for a job elsewhere. *The Oakville Daily* Duo? He and Carleigh?

The thought gave him a worse case of indigestion than eating at The Oakville Greasy Spoon over on Fourth Street.

It hadn't been a good day. Who in their right mind wanted to be half of *The Oakville Daily* Duo? Carleigh slouched at her desk, trying not to let despair flood her mind. She still needed to come up with an idea for next week's "Caleigh's Creative Corner" and she had two articles to write before Monday. Not to mention finding two national news articles to include in the weekend edition.

She. Just. Could. Not. Focus.

Time for more coffee. Carleigh did a few shoulder rolls then trudged to the coffee counter. In her own world and worried about her lack of motivation, Carleigh ran smack into someone.

"Oops." She looked up to see Trey in front of her, mug of coffee in his hands.

Although now the mug wasn't so full of coffee. The dark liquid had sloshed over the side onto Trey's white tennis shoe. "Sorry."

Trey glanced down at his shoe, which was no longer white, but mudded with coffee. "Someone's mind isn't in the game."

"Yeah. Sorry about spilling the coffee. I'd offer to take your shoe to the dry cleaners, but I don't think they dry clean shoes." At her ridiculous rambling Carleigh felt the heat climb up her cheeks. Could this day get any worse?

"Actually, they do dry clean shoes. When I was doing that front page article last year on the new dry cleaning machines at Sharon's Dry Cleaning, Sharon told me they actually can dry clean shoes."

The man was just so full of random facts. "Oh. Wow. Okay. Well, do you want me to take your shoe there and get it cleaned?"

He peered at her through the green eyes of an antagonist. "Don't worry about it. I'm sure with a little elbow grease, the coffee stain will come right out."

"All right, then. If you'll excuse me, I need some coffee."

"You too, huh?"

"Yeah. Pretty stressful all these changes."

Trey regarded her again, a smirk lining his face. "So, I take it you're as excited as I am about being part of *The Oakville Daily* Duo?"

"Probably less excited."

"Doubt that. This has got to be the worse day ever. Well, if you don't count yesterday when we were told we would be partnering on all articles. That was tragic."

Carleigh sighed. "True. How will we ever succeed at this?"

"By doing what we always do. Put up with each other and, when possible, ignore each other."

"Good point."

They stood there awkwardly until Carleigh eyed the coffee pot only steps away. "Well, better get back to work."

"Hey, check that out." Trey nodded toward the front desk. Lindy had gone to lunch and a delivery person from the flower shop was setting an oval-shaped ginormous vase of flowers on Lindy's desk.

"Wow. Those are beautiful."

"Yeah. Wonder who they're from."

The curiosity was nearly killing Carleigh. Chalk it up to being an investigative reporter and wannabe fiction novel writer.

"Let's go see if we can find anything out," Trey said, nudging her toward Lindy's desk.

How had the man read her thoughts? Uncanny. Frightening. Unsettling. Disturbing.

Carleigh followed Trey and together they slunk toward Lindy's desk, on the lookout for any witnesses who could thwart their investigation. Howard's door was shut, so he was probably working on editing, Bubba was in the back room working on the presses, Margie was on a work-related errand, and Chip was wherever he'd wandered off to for the moment. "All clear," she whispered.

Trey did a hasty sweep of the room himself, and then leaned in, as if to smell the flowers. "There's got to be a card in here somewhere." He emerged from the bountiful bouquet, his eyes watering. "About poked my eye out, but here it is."

"You're going to read it?"

"Wouldn't you?"

"Yes, but, well..."

The bell on the door jangled and a customer walked in. "I just need to leave a payment for my subscription," he said.

"Thank you. We'll see that your account gets credited." Trey took the check from the customer and left it on Lindy's computer keyboard.

"How do you do that?"

"Do what?" Trey asked.

"Act so calm and collected. My heart rate is extremely elevated right now."

Trey shrugged. "It's all part of being an effective journalist."

"Or something like that," Carleigh said, rolling her eyes.

"Hey, are you giving me a compliment?"

Never. "About what?"

"About being so calm and collected. That sounded like a compliment."

"It was no such thing." She pursed her lips. This guy really had an ego. "Back to our regularly-scheduled program. What does the card say?" If they didn't hurry, Howard would emerge from his cocoon or Lindy would return to work. Carleigh's heart rate ramped up even more.

Trey opened the card. "It says, 'To Lindy from your secret admirer.'"

"What?"

"Shhh! You'll give us away."

Carleigh closed her gaping mouth and pondered what the card said. "Lindy has a secret admirer?" she whispered.

"Yeah. Pretty crazy." Trey stuffed the card back inside the envelope and onto the card holder in the bouquet. "Who would have thought?"

Who would have thought, indeed?

"Who do you think it's from?" Did Trey have a suspicion?

"How should I know? I'm not a member of the secret admirer association."

Carleigh narrowed her eyes at him. "There's a secret admirer association?"

"How should I know?"

Thankful for the brief interruption to an otherwise dreadful day, Carleigh grabbed her coffee and returned to her desk. While she was happy for Lindy, a jolt of something unidentifiable settled into her heart.

What would it be like to have a secret admirer? A potential true love?

Trey returned to his desk with the intent of pumping out his article about how the local basketball coach had served in his capacity for over twenty-five years. He also needed to finish "Trey's Sports Corner."

But it wasn't happening.

He reclined in his office chair and clasped his hands behind his head. Really weird about Lindy's secret admirer. If he went to the flower shop in his photojournalist capacity, he could probably find out who had sent it, that is, if Lindy wanted him to find out. A secret never remained a secret for long in Oakville.

His thoughts then reverted to the fact he had been forced into *The Oakville Daily* Duo role. When he started at the paper two years ago, he dreamed of being a one-man-show. Capturing important articles, preserving them with photos, and maybe even someday winning an award. He did not, however, plan on having to be a team with Quirky Carleigh.

And she was quirky, all right. He inspected his stained shoe. He could have insisted she take it to Sharon and have it dry cleaned, just to be a pain, but a $14.99 pair of shoes wasn't worth it. With his luck, it wouldn't be long before the other shoe matched.

How would this whole duo thing work between them? They couldn't be in each other's presence five minutes without arguing. She had a way of really getting under his skin. Today it was the malicious destruction of his tennis shoe. A few days ago, it had been the whole breaking-and-entering episode. The fact she was always chipper annoyed him too.

Now they would be working side by side for what might as well be twenty-four seven. At least he would have a reprieve from her this weekend before seeing her again on Monday.

From his vantage point at his desk, he could see her if he veered over to the right. She was deep in thought, staring intently at her computer screen. He'd noticed long ago that whenever she was exceptionally nervous, she'd bite her lip or tap her fingers. Just as she was doing now.

"Thanks, Howard, for causing your two best reporters to have major writer's block," he muttered.

A thought came to him then. What would Carleigh do if she received flowers from a secret admirer? He'd seen the interested expression on her face when she first saw the flowers and again when Trey read the card.

He shoved the thought aside. There was absolutely, positively, no room in his addled brain for any thoughts of Quirky Carleigh.

And if he didn't get to work on his articles, Howard would demote him to obituaries.

That couldn't happen.

Finally. The work week was over and Carleigh could look forward to enjoying her days without seeing Trey. Well, two days anyway.

Before she left, Bubba loaded two stacks of newspapers into her 1999 four-door sedan. "Have a good weekend," Bubba said, waving as he returned to *The Oakville Daily.*

"You too, Bubba."

Bubba was an all-around nice guy. Carleigh likened him to a mid-forty-year-old teddy bear with a bushy brown beard. He was the printing press coordinator and printed all the papers with the assistance of a home-schooled intern named Justin. Bubba was also the janitor. He had a wife, three kids, and attended the same church as Carleigh. Large in size and heart, he could be counted on whenever anyone needed help.

Carleigh drove toward the post office, her first stop. She, Trey, and Margie delivered newspapers to the six newspaper dispensers around Oakville on their way home each evening.

Several years ago, before Carleigh became an *Oakville Daily* employee, the newspaper nearly had to close. With free online news and fewer people reading actual print news, *The Oakville Daily* had taken a hit. Subscriptions had decreased. Back then, most of the articles were national, or at the very least, regional.

About six years ago, the former owner, in an attempt to avoid the inevitable closing of *The Oakville Daily* and possible bankruptcy, sold it to Howard, who was determined to save the floundering newspaper.

While it took some time, Howard achieved his goal. He revamped *The Oakville Daily* from news anyone could get anywhere, including online, and turned it into a personal paper the people of Oakville reveled in. He focused on news around the town as his main goal. Sure, he still included an article or two in every issue about regional or national news, but for the most part, *The Oakville Daily* was all about Oakville. He published newsworthy items about businesses, celebrations of Oakville residents, and opinion pieces. He made it a priority to cover the local school and homeschool events. Photos graced the pages, and Howard, born and raised in Oakville, became the town's hero.

Now he was the owner, CEO, editor, office manager, and opinion piece coordinator. Grouchy and with no filter at times, Howard's heart was one of pure gold, and he cared for his employees. Each of the six permanent full-time employees and the five part-time employees, which included Margie, three newspaper delivery people and the printing press intern, loved their jobs. While the full-time employees wore many hats to help keep *The Oakville Daily* afloat, no one minded. Howard took care of his employees, and his employees in turn offered their loyalty and strong work ethics to his business.

Carleigh pulled into a parking lot in front of the post office. She wouldn't trade this job for anything, save one thing—to become a full-time novelist. That was her dream. But in the two years she had worked for Howard, she had grown both in her writing skills and her appreciation for the town she was born and raised in.

She opened the newspaper dispenser, removed the coins and placed them into a bank bag, and retrieved the few remaining newspapers from yesterday. She then placed the current day's newspapers into the dispenser and dropped the bank bag off with a completed deposit slip at Oakville Bank.

Howard trusted his three reporters to be honest and forthright with any money they retrieved from the dispensers and rewarded them for their hard work with an employee pizza party during work hours on the fourth Thursday of each month.

Carleigh next zipped to Buy it All Grocery and to her second newspaper dispenser. It worked out well today because she also needed to run into the store and get a few items, namely strawberries to take to Mom and Dad's house tonight for dinner.

Just the thought of spending some relaxing time with her parents calmed her frazzled nerves. She and Sullivan Theodore looked forward to this day each week.

There were two grocery stores and one health food store in Oakville, but Buy it All was Carleigh's favorite. She entered the modest store that had only received minor updates since it was built in the 1970s. The narrow aisles, white tiled floor, and items crowded on shelves were part of its charm.

Carleigh proceeded to get a gallon of milk, some dog treats for Sullivan Theodore, a frozen pizza, and a tub of spinach before entering the fruit department at the far end of the store for some fresh strawberries.

Mom was making strawberry shortcake tonight, the family favorite. *Good. Looks like there is a plentiful selection.* She reached for a tub of strawberries when she noticed another arm belonging to someone else reaching for the same tub at the same time. "Oops, go ahead." She backed up a bit to allow the other person to retrieve the strawberries they needed first.

No one answered and no one stepped forward, but she did hear a somewhat recognizable snicker nearby. She swiveled her head to see none other than her writing nemesis laughing, apparently at her.

"What?" she asked.

"You crack me up, Carleigh."

"Why is that?" The audacity of the man. And why was *he* here?

"Because no one else was reaching for strawberries."

What was he talking about? "Excuse me?"

"Didn't you see they just put in a mirror to the side of the berries?"

His words didn't compute in her tired mind. A mirror? "Really, Trey, what are you talking about?"

"Check it out." Trey walked the few steps between them and pointed at the mirror gracing the side of the refrigerated berry section. "It was *your* hand you saw reaching for strawberries. Not someone else's."

The realization hit her like a wildly flung weekend edition of *The Oakville Daily* toward a residential door. The heat crept up her cheeks and she literally wanted to die. Trying her best to regain her composure, Carleigh

45

faced Trey and placed her hands on her hips. "Are you stalking me?"

"What? Stalking you? No."

"Then why are following me to Buy it All? Don't you have newspaper dispensers to fill?"

"Already done." Trey puffed out his chest like he was some sort of hero.

Uncomfortable silence followed, as it always did whenever they had an "encounter." He laughed again and shook his head. "Careful about those mirrored refrigerators, Carleigh. They'll get you every time."

She had every mind to throw the bag of Sullivan Theodore's doggy snacks at Trey, but refrained when an elderly woman hobbled around the corner. "Oh, it's so nice to see you both," the woman exclaimed.

Carleigh attempted to change her facial expression from one of serious disdain to one of pleasant proportions. "Hello, Mrs. Roper. How are you?"

"Quite well. Your article on how to make a tie-dyed shirt for your pet was quite enlightening. I made several for my cats."

"Thank you, I appreciate that compliment. I'm honored you enjoyed the article."

Mrs. Roper smiled and continued. "And you, Mr. Trey, I very much enjoyed your write-up about how parents can encourage their kids in sports. I passed it on to my great-grandchildren. Well done, young man."

The appreciative expression on Trey's face from Mrs. Roper's comment almost made Carleigh forgive him for taunting her about the mirrored refrigerator.

Almost.

# Chapter Four

TREY OPENED HIS TRUCK door and was just about to walk up the front steps of his house when his neighbor, Mr. Fortuna, waved at him. "Can I speak with you for a minute?"

"Sure. How are you?" Trey transferred the two bags of food to his other arm.

"I'm well. Mrs. Fortuna has been after me since my last birthday to invite you to church. Do you have a church home, Son?"

Trey thought about it for a minute. When he first moved to Oakville to take the reporter job two years ago, he continued to drive the hour each way to his hometown church to attend with his parents. Winter weather, combined with a desire to join a local men's Bible study, prompted Trey to do a full-out church search in Oakville about six months ago. So far, he'd visited five of the six Bible-based churches in town on a rotating basis. "Not a church home, Mr. Fortuna. I'm still in the search phase."

"Have you tried Oakville Community Church?"

"As a matter of fact, I went there a couple of times several months ago, but then one of the people I interviewed for an article invited me to her church, so I went there and to a couple of other churches."

"Could I convince you to try Oakville Community Church this Sunday?"

Mr. Fortuna may barely be five-three in stature and seem unimposing, but he was extremely persuasive. He waited patiently while staring at Trey with what could be termed "laser eyes."

"Sure, I'll attend. Does it have a men's Bible study? I've been hoping to get connected into one of those."

"We sure do. It has some young fellows like yourself in it and some more seasoned fellows in it too. I joined up twenty years ago and haven't looked back. Service starts at ten."

"I'll be there."

Mr. Fortuna wiped the perspiration from his brow. "Thanks, Son. You saved me from sleeping in the dog house tonight. The missus will be thrilled I asked you and even more thrilled you accepted."

"Glad I could help you out." Trey unlocked the door, carried in his groceries, and let Jaxx into the house. Jaxx, as usual, was happy to see him. "Good to see you too, boy. It's been one long week. Have I told you how annoying Quirky Carleigh is?" He gave Jaxx a pat. "Tomorrow is supposed to be partly sunny with no wind. How about a walk?"

As if Jaxx understood, he stood on his hind legs, bracing his forepaws on Trey's leg, wagging his tail. "That's what I thought. It will be good to get out and get some fresh air. You can't imagine the week I've had. As if the whole *Oakville Daily* Duo situation I told you about isn't bad enough, I ran into Carleigh at the grocery store. Seems she's everywhere."

Jaxx bobbed his head in agreement. That was the nice thing about Jaxx. He was a great listener and he never argued. And never broke into people's homes.

Just an all-around well-behaved dog.

The next day, Jaxx leaped on Trey's bed, leash in mouth. "Give me a few minutes to down some cereal and we'll head out," Trey promised.

The temperature was a warm fifty-two degrees with the sun shining brightly. With such an amazing May day, what could possibly go wrong?

Trey zipped up his hoodie and put the leash on Jaxx, who jumped around as if he'd never gone on a walk in his life. "All right, buddy, let's go. I saw a path leading around the pond near the park. How about we take that route?"

Jaxx tugged on his leash. He probably didn't mind if they ventured to the next town, as long as they went for a walk.

When Trey moved into his two-bedroom house six months ago, the weather hadn't been conducive to going on extended walks. Winters were harsh in Oakville, so Trey had kept the walks short, usually just down the block. It sure beat living in the apartment he'd resided in for a year-and-a-half when he first moved to Oakville. His rental house was centrally located and he liked the neighbors he'd met.

Well, except Carleigh, whom he'd just learned lived somewhere in the neighborhood. Hopefully not near the pond or park.

He dismissed the disturbing thought from his mind. Today he'd relax, revel in the fact he wouldn't have to see Carleigh, and enjoy his time with Jaxx.

They sauntered up the sidewalk about a block toward the park when he spied her.

And she spied him.

Was it too late to turn around?

Carleigh, with the troublemaking fluffy rat-dog on a blue leash, walked only a few yards ahead of him.

"Let's turn around, Jaxx," Trey muttered.

The dog either didn't hear him or ignored him and continued with haste toward Carleigh and her pet. When Jaxx reached them, he slowed down and gave a doggy greeting to Carleigh's fluffy nuisance.

"Uh, hi," Trey said.

Carleigh looked at him, but he couldn't read her gaze through her hideously large sunglasses. "Hi."

"Enjoying the weather?"

"Yes."

"Have any more encounters with mirrored refrigerators or doggy doors?"

"Very funny. Are you stalking me?"

"Not at all. I happened to think it would be a good idea to take Jaxx for a walk since it's such a warm day. We haven't yet been down this way. Isn't there a pond or park or something that the path meanders around?"

"Yes. We take this route often. When the weather is nice, anyway."

They walked in silence and Trey shoved aside the thought that she looked pretty cute in her bright pink hoodie and purple exercise pants. "What's your dog's name again? Theodore something or other?"

"Sullivan Theodore IV. Sullivan Theodore for short. And your dog is Jake?"

"Jaxx."

"Right."

"So, uh, do you care if we walk with you?" The words slipped out before he could stop them. Yes, the stressful past week definitely fouled up his common sense.

She looked at him again, and he imagined her narrowing her gaze at him. "All right."

"Seems like the dogs get along well."

Trey just needed to be quiet while he was ahead. Thinking before speaking had never been his strong suit. And then the crisis occurred.

To be fair, the crisis wouldn't have happened if Trey hadn't asked if he and Jaxx could walk with Carleigh and Sullivan Theodore.

He never should have suggested it.

But it was too late now.

She never saw it coming. Not even given Sullivan Theodore's at-times obnoxious behavior.

She couldn't really blame the squirrel. Sure, he was an antagonizer, but running across the park from point a to point b didn't make him a criminal.

Not really.

It all happened so fast. One minute, Carleigh was walking with Trey. Their arms kept bumping since she was right-handed and he was left-handed, and they both used their dominant hands to control their respective dog leashes. Awkward at best, heart-fluttering at worst.

Which was beyond bizarre.

After all, this was Trey. Why would her heart flutter if his arm brushed hers?

She should have had a cup of coffee before the walk. Missing out on her caffeine jolt addled her brain.

There wasn't time to really contemplate the heart-fluttering because the crisis interrupted all rational thought.

The squirrel darted in front of them. At that moment, Sullivan Theodore jerked the leash free from her hand and began an all-out race toward the squirrel. From the corner of her eye, Carleigh could see that Jaxx had done the same. Both dogs bolted after the squirrel in a zig-zag fashion.

For all of his training to stay on the cement pathway, Sullivan Theodore ignored it and barreled across the muddy grass. He came dangerously close to the pond before changing direction and dashing toward the pavilion. The squirrel taunted the dogs ever so often, stopping and sitting on its hind legs while rubbing its little hands together, an evil glint in its eye.

"Stop, Sullivan Theodore!" Carleigh dove for the leash. Thankfully he had a harness rather than only his traditional collar or he may have been choked as he ran. His tail wagged and a guttural growl rose in his throat, but he did not stop.

Neither did Jaxx, who was barking loudly, as if to warn the squirrel of imminent danger. Trey was in much the same predicament. He chased Jaxx, commanding his dog to stop, but as if Jaxx and Sullivan Theodore were in cahoots, they ignored their masters and forged ahead in pursuit of the squirrel.

Mud caked Carleigh's pink tennis shoes and the knees of her leggings, and she nearly tripped over a tree branch. "Sullivan Theodore!" she yelled again, using what scant little breath she had to painfully call him.

A runner she was not.

Especially when it was against her will.

For example, in P.E. class in school when they had to run the mile or the time that bratty kid in third grade chased her all around the playground, or now with Sullivan Theodore reminding her that he wasn't the innocent angel she pretended him to be.

Carleigh huffed precious air from her lungs, begging her cardiovascular system to cooperate during this emergency. How could it be that such a tiny dog couldn't be stopped? She stooped and managed to grasp the leash so that the Shi Tzu would be forced to halt to no avail. Sullivan Theodore jerked on the leash all the more as if in a tug-of-war, pulling her back into the race.

"Jaxx!" yelled Trey. "Stop!"

The squirrel skittered up a massive oak tree near the water fountains, and Carleigh thought this might be the end of their adventure. But it was not to be so.

As Sullivan Theodore made one last attempt to seize the rodent, he pulled extra hard on the leash. At that same time, Carleigh's legs flew out from under her and she slipped on the squishy mud-laden grass and fell forward to her demise.

Well, not exactly to her demise, but it would have been better to disappear completely off the face of the earth than to be lying face down in the wet grass while Sullivan Theodore IV barked his head off to call attention to the situation.

The air left her lungs and her knee throbbed. She uttered what could only be described as a tortuous moan while Sullivan Theodore jumped on her back and continued to bark excessively.

Carleigh saw two sweatpants-covered legs in her peripheral and a hand reaching down to her. "Can I help you up?"

She rolled over, causing Sullivan Theodore off to jump off her back, and moaned again. A crowd had begun to form and somewhere she heard, or thought she heard, the click of a cell-phone camera.

Wishing she could be prideful and ignore the offer of help, but knowing it would be wise to accept it, Carleigh stretched her left hand toward Trey while keeping Sullivan Theodore under tight rein with her right.

With an efficient swoop, Trey assisted her to feet, so much so that she nearly collided with his chest. Somewhere in the recesses of her battered thoughts, she knew her prescription sunglasses had flipped off her face, and her blurred vision only enhanced the direness of the situation.

Carleigh tried to ignore that her face was inches from Trey's. He held her hand in his while he grasped Jaxx's leash with the other. She dared to look up at him. "Are you all right?" he asked.

"No. I mean yes." She was all right in that she wasn't severely injured and there was no need to call 9-1-1. But her pride, well, that was another thing.

"Wow. I didn't realize."

"Realize what?" That she was a klutz? A dolt. An oaf? That her legs didn't work well when pulled out from under her? That she wasn't made to ice skate on muddy grass? All of the above?

"That your eyes are brown."

"What?"

"Yeah. I had no idea your eyes were brown. They've always been hidden behind your glasses and now I see they're brown."

"My eyes have always been brown and my regular glasses have clear and transparent lenses that don't hide the view of the color of my eyes."

"Just never realized is all. They're pret..."

She inwardly winced, willing herself to wake up from this nightmare. Wasn't she supposed to have a break from Trey's company for two days? If he and Jaxx hadn't insisted on walking with her and Sullivan Theodore, none of this would have happened.

They stood for a tense moment staring at each other, heat whooshing up her neck and face. They'd both made realizations—Trey apparently noticing she had brown eyes and Carleigh realizing that she was nearly hugging the enemy.

The dogs began winding their leashes haphazardly around their humans' legs as they played some sort of game of chase with each other. Sullivan Theodore at seven pounds and Jaxx, as a German shepherd, at probably eighty pounds or so.

The winding of the leashes caused Carleigh and Trey to be bound even closer together. Carleigh thumped into his chest again and they nearly tumbled over.

Several people stood nearby watching the entire scene.

"Hey, let's take a picture for *The Oakville Daily*," someone said.

And that's when Carleigh knew she would never emerge from this episode unscathed.

# Chapter Five

HE REALLY NEEDED TO think before he spoke. Just because he noticed for the first time ever that Carleigh had really pretty brown eyes didn't mean Trey had to say it out loud.

The dogs wound the leashes tighter and tighter around them, forming an instant alliance—an ironic alliance considering their owners' feelings toward each other. Conspiring with the enemy against two delinquent dogs was not on his agenda today. Yet, here he was, his face only a few inches away from Carleigh's, providing ample opportunity for nosy onlookers to snap photos with their cell phones of the entire incident.

For the leash issue, not to mention running off in the first place, Jaxx would be grounded until he was two-hundred and forty in dog years.

"Can you look this way?" someone asked.

Trey turned his head and noticed a geeky-looking kid holding his phone up, taking rapid- fire photos. Several other people followed suit.

"Hey, isn't that Carleigh and Trey from *The Oakville Daily*?"

"Wow, did you see how all that went down?"

"Wonder if we could talk Howard into writing a story about all this for the front page. He's always looking for feature stories."

"Hopefully he'll choose my photos since I saw them first and I've always wanted my pictures to be published in *The Oakville Daily.*"

"Wait. Are they dating?"

At the last statement made by some teenager, Trey winced and knew his ears had probably turned bright red. A stupid phenomenon he'd inherited from Grandpa Montgomery whenever he was thoroughly embarrassed.

Like now.

He could hide his lack of composure better than most—he was highly practiced at it—but those red ears gave Trey away every time.

A jolt threatened his balance because the dogs chased each other even faster, round and round, causing the leashes to tighten. An "oh, no" interrupted Trey's thoughts.

Carleigh's sunglasses, which she'd lost moments before, lay at the feet of the geeky kid who had galloped forward, his cell phone still angled for the best shots. In one tragic movement, the kid stepped on Carleigh's glasses, breaking them while not even noticing he had done so.

"Hope you bought the warranty." He could see the entire fiasco bothered her. "Let's fix this mess," he suggested. "Jaxx, Theodore, stop right now!"

"It's Sullivan Theodore."

"Right. Stop right now!"

Both dogs ceased their antics and glanced up at Trey. He did his best to give a stern dad-look, much like the one he'd received numerous times as a kid. "Go that way." He attempted to explain to the canines to chase each other counterclockwise so as to untangle him and Carleigh. But instead of obeying, Jaxx barked and Sullivan Theodore cocked his head to one side, then the other.

It was hopeless.

The tightening of the leashes wound Trey and Carleigh even closer. Trey would've toppled over were it not for his oversized feet. He attempted to shift for better footing just as Carleigh fell into him. "Uh, this is awkward," he muttered. He placed his hands on her arms to stabilize her.

Trey met her eye and quickly glanced away.

Awkward was right.

How could he get them out of this mess?

After an eternity, Trey found his voice again. "Sullivan Theodore is a bad influence on Jaxx."

"Au contraire, Pierre. If you and Jaxx hadn't started walking with us uninvited..."

"You didn't object."

"You asked to walk with us."

"But you didn't have to say 'yes.'"

"How could I object when you and your bear-sized dog just bumble on in, interrupting the peaceful stroll Sullivan Theodore and I had planned?" Before he could object, she continued, speaking swiftly as though she moonlighted as an auctioneer. "And furthermore, if Jaxx hadn't decided to chase that squirrel, none of this would have happened."

He removed his hands from her arms, shifted his feet again, and prayed they remained upright. "Whoa. Wait just a minute here. It was Theodore who started chasing the squirrel. Jaxx had no choice but to follow along."

"No choice? So, are you calling Jaxx a follower?"

Was there no winning with this woman? "No. I'm saying Theodore was the instigator. Your little fluffy rat-dog is a bad influence on Jaxx."

"Fluffy rat-dog? He is no such thing. Besides, as Jaxx's dad, you should be teaching him that if another dog jumps off a bridge, he shouldn't follow and do the same. Didn't your parents ever teach you that?"

Trey laughed. Jaxx's dad? He loved the dog and was thankful for him, but he didn't consider himself the dog's dad.

Well, not really.

The geeky guy had inched closer. "Mind if I get a few quotes?"

"Who are you?" Trey asked.

"Name's Kyle. I write for the Oakville High School newspaper. My goal is to write full time for a national publication by the time I'm nineteen. This will get me well on my way once I publish my story in both *The Oakville High Chronicles* and *The Oakville Daily*." He withdrew a notebook from his pocket. "Now, I know your names, but what were you doing when this occurred?"

An elderly woman with billowy white hair and red lipstick saved the day. "Now, now, Carleigh. Can I be of any help?"

Heroes sometimes came in the most surprising packages.

"Mrs. Bassanelli, thank you so much. Can you help us?" Carleigh asked.

"Let me see what I can do. You poor dears." Mrs. Bassanelli spent the next several few minutes untangling them.

Kyle intruded once again. "Can you tell me how to spell your name, ma'am? Does it end with a 'y,' an 'I,' or an 'ie?' And how is it that you came upon this situation?"

Mrs. Bassanelli waved him away. "You will never be a good reporter if you're that obnoxious. Now go away and let these people be embarrassed in peace."

"Ma'am, I was only trying…"

"Go away, young man."

Kyle appeared offended but slunk away, head down, as he presumably scrolled through the four-hundred and fifty-seven photos he'd snapped of Carleigh and Trey's embarrassing moment. Other people who had gathered also disbursed, leaving just the three of them and the dogs.

"Kids these days," Mrs. Bassanelli said through pursed lips. After several frustrating minutes, she finished untangling them "This is such an unfortunate mishap." Mrs. Bassanelli scrutinized them from head to toe, then focused on Carleigh. "You poor, poor dear. I hope the mud and grass doesn't stain your clothes."

"Thank you, Mrs. Bassanelli. You are a lifesaver."

The older woman handed Carleigh her glasses. "Think nothing of it, dear."

Carleigh placed one side of the broken glasses on her face. One of the lenses was missing and the frame was bent. "There. Now I can see somewhat to go home."

61

Trey bit back a laugh. If she knew how ridiculous she looked with only one lens and the glasses teetering precariously on one side of her face, she'd remove them in an instant. The mud and grass caked to her face and hair added to her unkempt appearance.

"I have something that will cheer you up," said Mrs. Bassanelli, wiping her hands on her black polyester slacks. "I was going to stop by and ask you, but this works better and it'll alleviate the pain you've suffered all in one fell swoop."

Carleigh nodded. "What is it?"

"Well, as you may or may not know, my Stella's birthday is next Saturday."

"Really?"

"Yes, and I've decided to throw her a huge birthday party and invite all her friends. I'd be ecstatic if you could come, Carleigh."

"Is Stella your child?" Trey asked.

"Yes, she is." Mrs. Bassanelli sized Trey up. "And your boyfriend here can come too."

"I'm not..."

"He's not..."

Mrs. Bassanelli either ignored them or hadn't heard their objections since she prattled on. "We'll have a clown, and of course some games. The bakery on Main Street is making the most adorable dog-friendly cupcakes, and I've purchased streamers, balloons, and hats from Oakville Party Supply. So far, we have about twenty who have committed to coming. Can I count on Sullivan Theodore and..." she pointed at Jaxx.

"Jaxx."

"Unusual name. Can I count on both of them to be there?"

"You want the dogs there?" It had been a while since Trey attended a birthday party, but times had changed.

"Absolutely! My Stella loves Sullivan Theodore IV, and she might like Jaxx too."

"That's really nice of you to let your daughter have pets over for her birthday."

Mrs. Bassanelli's brow furrowed. "Yes. Well, anyway, can I count on you both? It's at two o'clock in the afternoon."

"Count me in, Mrs. Bassanelli. Sullivan Theodore and I will look forward to it."

"Delightful!" the woman clapped her chubby hands which boasted glittery red fingernails. "And you?"

"What about it, Trey?" Carleigh asked. Her eyes seemed to be daring him to say "yes" before she smiled at him for the first time ever. "Besides, it's the least we can do since Mrs. Bassanelli rescued us."

Trey got the hint. "All right. Jaxx and I can make it. What would your daughter like for a gift?" Gifts for little girls were completely out of his realm. He thought of his cousins, two of whom had young daughters. Maybe he could ask for some advice.

"Superb! So glad you can come! You'll find a list of things she'd like on the registry at People's Pets."

"People's Pets?" That was unexpected.

"Yes. Make sure you look at the registry. My Stella is quite particular and her favorite color is purple."

Confusion clouded his mind. "You registered your daughter at People's Pets?"

63

Carleigh giggled. Mrs. Bassanelli gave him a look suggesting he might be a few letters shy of a computer keyboard.

"Of course, I would register my Stella at People's Pets. Where else would I register her?"

"The toy store? The clothing store?" Trey shrugged.

Mrs. Bassanelli rested a hand on his arm. "Poor dear. You can find toys and clothes at People's Pets."

"Really?" Who knew?

"Yes. Now I'd better run. It was marvelous seeing you, Carleigh, and meeting your boyfriend."

"I'm not..."

"He's not..."

"So lovely that you both work together and are both writers." Mrs. Bassanelli squeezed Carleigh's arm. "And especially lovely that you'll both be attending my Stella's birthday party next Saturday."

The woman ambled off, leaving Trey and Carleigh behind with the dogs. They walked toward their homes, silence between them, which was fine with him.

But he really had to know. Call it reporter curiosity, but how was it that someone as elderly as Mrs. Bassanelli could have what sounded like a young daughter? "Is Mrs. Bassanelli raising her granddaughter?"

"Her granddaughter?"

"Yeah. She made Stella sound like she's a little kid. I would have imagined at least a teenager."

Carleigh started laughing again. While it was at his expense, he realized he kind of liked the sound.

"You poor dear," Carleigh said, changing her voice to sound like the animated Mrs. Bassanelli.

"What?"

"Stella is a dog."

# Chapter Six

CARLEIGH READIED HERSELF FOR church the next morning. She pulled her shoulder-length brown hair into a low ponytail and applied her makeup. Finally, a day without having to see Trey Montgomery. "Thank the Lord for small favors," she muttered.

Yesterday had been a disaster of behemoth proportions. The only bright spot was seeing Trey's face when he realized Stella was a dog. That made the sore knee, the broken glasses, the humiliation, and the grass-stained purple leggings worth it.

"Can you believe it?" she asked Sullivan Theodore, whom she had forgiven for yesterday's events, "That Trey thought Stella was a little girl? He is so obtuse." Sullivan Theodore nodded as if he understood. "Now, you be a good boy and I'll see you after church."

The drive to Oakville Community Church took Carleigh all of five minutes, and when she arrived, she parked next to Mom's silver SUV. Church had always been an important part of her life, and a warm feeling rose within her at the sight of the place of worship.

She spied Bubba, his wife, and three kids across the parking lot and waved. Four of the women in her Bible study were cloistered just inside the front door, and Carleigh stopped and chatted before meandering through the foyer.

Isla, her twelve-year-old prayer partner, embraced her in hug. "Thank you so much for praying for my dad," said Isla.

"How is he doing?" Isla's dad had recently undergone heart surgery.

Isla grinned, her mouth full of braces. "Doing much better. Mom says now we need prayers as he recovers because he can be a bit stubborn."

"I'll definitely keep your family in my prayers."

"Thank you. Are you coming to the next prayer partner meeting?"

Carleigh enjoyed the opportunity to be a positive role model for her younger sister in Christ. "I wouldn't miss it."

Mr. and Mrs. Fortuna were the greeters today, and Carleigh smiled and said "hi," as she took a bulletin from them before entering the sanctuary. Her parents wouldn't be difficult to find. They sat in the same place they had for the past fifteen years. The far right-hand side, four rows from the front.

Nothing could extinguish her jubilant mood, and Carleigh said "hi" to a dozen other people before making her way to where her parents had claimed their seats.

And that's when she saw him.

Across the sanctuary, Dad stood talking with Trey.

No. It couldn't be. Didn't he attend one of the other churches in town?

"Sweetie," said Mom, bestowing a hug on Carleigh. She took a step back. "Is something wrong?"

"Why is Dad talking to the enemy?"

Mom turned her head. "Oh, Trey was wandering around aimlessly, and you know your dad. He took Trey under his wing and invited him to sit with us."

Carleigh informed her dad of her opinion when he joined them just before the service started. "Dad, you're a traitor. A turn-coat. A Benedict Arnold."

Dad had the audacity to appear shocked that he could ever be a traitor. "It's good to see you, honey," he said, smirking. Mom laughed and elbowed her husband.

Pastor Gehrig began speaking. "Welcome to Oakville Community Church. We're glad you're here. Please have a seat for a few announcements before we begin worship."

Dad always sat on the edge seat with Mom next to him, and Carleigh next to her. Perhaps today Dad could sit in the seat one over from the edge so there would be somewhere for Trey to sit. "Psst, Dad..."

Her father leaned forward. "Yes?"

"Can Trey sit by you?"

"I'm fine here, Carleigh, really," said Trey, plopping down next to her.

There were five other Bible-based churches in Oakville. Why did Trey have to choose this one? Carleigh shuffled in her seat, doing her best to ignore Trey's long legs extended beneath the next row of chairs in front of him.

"How have you been?" Trey whispered. "Did you have a good day yesterday?"

68

"The best."

Trey chuckled and returned his focus to Pastor Gehrig.

"Why are you here? Are you stalking me at church?"

"Hardly. Mr. Fortuna invited me. I've been searching for a church home."

After the announcements, they began worshipping the Lord. Carleigh tried her best to relax, but there was just something anxiety-provoking about sitting next to Trey. Especially in light of the fact he really did have no personal space. Matters were made worse when several people crowded in the chairs next to, behind, and in front of them, causing their proximity to be much closer than Carleigh found comfortable.

She caught a whiff of his cologne. Instinctively, she inhaled the woodsy scent.

The words of the worship music appeared on the screen and the congregation began to sing. Trey's voice was strong and on-key, something she personally found surprising.

Several minutes later, Pastor Gehrig took his place at the podium. "Today's message will be on loving and praying for your enemies. We have many scripture passages to look at today, but please turn to Matthew 5:43-48. We'll start there."

Thankfully, Dad hadn't invited Trey to lunch or she might have disowned herself as his daughter. The rest of Sunday was relaxing and the perfect antidote for what could potentially be a stressful week working with Trey on *every* story.

On Monday morning, Carleigh arrived at work a few minutes early. Lindy's bouquet emitted a heavenly scent as she approached the front desk. "Your flowers are beautiful."

"Thank you," beamed Lindy. "I can't even begin to imagine who they might be from."

Lindy told Carleigh last week the flowers were from a secret admirer, even though Carleigh already knew from her investigations with Trey. "Oakville is a small town. You could probably find out."

"Probably. But there's something exciting about not knowing." Lindy paused, a frown creasing her brow. "I don't want to be disappointed."

Carleigh wasn't surprised Lindy had a secret admirer. A couple years older than Carleigh in school, Lindy Chou was a popular, pretty, and petite girl on the tennis team who, with her doubles partner, won the state championship in their division.

"Carleigh and Trey, meet in my office," announced Howard.

"Wow, he's getting started early," said Lindy.

"He sure is. Wish me luck."

At Howard's request, Trey shut the door and closed the blinds peering into *The Oakville Daily* office. "Now then," said Howard. "A couple of things. First of all, you two will have the Buy it All customer appreciation day to cover this week, as well as the interview with Zander Velasquez and Mrs. Velasquez."

A knock on the door interrupted Howard. "Come in," he said.

Chip entered. "Sorry I'm late, sir."

Howard checked his watch. "No problem. I was just planning our duo's schedule for the week."

"Have you already told them about tomorrow?"

"No. Why don't you go ahead?"

The suspicious gleam in Howard's eye left an unsettled feeling in Carleigh's gut.

Howard's phone rang then. "Yes?"

"Howard, it's a man named Kyle who says he has the story of the century for you."

"What a surprise. And let me guess...he has photos as well. Put him through."

Trey nudged Carleigh. He mouthed the words, "That Kyle kid from Saturday." Trey was likely correct.

Howard held the receiver in his hand, but eyed Carleigh and Trey before taking the call. "You can't believe the number of photos that have been emailed to me from the fine folks of Oakville pertaining to your little adventure on Saturday." He beamed, his eyes protruding behind his glasses and his plump cheeks rounded into a satisfied smile. "You two are already celebrities in this town and we haven't even announced our plans to the public about *The Oakville Daily* Duo. This is turning out better than I expected."

Carleigh avoided Trey's eye and fixed her attention straight ahead at the framed certificate on the wall behind Howard's desk designating *The Oakville Daily* as Oakville's number one news source. She did not want to be part of *The Oakville Daily* Duo any more than she would want to swear off fashionable shoes for the rest of her life. And she didn't even want to contemplate the photos that had captured her and Trey's fiasco last Saturday.

Giving into the temptation to see how her adversary was handling the disheartening news, she allowed her eyes to shift slightly for a peripheral glance at Trey. He sat upright, seemingly cool-as-a-cucumber. However, there was a giveaway, one that Carleigh had begun to notice more often. The ear that faced her went from its usual color to a vibrant red.

Carleigh stifled a smug smirk and watched as Howard tapped line one to take the call.

"Really? Our very own Carleigh and Trey? And you say you have photos as well?" Howard thrummed his fingers on the desk. "I'm eager to see them. Yes. Please stop by after school and we'll talk then."

Howard hung up the phone and grinned at Carleigh and Trey. "You two had some adventure this past weekend from the sounds of it."

"Yes, sir," said Trey. His voice lacked any indication of nerves, and he appeared unruffled as always, save for the change in ear color.

"I look forward to hearing what this kid, who writes for the school paper, has to say about that adventure."

"It's really not that exciting," insisted Carleigh. She wished her own voice would exhibit a tone of tranquility, as Trey's did.

"I'll be the judge of that." Howard took a drink of his coffee. "Now then, Chip. Tell them what we have in store for them on Wednesday."

"All right." Chip stood and, as was his usual high-energy custom, jogged in place. "To kick off the promotion of *The Oakville Daily* Duo, we will have a photo session. I'll be the photographer and we'll go out to The Falls and take some photos of the two of you together for our front-page article and promo piece that Margie and I are collaborating on."

"Since when did you become a photographer *and* a writer?" Trey asked.

"Oh, I have no intention of being either, but..."

Howard cut in. "Remember that here at *The Oakville Daily*, we all wear many hats, sometimes temporary hats, sometimes permanent hats. Chip will be doing the photography on a one-time basis with Trey giving him some guidance. Margie will write the article. Maybe we'll even have an open house to celebrate so people can meet the two of you, get acquainted, give you some story ideas, and hopefully, become subscribers if they aren't already."

Carleigh realized she'd been holding her breath. "Is a photo session really necessary?"

"Of course it's necessary, and I can't wait to see how Margie puts the story together. Chip is the brainchild behind this and I, for one, think it's a phenomenal idea. Well done, Chip."

"Thank you, sir. Always ready and willing to help make *The Oakville Daily* the number one paper in Oakville." He snort-laughed.

"Now then. I'm confident that after yours and Margie's story and the story we receive from Kyle, there truly will be no competition for *The Oakville Daily*."

Carleigh heard Trey groan.

Her thoughts exactly.

# Chapter Seven

TREY HAD SETTLED IN comfortably to work on a couple of articles when Howard dropped an envelope on his desk. "It's a letter to the editor. An interesting one, and one that doesn't include a full name and phone number, but we'll take it. Can you take care of it for tomorrow's paper? I'm leaving early today to surprise Karen for our anniversary."

"Happy Anniversary."

"Thanks. This makes the big three-five. I'm planning some activities for Karen for the entire afternoon, including taking her out to the new Italian restaurant, so there's some prep work to be done."

"Howard, there's a call on line one. Story idea," announced Lindy.

"I'll take it in my office."

Five minutes later, Howard emerged with a grin on his face. "Emergency meeting for *The Oakville Daily* Duo!"

Trey looked up from his computer screen. Clearly, Howard was more thrilled about the new name for his two star reporters than anyone else was. Carleigh stood up at her desk and made her way toward Howard. Trey did the same.

"That was Mrs. Peters. She's home now from the hospital after having her triplets. She thought her story would be of interest to our readers. Can you two head over there in the next half hour? She needs you there before she puts the babies down for a nap."

Deadlines took a backseat when Howard insisted on story coverage. In the "olden days," one photojournalist would take the job. Now, however, he and Carleigh would have to cover it together. Waste of time in Trey's opinion.

"Sure, Howard," said Carleigh.

"Good. Take the van. Lindy has the keys at the front desk. I need to go get stuff arranged for Karen. Oh, one important thing…be extra careful driving the van. Wear your seatbelts, drive the speed limit, and no driving through mud puddles. It's a classic and irreplaceable. Also, be sure to replace the sun shade on the dash when you return. Understood?"

Trey had to remind himself he wasn't a teen borrowing Dad's car for the evening. "Sure thing, Howard."

"Good. Get to it, *Oakville Daily* Duo."

"Try to hide your enthusiasm," quipped Margie. A motherly sort, Margie could be quick-witted when the need arose.

"You know, Margie, sometimes I think you're the lucky one doing the obits and being the special assignments coordinator."

"Someday, you'll have seniority and you'll get the superior assignments," Margie said, putting on her reading glasses. Margie didn't really need to work because her husband was a prominent lawyer in town, but she had recently become an empty-nester and needed something to fill her days. Howard convinced her to work for *The Oakville Daily* and Margie agreed, provided the position offered a relatively low stress level, hence the obits and special assignments title. She was also either related to—or knew just about everyone—in Oakville. Her flamboyant personality and extensive experience heading up and teaching arts, crafts, and drama at the local home-school co-op for twelve years emerged in her dedication as a valued employee. Her administrative skills were also highly valued and contrasted Howard's "organized chaos."

Trey laughed at Margie's comment and grabbed his coffee mug. Maybe they could stop by and get a real cup of coffee at Coffee Drive-Thru on Fifth Street since it was close to Mrs. Peters's house.

It had been some time since Trey rode in the minivan at the beginning of his career at *The Oakville Daily*. Howard had given him a tour of the town, which Trey welcomed since he was new to the area. This would be the first time Trey would actually *drive* the work vehicle.

He headed outside to the back of the brick *Daily* building where the van was parked. While he had obviously seen it before, the appearance of it still shocked him nonetheless.

The minivan had seen better days. The 1990 eyesore was bright green with the words *The Oakville Daily* in huge black block letters on each side. Below the words was the phone number and an old fax number. On the back of the van were the faded words, *"We deliver the news to you."*

When Howard took over the newspaper, finances were tight and he hadn't replaced the minivan. As the years passed, he declared that since the vehicle was paid for and had low insurance premiums, he'd keep it until it died. Trey figured the real reason Howard kept it was because he was quite fond and protective of the vintage automobile.

"This thing is hideous," said Carleigh. "How about you drive?"

Trey manually unlocked the passenger side door for Carleigh.

Bubba loaded the camera equipment into the back. "Be careful and take the corners slowly."

"Thanks, Dad. What time should we be home?"

Bubba placed a fleshy arm on the sliding door. "Be home by curfew, Son." He laughed a contagious belly laugh and sauntered toward *The Oakville Daily*.

Trey climbed into the driver's side, removed the sun shade from the window, fastened his seatbelt, and started the vehicle. After protesting a couple of times, the engine finally roared to life. Talk radio emitted from the speakers. "Reassuring to know the radio still works." He reduced the volume and positioned his coffee mug in one of the cup holders below the dashboard. "I thought we could go to Coffee Drive-Thru on the way and get some decent coffee. What do you say?"

"Sure." Carleigh clicked her seatbelt and adjusted the seat with the manual adjustment. "This thing was primo in its day. Check out all the cup holders."

"Impressive. Perfect for the growing family."

Trey started down Eighth Street and turned onto Main toward Coffee Drive-Thru. "It's a snappy little unit."

"It fits you. Maybe Howard will let you trade your truck for this."

"Very funny. I'm a truck guy. I'm actually allergic to minivans."

"But it is a 'snappy little unit.'"

Trey harumphed. "I'm just surprised it even rolls along. It's like one of the first vehicles ever made."

"Actually, it reminds me of a getaway car."

"Only without the oomph to actually make a getaway."

Carleigh's laughter filled the van and he liked the sound of it. He shook his head. No, he did not. She was his rival. The sooner he got some quality coffee in his system, the sooner his thoughts would be rational. He stepped on the gas and the van lurched. "Wow, this thing has some pep."

"Uh, Trey?"

"Yeah?"

"There are flashing lights behind us."

"Come on, Carleigh. That's not even funny. I'm already freaked out about driving Howard's classic car."

"No, seriously."

Trey peered into the review mirror. Sure enough, a police car was following them.

"Were you driving over the speed limit?" Carleigh asked.

"No. We haven't driven far enough to even reach the speed limit."

"Well, you did say it had some pep."

Trey put on his turn signal and pulled over to the side of the road. Unfortunately, Main Street was the most popular street in Oakville and several people passed by, their heads lolling out the window to see who was driving *The Oakville Daily* minivan.

"Great. This will be in the paper tomorrow."

"Don't worry. I do the police blotter. Oops, I think it's Officer Zemski. He's a stickler for the rules."

"Thanks. That makes me feel better."

Carleigh offered a chipper smile. "Glad I could be of help."

Officer Zemski walked up beside the window, a serious expression on his bearded face. "Hello there, Trey. Do you know why I pulled you over?"

"I was speeding?" The words practically fell from his mouth in guilt.

"You were?"

"I don't know. Maybe?"

Officer Zemski's mouth formed a stern line. "License and registration, please."

Carleigh opened the glove box and the entire thing fell out, dispersing a host of miscellaneous papers, napkins, pens, a tire pressure gauge, about six dollars in pennies and nickels, and some severely expired sunscreen.

"Um, just a minute please, Officer." She and Trey both unlocked their seatbelts and bent over to pilfer through the mess.

"Maybe you should clean this thing out every once in a while," suggested Officer Zemski.

"We haven't driven it in a long time. Howard just gave us an important assignment," said Trey. Maybe Officer

Zemski would allow him to get out of a ticket if he stressed the necessity of driving the van.

He handed Officer Zemski his driver's license. "Not a flattering picture," the officer said.

Carleigh finally found the registration and handed it to Officer Zemski.

"Sit tight. I'll be right back."

Trey did his best to remain cool and unfazed. He had practice at appearing calm. He could do this.

"Your ears are red."

Great. Carleigh noticed his most embarrassing feature. "Thanks."

"Sure. We photojournalists are paid to notice the details."

More people drove by. Some honked, some stared, and one took a picture or video with their cell phone. "We thought Saturday's adventure was bad. This will really be bad when we read about it in *The Oakville Daily*."

"How do you stay so calm in stressful situations, well, besides your red ears?"

"Lots of practice."

Carleigh gave him a look like she wanted him to elaborate, but he wouldn't. Some things were private and most things about him she did not need to know at all.

Officer Zemski returned to the window. "Here's your license and registration. I'm pleased to discover that you've only had one minor infraction in the past few years."

"Yeah. I didn't see the mailbox with all the snow."

"Good to know. Now, you weren't speeding, but you do have a tail light out."

Trey released a huge breath of relief. "Thank you, Officer. You had me a nervous there for a minute."

"Just keeping you on your toes. Get that tail light checked out and keep up the excellent work on the articles." He shook Trey's hand and returned to his vehicle.

Trey plopped back against the soiled cloth seat. "Now then. That was a close one. Shall we continue on?" he asked.

"You're beginning to sound like Howard."

"Let's just say I am in dire need of some quality coffee."

After the interview with Mrs. Peters, Carleigh and Trey climbed back into the minivan. "I can't believe it's two o'clock. So much for getting this wrapped up before the babies take their naps," said Trey.

"The babies were adorable, but Mrs. Peters can really talk. I remember that from when she was a clerk at the grocery store. Mom could never get away if she went to her line."

"We'll have to hurry if we're going to get all this stuff done before deadline tomorrow. Howard gave me a letter to the editor to handle too."

"I need to finalize my interview questions for Zander and Mrs. Velasquez."

To-dos rammed through Carleigh's mind. Trey might need to make another dash through Coffee Drive-Thru to help her maintain her sanity. But before she could suggest it, he rounded the corner from Mrs. Peters's street onto Fifth. A bit too hastily. It was almost as if the minivan went up on two wheels. She clutched the door handle.

"Ummm, Trey?"

"Don't tell me Officer Zemski is following us again."

"Nope. It's worse."

"Worse?"

"The minivan is falling apart. I just saw a hubcap rolling away when you took that corner."

Trey shook his head. "It was probably from another vehicle."

"Nope. No one else is on this street right now. It was ours. And there it goes." She pointed to the right. A gray hubcap rolled along its merry way down the street and onto the sidewalk.

"Howard will have our hides if we don't stop and get that."

"Your hide. And yes, do stop and let's get it. If it has to be replaced, it's vintage and would probably cost one month's worth of pay."

Trey stopped the minivan and climbed out. Carleigh watched as he ran after the hubcap. It seemed to elude him and he stepped up the pace, taking gigantic strides. She giggled. She really didn't feel sorry for him. Not after all he put her through on a daily basis. Finally, Trey caught the hubcap and returned to the van. "Hopefully nobody got that on camera."

"I think we're in the clear. We'd better get back before we have any other misfortunes."

Trey threw the hubcap in the third-row seat and drove back to *The Oakville Daily*.

He carefully parked the van in its place and they jointly replaced the sun shade in the front window.

When they returned to the office, she watched with amusement as Trey unfolded a letter from an envelope. Could this be the letter to the editor?

The Oakville Daily didn't receive many letters to the editor, but it did receive some, especially in election years. His eyes enlarged and curiosity got the best of her. She moseyed over to his desk. "Anything interesting? I need a break from typing up my notes from the Peters story."

"Yeah. It is interesting. Take a look."

He handed her the letter, which was typed on typical white paper. She read the words:

```
Dear Editor,
    I want to thank you for the excellent
service I have received from The Oakville
Daily. Your receptionist, Lindy, goes
above and beyond for customers. She is
efficient, courteous, friendly, smart,
polite, and has an exceptional sense of
humor. Thank you for hiring her. Because
of her, I read The Oakville Daily daily.
    Sincerely,
    S.A.
Oakville
```

"No name and phone number? I'm surprised Howard will allow us to print that."

"I know. He mentioned something to that effect, but said to publish it anyway."

"Bizarre." Carleigh swiveled to Lindy's direction. Lindy was on the phone. "She does do a good job, but this letter is..."

"Above and beyond?"

"Exactly."

"Wait." Carleigh read through the letter again. "Check out the initials on the letter."

"S.A."

"Yes. Secret Admirer."

Trey slapped his knee. "You're right! I bet it's the same guy who sent her the flowers."

"Yes, but question is...who could it be?"

"No idea."

Carleigh thought it might be fun to attempt to solve Lindy's secret admirer's identity, but pondered if it was a wise idea to again join forces with her adversary. Of course, he might have a worthwhile idea or two. "Do you want to try to solve the mystery of the identity of Lindy's secret admirer?"

"Count me in."

"*Oakville Daily* Duo, Margie, and Chip, in the conference room, pronto."

Howard's impatient tone interrupted Trey's story flow for an upcoming sports article, and he flashed the "emergency writer signal" to Howard—the one-minute sign—and continued to type up his thoughts.

When he finished transferring his thoughts from his mind to the computer screen, Trey glimpsed Howard leaning against the doorway to his office, arms crossed, tapping his foot against the floor. "Glad you could join us," he said, as Trey entered. The others already crowded around the weathered brown table in the small conference room. "Now then. I wanted to touch base with everyone regarding the article about Carleigh and Trey's adventure in the park."

Trey groaned. "Can we put another article in its place?"

Margie gave him what he could only refer to as a "motherly look" with her short brownish-gray hair and her slightly-pursed lips. Had she perfected this "look" on her own children during their growing up years?

"Now, Trey," she said, her voice soft but firm, "I have worked hard on this article, and Chip has devoted many hours to the photo layout. We are not going to put another article in its place."

"I thought that Kyle kid was writing the story."

Carleigh didn't say anything but nodded. Amazing that she actually agreed with him. Make that twice in one day.

Margie and Chip shared a knowing glance while Howard steepled his fingers. "Let's just say I didn't care much for that Kyle kid. He would do well writing for a glossy tabloid, but not for a publication with integrity, such as *The Oakville Daily*. Instead, I offered to publish a few of his photos, give him a byline for them, and have Margie write the article. Chip is in charge of graphics."

Trey released a huge sigh. No telling the type of article Kyle may have written. Howard had their backs, and for that, Trey was grateful. "That's actually good news."

"Why, thank you," said Margie. She pretended to bow.

Howard retrieved a folder from a nearby filing cabinet. He placed several pictures on the table. "Here are the photos we've chosen to use. It was tough. We had over thirty-five photos from about ten people, including that Kyle kid."

The first was of Carleigh and Trey running after their dogs. A caption had been attached to it that read: *When choosing to get some exercise outdoors, be mindful of the mud from the recent spring rains.*

The second was of Trey assisting Carleigh to her feet. The caption for it read: *Trey Montgomery shows his gentlemanly side in assisting Carleigh Adams to her feet after her unfortunate fall.* Several more had captions as well for a total of seven photos.

Carleigh cleared her throat. "Thank goodness you don't have the one with the leashes wound around us."

She was right about that. Trey could only imagine how ridiculous they looked in that picture. At least the ones that Howard had chosen to use weren't really that bad after all.

"Truth be told, I do have that photo with the promise that if I use it, I will give Kyle credit. But it doesn't fit with this article."

"Will you let us know if you use it?" Trey asked.

"Absolutely." Howard picked up the photos and placed them back into the folder. "This is the rough draft of the article that I just need to edit and it will be ready for tomorrow's issue." He handed a copy to both Trey and Carleigh.

Trey scanned the title. "As You Venture Out This Spring, Watch for Mud."

Margie beamed. "Isn't it whimsical? It took me awhile to come up with that title."

He didn't say anything, but instead perused the article.

As two of our very own *Daily* reporters discovered this past Saturday, mud can be a dangerous part of spring. Carleigh Adams and Trey Montgomery, better known as *The Oakville Daily* Duo, were walking their dogs together when the slick mud from the recent spring rains wreaked havoc on their otherwise enjoyable outing.

When their dogs, Sullivan Theodore and Jaxx, chased a squirrel, *The Oakville Daily* Duo had no choice but to participate in the chase of a lifetime. Fortunately, no ligaments were strained and no bones were broken during Carleigh's unfortunate fall. Her sunglasses, however, met their demise and succumbed to an untimely death.

Margie had proceeded to give a few tips about safely navigating mud-covered walkways and fields. All in all, the article wasn't too bad, especially since it could have been much worse if Howard had chosen the leash photo or allowed Kyle to write it.

"We want the people of Oakville to be intrigued by our *Oakville Daily* Duo. This article is the precursor to the front-page article we'll soon publish detailing that you two will now be covering the news as a team. Margie will write that article as well, and as I mentioned previously, Chip will take you two on a photo session Wednesday right after lunch."

The thought did not sit well with Trey. Did they have to make such a gigantic deal out of him and Carleigh being a team? While he knew it would work well from a marketing aspect, he really didn't need anyone thinking of them as any sort of team.

This week had already started out with the minivan ordeal. Wednesday they'd have their "photo session" as Howard called it, and Saturday he would be attending a birthday party for a dog.

Why did he feel like he was smack-dab in the middle of a reality TV show?

Good thing tomorrow would be an uneventful day covering Buy It All's customer appreciation day.

He needed uneventful.

# Chapter Eight

THE BUY IT ALL parking lot was packed. As the more popular of the two major grocery stores in Oakville, people were doubly excited to hear that the shopping mart was offering free hot dogs and pop and donuts from Karen's Bakery. There would also be exclusive drawings for those who stopped by and entered.

Trey offered for Carleigh to drive the van today, but she declined. With her luck, she'd hit something and dent Howard's vintage vehicle.

Her mind was still reeling from yesterday's events and the photos Howard had chosen to publish. It could have been a lot worse, but the second one with Trey helping her up emphasized her terribly muddy clothes. There had been a couple pieces of grass sticking haphazardly out of her hair, and a mud splotch on her right cheek. Neither Trey nor Mrs. Bassanelli had offered to tell her about her grass-filled hair or muddy face.

At least today would be a calmer day. She never realized that working for *The Oakville Daily* could be so adventurous. Of course, back before she became part of the "duo," things were much more manageable.

Trey whipped into a parking spot, narrowly missing the back bumper of a pickup truck parked in front of them. "Maybe Howard should pay to have you go back to driver's ed," she quipped.

"Nah. I'm an experienced driver. This green machine has just taken some time to get used to with it having a pointy nose and all."

Carleigh never figured vehicles to have pointy noses, but Trey might have a point, no pun intended. She doubted he was an experienced driver, however.

"You ready for this?" he asked.

"Ready as I'll ever be."

"Now, remember, stay away from the mirrored refrigerators."

Carleigh slugged Trey in the arm and he began to laugh. She supposed he was sort of attractive when he laughed.

Sort of.

She sipped coffee from her mug and pretended her mind did not just insinuate that Trey was attractive in any capacity. If Howard insisted they continue to spend time together, her mental health would suffer for sure. Already her eyesight needed to be evaluated.

A crunching sound interrupted her thoughts and Carleigh jolted forward as something hit the van. The person who had parked next to them misjudged the parking spot and had rammed into the van's rear fender.

"Was that what I think it was?" asked Trey.

"Yes, someone just hit the van."

Trey face palmed his forehead. "We really need to take our own vehicles to these assignments. Howard is going to kill us."

"Yes, well, I'd say it was nice knowing you, but..."

"Feeling is mutual. Should we assess the damage?"

Carleigh dreaded what may have happened to Howard's prized vehicle. She peered out her window again. The person had reversed and was attempting to re-park. This time the driver barely missed the van's passenger side door. "Maybe I'll wait here until she shuts off her engine. Safer that way."

"Good idea."

They waited for what seemed like an hour. People streamed into Buy it All and the aroma of barbecued hot dogs filled the air. Carleigh's stomach growled.

But first things first.

After the other driver switched off the engine, Carleigh safely wedged herself out of the van. The other car, an already-dented, faded brown-and-orange classic automobile, parked crookedly, straddling the intersection of several parking lines.

An elderly woman with curlers sat in the driver's side. Carleigh and Trey walked over to the dented rear fender. "Not as bad as I thought," muttered Trey.

The crimp in the fender could have been worse, but it would be obvious to anyone with any sort of vision to see that it had, indeed, met with an unfortunate collision. "Do you want to tell her the news or do you want me to?" Trey asked.

"You can."

Trey knocked on the woman's window. She rolled it down. "Yes?"

"Ma'am, did you know that you just hit our van?"

"I what?" Her eyes grew large and magnified under overly thick pop bottle glasses. She grabbed a crocheted purse from the seat beside her and climbed out of the car. She could have been something from a movie with her colorful moomoo house dress, nylon stockings, and white slip-on sneakers. She peered from the minivan to the front of her car and back to the minivan. Some of the van's green paint was on the front portion of her dented car. "Oh, mercy." She reached inside her dress pocket and pulled out a tissue. "I am so sorry."

"We'll have to call and have the police stop by to document it." To his credit, Trey's tone was courteous and kind.

"Will I be in trouble?"

"I'm not sure what he'll say, but you do have insurance, right?"

"Yes. Yes, I believe so."

Moments later, a police car entered the parking lot and Officer Zemski emerged.

It was going to be a long day.

When they returned to *The Oakville Daily*, Carleigh had a feeling that Howard was going to kill them for denting his cherished vehicle. She should probably type up a quick Last Will and Testament of Carleigh Adams, leaving Sullivan Theodore IV and all of her earthly possessions to Mom and Dad. But she wouldn't think of that now—or at least she would try not to think about it—because duty called, and she wanted to do a thorough job for the owners of the grocery store.

This was the part of her job that Carleigh lived for—the interviews. She moseyed around Buy it All asking customers and employees questions. Trey recognized the wide variety of photo ops and took dozens of pictures and joined her in chatting with the owners, husband and wife team, Kevin and Amy. Carleigh had attended school and was friends with their oldest daughter. "It looks like an impressive turnout," she said, noticing that while Buy it All did steady business, today was exceptional.

"We're just so grateful for our customers. When Dad and Mom passed this business to us ten years ago, we knew we wanted to keep it the same as it's always been in the sense of excellent customer service and a readily available variety of products—things that have been the cornerstones of this store for three generations." Kevin wrapped an arm around his wife's shoulder. "God has blessed us richly with Buy it All, and we hope that in some way, we can be a blessing to others."

They conversed for a few minutes more before Amy said, "Now, don't you two forget to sign up to win. We have some sensational prizes. Every hour on the hour, we're giving away a case of Oakville Frosted Cookies. As you know, those are made right here in Oakville and shipped all over the country. We also have, for third prize, a month's worth of dairy products; a family-sized ice chest perfect for picnics for the second prize; and for the grand prize, a barbecue grill."

"We'll be sure to sign up," said Carleigh, as she made her way to the sign-up table, followed by Trey.

"Man, I sure would like to win this barbecue grill." Trey ran his hand along the top of the grill. "It would look incredible on my deck."

After interviews, they went outside and sat at one of the picnic tables that had been placed in the roped-off area of the parking lot. The day was ideal for not only the grand opening, but also a town-wide barbecue.

"It's that time again!" Kevin announced over the loudspeaker. "Time to draw another name from our hat for a case of Oakville Frosted Cookies. As you know, Buy it All is a loyal supporter of Oakville Frosted Cookies and sells them by the dozens each week. This case of twenty-four is the ultimate for anyone who loves the best cookies in America." Kevin should have been a radio announcer with his deep, steady voice. He beamed, his face shining in competition with his vivid Hawaiian shirt. "Amy, who should we have draw the next winner?"

The crowd murmured their excitement, and Carleigh recalled that each year, it was an honor to be chosen to pick a winner. This year was no different. "I think we'll ask Carleigh Adams from *The Oakville Daily* to pick our next winner." Amy beckoned Carleigh to join her and Kevin.

"Oh, wow, thank you for the honor." Carleigh reached into the cowboy hat and withdrew a slip of paper. Without looking at it, even though she was tempted to do so, she handed it to Amy.

"Thank you, Carleigh. And the winner is...drumroll, please...."

Kevin pounded on a hide drum. Amy opened the folded paper. A pin drop could be heard as the audience hushed to complete silence. "And the winner is...Trey Montgomery!" The crowd went wild with clapping, as if Trey had won a million dollars instead of a case of Oakville's prized cookies.

Trey's jaw slacked and Carleigh snapped a photo with her cell phone. Who knew that she would choose him to win a case of Oakville Frosted Cookies?

"Is that rigged since she chose her boyfriend?" someone in the audience asked.

Heat rose up her neck and face. "He's not my boyfriend," she said, her voice almost a growl. She attempted to locate who it was who had uttered those appalling words. Meanwhile, Trey stepped toward Kevin and Amy and retrieved his prize.

"Join us next hour for another winner and this evening at six-thirty when we announce the winners of our other prizes." Kevin rested the microphone on the table and the crowd cheered.

Numerous people congratulated Trey, and several asked if he was willing to offer a share of his winnings.

"I snapped a magnificent photo of you receiving your prize," Carleigh showed him the picture on her phone.

"I'm not trying to sound ungrateful, but man, I sure did want to win that grill."

"Too bad it's only one entry per person."

Trey was so dejected she almost felt sorry for him. Almost.

An hour later, Carleigh and Trey briefly left Buy it All to let Sullivan Theodore and Jaxx out for a bathroom break.

"Man, Howard is really going to kill us over that dent. He treats this thing like it's an expensive sports car."

"So, like a glorified station wagon or something?" She attempted to disguise a smart-alecky grin.

Trey's eyes enlarged, and he sent her a horrified glance that took his attention off the road for far too long. "A glorified station wagon? Carleigh, where have you been? The 1970s?"

"My parents were born in the later 1970s, so no, I haven't been hanging out there. I just have fond memories as a little girl riding in my Grandma Adams's 1978 station wagon to get ice cream during the summer. She loved that thing and Dad always talked about how it was in pristine condition and had so few miles on it even three decades later. It had brown panels and was the longest car I've ever seen. Thankfully I didn't have to practice parallel parking that monstrosity."

Memories of Grandma Adams flooded Carleigh's mind. Grandma passed away seven years ago, leaving a huge void in the lives of all who knew and loved her.

"Well, an expensive sports car is nothing, and I mean *nothing* like your grandma's 1978 station wagon, even if it did have wood panels. I've seen one of those things because my dad owns a mechanic shop. They're pretty cool, but no, the sports car I'm thinking about has a hefty price tag and can go from zero to sixty in three-and-a-half seconds."

Carleigh attempted to calculate how many years she would be working at *The Oakville Daily* before she'd come close to making a down payment on such a car. "Well, here's hoping Howard exercises some grace when we tell him. At least it's a minor dent."

Trey tapped his fingers on the steering wheel and turned onto Maple Avenue. "True. And I could probably have my dad help me pop out the dent."

Carleigh perused their neighborhood with fresh eyes. A meadowlark sang in the distance. The neat and tidy craftsman-style homes lined either side of the street, comfortably spaced and indicative of a quaint, yet updated 1940s village. She'd been fortunate to find a home to rent, and even more fortunate to find one with a sizable back yard for Sullivan Theodore.

If only she'd known Trey lived so close by, she might have opted for another neighborhood. She cringed when she recalled the incident with the doggy door.

"Mine is the yellow one on the right."

Trey pulled up to the curb of her house. Pink, white, orange, and purple tulips had begun to show their faces from the front flower bed. Soon, she would need to take a much-needed trip to Oakville Trees and Nursery for some petunias and pansies.

"I'll be right back." Carleigh opened the minivan door and walked toward the house. She opened the front door,

98

and Sullivan Theodore bounded toward her, leaping into her waiting arms. Carleigh snuggled him and gave him a pat. "How about a snack?" she asked. The snacks were in the cupboard across from the sink, and she opened the door to retrieve a few.

Sullivan Theodore rushed out the door and into the front yard. Carleigh tossed the bag of doggy treats on the counter and raced after him. "Sullivan Theodore, come back here now!"

But her pet didn't mind. He raced toward Trey, his tail wagging. All Carleigh could think of was chasing him down the street if he spied another squirrel.

"Well, hey there, Theodore. Been in any trouble lately?"

"Can you please nab him?"

Trey leaned over to do her bidding when Sullivan Theodore leaped over his arm and took off down the road.

"Not again," moaned Carleigh. "I'll be right back."

"Need some help?"

Pride nearly stopped her from accepting his offer, but if he did help, then they would find Sullivan Theodore faster and be able to get back to work sooner, so she acquiesced. "Sure, thanks."

Carleigh's heart pounded. She slipped off her stylish high-heeled sandals, silently reminding herself to retrieve them again on the way back, and took off as fast as she could in the direction her pet had gone.

Trey caught up to her, then passed her. "I think he went toward my house."

Several minutes later, they still hadn't located Sullivan Theodore. A few cars drove by on the street, and Carleigh prayed they would be mindful and cautious to watch for a tiny white dog zig-zagging through the neighborhood.

When she couldn't find him, she rushed back toward the house. Where could he be? She'd checked everywhere between her house and Trey's. In front yards, back yards, and side yards. She'd called his name so many times she was nearly hoarse, and her aching feet were black from running outside without shoes.

"Did you find him?" Trey asked sidling up next to her.

"No, I was hoping he hadn't gone far."

"We'll keep looking. We could call animal control and ask for their help."

The animal control guy was extremely accommodating and would rather assist someone finding their pet than take it to the shelter. Carleigh fought back tears that threatened to form in her eyes. Why had she gotten sidetracked and left the front door open again?

They sat on the porch while Carleigh called animal control. "He's on his way."

"Good. Let's go look for him again. We'll find him."

Her gaze met Trey's. "Thanks, Trey, for helping. I really appreciate it."

"Yeah. No problem. I know how I'd feel if it was Jaxx who'd run off. Not that he would because he's an obedient and well-behaved dog, but..."

She was about to give him a crusty, when she noticed a kindness in the depths of his eyes. They sat there for a moment, their eyes connecting.

Maybe Trey the Irritating Montgomery had a considerate side.

Highly unlikely. Impossible. Implausible. Remote.

But still, his kindness was just what she needed at the moment while she agonized about Sullivan Theodore's whereabouts. She prayed several more times, berated herself at least a dozen times for not watching him more closely, and contemplated her next move.

A few minutes later, she glanced up to see a peculiar sight. "Sullivan Theodore?"

Trey followed her gaze toward the minivan. A white dog with a navy collar sat in the window of *The Oakville Daily* minivan. He was on the dash, his face pressed against the window, his pink tongue swirling doggy saliva all over it.

Carleigh jumped to her feet and sprinted towards the van to secure her pet before he ran off again. "How did he get in there without us noticing?"

"Your dog is a regular Houdini?" Trey asked. She followed his shifty gaze to the driver's side door he'd left open, allowing Sullivan Theodore access to the front seat of the van.

She reached for her pet and held him close. "You are in so much trouble."

Sullivan Theodore pasted on one of his innocent faces, the one where he appeared sweet, honest, and completely virtuous.

Which he was not.

Carleigh secured Sullivan Theodore in the house while Trey canceled the call to animal control. Then they drove to Trey's to let Jaxx out, which proved to be a much less-exciting venture, and returned to Buy It All.

As they rode back in silence, Carleigh figured maybe Trey did have a nicer side. He was still her adversary, but the way he'd offered to assist her with Sullivan Theodore did hint at the possibility of him possessing some admirable qualities.

Just hinted, though.

Four hours later, Kevin announced that in ten minutes, he'd share with the customers who had won the other prizes. Trey still tried not to be bummed about not winning the grill. At least he had enough cookies for everyone in his new men's Bible study group for when it was his turn to bring treats.

If the cookies lasted that long.

Customers milled around the store, purchasing items and visiting with other patrons. It was part of Oakville's charm that such a large swarm of people would attend the event. While his hometown would still be considered a smallish town, it was at least twice to three times the size of Oakville.

Trey had seen numerous people he knew and had chatted with dozens more. Oakville was really growing on him.

His shoulders ached from lugging around his camera equipment. Thankfully, he'd been able to take a brief break and run home and let Jaxx out. He hadn't expected to make this story an all-day event. Of course, the whole fiasco with Sullivan Theodore had set them back a bit.

Yet here he was while Carleigh interviewed one hundred and fifty people and he snapped three million photos. Not that he didn't love his job, and the photography part was actually his favorite, but he still had deadlines to meet at the office.

Like the article for this week's "Trey's Sports Corner." He'd decided to write about the struggles of an underdog. A kid who wasn't athletic, who could only dream of making the team. Maybe next week, he'd write about a team member who showed up for each practice, worked hard to learn the tricks of the game, and still was only a benchwarmer when game time arrived. The third installment would be a piece on how to encourage your kid, even if they aren't following in your footsteps as a star athlete. He knew something about that.

He'd often received positive feedback about "Trey's Sports Corner," although with this new segment he was planning, it would have to go beyond the two-paragraph allotment. He was confident Howard wouldn't have a problem with that.

That was one positive thing, among many, about working at *The Oakville Daily*. Howard gave his reporters a lot of free rein.

If only he had given Trey free rein on *not* being part of *The Oakville Daily* Duo.

Several steps away, Carleigh burst out in laughter at something a customer had said. Her rosy face shone and she removed her glasses and wiped her eyes. "That is so hilarious!" she exclaimed before she and the customer proceeded to laugh again. He could see she was genuinely amused and for the slightest of seconds, he was drawn to her contagious giggle.

Today she wore a bright purple shirt and some jeans. The woman had no clue what it meant to be subdued in the color of her clothing choices. She'd left her hair down and it brushed against her shoulders. If he was honest, he would have to admit to himself that she was far from plain.

Not that he noticed her appearance because he really didn't. Not too often, anyway.

She swiveled her head toward him and caught his stare. Trey knew his ears were likely red, and he quickly remedied any embarrassment by turning and speaking to a passing customer, as if he was never staring at her in the first place. Maybe Carleigh would even think it was her imagination that his eyes were even glancing in her direction at all.

He hoped so.

Kevin was busy announcing the winners of the dairy prize and the ice chest. "And now, last but not least, the moment we've all been waiting for—time to see who wins the grand prize of a barbecue grill purchased at our fantastic Thambert's Hardware Store." The entire town of Oakville had arrived for the later hours of the customer appreciation day after getting off work and a thunderous roar of claps filled the outdoor area. "We are so thankful for this beautiful day God gave us. It could have been raining like it does most often during the month of May, but instead we've been blessed with abundant sunshine. We are also grateful to you, our customers. Amy, who should we have choose the grand prize winner?"

Amy took the microphone from her husband. "How about for the drawing for this most important prize, we choose none other than Trey Montgomery from *The Oakville Daily*?"

Trey wanted to decline, but when he saw Amy's exuberant expression, he decided not to say anything. Instead, he reached into the cowboy hat and drew out a piece of paper.

Silence fell over the parking lot, much different than a few minutes before when everyone was conversing with each other. Trey prepared to snap a photo.

"Thank you, Trey. And now, I've been given the honor of announcing the winner in this historical moment." Amy nodded at her husband and he played the drum roll once again. "The winner of this year's Buy it All customer appreciation day grand prize is...Carleigh Adams!"

Trey knew he should lift his jaw from the ground. He just couldn't believe it. Carleigh had won the grill? Did she even have a deck? Or a penchant for grilled burgers on a hot summer night? Did she even know how to use a grill? People bumped into Trey in their quest to congratulate Carleigh. He tried to maintain his composure and snapped the photo when she went up front to receive her prize.

But he still couldn't believe it.

"This is so exciting!" She beamed, raising her hand for a fist bump.

Trey reluctantly obliged because he didn't want to be a sore loser.

"Do you want to trade the grill for my case of cookies?" he asked.

"No thanks, but do you think we can fit it in the minivan?"

"Yeah. I think we can manage. Maybe you could let me borrow it for a week or so."

"Um, yeah...no. We are for sure not sharing custody of my grill. My parents are right over there. I can't wait to hear what Dad says about my win."

Trey snapped a few more photos, then put his camera away.

At least tomorrow would be a better day.

Oh, wait. Scratch that thought. Tomorrow was the photo session for *The Oakville Daily* Duo.

# Chapter Nine

TREY ARRIVED AT WORK early in the morning to explain the dent in the minivan to Howard before his boss discovered it on his own. He'd have to seamlessly merge in the devastating news after the discussion of other topics.

"Now then. Did the event go well?"

"Yes, sir, for the most part."

"For the most part?"

"Carleigh won the barbecue grill grand prize."

"Our very own reporter won the grand prize. That's really something."

Although not one to wallow in self-pity, Trey really did wish he'd won the grill. Carleigh yapped on and on about it all the way to her house where he assisted her in unloading it and pulling it around to the back where she did, in fact, have a deck. All the while, the fluffy rat-dog stood at the glass door and barked nonstop. Carleigh assured him that those were "happy barks" since Sullivan Theodore knew a barbecue was advantageous for him as well.

"Did you win anything?" Howard's voice brought Trey back to the present.

"Yes."

"Well?"

"A case of Oakville Frosted Cookies."

"Really? Those are known all around the country, maybe even the world. That's impressive. Congratulations." Howard slapped Trey on the back.

"Thanks. I plan to take some to my men's Bible study when it's time for me to bring snacks."

"Just think, both members of *The Oakville Daily* Duo won prizes. That should be a record or something. Speaking of which, don't forget about your photo session with Chip right after lunch. I can't wait to get this *Oakville Daily* Duo promotion out in the open so people can begin knowing the two of you as that."

Trey could wait. He could be a very patient man if need be.

"Are you able to make the photo session?"

"Yes, sir. It's just that, well, Carleigh and I are not exactly..."

"Comrades? Yes, Trey, everyone in the office knows you two compete with each other and view each other as the 'enemy.' You two have different writing styles, but it works. You make a top-notch team."

Trey would revel in the fact that Howard valued their writing, but he'd leave the "top-notch team" part out of his troubled mind. He checked the time on his fitness tracker watch. He really needed to tell Howard the bad news before everyone else arrived. "Uh, Howard, I need to tell you something."

"Don't worry. I already know that you and Carleigh were pulled over in the minivan by Officer Zemski the other day. A few customers were kind enough to snap photos of the event. I'll forward the emails to you and Carleigh and you can decide which picture or pictures should make the paper."

Trey inwardly groaned. When he was a kid, he appreciated making the paper. As an adult, not so much, and unfortunately, it occurred all too often these days.

"It's not that. It's something else."

"This doesn't sound good. You're not quitting, are you?"

"Definitely not. I love this job." *Well, for the most part anyway.*

"Carleigh's not quitting, is she?"

"Not to my knowledge."

"Okay, then I can handle whatever news you are about to give me."

Trey tapped his foot. He seriously doubted Howard could handle this news. "You might need to grab a donut, sir."

"This isn't boding well if I have to have 'comfort food' just to hear what you have to say. Now on with it, pronto."

Trey cleared his throat and explained to Howard the occurrences of yesterday's distressing event.

"So, someone just rammed into you in the Buy it All parking lot?" Howard asked. Already, Trey could see through Howard's glasses that his boss's eyes were wet.

"Yes."

"I'm not sure I'm able to see this." Howard followed Trey out to the back of the building. While he was sure he was exhibiting a calm exterior, inside Trey nerves were on edge. This was Howard's "baby."

"It's not as bad as you think and not as bad as it could have been."

Howard's footsteps were heavy and sluggish and Trey slowed his own long-legged pace to accommodate Howard's delaying the inevitable. "Do we know who did it?"

"A woman named Mrs. Moeller."

"Mrs. Moeller? Oh, no. Please tell me she did not dent my prized vehicle with her outdated car."

How could he tell the truth without causing his boss more sorrow? "Yes, it was an incident involving her outdated car, but the dent is small, and if there's a problem with the insurance or Mrs. Moeller is uninsured, I can probably pop it out quite easily. My dad is a mechanic and he also restores classic vehicles in his spare time. He's taught me a thing or two."

"Thank you, Trey. I might take you up on that. Although just between you and me, Mrs. Moeller shouldn't be driving anymore. She's upwards of ninety."

"Carleigh made reference to something similar while we waited for Officer Zemski to arrive."

Howard stopped and lingered a few feet from the minivan, hesitant to take those final steps. "We need to take this slowly."

"Take all the time you need."

Howard took one lethargic step, then another, his scuffed loafers trudging along the sidewalk. If he procrastinated long enough, they'd need to reschedule the photo session.

Sweat beaded on Howard's brow. "This is tough. The minivan is a sign of how *The Oakville Daily* has survived through the years. Through easy times and difficult times."

Trey took pity on his boss and his existential crisis over the minivan. He knew he'd be bummed for sure if anything happened to his pickup. "It's on this side." Trey led him to the passenger side.

"Oh, no." Howard rubbed the back of his neck. "This is not good."

"Like I said, sir, I can pop out the dent. It'll be just like new."

Customers yapping it up over at Oakville Farm Supply across the street were the only sounds amid Howard's melancholy state.

Howard shuffled forward and smoothed a hand along the fender where the dent now resided. "I remember in the not too distant past when this was a streamlined vehicle. Straight body, no defects."

"It can be that way again. Do we have insurance?"

"We do, but it's only liability. Not sure what Mrs. Moeller's company will do for us. You'll have to give me all of that information and we'll have to obtain a copy of the police report."

"Officer Zemski said he'd be over with a copy of the report sometime this week. It seems he understands your affection for the minivan."

"Zemski and I go way back. We used to bowl together on the bowling league." Howard sniffed. "Well, what's done is done. While this is disturbing news, all we can do is move forward."

"Might I make a suggestion?"

"Sure."

"Maybe you could retire the minivan and use it as a memento of days past. You know, have it on display for the treasure that she is." Trey held his breath.

For a moment, Howard's misty eyes seemed to return to their normal appearance. "Not a completely bad idea. I could enter it in those classic car shows and take glossy photos of it to put in the car collector magazines." He paused, and Trey released the breath he'd been holding. "But no, we need to keep her in service. She's been a faithful soldier in this quest to bring Oakville quality news. Besides, you and Carleigh will need it for interviews and to cover stories."

"All right."

"Oh, and thank you for fixing the tail light the other day. Bubba had to tend to the printing press issues, and I appreciated having you as a backup."

"No problem."

This time, it was Howard's turn to sigh. "Now then. I can't promise I can put this behind me, but at least, like you say, it's not as bad as it could have been." His dejected face showed his true emotions. "You were right, though. I do need one of Karen's donuts to get me through this."

Trey thought all was well until he heard Howard's heavy footsteps clunk toward the front of the van. "What is this?"

Trey's gaze followed Howard's finger, which pointed to a smeary caked-on slobbery mess on the window.

"Uh, there was a little accident."

"Another one? You do have a valid driver's license, correct?"

"Yes, sir."

Howard pointed to the dried dog saliva mixed with who knew what else. "Then what happened here? Did someone spill something?"

"No, it was a dog incident."

"What kind of dog incident?"

How could Trey explain the situation to an already-ramped up Howard? "You see, Carleigh's dog climbed into the minivan unbeknownst to us, pressed his furry face against the window and licked it."

Howard inspected the smeared mess, which was more extensive than Trey remembered. "Looks like a bunch of spitty-boogery dribble," he growled. "And what was Carleigh's dog doing in the minivan? This is not a pet taxi."

Howard's verbiage gave Trey an image of *The Oakville Daily* minivan painted yellow with a taxi sign and paw print decals on the side transporting Jaxx, Carleigh's dog, and a host of other Oakville canines. He stifled a chuckle. To laugh at Howard's annoyance would be career suicide. "We stopped to let the dogs out and Theodore climbed in somehow without us knowing. He frequently misbehaves."

"This is not good news." Howard placed his hands on his hips. "I'll be chatting with Carleigh about this and the window will need to be returned to its former condition. And in the future, no pets in the minivan, understood?" He scowled and ambled back to *The Oakville Daily.*

Carleigh would be in for it for sure and Trey felt a smidgeon sorry for her.

But only a smidgen. She really needed to do something about that criminally-minded dog of hers.

Trey was about to return to his desk when Howard asked if he could come into his office for a minute. "I have one other item I need to ask you about."

Was he still upset over the dent and dog slobber incidents? Trey couldn't imagine what it might be that Howard needed to speak to him about, but he followed his boss into his office.

"We have two simultaneous items that need to be covered on Friday evening. I was afraid that might happen after we decided to go the 'duo' route, but it won't be a problem this time."

Trey didn't point out that there had been no "we" in the decision to go the "duo route." He thought about Friday's calendar. "I know that the Oakville Athletic Awards Ceremony will be held at the high school at seven p.m. What else is going on?" For a town with a population of just over three thousand residents, Oakville boasted numerous activities.

"There's the Homemade Kazoo Festival in the Oakville Hotel conference room at the same time."

"Homemade Kazoo Festival? Never heard of it."

Howard chuckled. "Not sure many have." He adjusted his glasses, and seemed to have recovered somewhat from the trauma of the minivan dent and dirty window. "Folks from several counties over, and maybe even other states, come from near and far to compete with their homemade kazoos. Apparently, they make these kazoos from an empty toilet paper roll, which they decorate with paint and then attach wax paper to the end of it. There are all types of categories including awards for the most creative and best-sounding kazoo."

"Sounds fascinating." Not.

"That's what I thought! If Karen and I hadn't already committed to watching our grandson that evening, we would for sure be attending. Folks take this event seriously, and it's an honor that the organizer contacted me and asked if *The Oakville Daily* would be interested in covering it. We're really starting to become a household name of sorts and are known for our journalistic integrity. Would you like to cover this event?"

Tough decision. Not. "While it sounds intriguing, I think Carleigh would be the best one to cover this event. I should take the Oakville Athletic Awards Ceremony." He truly did believe Carleigh to be the best reporter for that assignment.

"That's gentlemanly of you to give her the Homemade Kazoo Festival, especially after she won the grill you wanted. And yes, I heard all about your thoughts on that from…" Howard cleared his throat. "From an anonymous source. Anyway, are you sure you want the awards ceremony gig?"

"I'm sure. She has a knack for covering those quirkier events and hobnobbing with the participants."

"That's true. She does extraordinary work, especially with her attention to detail." Howard stroked a non-existent beard. "Now then, I'll assign Carleigh to the Kazoo Festival and you can take the awards ceremony."

Chip was a little too chipper for Trey's taste when he popped into work that day. "Are you and Carleigh ready for your photo session?"

"Not really."

"You're not? I can ask Howard if we can delay the time by an hour or so."

"No, it's not that, it's just that...I wish we didn't have to be a duo."

Chip's expression fell. "What? But it's the best idea since buttered popcorn. Anyway, Howard said we could take my vehicle because he wants to give the minivan a rest. Can't wait to show you my new set of wheels. It's top-of-the-line in mid-sized SUVs. Leather heated and cooling seats, GPS, and its off-road capability is impressive."

Trey didn't want to be the bubble-popper of Chip's enthusiasm. "Can't wait to see it either. I remember you saying you were going to pick it up yesterday."

"And I did. Well, I've got a lot to do, so I'll see you after lunch." For several seconds, Chip gaped into space toward the front of the building where Lindy had not yet arrived, then sauntered off toward his workspace.

Carleigh was already sitting at her desk, her fingers flying across the keyboard. He wanted to tell her about Howard's reaction to the minivan, but decided that could wait until they were on their way to the photo session.

He groaned again and set to work on his deadlines. Two articles needed to be completed before the session, as well as photos selected for the Buy it All event.

And prolonging the time was just fine with him.

"Carleigh, I need to see you in my office," Howard called a short time later.

Because Howard left the door to his office open, Trey could hear most of the conversation. He definitely expressed his alarm over the dog slobber. Then he launched into the whole awards ceremony-kazoo event. Surely giving Carleigh the Homemade Kazoo Festival would put him in her good graces. She really wasn't a sports person anyway.

Carleigh emerged from Howard's office and she tossed a glare Trey's way. He looked around and then pointed to himself as if to ask if that crusty look had been directed at him. She nodded and sidled up to his desk. "I have two bones to pick with you, Trey Montgomery."

"Only two? How did I get so fortunate?"

Her eyes narrowed. "Bone number one: thanks for getting me in trouble over Sullivan Theodore hopping into the van and messing up the window. Howard is more stressed about that than the dent, and he wants it buffed to a sheen, which I was already going to do anyway." She paused for a breath and tapped her polka-dot-decorated fingernails on his desk in a rhythmic pattern. "To turn Sullivan Theodore in before I had a chance to tell Howard myself was uncalled for, unexpected, and rude."

"Look, Carleigh. I didn't mean to throw Theodore to the dogs." He smirked at his clever quip, but he was the only one who thought it was amusing. "Howard asked and I told. Not like I offered up the info all willy-nilly."

She clearly wasn't convinced. She pressed her mouth into a straight line and sped up her finger tapping. "Bone number two: why didn't you take the Homemade Kazoo Festival?"

"I thought you would want it."

"I have mentioned before how excited I was to interview the coaches and winning participants for the awards ceremony since I am a former graduate of Oakville High."

"Oh." Yes, he did vaguely recall her mentioning something about that.

Her forehead furrowed into a distressed glower. "You're impossible, Trey Montgomery. Irritating, aggravating, and bothersome."

He may be impossible, irritating, aggravating, and bothersome, but she was sort of cute when she was flustered.

But just sort of.

# Chapter Ten

THE MOMENT CARLEIGH HAD been dreading arrived all too quickly. While finishing up three different assignments, her momentum had been interrupted by grabbing a bite to eat, letting Sullivan Theodore out, and preparing to return for Chip's photo session.

"This is going to be painful," she told Sullivan Theodore.

He angled his head and tipped his ears toward her.

"I mean, if it was anyone else, it might be okay, but Trey the Irritating? Ugh. Riding with him and trying to make conversation. No thanks. Good thing Chip will be there. And get this..." she took a bite of her sandwich. "Trey turned you in for the slobberfest on the minivan window. Can you believe that?"

He gave a grouchy yip in response.

"I know, right? Totally disloyal, double-crossing, and perfidious." She gave her dog a pat. "And that's not the worst of it. There were two simultaneous events scheduled for Friday. Howard overbooked us, and I got the shaft. Trey chose to cover the awards ceremony at the high school, and I have to cover a kazoo festival. Yes, you heard that right. A kazoo festival. All these years of practice and preparation, and it's come to this."

Sullivan Theodore placed his paws on her leg in a comforting gesture, and she handed him one of his favorite doggy treats. "Then this photo session. Two good things about it, though, if I tune into my optimistic nature are that Trey will not be driving and we won't be taking the green minivan." Gratitude spilled from her on those two counts. "We sure don't need another accident like we had yesterday or another scenario with Officer Zemski."

Carleigh finished eating, let Sullivan Theodore out one more time in the backyard, gazed at her new barbecue grill that she had no idea how to use, and then locked up the house and headed back to work. Surely it was the upcoming appointment that had her stomach in knots and not the overly-enthusiastic consumption of her veggie sandwich.

When she arrived at work, Trey and Chip were waiting for her by Chip's sleek new SUV. "Wow, this is impressive."

"Thanks. I have been saving up for a down payment for a couple of years now. Good thing I have a side job doing freelance marketing because I'll be paying it off for the next century. But this baby is brand new off the auto line and it's got a full warranty and all the bells and whistles."

Chip and Trey spoke of technical vehicle topics of which Carleigh had no interest. "Where are we going to take the photos?" she asked, once she could get a word in edgewise.

"The Falls. Howard wants a nice background. Should we go? I'm eager to test this baby out on the open road."

Chip glanced toward *The Oakville Daily,* straining his neck to see something or someone.

"Here, let me get the door for you." Trey opened the front passenger door.

"Now that's a gentleman for you," quipped Chip.

Carleigh thanked Trey and climbed into the stylish interior of the SUV. She appreciated Trey's gentlemanly action, but it didn't make up for her having to cover the kazoo festival or being on the outs with Howard over the slobber because of Trey's tattling.

She inhaled the aroma of "new car smell" and ran her hand over the smooth dashboard with all kinds of gadgets. Mom's SUV Dad purchased for her birthday was plush and only a few years old, but nothing like this vehicle. "This is really posh, Chip."

"Thanks. I'll owe on it for five years, but it'll be worth it."

Trey and Chip chatted about guy things while Carleigh watched the passing scenery. Even having lived here all her life, she never tired of the rolling green farmland and the snow-capped mountains in the distance. She never wanted to live anywhere else.

"Well, here we are." Chip pulled into the parking area of the county park known as "The Falls."

Gushing crystal-clear water tumbled over the side of the hill. Carleigh inhaled the fresh watery air. Maybe she'd just take the rest of the day off and veg in the beautiful scenery. If she had Sullivan Theodore and a new release from her favorite Christian romance author, life would be perfect.

"I thought that would be the best spot." Chip pointed to a location not far from the SUV.

"All right. I'll be right over." Carleigh climbed back into the SUV for a touch-up. She reapplied more mascara and lip gloss and brushed her hair.

"I should do some touch-ups too," Trey said, taking a glimpse of himself in the vehicle's window. He combed his fingers through his hair.

"I'm surprised guys care about that."

"They don't. But it's like school pictures. You don't want to look like a total dope."

They wandered over to the area where Chip had set up the tripod. "I'm really not a photographer, so I'll probably have to take a couple thousand pictures, but you guys will help me out, right?"

Carleigh smoothed a wrinkle in her blouse. She'd purchased it yesterday from her favorite downtown clothing store just for this particular event. If Howard was going to have them in all kinds of promo materials, she might as well look stylish.

"Now, both face me," ordered Chip, barely settling down his hyper personality long enough to set up the camera.

She and Trey faced him and on the count of three smiled. The camera clicked once, twice, then two hundred more times with the same pose. Chip unfolded himself from bending over to peruse a few of the photos. "Okay, now a different pose. If you could please face each other."

"Do we have to?" Trey asked.

"I think it would be better to face you," Carleigh added.

"No. No, I want you to face each other for this one. Like you're chatting about an article."

Carleigh changed her stance to face Trey, and as she did so, her foot slipped on the muddy ground and she nearly took a tumble.

Trey reached out for her, his hands on her upper arms, warm and firm. "Are you okay?"

Her heart raced and words were difficult to find for a moment. "Yes." Physically she was fine, but inside she was totally humiliated. She. Did. Not. Need. A repeat of what had happened at the park, especially not in her new jeans and cutesy high heels.

Trey still appeared concerned for her welfare and they stood staring at each other for a minute. He did have nice green eyes. Small blue flecks interspersed them and he had good hair for a guy, not too fluffy or balding. And he didn't have an abundance of facial hair, which was a plus. Carleigh did not like plentiful facial hair on a guy.

*What on earth? Why are you thinking about this guy's good qualities? Carleigh Jo Adams, need I remind you he is the enemy?*

"Nice. I like that pose. Now smile at each other."

Carleigh attempted to do so in an authentic way, rather than appearing like she was gritting her teeth, but it was difficult. She thought of the doggy door episode, the park adventure, the kazoo festival, the Sullivan Theodore minivan fiasco, the competition for articles before the 'duo' days, the time he'd adjusted her office chair as a prank on April Fool's Day so that it sat at just three inches from the floor, and...

"Not a growl, Carleigh. A smile," Trey said, offering his own to her.

But his smile was far from trustworthy, especially with the suspicious glint in his eye.

A soft breeze blew then and she noticed a pleasing scent of aftershave, cologne, or deodorant. If only she had allergies, she could sneeze and they would no longer have to face each other, but she'd been blessed with no allergies at all, not even hay fever.

"Now turn slightly toward me." Chip was enjoying this far too much.

"Do you need assistance?" Trey asked, his arm ready to offer it.

"Umm, no thank you."

"Not from the enemy, huh?"

"Exactly."

They were now semi-turned toward each other. "Put your heads closer," barked Chip.

Carleigh rolled her eyes. "He's relentless."

"That, he is."

Carleigh and Trey merged closer.

"Perfect!" yelled their photographer. "Now move right over to face the opposite direction and I'll move the tripod."

"This is taking forever."

Trey nodded. "Yep. Hey. Quick question...why would you choose to wear those ghastly shoes?"

"Ghastly shoes? What on earth?"

"Yeah. You've already almost fallen once and the mud is really clinging to those heels."

"You obviously have no fashion sense."

"I'm all for practicality."

Carleigh shook her head. The guy was impossible. "Some people prefer to look stylish, especially for the most important photos of their career."

"Maybe. But if you had been wiser in your choice of footwear, you wouldn't have nearly fallen. Good thing I was there to rescue you."

If he was fishing for a compliment, Carleigh would not be the one providing it. "You're so prideful."

"Prideful? No, I'm not. So what's with you wearing those shoes?"

"These shoes are perfectly fine. What about *your* choice of footwear? Much too casual, informal, and blasé."

Trey snickered. "Casual, informal, and blasé? Maybe less so if you hadn't spilled coffee all over them."

"Hey, I offered to take them to dry cleaners."

"I'm noticing a trend in spilling things and slipping..."

Carleigh narrowed her eyes at him and placed her hands on her hips. "Don't you even say it."

"That you're a bit clumsy?"

"Children!" interrupted Chip, still snapping photos. "Can we please stop arguing and get back to the task at hand? Some of us have day jobs."

Carleigh shook her head. "I can't believe Howard would think this is a worthwhile idea."

Chip took several more photos, some when Carleigh was still recovering from her irritation with Trey.

"Come look at some of these photos."

Begrudgingly, Carleigh traipsed over to where Chip was scrolling through the pictures. Mud caked to her shoes and she attempted to scuff it off in the deeper grass. She would avoid getting Chip's new interior muddy at all costs.

She and Trey leaned in to see the screen on the camera. "Some of these are really good."

Chip flipped through the photos. Some did have potential. Others, like the one of Trey making a face at Carleigh or the one with Carleigh gritting her teeth, needed to be removed. "I see some good ones and some that can for sure be deleted."

"No. Howard said you'd say something to that effect and that I shouldn't delete any of them until he sees them."

"But my eyes are closed in that one," she countered.

"And I'm yawning in that one," added Trey.

Chip ignored them. "Look at this one."

In the photo he referenced, she and Trey could have been posing were it not for the fact that this had been one of those spontaneous pictures. They were facing each other, her head tilted slightly, and both of them sporting broad smiles.

"Now that is what I call an engagement photo," said Chip.

Trey coughed. "A what?"

"An engagement photo. You two are posing like this one was a pre-wedding photo."

"Delete it, please," Carleigh begged.

"Nope. Not until Howard sees it. But man, that really does look like an engagement photo."

Trey slugged Chip in the arm, causing the skinny man to teeter somewhat. "No engagement photos, not with Carleigh."

"That's offensive, Chip. Please rescind that thought." Chip was such a traitor.

But Chip only chortled with his trademark snort-laugh and placed the camera back in its bag.

The entire way back to the office, Carleigh scowled out the window. There was only one thing worse than being a part of the duo. And that was having an engagement picture with Trey. She'd have nightmares tonight for sure.

# Chapter Eleven

TREY ATTEMPTED TO FINISH his pending workload when they returned to *The Oakville Daily*, but his mind was still processing all that had happened during Chip's photo shoot. Carleigh was tapping her fingers on her desk and biting her lip. Had all the craziness of this afternoon caused her to be distracted too?

He returned his attention to his computer screen. Today had been a nightmare in the making, and Chip hadn't helped one bit.

Engagement photo?

Not on his life.

Trey cringed when he remembered Chip's comment. Maybe someday he'd get married and hopefully have a marriage like his parents shared, but when that time came, he would not be marrying Carleigh.

No way, no how.

But...while he had dissed her choice in shoes, truth was she did look rather cute in them and those bright colors she always wore. She could be a lot of fun to hang out with when they were getting along. And when she fell and he steadied her...

Trey shook his head. No. He was not sort of, kind of, in a far-off, obscure way, falling for Carleigh.

Absolutely not happening.

Why then had she filled his thoughts from the second they climbed back into Chip's fancy SUV?

Trey unlocked the doors to his truck and loaded the camera equipment early the next day. Carleigh settled into the passenger side. "Not bad," she said.

He puffed up at her compliment, fastened his seatbelt, and started the engine. "Thanks. I still have about a year's worth of payments, but the payoff is getting closer."

Trey eased the truck from its parking spot at *The Oakville Daily* and maneuvered it onto the street. The minivan was in the shop today, and it was a relief to be driving his own vehicle for an assignment. He was proud of his newer model truck for which he'd saved up for years for the down payment. When the time finally came to make his purchase, Mom and Dad had loaned him the money. Now he paid extra each month in eager anticipation of paying it off sooner than expected.

"You actually drive like a somewhat-sane person in your own vehicle."

"Thanks, I think. This is so much easier than that pointy-nosed van."

"More comfortable too." She eased into the gray cloth seats.

Trey dismissed the thought she looked like she belonged in the passenger side of his truck.

"Oh, by the way, I'm still not thrilled about having to cover the kazoo festival tomorrow evening. Care to trade?"

"No way. Besides, you are perfect for that assignment."

"And why would that be?"

"As I mentioned to Howard when he asked me which assignment I wanted, you have a knack for covering those quirkier events and hobnobbing with the participants."

Carleigh sat up in the seat and faced him. "Whoa. Hold the phone. Did you just say that Howard gave you a choice?"

"Yes."

"I thought he assigned it on his own."

"Uh...no." Trey thrummed his fingers on the steering wheel, regretting he ever mentioned about Howard asking him about which assignment he wanted. His big mouth always got him into trouble. He wished he had a knit cap on right about now to cover his likely-reddening ears.

"I can't believe that. You know I went to school here and know most of the teachers and coaches at the awards ceremony. And yet, you chose to give me the kazoo festival."

"You probably know all of those people too. Besides, like I said, you have a knack for covering those types of events."

"But aren't you the musical one?"

Trey thought about that for a moment. "The musical one? I might be somewhat musical, but I don't play the kazoo."

Carleigh crossed her arms. "This just goes to show that we will forever be adversaries."

"Even though we now have an engagement photo?"

"Hmmf. That is not even funny."

"Hey, do you want to try to solve who sent Lindy the flowers?" Trey asked after the interview for today's assignment. Fortunately, it had gone smoothly and efficiently.

Spending more time with Trey than was absolutely necessary was really not something Carleigh wanted to do, especially in light of the whole kazoo and engagement photo fiasco. Besides, she had a ton of stuff to work on back at the office, not to mention this current assignment. Unfortunately with Sullivan Theodore's mischievousness, she'd spent precious article time yesterday detailing the minivan widows.

Still, it would be interesting to know who Lindy's secret admirer was.

"What do you say?" Trey asked again.

"All right."

Trey sped into the parking lot of Louella's Flowers and Gifts. "How do you propose we do this?" Carleigh asked.

"Just watch the master."

"Should I be scared?"

Trey just laughed and shut off the engine. "Follow my lead and let's see if we can solve this mystery."

"Are you sure you aren't really a detective in disguise?" Carleigh followed Trey to the front of the business, where he opened the door for her, which she appreciated, but pondered a hidden motive. "Trying to get on my good side after the kazoo incident by being a gentleman?"

He grinned. "Something like that."

Louella Greene had owned the florist shop since Carleigh could remember. A short woman in her late fifties, Louella had a charming personality, a dramatic flair, and a compassionate heart. She also was a bit scatterbrained.

"Hello. Haven't seen you in a while," she said, directing the latter part of her comment to Carleigh. Louella arranged a bouquet of beautiful red roses and baby's breath. "How have you been?"

"Busy, but good." Carleigh inhaled the delicious scent of fresh flowers. She could move into this place without one ounce of hesitancy.

"Let me guess. This is your boyfriend?"

"Absolutely not," Carleigh answered a little too quickly. From the corner of her eye, she saw Trey's amused expression.

"Oh, sorry about that. You two are just such an adorable couple…"

*Adorable couple?*

Louella continued, "I guess my imagination got ahead of me, and most couples come in to pick out flowers for

132

their upcoming...well, never mind." She fussed with the flower vase. "So, what brings you in today?"

Had Louella thought they were in to pick out flowers for a special occasion for themselves like a wedding? She cringed. Surely not.

Trey piped up, filling in for Carleigh's momentary loss of words. "We're actually doing a story on secret admirers."

They were?

Trey continued, leaning an elbow casually on the counter. "It seems that sometimes secret admirers send flowers to the object of their affection."

He was right, he was the master when it came to soliciting information. Carleigh would have to remember that if he became all suave and inquisitive in chatting with her.

"I suppose that's true," said Luella. "A story on secret admirers? How romantic. Although, you should have written it for Valentine's Day."

"True. But inspiration can strike at the most inopportune times."

Carleigh took a step back and watched the interaction. Louella was a romantic at heart, and how could she not be, owning a florist shop? And Trey had really captured Louella's attention with his story idea.

"I suppose so. This is an intriguing subject. Are you going to write about how sometimes these secret admirer stories end with a romantic wedding on a beach in South Carolina?" She placed her hands under her chin and swooned. "I always wanted to be married on a beach in South Carolina. The ocean waves splashing against the sand in the background, the sun shining, and the smell of the salty sea in the air...Oops. Sorry. I digress."

"Unfortunately, we're over 2,000 miles from South Carolina, but I—we—do want to write in our article about how many of these secret admirer episodes do end in trips down the aisle."

Louella held her hand out and studied her wedding ring. "My hubby, Lew, and I were high school sweethearts, but he did leave me some anonymous notes in my locker at school, so for about a week, I didn't know who had sent the notes. Then, because I've always been interested in handwriting analysis and I was the English teacher's aide, I compared the notes to the assignments. Low and behold, the secret admirer mystery was no more." Her face lit up. "We've been married for thirty-nine years now. Of course, not on a beach in South Carolina, but rather in our church here with a small reception in my parents' backyard, but I wouldn't trade it for anything."

Carleigh scribbled the notes on her notebook, wishing she could run out to the truck and grab her phone to record, but not wanting to miss any of Louella's passionate story. "Did he admit to being the one to send you the notes when you confronted him?"

"He tried to act coy at first. You know men. Always so goofy about that type of stuff. Lew denied it, but when I showed him I had proof, he admitted to it. Homecoming was the following week and he asked me to the dance. We dated all through high school and married after we graduated. He still leaves me notes sometimes."

Carleigh could see the admiration Louella had for her husband. "How romantic. You two sound like you're still very much in love. Happy endings are the best."

Louella held a hand to her heart. "After all these years of raising four kids, a mortgage, and us owning this florist shop and his plumbing business, yes, we're still very much in love."

"Do you ever have men come in and purchase flowers and have the flowers delivered from a secret admirer?" Trey removed his camera from his bag as he spoke.

"Before I answer that, I just have to say I am so honored to be in your story. I've wanted to be on the pages of *The Oakville Daily* forever, but I've just never done anything famous to earn that recognition. So, thank you for coming in today."

"You're welcome. And I'd like to get a few photos after we talk."

"Absolutely. This is truly exciting. My humble florist shop on the pages of *The Oakville Daily*. Well, it isn't the first time because I've paid for ads over the years, especially around Valentine's Day, Mother's Day, and prom, but this is remarkable."

Trey chuckled. "So, do you ever have men come in here and purchase flowers to have delivered from a secret admirer?" He asked again.

"Actually, yes. I can think of about four times off the top of my head. But I have to warn you, I do have to respect their privacy on such matters."

Carleigh glanced at Trey. How would he handle obtaining the information from Louella if she kept her promise to her customers and wouldn't give out names?

"We don't want to do anything that would cost you customers."

"No, and I would never betray their confidence."

Louella spent the next few minutes speaking about three of the scenarios. "Two of them got married." She said their names and Carleigh knew exactly of whom she spoke, although she never knew that's how the couples had met. "And then there was the recent incident. Of course, that will be a continuing saga from what I understand."

"What do you mean?"

"Well, he is sending flowers to his object of affection every couple of weeks for the next three months like clockwork."

Trey lowered his voice to almost a whisper. "Would this happen to be Lindy Chou at *The Oakville Daily*?"

Louella's eyes grew large. "Ooh, I've said too much."

"We don't plan to print anything about this latest one since it's still active..."

"We don't?" Trey stared at her pointedly.

"No, we don't because we wouldn't want to cost Louella a customer, or worse, her reputation. Do you think it would be all right to discuss the other three in our article?"

"I can call them and ask and let you know."

"Perfect. We can even write the article without their names or give them false names. All right, proceed with your line of questioning, detective," Carleigh told Trey. While Howard wanted her to do the interviews, it was entertaining to watch Trey in action.

"So, Lindy Chou received some flowers last week and you indicated she will be receiving deliveries every couple of weeks over the next three months."

"Yes, that's what he asked and he even gave me the dates of delivery."

"Do you know who it was?"

Louella cast him a warning look. "Even if I did, which I don't, I wouldn't tell because his identity has not yet been revealed to his beloved."

Carleigh giggled at Louella's dramatic wording. "No, and we don't want to know his name."

"We don't?"

Trey really needed to refrain from contradicting her. "Not yet, we don't. When it is revealed, perhaps we can do a 'part two' of the article."

"Ooh, I love that idea." Louella gushed.

"So, he just waltzed in here and ask to have the flowers delivered?"

Trey should really be a detective with the way he hounded his subjects.

Louella closed her eyes as if to recall the moment. "It was just like it was yesterday. I remember clearly that I had sent my delivery guy on a run with a bunch of deliveries. My assistant florist was at lunch, and I was here manning the fort. This man walks through the door in a black trench coat, a black cowboy hat, and dark glasses. I almost had a heart attack. I thought, oh, no, I'm being robbed. My heart pounded and I wished I had one of those convenient buttons on the bottom of my counter that rang directly to Oakville PD. I remember my breath came in short gasps and I thought of my husband

and my children and my grandchild who will be born in two months. Would my wonderful life all come to an abrupt end? I rehearsed in my mind right then and there about telling him to take the roses, the carnations, the baby's breath— take it all. Just please don't harm me." She stopped for a breath. "I've never worried before about safety, not here in Oakville. After all, most of our crimes are petty in nature. And this man—he wasn't particularly scary. He had this curly red hair billowing out from beneath his cowboy hat. Almost clownish."

"Clownish?" Carleigh searched her mind to come up with someone who fit that description. All was doable until Louella mentioned the clown hair.

"Yes. It was curly red hair. He was not well groomed at all and he actually smelled like he'd had onions for lunch."

Trey rejoined the conversation. "So, what did he say?"

"He said he would like to place an order for some flowers, and I said, 'Oh, you're not here to rob the place?' He said, 'No, just need to place an order.' I breathed a million and two sighs of relief and thanked the Lord for protecting me that day. I'm still thanking Him. Anyway, he said he was not concerned about the expense, told me who they were to be delivered to and the planned delivery schedule, then paid in cash."

"Did you see the vehicle he drove?" Surely, in a town the size of Oakville, knowing the make and model of the vehicle would assist them in finding out who Lindy's secret admirer was. Carleigh held her pencil in the air, awaiting Louella's response.

Louella shook her head. "No. He was on foot and must have parked somewhere else. He plopped the money on the counter with a generous tip. Funny thing was that he had a fake Southern accent, almost like he was masking his real voice. I wondered briefly if he was an actor. So, I racked my brain again trying to think if I'd seen him at one of the community plays or something, but nothing came to me."

"He went through a lot of trouble to do all of this," Trey said.

"Yes, he did. I don't know Lindy really well, but I've interacted with her when she took my payment for the ads. She seems like a nice girl. Hopefully this man is on the up-and-up, as you never know these days. I was reading one of my Christian suspense novels the other night and sometimes creepy people can seem friendly at first."

Trey nodded. "Did he write on the card or did you write the note for him?

"As so often happens with orders, because a lot of them are by phone or online...did I tell you that my son developed a website for me? It's all updated and people can order online or even pay their bill online." Louella's face lit up at the mention of her new website. "Anyway, the man told me what he wanted to have written on each of the four cards and I wrote it down. The others are stashed away until they'll be used in conjunction with the delivery of the flowers."

"Interesting," said Carleigh. "Too bad he didn't write it because that would be amusing to find out who he was based on some handwriting analysis."

"Ooh, I agree. It's been a while since I've done any comparisons like that, so I would have been up for the challenge, especially since his clothing style was a bit unusual."

"Is there anything else you can remember about him?" Trey asked.

"No, nothing that comes to mind. I hope after three months, Lindy discovers who her admirer is so I can know. He really was a mystery man. I've never seen him before in town, and I know just about everybody, having been born and raised here. I figure he drove over from one of the other towns. I'm honored he did business with my florist shop, but I really do want to know who he is. For peace of mind."

Trey snapped some photos of Louella's most impressive bouquets, a photo of her standing near the sign of her business, and when he returned from his flower deliveries, a picture of her delivery driver, an ancient man who was hard of hearing.

As they left the shop, two thoughts competed for attention in Carleigh's mind: who was Lindy's secret admirer and what would it be like to have a man go to such lengths to declare his interest?

Odds were it would be a while, if not forever, before she discovered the answer to either of those questions.

# Chapter Twelve

TREY ATTACHED THE LEASH to Jaxx's collar, grabbed the haphazardly-wrapped present for Stella, and headed out the door. Why he was attending a birthday party for a dog was beyond him. The chew toy he'd purchased and wrapped squeaked beneath his arm, as he shoved his house keys into his pocket. Jaxx barked in response, as he always did whenever he heard a squeaky toy. It had been an ordeal keeping the new toy away from him. Hopefully neither Stella, nor her owner, would realize there were a few bite marks in the floppy chicken chew toy. At least it wasn't obliterated by bite marks like Jaxx's own toys.

"I know you'd like a new squeaky chicken toy of your own. Maybe I can stop by People's Pets and get you one to add to your extensive squeaky toy collection. Until then, no more chewing on birthday gifts and things that don't belong to you."

Jaxx put a paw over his eyes, probably in embarrassment. When Trey adopted Jaxx as an adult from the pound, it immediately became clear Jaxx had a penchant for chewing on things. He had chewed through a leash, several tennis shoes, a pair of Trey's socks, and the leg of Trey's dining room chair. Trey had, for the most part, broken Jaxx of his chewing issues he had obviously developed years ago before Trey owned him. Issues likely due to nervousness and separation anxiety. But Jaxx did lapse into his former chewy self at times and gnawed on things other than his squeaky toys and rawhide chews.

Trey spied Carleigh down the street walking Sullivan Theodore. Her bright neon-yellow shirt diminished any hope of camouflaging herself. She only lived three doors down from Mrs. Bassanelli. If he hurried, he could enter Mrs. Bassanelli's house with Carleigh, rather than by himself, which he dreaded doing. He may not be an introvert, but he was no extrovert. Rather, he was somewhere in the middle—an ambivert—who liked to take his time and peruse his surroundings before getting too chatty. And if he could peruse those surroundings with Carleigh, who no doubt would know everyone at the party, life would be that much easier.

He waved a couple of times, attempting to get her attention. Jaxx yanked on his leash and stepped up his pace. Trey did the same and waved again. This time Carleigh saw him. Cars crowded around Mrs. Bassanelli's house, taking up spaces in front of nearby houses. A familiar old dumpy vehicle squealed its tires and parked across the street, halfway on the sidewalk.

Trey broke into a jog, Jaxx eagerly obliging, and met Carleigh just outside the white picket fence in front of Mrs. Bassanelli's immaculate green-with-brown-trim home. "Thanks for waiting."

"Sure."

He noticed her hands were full. "Here, let me take that for you," he said, nodding at a present.

"Thanks."

Trey should offer to also carry the cumbersome purse-like contraption in her other hand, but he couldn't manage it with both presents and Jaxx. Besides, while he would like to get back into her good graces after the kazoo festival incident—although he wasn't sure why—carrying a purse pushed the limits of his penance.

"Did you bring anything else?" she asked.

"No. Did I need to bring something else?"

"Yes, a side dish."

"Side dish?"

She pointed to the purse. "Mrs. Bassanelli asked us to bring a side dish for the party."

"It's a potluck?"

"In a way, I guess, but this way all of the guests eat lunch and it's not a burden on anyone."

Trey focused his attention on the purse and then on Mrs. Bassanelli's house. Lively commotion could already be heard even outside on the sidewalk. He really needed to just send Stella's gift with Carleigh and return home. He had no business going to a dog party that included a potluck. "I could call in a pizza."

Carleigh laughed, causing his muscle tension to ease a bit. "No, that probably wouldn't be a good idea. Mrs. Bassanelli is big on everyone bringing something made with joy to share with others. Oakville Pizza Company wouldn't cut it."

"So..."

Awkward silence filled the space between them and Jaxx tugged on his leash. "So..." he repeated. "Can I share your side dish?" Oh, the humility he had to endure! His ears were probably a vibrant red hue right about now. But he maintained his collected composure by adding a grin to his request.

"Share my side dish?"

"Yeah. You know, since we're friends, maybe we could say we went in on it together."

"I wouldn't say we are friends."

"No, I guess not." Why did a tinge of disappointment fill him at her words? They weren't friends. They were competitors in the game of the written word. "Do you think Mrs. Bassanelli will be mad at me for not bringing something?"

"She won't be mad, but she will be disappointed. I've been to her get-togethers several times, and she really takes this whole 'everyone bring something made with joy to share with others' thing seriously. She might make you go back and whip something up really quick."

Was Carleigh teasing him? "Are you serious?"

"There's no telling with Mrs. Bassanelli. She's a dear woman, but she is spontaneous. Besides, this party is extremely important to her, and everyone wants it to go off without a hitch. Mr. Bassanelli died last year, and this is Stella's first birthday without her dad."

Trey still wasn't accustomed to pets being considered children. "So, what do you suggest I do?"

"Well..."

The car door of the old dumpy car across the street screeched open and an ancient woman in a dress emerged with a dog. "Oh, no. Look who's here."

"Mrs. Moeller. Haven't seen her in a while."

"No, not since she dented *The Oakville Daily* minivan."

"I'm not surprised she's invited. She and Mrs. Bassanelli go way back. I think she may have even been Mrs. Bassanelli's teacher or something." Carleigh paused. "Look, we can share my side dish, but you owe me one."

"All right. I really appreciate it."

"Sure."

"So, what is it? You know, in case they ask."

"It's a pasta salad."

Mrs. Moeller hobbled across the street. Trey opened the door for Carleigh and Mrs. Moeller, and slipped inside Mrs. Bassanelli's home.

Regretting it instantly.

Dogs ran around everywhere, their yips mingling with the commotion of women's voices, some shrill and some more subdued. Aromas of all types lingered in the air. From what Trey could see, the place was packed entirely with women. A few were as old as his mom, but the vast majority were old enough to be his grandma, great-grandma, or even his great-great grandma.

"Hey, I know you," Mrs. Moeller sniveled.

Trey forced himself farther into the room. He turned to Mrs. Moeller. "Hello."

"You. You are the one who said I dented your station wagon."

"Uh. Minivan."

"Station wagon, minivan, no difference. One is just higher off the ground is all." She stood, narrowing her eyes at him, a bulldog at her side.

"So good to see you both!" exclaimed Mrs. Bassanelli, saving the day. She rushed toward both Trey and Carleigh and enveloped them in a hug. Trey caught a whiff

145

of Carleigh's hair. A light citrusy scent, competing with the food, dog smell, and stale perfume of the room. He inhaled. She turned her head and about collided their faces together, her eyes meeting his.

He took a step back out of Mrs. Bassanelli's hug. "Good to see you, too."

"Everyone," Mrs. Bassanelli clapped her wrinkled, well-manicured hands. "You all know our dear Carleigh girl, but I'd like to introduce to you her boyfriend, Trey. They work together at *The Oakville Daily*."

Trey inwardly groaned. "I'm not her..."

"And he's not my..."

"Oh, yes, *The Oakville Daily* Duo! I saw the pictures and read the write-up," exclaimed a tall willowy woman holding a tan teacup Chihuahua. "My name is Mrs. Gomez. So nice to make your acquaintance."

Trey shook the woman's hand and narrowly missed being bitten by the teacup Chihuahua.

"Now, now, Mighty, it's all right. You see, Mighty is extremely protective."

"We are so glad you could both make it. Can we have a round of applause for this handsome couple?" A room full of women joined in Mrs. Bassanelli's clapping. "Well, well, what did you bring us that you made with joy?"

"My mom's...um, you see, this is from both Trey and me, so a joint effort. It's my mom's famous pasta salad recipe passed down through the generations."

"Scrumptious!" declared Mrs. Bassanelli, reaching for the purse. "I'll just go set it on the table. Now, everyone, remember not to take supersized portions. We all want

146

to sample this delicious recipe passed down through the generations."

"I'm Lil. Nice to meet you. I find it endearing that your boyfriend assisted in making the side dish," said an elderly woman with bright eyes, gray curly hair, and an ebony face. "My dearly beloved, Earl, God rest his soul, wasn't the type to help me in the kitchen." She reached up and gently pinched Trey's cheek. "Something tells me you're a keeper."

Trey knew his ears had gone beyond red to some sort of deep crimson. Good thing he could maintain his composure. Carleigh's boyfriend? That he had helped in the kitchen to make a pasta salad he knew nothing about? That he was the only guy here in this room full of crazy women and just as many dogs?

This might be prime time for the floor to open up, swallow him whole, and transport him to another universe, like in those sci-fi books.

Mrs. Bassanelli peered at her gold-chained watch. "The clown will be here soon. How about we all go out back and let the dogs play and get reacquainted before lunch?"

Everyone concurred and Trey and Carleigh followed the women to Mrs. Bassanelli's expansive backyard. Carleigh whispered, "She actually has an acre lot because Mr. Bassanelli purchased three house lots at once back in the day."

"Attention, attention!" Mrs. Bassanelli motioned for her guests to draw closer to the patio table. "There is a party hat for each dog." She handed each of the women a pointy birthday hat, made especially for dogs. Carleigh placed the silver pointed hat with a blue puffy ball on it on top of Theodore's head.

"This one is for Jaxx," said Mrs. Bassanelli, handing him a white hat with purple paw-print polka-dots on it and fake blue fur around the perimeter. He held it in his hand for a moment and looked over at Jaxx.

"Uh, Mrs. Bassanelli, do you have another hat I could trade this one for?"

"No, that's the last one. It was the biggest, so I thought since Jaxx is oversized, it would fit best. Is there a problem?"

"It's just that Jaxx is a manly dog and..."

Mrs. Bassanelli tossed aside his concerns. "I'm sure Jaxx won't mind."

Trey wasn't so sure.

Despite his reticence, Trey was able to force himself to place the nauseating hat on top of his poor dog's head. Jaxx took one for the team and trotted off.

Trey thought of how the backyard could have been a reprieve with its mammoth pines, towering Oak trees, and swimming pool, but with a million dogs in party hats running around and the constant cackles from the women, it more resembled a nightmare. "I think I just remembered something I needed to do," he said, hoping Carleigh would understand.

But Carleigh was nowhere near him. She'd meandered off to visit with the other women, leaving him to his flounder in his awkwardness.

She shouldn't have left him to his own devices. Trey did look like the proverbial fish out of water, standing alone in the shelter of the deck next to the pool, hands in his pockets. Jaxx joined the other dogs in dashing around the host's vast backyard.

Mrs. Bassanelli reached for Stella, an uppity white poodle with a pink tutu, pink bows on her ears, and a pink collar. Anyone else who would have picked up Stella would have received her "opinion" on the matter. But Stella loved her owner almost as much as Mrs. Bassanelli loved her pet. She snuggled into the crook of Mrs. Bassanelli's arm. "I'd like you to meet Stella," she said to Trey.

Carleigh returned her attention to Lil, who owned a Pomeranian named Sunny. Every so often, she glanced over at Trey to be sure he was surviving the ambush of elderly women chatting with him. She also checked on Sullivan Theodore, just to be sure he was behaving himself.

"I do believe I just heard the doorbell. It must be the clown." Mrs. Bassanelli rushed along on squatty legs toward the front door and returned a short time later. A clown with glasses, a curly red wig, a fake red nose, and oversized shoes accompanied her. His face paint did little to hide his cantankerous expression, and he continually hiked up his pants, already held up on his thin frame by striped suspenders. The clown clutched a notebook in his hand, along with a cell phone and an oversized black trash bag.

"Attention, attention," said Mrs. Bassanelli, tapping on the outdoor patio table. "I want you to meet our clown. Sir, what is your name?"

"No name," he grunted.

"How clever. This is No Name, the clown."

Instead of waving enthusiastically, the peculiar man nodded toward the women, his eyes scanning the backyard. Did he feel overwhelmed by the sheer number of canines?

The clown retrieved a ball from the trash bag and threw it for the dogs to fetch. Some dogs took interest in the activity, while most continued doing their own thing. After some time, No Name placed the ball back in his bag. He took a step backwards and accidentally tripped over one of the many dog water dishes around Mrs. Bassanelli's yard. "Stupid," he scowled.

Several of the women passed around concerned glances, and Carleigh prayed the bad-tempered clown would not ruin Stella's party for Mrs. Bassanelli.

"All right, everyone, let's have a bite to eat before we play games." Mrs. Bassanelli nearly did a jig in all of her excitement.

"If Mrs. Bassanelli could, I think she'd have a birthday party every day for Stella," chuckled Lil.

A massive drove of women congregated in Mrs. Bassanelli's gourmet kitchen. After lunch, the host suggested several games. "The first is musical chairs. Would you like to be in charge of the music?" she asked the clown.

"Nope."

Mrs. Bassanelli appeared to be taken aback at the clown's brash answer. She not-so-quietly murmured to Mrs. Gomez, "Guess that's what I get for ordering a clown at the last minute. I just knew Stella would love a clown at her party, and so I went with the only one I could find on such short notice. This man had no reviews at all on the Oakville social media page, Oakville Thumbs Up, Thumbs Down. Now I know why. Maybe his name should be No Joy instead of No Name." She cleared her throat and raised her voice toward the clown. "No problem. I'll take care of the music."

"Will you be giving instructions?" Mrs. Moeller asked, a forgotten, dangling curler waving in the gentle breeze at the base of her neck near her crocheted collar.

"Yes. All of the dogs must be placed on their leashes and marched around a circle created by the oak and birch trees over there."

Mrs. Bassanelli continued the instructions and started to play "Happy Birthday" sang in dog barks on an old cassette in a boombox. The song played over and over again until she clicked the "stop" button. When the music stopped, Carleigh encouraged Sullivan Theodore to sit. Sure enough, he was one of the first to sit and was able to remain in the game. Little by little, dogs were excluded from the game, including a Yorkshire terrier named Duke, a yellow lab named Crabby, and Mrs. Moeller's bulldog, Wrinkles. In the end, Mighty beat out all thirty dogs, including Stella, and won a bag of dog treats.

"Time for the photo session," bellowed No Name. He dumped out two pillows from the black trash bag: a well-used soiled brown pillow with an orange fringe and a flattened stained dog bone pillow. "Come pose by these, one at a time."

The owners assisted their dogs while No Name snapped the photos. Some of the dogs growled, some whimpered, and none offered doggy smiles for the camera.

"I'll need to get everyone's names and addresses and which dog is theirs so I can mail you the photos," No Name said, a slight smile forming on his painted face for the first time. Each of the owners gave him the requested information, of which he scribbled down in his tattered notebook. Mrs. Bassanelli then handed him a check and sent him on his way.

"I gave him no tip," she announced to her guests. Her statement was met with roaring applause.

"He didn't deserve a tip with his sour disposition," said Lil. "He shouldn't be working with dogs. He just doesn't have the personality for it."

"I agree," said Mrs. Bassanelli. "But we shan't allow such a distasteful man to ruin Stella's birthday."

The guests began to mingle again and Carleigh wandered over to Trey, who seemed to be the most popular guest. "How are you doing?"

"All right for being the only guy here."

"And one of the youngest guests."

He chuckled, and she pushed aside the thought that she liked his laugh. He lowered his voice. "What time does this thing end?"

"Mrs. Bassanelli is known for her never-ending afternoon parties, but I imagine it should be over around five or so. People will need to get home in time for dinner."

"Glad it was a nice day for the party."

"Yes, me too. Mrs. Bassanelli needed this to go smoothly since it's Stella' first birthday without Mr. Bassanelli."

"Do you know the story behind the pool?"

"Mrs. Bassanelli was actually in line to become an Olympic swimmer. Unfortunately, she injured her knee in a car accident and was unable to compete. Mr. Bassanelli put in the original pool for their twentieth anniversary as a surprise for his wife. It's been updated twice, and Mrs. Bassanelli still loves to swim."

Trey nodded. "Well, it's almost warm enough."

"I'm thankful it's a pleasant day. Sometimes days in May can be rainy and miserable."

They spoke for a few more minutes before Carleigh was tugged away by the yellow lab's owner, Peggy, who wanted to discuss an idea for an article.

Trey remained by the poolside, drinking a glass of Mrs. Bassanelli's famous fruit punch. The dogs had become all the more rambunctious with Sullivan Theodore leading a charge of canines back and forth across the yard. If only she had that much energy, Carleigh could really crank out the articles for *The Oakville Daily*.

Jaxx barked often, as if to keep his charges in line as he ran alongside several smaller dogs.

It happened all so suddenly that no one could have seen it coming. Not Carleigh, who was chatting with Mrs. Bassanelli about the dog cake she'd special-ordered, nor Trey who had just returned to the side of the pool after getting an earful from Mrs. Moeller.

The dogs dashed away from the yard and toward the patio where the pool was. As if in a herd, they rushed toward Trey. No time to shout a warning for them to stop and no time to warn her *Oakville Daily* Duo partner. The dogs had no mercy on their unsuspecting victim.

A most unfortunate event, in the guise of a stampede, occurred that day at Stella's birthday party.

One moment Trey was standing on the patio near the pool, and the next, he was *in* the pool.

# Chapter Thirteen

HE HADN'T SEEN IT coming. Not that he had been prepared for anything at this wacky party. One minute he was standing near the pool drinking some fruit punch and wondering how he could graciously excuse himself from the party and the next minute, he was teetering precariously, doing some sort of zany dance move as he attempted to maintain his balance.

The tiny Pomeranian did him in with a final push.

He landed on his back in the pool.

A pool that had not yet had the heated function turned on for the season.

The cold water sucked the air right from him and he floundered for a few seconds. Pushing himself up above the water line, he gasped, then regained his composure and swam to the side of the pool. He was thankful Mom had made him take swimming lessons from that dreaded militant swim teacher when he was a kid.

He shivered and wished it were much warmer outside than seventy degrees, especially with icy water. If he didn't get out soon, he'd probably get hypothermia.

The guests lined the edge of the pool, asking a myriad of questions.

"Oh, no. Is he going to drown?"

"What on earth happened?"

"Can he swim?"

"Today isn't warm enough to go for a swim, young man."

"Carleigh, would this make a good story for *The Oakville Daily*?"

Jaxx jumped in, splashing the women on the side. They shrieked and took a step back. Trey just wanted to get out of the pool, run home, and never see these people again. He searched the crowd for Carleigh. She stood in the front with concern lining her face and a hand extended.

He climbed out and Mrs. Bassanelli handed him a towel. "I'm so sorry that happened. You poor dear." She wrapped an additional towel around Jaxx.

"Are you all right?" Carleigh asked.

"Yeah. The only thing wounded is my pride."

The women surrounding the pool clapped and voices chorused in the excitement of Trey being safely on land once again.

"That was a close call."

"Poor guy. I thought he was going to drown."

"Thank the Lord that the pool is only six feet deep."

"Did you see how his dog courageously saved him?"

"I wonder why he thought he should go for a swim?"

"Isn't that the reporter from *The Oakville Daily*?"

Trey's teeth chattered, and whispers amongst the women continued. Had he been able to choose what to do on a pleasant and sunny Saturday, it would not have been to attend a dog's birthday party. And it certainly would not have been to go for a swim in Mrs. Bassanelli's pool.

"Now that we know Trey is going to survive his harrowing near-death experience, let's proceed, shall we?"

Mrs. Bassanelli sat at a decorated outdoor table with Stella in her lap. She "worked" the dog's little paws as if to open the gifts. She oohed and awed at each present.

Until she got to Trey's gift.

"Well, what have we here? What do you think this is, Stell?" Mrs. Bassanelli asked in an exaggerated voice. "It says on the tag that this one is from Jaxx."

Stella yipped.

"This one has us perplexed." Mrs. Bassanelli gave a wide-eyed look at her audience. Trey figured the woman majored in theater at some point in her life.

Ripping the paper off the gift with Stella's "assistance," Mrs. Bassanelli uncovered the floppy chicken toy.

"Oh."

But it wasn't an "oh" of delight, or an "oh" of joy. It was more of an "oh" of disgust.

He stood on tiptoe in an attempt to see over the tall fluffy gray hair of the woman in front of him. Mrs. Bassanelli's brow furrowed and she had a look of disturbance on her wrinkled face. Stella sniffed at the toy, whined, and turned her back.

"Oh, dear. This toy has been sampled."

The audience uttered several gasps and Trey held his breath. One of the legs of the chicken toy had been bitten off. He frowned at Jaxx. When had that happened? He'd thought there'd been only a few minor chew marks.

157

"I know, I know, Stell. You don't like chickens." Mrs. Bassanelli set the toy on the table and gently patted her dog. To the audience, she commented, "It stems from that time when Stella visited my sister's farm. The free-range chickens chased her and backed her into a corner of the yard. Poor Stella was trapped by the honeysuckle bush. She had nightmares for days after that."

Mrs. Bassanelli perused the crowd. "Now don't think I'm ungrateful. I know chickens are popular these days and regifting is all the rage. Thank you for the gift, Jaxx."

Trey wanted to slink away at the woman's comment. He had no idea Stella didn't like chickens and no idea that his gift would appear used. He made a mental note to never again attend a dog's birthday party.

He just wasn't cut out for such things.

The presents seemed to go on forever, and Trey's soggy pants clung to his legs, one of which was falling asleep. The clock said four-forty-five. Surely after all these hours, the party was nearly over. As if she'd heard him, Mrs. Bassanelli announced they'd now receive door prizes before the "party of the century" as she called it, came to a conclusion.

"This is truly Stella's favorite part of the event. She and I choose winners for the each of these gifts. We hope you will enjoy receiving them as much as we enjoyed choosing them."

Women's voices again chorused in response to Mrs. Bassanelli's statement.

"This is my favorite part."

"Ooh, I hope my dog wins."

"This is so positively, utterly thrilling."

"Do you think my dog has a chance?"

"I have been counting down the minutes until this moment."

Mrs. Bassanelli handed a tambourine to Lil. "Would you be the drumroll girl?"

"Me?"

"Yes."

"What an honor." Lil placed a hand on her heart.

Mrs. Bassanelli adjusted her glasses and read from a worn notebook. "And now, for the first winner..."

The crowd hushed and Lil shook the tambourine.

"The award for our smallest guest goes to Mighty!"

Mrs. Gomez stepped up with her teacup Chihuahua to receive the gift. She held Mighty in one arm and unfolded a piece of paper with the other hand. "I know it's a lengthy list, but there are so many people to thank. First, I'd like to thank Mrs. Bassanelli for hosting this amazing party and for inviting us. We are thrilled to be in the in-crowd. Secondly..." Mrs. Gomez continued for roughly fifteen minutes thanking everyone from her friends to the mailman who delivered the advertisement about Mighty's mom having a litter of pups.

"Now, this next one was toilsome, so I decided to make it a tie. For the biggest guest, we have a three-way tie between Lucy, Jaxx, and Blue.

Lucy was a Dalmatian. Her owner, a woman named Tara Beth, rushed to stand next to Mrs. Bassanelli. "Even though it's a three-way tie, I'm ever so grateful. This will look marvelous on Lucy's resume."

Blue was a Labradoodle owned by a woman with frizzy black hair and a crusty demeanor named Gail.

"Trey, are you coming up to receive Jaxx's award?" Mrs. Bassanelli asked.

He staggered forward, the towel still around his neck. "Thanks."

Tara Beth and Gail made statements and Mrs. Bassanelli then turned to Trey. "Now for you, young man. Would you like to say something?"

"Uh, sure. Thank you to Mrs. Bassanelli for hosting this party and thank you to Lucy and Blue for sharing the prize with Jaxx."

"Is that all?"

"And thank you to all of you here."

Mrs. Bassanelli arched an eyebrow, then ushered him toward the crowd. She proceeded with giving awards to the best-dressed guest, the quietest guest, the cutest guest, and the bubbliest guest, which she gave to Sullivan Theodore.

"We have one more prize, and let me say there are times in our lives when things don't go according to plan. It's in those times when we discover the strength God has blessed us with." She paused and dabbed at her eye with a handkerchief. "This guest has had a hard go of things. First, he has to share the meal made with joy brought by another guest. Then he falls into the pool and almost loses his life. Lastly, he sadly gives a used toy as a gift. But throughout all this hardship, Trey has endured. It is to you that we give our most prestigious award. The door prize for being such a trooper through life's most challenging times."

Trey knew his ears reddened and his jaw dropped to the floor. And as he walked forward to receive the gift, which was a miniature trophy in the shape of a dog bone, he knew more than ever that this was the absolute worst day of his entire life.

Carleigh waved goodbye to the ladies at Stella's party and stepped out the door with Sullivan Theodore. It had been a lengthy birthday party, but a memorable one. Many of the elderly ladies in attendance also attended Carleigh's church and several had been friends of the family for years. It was a pleasure to see them again.

Mrs. Bassanelli loved to host parties and Stella's birthday party was no exception. It was beneficial for the widow to have something to throw her time and energy into after the unexpected loss of her husband.

"Carleigh!"

She peered over her shoulder to see Trey jogging toward her, Jaxx in tow. "Let's turn around," she told Sullivan Theodore, who was happy to oblige so he could visit with his friend, Jaxx, again.

"Yes?"

Trey threaded a hand through his hair, causing an even more ruffled look to his messy, but masculine appearance, and his eyes were a brighter green than usual. Even with the incident in the pool and his clothes wrinkled and with a decidedly day-old slept-in look, Trey was attractive in a disheveled sort of way.

Not that she would admit that to anyone or even to herself.

"So, did you tell Mrs. Bassanelli the truth about me not helping with the joyous meal?"

"Joyous meal?"

"Yeah, the meal that we were supposed to take and I forgot one so you shared with me? Did you tell her the details on that?"

"No."

Trey shook his head. "Then how did she know?"

"No clue."

"Are you sure you didn't mention it to her?"

"Positive. Why would I do that?"

"Well, we aren't exactly friends."

Carleigh shrugged. "Just because we're adversaries doesn't mean I'm going to share something that embarrassing with Mrs. Bassanelli."

Trey stared at her as if he was trying to determine if she spoke the truth. "I suppose Mrs. Bassanelli may have surmised it. She is a pretty sharp cookie."

Carleigh took pity on him, standing there with Jaxx's leash in one hand and the presents for winning the door prizes in the other. "I'm really sorry about what happened in the pool, and I'm glad you're all right. On the bright side, you won two door prizes. That has got to be history in the making at one of Mrs. Bassanelli's parties."

He raised his eyebrows. "About the party. That is the last one I hope I ever have to attend."

"I heard her mention she's thinking of hosting a doggy carnival in the fall. I'm sure you'll be on the list."

"No thanks and no thanks."

"Well, I better go. It's been a long day and we have church tomorrow."

They dawdled for a minute longer before deciding to go their respective ways. When Carleigh glanced back, Trey stood there still staring in her direction.

The poor guy. He had to be traumatized after today's events. Even though he was ornery, she did feel sorry for him. For all he had endured, Mrs. Bassanelli was correct when she mentioned that Trey Montgomery was indeed a "trooper."

# Chapter Fourteen

TREY PROPPED HIS FEET up on the coffee table and stared aimlessly at nothing. What a bizarre day. One he never wanted to repeat again.

How had he even survived? The whole joyous meal ordeal and Mrs. Moeller's tongue-lashing would have been sufficient, but add to that the pool episode and the ridiculous door prizes—both of which tested his sanity.

And to think he once entertained taking up extreme sports. Who needed extreme anything when they could be invited to a dog's birthday party thrown by the eccentric Mrs. Bassanelli?

Trey's ears still rang from the constant cackle of women's voices, and the pungent odor of their overwhelming perfume still inundated his nose. He'd probably be scarred for life. If he ever had to attend another dog birthday party they would need to sedate him.

Jaxx rested a paw on Trey's arm, and Trey gave him a scratch behind his ears. "Glad you came out of it unscathed for the most part."

Jaxx bobbed his head. He at least smelled fresher now that Trey had thrown him in the bathtub after his heroic efforts to rescue his owner.

Trey closed his eyes and rehashed the eventful day. Thankfully, no one mentioned they'd be submitting a barrage of cell phone pictures of the party to *The Oakville Daily*. After all, a man had his pride.

The women *had* taken a gazillion photos, especially Mrs. Bassanelli, but to his knowledge, no one had snapped one of him taking his "leisure" swim. If they had, he was certain Margie would give the photo a witty caption such as "Herd of Dogs Mauls Unsuspecting Reporter, Causing a Big Splash."

There was always a silver lining to every dark cloud, as Mom often said. The silver lining in this instance was that Howard would receive no pictures of one half of his *Oakville Daily* Duo from today's party.

A strange thought then occurred to Trey. Another guest had a camera too. Well, not exactly a guest, but an entertainer. The grumpy clown had sported a clown wig and was tall and thin. Louella had described Lindy's secret admirer in a similar light. What if the clown was her S.A.? He'd need to run that thought past Carleigh. Not that he was in any hurry to see his rival again.

Still, he'd make a mental note to ask her her thoughts on the subject. Could be that they could solve the whole secret admirer mystery in one easy swoop. Maybe that could be the silver lining of the asinine dog party too.

That was, if Lindy wanted the case solved. If her secret admirer was the grumpy clown, she would be better off not knowing. Something about the guy seemed sinister, and even with all the makeup, he appeared old enough to be Lindy's dad.

Trey reached for the copy of *The Oakville Daily* on his coffee table. This week, he'd written on a particularly sensitive topic for "Trey's Sports Corner." He'd read it more times than he could count, what with edits and after it appeared in print, but the topic was a personal one, and he prepared to read it again.

So he would be ready for tomorrow.

Last fall, Ashanti Hickman, a freshman at Oakville High, sat on the bench during a girls' junior varsity volleyball game. Trey had been there to cover the game and to take photos. At one point, he sat next to Ashanti and asked if she was enjoying the game and what position she played.

"I don't really have a position. I'm too short to be a setter and I can jump about as well as an elephant. I also am new to overhand serving, so I guess my position is as a benchwarmer."

Trey recalled that elephants were the only animals that couldn't jump, but even so, Ashanti's heartfelt revelation wasn't humorous in the least. A tear had slid down her cheek as she continued to relay her story.

"My older sister, Anabella, is an all-star athlete. She's been on the varsity team since freshman year, and I think they would have let her play on the varsity team in junior high if it had been allowed. Mom was an all-star too, and both went to state for Oakville. And then there's me."

The frustration in Ashanti's voice gave way to melancholy, and Trey didn't know what to say. He sat for a time just listening and praying he'd say the right words and not mess it all up. The crowd cheered and he realized he likely just missed a really good play.

But he could get more photos and stats later.

Something about Ashanti's sorrow tugged at him.

The young girl was now looking up at him, as if waiting for him to acknowledge what she had said.

When he said nothing, she continued. "As you can see, today I am the only benchwarmer. Usually, there are three of us. But the other two aren't here today. One is sick and the other one had an orthodontist appointment. So here I am, wishing I was the athlete Annabella is, and trying to find a way to make my mom proud of me." She sighed. "I'm sorry for all the TMI. I'm sure you have more important things to do than listen to a whining girl sitting on the bench."

The team on the court, the coach, and the crowd were all mesmerized by the game. Everyone but Ashanti. He prayed again for the right words.

"I'm sorry, Ashanti."

She shrugged. "Not much you can do about it unless you can make me into an all-star volleyball player or turn me into Anabella. That works too."

"I'm sure your mom would miss you if there were two Anabellas."

"We'd be going to state, so that would be all that matters."

Trey wondered if Ashanti's mom really was as hard on her as Ashanti said, but he kept that thought to himself.

"When I was in school, I sat the bench during football."

"I doubt that."

"No, really. I did. I watched my friends and just about everyone else at my school play entire games. Me? I made sure the bench didn't up and fly away with a strong wind. The coach even forgot that I was a player one time and asked me to go refill the water keg. Talk about embarrassing."

Ashanti laughed a little, and Trey was glad he was at least taking her mind off her misery.

"Was your older brother the MVP of the football team like Anabella is the MVP of the volleyball team?"

"No, I'm the oldest, but I do have a younger brother who is a star football player. He's everything I wasn't when it comes to that game. My dad was a star football player too, so he's super proud of my brother. I feel like I let my dad down."

"That's how I feel too, only with my mom."

Trey rested his arm on the camera bag. "Do you even like volleyball?"

"Not really. I play it because Mom loves the game, and I guess she expects me to play too, even though Anabella has taken up the family torch."

"Hmm."

"So did you just stay on the bench the whole season year after year or did you ever get better?"

Trey took a trip back to the not-so-distant past. "I imagine I got somewhat better, but it never was my sport. I stopped playing, if you could call it that, after freshman year. I had run track since grade school, but starting my sophomore year, I really made it my sport. I trained, ran 5k races, studied the sport, and excelled at it. I loved hockey too, but since there were no hockey teams, track became my ambition. While I was never the fastest, I've always had endurance, and I've even won a few times at state."

"Really?"

A smile from Ashanti. He was doing something right.

"Yeah. I still love to run."

"Even though you're old?"

It was Trey's turn to chuckle. He remembered when he thought someone in their twenties was old. "I still worry that I disappointed my dad, though."

"Have you ever asked him?"

"Nah. But maybe I should. Have you ever talked to your mom about this?"

"No. I guess I'm too afraid of how let down I've made her."

The scoreboard reflected that Oakville had just scored another serve. He needed to get his head in the game, but some things were more important.

"Look, Ashanti. Maybe you should think of playing another sport. One you enjoy and leave volleyball in the dust."

"Won't I be a quitter then?"

"I'd say wait until the end of the season, because no, you don't want to be a quitter. But you should be exploring other sports. What about basketball?"

"Too short."

"Short people play basketball."

"I don't really like it."

Trey nodded. Basketball wasn't his sport either. "What about tennis? Or soccer? Track? Maybe skiing?"

"You know, I'm going to try track. I think I'm kind of fast, at least in P.E., I am. Do you have some pointers?"

169

Trey shared some of the tips he'd learned over the years. "Be sure you talk with your mom about this too. You'd probably be surprised to hear what she has to say."

"If you promise to talk to your dad."

"I'm already out of school, have been for a while, seeing as how I'm old."

Ashanti giggled. "You're not super old, just kind of old. Anyways, you have to talk to your dad about it, and I'll talk to my mom."

"All right. It's a deal." Only Trey didn't really want to talk to Dad about something so far in the past, even though it still weighed on his mind from time to time. "Oh, and Ashanti, one other thing..."

"Yes?"

"When you go out for track in the spring, I'll need some quotes from you for my write-up about the Oakville track meets."

"Really?"

"That is if you end up liking track. If not, no worries. I'll find you on the tennis court or the soccer field."

"It's a deal."

Trey gave her a fist bump. "Well, I better snap some more pictures. My boss expects a lot of them for the games."

"Thanks for your advice. I can't wait until spring."

All these months later, Trey had finally been ready to write up an article about expectations in sports for "Trey's Sports Corner." And Howard had agreed that two paragraphs wouldn't cut it, so he'd given Trey all the leniency he needed.

Ashanti later joined the track team and excelled.

170

Now there was only one thing Trey still needed to do. Talk to Dad about football.

# Chapter Fifteen

TREY LEFT FOR HIS hometown of Chesterton early Sunday morning and arrived in time to attend church with his parents. While he enjoyed living in Oakville, there was something special about taking the one-hour trip back home on a regular basis to visit his family.

Besides, the break from Oakville would do him some good. There were times he felt like he'd been plopped in some off-the-wall reality TV show and was unable to escape to real life.

He still had a pounding headache from Stella's birthday party, and Jaxx had been extra obnoxious since hanging around those other dogs.

After church, Trey headed to his parents' house for lunch. Because the weather was a pleasantly warm day of seventy-one degrees, Dad was grilling hamburgers on the grill, one of Trey's favorite meals.

"Did you hear the awesome news?" asked Austin, Trey's fourteen-year-old brother, who was bursting with excitement. "I barely could get through church without telling you!"

"What news?"

"I won an award at the awards ceremony for MVP on the football team."

"Austin, that's awesome!" Trey raised his hand and they shared a fist bump.

"Yeah, and next year as a freshman, it's looking like I'll get some serious varsity playing time."

"I'm proud of you, bro."

Austin beamed, his round face a miniature replica of their dad's. He was built like Dad too. Stocky and big for his age. Quite the contrast to Trey, who at six feet and one hundred, eighty pounds boasted lean muscle and a runner's body like his uncle on Mom's side.

"You'll have to come to some of my games next year. Maybe you could write about them."

"I will absolutely come to some of your games next season." Trey wouldn't miss Austin's games for the world. Despite the age difference, he and Austin were very close.

"Trey?"

"Yeah?"

"Do you ever regret that you didn't play football much in high school?"

The question was an innocent enough one, but the answer niggled at Trey more than he'd ever let on. "Not really. I was busy doing other stuff."

To Trey's relief, Austin accepted his answer. Trey still needed to talk to Dad and keep his promise he'd made to Ashanti last fall.

"Are you still working with that annoying lady?"

Trey chuckled. "Carleigh? Yeah. Our boss has teamed us up and is calling us *The Oakville Daily* Duo. It's crazy."

"Ugh. I would hate that. Too bad there's no one else you could team up with."

"It would sure make my life easier." He thought of the most recent escapades he'd had to endure with Carleigh as his team member.

"Too bad she's so annoying. Otherwise, you might kinda like her."

"Uh, yeah. No." The "engagement photo" as Chip had called it popped into his mind. He would never like Carleigh in that way.

Mom kept every newspaper clipping featuring her boys. The local newspaper—while larger, but not as thorough as *The Oakville Daily*—featured several stories from back in the day when Trey attended high school. He perused the articles, painstakingly framed and lined up on a bookshelf. The first three shelves were his and included articles about his time in Chesterton Christian Athletes, his track meets, and the missions trips he took with his youth group. The bottom three shelves were Austin's and showcased his church activities and sports achievements. On the wall hung a framed article of his parents' mechanic shop with the entire family standing around Dad's prized classic, souped-up car he'd restored.

An additional bookshelf held Dad's numerous football awards, including state championships, MVP two years in a row, his football helmet, jersey, and class ring.

Mom's cheerleading outfit, a basketball trophy, and several photos of her high school years shared space on the shelf.

Yet, even with all the framed articles and Trey's three trophies sitting on the shelf alongside the articles, Trey felt like he'd let his dad down.

Not that Dad had ever mentioned or even insinuated it—or ever made him feel that way—but Trey had always wished he'd been a football player like Dad. That he'd disappointed him by not trying harder to follow in his footsteps.

"How goes things in Oakville?" Dad asked, pouring a generous amount of ketchup on his burger.

"He has to team up with that annoying lady," Austin offered.

Mom's brow creased. "Is this Carleigh we're talking about?"

"Yes."

"I liked her when we met her a few months ago while visiting Oakville."

Trey forked some watermelon onto his plate. "She's nice enough, but we compete on everything and now Howard has teamed us up and is calling us *The Oakville Daily* Duo. We are stuck together for every assignment whether we like it or not, unless there a conflict and there are two assignments at once. But that's rare."

He could see the wheels turning in Mom's mind. "Maybe you'll become friends now that you're always paired together."

"Not likely. She has this criminally-minded little dog named Theodore something-or-other. As a matter of fact, we were invited to this birthday party yesterday. It didn't go well."

"A birthday party?" Dad piled a heap of chips on his plate. "For a coworker?"

"No. It's a woman in the neighborhood. She's an elderly lady, and I didn't realize at first it was a birthday party for a dog."

Austin let out an obnoxious snort. "No way. A dog birthday party? Say you didn't go."

"I did go, and it was a mistake."

"Why would you go to that?" Austin held his burger in midair. "Your lack of good judgment concerns me, Trey."

"Mrs. Bassanelli, the owner of a dog named Stella, is a recent widow. Carleigh thought it would encourage her if we went and supported her since this was Stella's first birthday without Mr. Bassanelli, who passed away last year."

Mom reached over and placed a hand on Trey's arm. "I knew I raised a kind and thoughtful gentleman."

"Yeah, well, it was all fine until I got there and noticed there were thirty dogs and about that many elderly ladies. I was the only guy and Carleigh and I were the only ones under one hundred years old."

The exaggeration elicited another obnoxious snort from Austin.

"I bet they loved chatting with such a well-mannered young man," said Mom. She was always looking on the positive side of things.

"Sounds awkward," said Dad, always the realist.

Austin took a swig of milk. "Did you play games and all that?"

"Oh, we played some games, all right. There were dog competitions and Stella 'opened' her presents. Jaxx didn't let me in on his little secret about gnawing off part of the leg of the chicken toy I'd gotten for Stella. It was embarrassing. Then the worst happened."

Dad stopped eating and focused fully on Trey. "This is quite the story. What happened?"

"A herd of dogs stampeded and knocked me into Mrs. Bassanelli's pool."

"Oh, my! Thankfully you're a skilled swimmer. It really paid off all those years taking you to swimming lessons."

"Only my pride was wounded, Mom. At least I got some nutty door prize for being such a trooper through it all." Trey shook his head. "I still can't believe I went. It was awful. It lasted forever and Mrs. Moeller, who ran into *The Oakville Daily* minivan, was there giving me crusty looks the entire time. I think I may have seen an evil glint in her eye when I came up for air after falling into the pool."

Mom, Dad, and Austin were laughing so hard Trey wasn't sure they'd ever be able to return to eating.

Listening to the circumstances of his eventful day shocked even him. How had he survived and lived to tell the tale?

After lunch, Trey helped carry in the dishes from the picnic table on the back deck. Dad rinsed off the dishes and Mom loaded them into the dishwasher. Trey always appreciated that his parents were a team in all things. Hidden from his parents' view, Trey watched as Dad kissed Mom's cheek. "Sure do love you, Sweets."

Mom always blushed, even though they'd been married forever. Trey admired the love between them. While he knew his parents' marriage wasn't perfect, he also knew that the devotion his parents had, first to God, and then to each other, was the cement that held their marriage together.

He wanted a marriage like that someday. Someone he could laugh with, share life's hardships and challenging times with, pray with, and share a future together. At twenty-four, that day would likely come at some point, and Trey just hoped he'd make God proud of the kind of husband he'd someday be.

But marriage was definitely not on his mind for the immediate future. Maybe when he was thirty-five or forty, but not in this decade.

After making sure Mom and Dad had clean-up covered, Trey poured himself a glass of lemonade and headed to the porch for a few minutes before he had to return to Oakville. He settled into one of the rocking chairs and thought of Austin's question regarding football.

Truth of the matter was, Trey didn't regret *not* playing football. He regretted *stinking* at it. He'd wanted to measure up in that one area, but it never happened. Instead, at the practices and games, he became adept at acting like none of it bothered him—watching his fellow teammates score touchdowns or excel at the sport; knowing the coach had favorites and he wasn't one of them; seeing Dad was in the stands at every game waiting for Trey to migrate from the bench to the field, which never happened; and the good-natured ribbing from the other guys on the team. But in reality, all of it *did* bother him. The habit of masking his feelings in that one area taught him he could hide other things that bothered him. Not a healthy trait, and he prayed for God's assistance in overcoming it.

The screen door leading to the porch squeaked open and Dad walked onto the porch and sat in the other rocking chair next to Trey. "Mind if I join you?" he asked, his own glass of lemonade in hand.

"Not at all."

"It sure is good to see you, Son."

"It's good to be here."

Dad crossed his ankle over his knee. Even sitting, Dad had a huge presence. His broad shoulders and muscular arms gave testament to the fact that long before Austin became his school's top lineman, Dad was breaking records as a lineman at his own high school. "Cool about Austin's MVP award for football, huh?"

"Very cool. I'm proud of him."

"Me too." Dad ran a hand through the buzz cut he'd retained long after serving in Operation Iraqi Freedom.

"He makes me so proud. He's always been athletic, and with his size, power, and speed, there really is no stopping him on the field."

Trey thought about Dad's comment. He'd never been envious of Austin's size or athleticism, but instead had been one of Austin's most ardent supporters. However, all throughout growing up, Trey wondered if Dad was disappointed that he himself hadn't followed in his father's footsteps when it came to football. From the time both boys were little, Dad had thrown the ball around with them. The difference was that Austin actually caught on and excelled, where Trey failed miserably. He'd not told anyone about the guilt of letting Dad down all these years, except when he'd divulged some of it to Ashanti.

"You're awfully quiet," said Dad.

"Just thinking."

"About what?"

"Nothing much."

They sat in silence for a few more minutes. One day, Trey would have the courage to ask Dad if he was disappointed in him.

But why the struggle?

He and Dad had always been able to discuss nearly anything. They were close and Trey valued their relationship.

So why the hesitancy on this one topic—the topic that had plagued him for several years?

Trey prayed for God to guide his words, then took a deep breath. "Dad, I'm sorry I never played football."

Dad stopped rocking his chair. "What brought that up?"

Trey shrugged. "Just saying."

"I've never really given it a thought that football wasn't your thing."

"All those times you talked about your high school glory days and then your oldest son is totally inept at the sport."

Dad put a hand on Trey's upper arm. "Being good at football isn't what makes a man, Son."

Trey gazed across the street at the neighbor's house. "It just seems like I let you down."

"Trey."

Trey turned his focus to his dad.

"You didn't let me down because you didn't want to play football. How long have you thought that?"

"Pretty much since I was on the team. You were this incredible star player and then there was me. I was never really football material."

"Being football material, as you call it, isn't what makes a man either." Dad set his lemonade on the nearby table. "I'll never forget the day you were born. I'm sure Mom has probably told you how excited she was. I still remember sitting in the chair by her bed and seeing her holding you for the first time. It was the most amazing sight—my beautiful wife holding this tiny miracle." Dad paused a moment, likely recalling that day vividly in his mind. "You know me, Trey, I'm not one to ever get emotional. But that day, when the Lord gave your Mom and me one of the two best blessings, I *was* emotional. I attempted to joke my way out of it and told the doctor

I was exhausted and now needed a nap. Truth of it was, I was scared to death about being a dad. Would I raise you and Austin right? Would I succeed with your mom in raising you boys for the Lord? Would what *really* matters be evident to you two in the way I lived my life?"

Dad crossed his other ankle over the opposite leg. "Son, being who God created you to be is who I ever only wanted you to be. Not a clone of me. Besides, as far as athletics go, you were quite the track star. And from the sounds of it, you've used your track skills to chase after rogue hubcaps." Dad chuckled at the story Trey previously relayed about chasing *The Oakville Daily* minivan hubcap.

"Well..."

"And you must be athletic to have been able to swim so well after the herd of dogs incident." Dad's eyes crinkled at the corners. "I'd say you're a multi-talented athlete."

Trey laughed. Dad was attempting to lighten what could be a heavy topic, something he appreciated. They sat for a while both staring at the red-brick house across the street that looked exactly the same as Trey remembered it during his school years. He saw Dad from the corner of his eye and knew he was waiting for Trey to continue the conversation about football.

Why was this such a challenging topic to broach?

And he knew, had always known, that it was because he didn't want the man he loved, admired, and respected to be disappointed in him. Even over something in the past. He cleared his throat. "But the whole football thing...it never came naturally to me. Never was something I inherited from the gene pool. You were a football star and Grandpa Montgomery played and coached football, and one of Mom's brothers went to college on a football scholarship."

"Yes, football was mine, your grandpa's, uncle's, and now Austin's thing. A way of life, even, being out there on the field. That doesn't mean it has to be your thing. Football isn't for everyone. Besides, God gave you other talents and gifts, like being a mentor and volunteering at the youth group with the younger kids, writing for the school paper, running regular track, being a part of the Chesterton Christian Athletes, and working at our shop after school. Who cares if you didn't play football?" Dad paused. "Is this because Austin won an award?"

"No. I'm proud of Austin. He deserves the award and I think it's awesome that he's following in your footsteps. I just...sometimes I wish it had been me."

Wow. If ever he needed a lock on his mouth, it was now. He was so not good at expressing himself, *even* if it was to the man he loved, admired, and respected most in this world.

"Son, I couldn't be prouder of you. There has never been a day when I haven't thanked the Lord for the man you have become and are becoming." Dad's voice was thick with emotion. "A strong faith, a love of God, family, and country, and having integrity and godly character are what's important."

"I know, Dad, and you've always modeled that for me. It's just...I wanted football to be my thing."

"I knew it wasn't and I never forced it, or at least I hope it didn't come across like I did."

Trey shook his head. "You never did force it, Dad."

183

"And I knew that working at the mechanic shop was never your thing, even though you were smart and caught on quickly when you worked there after school. These things didn't disappoint me. As I said before, I want you to be the man God created you to be."

When Dad returned from fighting in Iraq, he'd realized his dream and he and Mom opened Montgomery Mechanics. He could fix any car, old or new, and had even expanded into RVs and motorcycles in recent years. "I liked working with you in the shop, but my dream has always been to write and take photos."

"I know that. And you excel at it. I read every single one of your articles and your photos are fantastic. It all started with that digital camera Mom and I got you for your sixth birthday. Remember that?"

Trey smiled, relieved that Dad wasn't disappointed in him. "I do remember that. I still have that camera. It's super slow and doesn't have much memory."

Dad laughed. "No, probably not. Technology has definitely improved. But I remember you took pictures all the time of anything and everything and never erased one photo. It was the start of where you are now. You're ambitious and have done well for yourself. I'm proud of you for putting so much hard work into landing that job at *The Oakville Daily*."

"Thanks, Dad. All these years, I thought I'd let you down."

"Not at all. But next time, don't wait so long to tell me that something is bothering you." Dad gripped his shoulder. "I love you, Son."

"Love you too, Dad."

It was as though a one-hundred-pound weight had been lifted from Trey's shoulders. His only regret now was that he hadn't mentioned it sooner.

# Chapter Sixteen

JAXX EAGERLY JUMPED INTO the front seat of Trey's truck. If the German shepherd knew exactly where he was going, he might not be so enthusiastic.

Trey drove the short distance to *The Oakville Daily*. In order to take some time off to take Jaxx to the vet, he needed to put in some extra time this morning to make up for it.

At seven a.m., no one was at *The Oakville Daily* yet, although Howard usually rolled in around seven-thirty. Trey parked in his usual spot and unlocked the door to his workplace. Jaxx sauntered in like he owned the place. "Behave yourself, Jaxx. I've got some things to do before we go."

Jaxx wagged his tail and sniffed around the room, likely noting the odors of paper, newsprint, flowers from Lindy's desk, and day-old pizza from the break room. Trey turned on his computer, started the coffee maker, and began the task of delving through a million and a half photos from a recent assignment. The building was quiet, except for the occasional car passing by, which caused Jaxx to stop what he was doing, ears perked up toward the direction of the noise.

Trey was so absorbed in his work he nearly lost track of time. He glanced up from his computer. "Jaxx?"

No answer, just a suspicious slurping, slobbering, chomping noise as though someone were smacking their lips or chewing with their mouth open.

"Jaxx? Where did you go?" The clock read 7:27. Howard would arrive any minute, and it wouldn't do for Jaxx to have gotten into some mischief. Sighing, Trey stood and wandered toward Howard's open office. "Jaxx?" He peered under Howard's desk and checked in the far corner behind the filing cabinets. No Jaxx.

*Where could he be?*

He honestly didn't have time for this. In fifteen minutes, he needed to leave to take Jaxx to his appointment. In that space of time, Trey still had an enormous amount of work to complete.

"Jaxx?"

The slobbering noise ceased, and Trey whipped around to see Jaxx standing behind him, tail between his legs. "Jaxx? Where have you been and what have you been up to?"

Jaxx swiveled his furry head from the left to the right, as if checking to see if anyone had caught him in whatever suspicious endeavor he had undertaken. He avoided Trey's eye, his head lolling to one side, and a chunk of something pink hung on the corner of his mouth. Trey stooped down to investigate, but the dog turned his head away. "You've never been good at hiding your guilt," he told his dog. "What have you been eating?"

With a shifty countenance, Jaxx shuffled toward Trey's desk, his tail still between his legs.

Howard emerged through the back door. Trey exchanged "good mornings" with his boss, then retreated to his desk.

"You're staying right by me this time, old boy." Not seeming to mind, Jaxx crawled beneath Trey's desk. An obnoxious chorus of repetitive squeaks pulled Trey's attention from reading his notes to the direction of the noise. "Jaxx?"

Another squeak sounded. Had Jaxx brought one of his squeaky toys from home? The dog took his time looking up from his location under the desk. It was obvious he carried some serious guilt. His brown eyes darted about before settling on a blue striped ball on the floor between his paws.

"Where did you get that?"

Jaxx placed a paw over the ball, as if trying to conceal it.

"I already saw it, so you might as well confess."

"Talking to anyone in particular?"

Trey bonked his head on his desk, as he peered up to see Carleigh standing not far from him. "Uh, yeah, Jaxx is here."

"Is it bring-your-dog-to-work-day and I missed it?"

"Funny. No. I have to leave in a few minutes to take him to the v-e-t."

"The vet?"

Jaxx whimpered.

"Shhh. He knows that word and what it entails. So why are you here early?"

"I have some extra stuff to get done."

"Oh, hey, can we talk later?" Trey still wanted to ask Carleigh's opinion on whether she thought the clown at Stella's birthday party might be the one sending Lindy flowers.

She eyed him and chewed on her lip. "Okay."

"Good. It won't take long."

Carleigh shrugged and returned to her desk.

A few minutes later, Trey led Jaxx to the truck. "Load up!"

Jaxx eagerly obliged, the toy half hidden in his mouth. At least he'd had the wisdom not to squeak it obnoxiously throughout the office as they left.

"Where did you get that toy anyway?"

The dog ignored him and began to once again squeak the toy. The piece of pink whatever-it-was had fallen on Trey's seat. When they stopped at the stop sign, Trey reached for it. Bright pink, rubbery, and of unknown origin. He pressed the slobber-covered toy between his finger and thumb, noting its pliability. "What is this?" He'd never seen anything like it before. "And where did you find it?" Likely where Jaxx had found the squeaky toy.

A few minutes later, Trey rounded the corner to the vet. Jaxx honed in on the building at the same time. He dropped the squeaky ball and blinked his eyes.

"Puppy dog eyes won't work here. You know you have to get your rabies shot."

Jaxx whimpered, slid down on the seat, and hid his face with his paws.

Lugging the German shepherd out of the truck and into the Oakville Veterinary Clinic was a challenge. Jaxx pressed his paws into the pavement and whimpered.

"For such a big tough guy, you really don't like the vet, do you?"

When Trey first got Jaxx, the dog struggled mightily with anxiety. Squeaky toys had become his friend, and chewing through everything his vice. He'd even chomped through his leash several times.

He'd thankfully improved and had mostly overcome his nervous and destructive tendencies, but the dog did resort to chewing on things every once in a while, especially when stressed.

After Jaxx's rabies shot, Trey took him home and returned to work. The day was getting away from him, and he still had multiple deadlines. Thankfully, the most stressful part of the day was past.

# Chapter Seventeen

CARLEIGH USED HER FIFTEEN-MINUTE break to make a speedy jaunt to Oakville Bibles and Gifts to choose a present for her prayer partner's birthday.

The charming and cheery gift store was located three businesses away from *The Oakville Daily*. It boasted a trademark red awning and creative window display and had just celebrated its fifteenth anniversary.

When Carleigh was younger, Mom's women's Bible study group founded the prayer partner ministry and precious Mrs. Barnes had been, and still was, Carleigh's prayer partner. Now Carleigh embraced the chance to be a blessing to Isla, her own prayer partner, just as Mrs. Barnes was to her.

Carleigh stepped inside and found a brightly-colored prayer journal with Isla's favorite Bible verse on the front. She requested it be wrapped in birthday-themed gift wrap, and returned to work with five minutes to spare.

Two hours later, she gave Lindy the thumbs-up signal, indicating she was at a stopping point in her article and ready for their lunch date. Three bouquets covered Lindy's desk, all with different varieties of eye-popping flowers. Her friend still had no idea who was sending the flowers, and Carleigh and Trey hadn't had a chance to rehash the clues to solve the mystery.

Lindy appeared at Carleigh's desk, purse in hand. "I am so ready for lunch. This has been a crazy-busy day."

"You're telling me. Let me just switch my shoes and grab my purse." Carleigh slipped off the shoes she had been wearing in favor of her pink wedge sandals. "I wasn't going to wear my sandals, but it looks absolutely gorgeous outside."

"Almost seventy-two degrees. I love summers in Oakville."

"Me too." Carleigh put on her pink wedges and stood. And that's when she noticed.

One wedge was clearly taller than the other. She stood, half-slumped, with one foot much lower than the other. "What on earth?"

"It looks like your wedge broke off your shoe."

"But how could that be? I've had them here since last week. How could it have broken?" Sure enough, when she removed the shoe and flipped it over, a portion of the wedge was missing. What appeared to be chew bites re-placed the former wedge. "It looks like someone chewed on my shoe."

Lindy began to laugh. Her petite frame tipping slightly on her own two-inch wedge sandals. "I'm sorry, that's just so...so funny. So, someone is chewing on your shoes. If that's the case, there's an employee of *The Oakville Daily* who is awfully hungry!"

Carleigh knew her accusation sounded ludicrous, but there was no other explanation. Haphazard bite marks lined various portions of the underneath of the left shoe. "It isn't even in a straight line, and there's a massive chunk out of this corner. My shoes are ruined."

"Shoe eaters apparently aren't picky about how they eat their shoes. Kind of reminds me of how some people eat corn on the cob."

"Funny, Lindy."

"Who do you think could have eaten it?"

"Wait! That's it! It was Trey."

"Trey ate your shoe? Wow, I always knew he was a little different, but shoe-eating? That's a steep departure from normalcy, even for him."

At Lindy's statement, Carleigh laughed, the first time since discovering her dilapidated shoe. "No, Trey doesn't eat shoes, but his dog does. And..." she peered beneath her desk. "It appears the squeaky toy a customer gave me for Sullivan Theodore is gone as well. So not only a shoe-eater, but also a thief."

"Wouldn't want to be Trey or his dog right about now."

"Guess I won't be wearing these." Carleigh put the shoe on her foot and limped around. "This stinks, too, because I had them special order these for me from Oakville Shoe Mart, and they took forever to get here. And they were expensive."

Lindy placed a hand on her arm. "I'm sorry, Carleigh. How about I treat you to lunch and then we stop by the shoe place and see if they can order you another pair."

"Maybe they can charge it to Trey's account." She glared in the direction of his desk. Trey was still at lunch, but when he returned, she'd be sure to share with him her opinion of finding her shoe half-eaten and Sullivan Theodore's new toy missing.

Trey hunkered down and began working on an article he was writing about the history of school sports when he sensed someone's eyes boring into him.

Sure enough, Carleigh stood in front of his desk, hands on her hips and a scowl on her face.

"Did you eat some bad food at the restaurant when you went out with Lindy?"

He thought the witty comment was humorous. She did not. She glowered at him, her eyes narrowed beneath her glasses. She stood at a lopsided angle, as though she was having a problem with her left foot.

"Notice anything different about me?"

He attempted to forget that she was cute, even when she was obviously angry at him. "Uh, you aren't wearing an eye-blinding color today?" He had noticed her more-subdued purple shirt this morning and how it made her face seem shinier.

"Eye-blinding color?"

Trey tried another tactic. "Is your hip okay? You're standing crooked."

"Very funny, Trey."

"No, I'm not being funny. When I ran track in school, one of the kids I ran with knocked his hip out of joint and stood crooked like you are now. It's just a question. You know, we're investigative journalists and all."

"Investigative journalists. Hmmf. And no, I didn't knock my hip out of whack. This is all your fault."

"The way you're standing?"

"Yes."

"How can that be my fault? Say, you are shorter than I remember. On one side, anyway." He covered a smirk with his hand. Maybe she was injured. He really shouldn't be laughing if that was the case. "Did you suffer an injury?"

"Trey Herman Montgomery." She tapped her right food on the ground.

"Wait. How did you find out my middle name was Herman?" Cue ears turning red.

By now a crowd had gathered. Chip, Lindy, Margie, Howard, and Bubba stood nearby, watching the spectacle.

Great. An audience.

"Oh, I have my ways of finding out middle names. Investigative journalism and all that."

Bubba chuckled. "She's got you there, man."

"Hey, no one repeat my middle name, please. I'm not exactly fond of it."

"Why not? Isn't it the middle name of all of the first-borns in your family since the 1800s?"

Carleigh's knowledge of his supposed secret perplexed him. How had she found out? Time to change the subject. "Look, Carleigh Jo Adams, I'm sorry about your injured foot or hip or shoe or whatever it is."

"How did you know my middle name was Jo?"

195

"Investigative journalism and all that," joked Chip.

"Nothing from the peanut factory," said Carleigh.

Trey stood. "Look, friends, there really is nothing to see here."

"Au contraire, Pierre." Carleigh raised her chin. "One minute, I had a fabulous new shoe from the Oakville Shoe Mart, and the next, it's damaged beyond repair."

"Hey, aren't those the shoes you wore for the engagement photo?" Chip asked.

"It wasn't an engagement photo, and yes, these are the same shoes."

"The very same shoes that were all caked with mud? Maybe there's an uneven balance of mud on one of them." Trey knew he was grasping, but he had a really bad suspicion that he was, indeed, responsible for the way Carleigh was standing. In an indirect way, of course. His eyes settled on the pink lower portion of the shoes. The same pink that matched the chunk of material in Jaxx's mouth that morning.

*Oh, no.*

"It's not mud." Carleigh removed her left shoe. "There are chew marks on the bottom of my shoe and a piece of the shoe has been completely bitten off. Know anything about this?"

"Really, Trey, you didn't strike me as the type that would eat shoes. If you're that hungry, we could establish a donation fund and buy you some boxed dinners over at Buy It All." Lindy laughed, obviously proud of her statement.

Trey was not amused. "I don't need food and I don't eat shoes." He took a deep breath. "Jaxx may have eaten part of your shoe."

"You think?"

"Yes, and I'm sorry. He had this bad habit of chewing on things when I first got him and sometimes lapses back into that bad habit when he's nervous. I think he may have suspected he had to go to the vet today, hence his anxious gnawing on your shoe."

"You need to keep your dog away from my shoes and from Sullivan Theodore. He's a bad influence. Besides, I had to special order these from Oakville Shoe Mart, and they were expensive."

Trey removed his wallet from his back pocket. How much were women's shoes these days? Ten dollars? Fifteen? Twenty? His own shoes with the coffee stain had been $14.99 at Oakville Shoe Mart. He removed all three fives from his wallet and handed the bills to Carleigh. "Keep the change, and I truly am sorry."

Lindy laughed, Bubba chortled, Chip smirked, Margie covered her mouth with her hand, and Howard shook his head and muttered something about being in the dog house.

"Fifteen dollars will not cover the cost."

Trey opened the top drawer of his desk and pulled out his emergency ten-dollar bill. "Here."

"Twenty-five dollars will not cover the cost."

Wow. For a shoe that was smaller than his own, Carleigh's shoe should not have cost more than the $14.99 of his own sneakers. "How much more?"

Lindy snorted. "You might just want to hand over your next paycheck."

"It can't cost that much. How much more, Carleigh?"

"They were $54.99 plus tax."

"Fifty-five dollars?"

"Well, if you add in tax..."

"No way." Trey leaned back in his office chair. "There's barely anything to those shoes and they're hideous."

"Trey, I realize you and Carleigh aren't married..." began Howard.

"Not yet, but they have had engagement photos," quipped Chip with a snort-laugh.

Howard released an exasperated breath. "As I was saying, I realize you and Carleigh aren't married yet, but..."

"*Yet?* With all due respect, Howard, Trey and I will never be married."

"What about *The Oakville Daily* Duo and all that?" Margie asked, her mom-voice attempting to bring reason to the conversation.

"Carleigh's right. We'll *never* be married."

"Well, whether that's the case or not, I realize that it's different for the two of you than it would be for a married couple, but, Bubba, I'm sure you will agree with me that you should never come between a woman and her shoes."

Bubba nodded. "Oh, yeah. I've been married for a couple of decades now and let me tell you, our closet consists of three rows of Vicki's shoes and a space for my four pairs of shoes. I have to keep over on my side of the closet or else I'm in the dog house for sure."

"Just own up and fork over the sixty dollars," suggested Howard. "It will save you a lifetime of misery."

"Don't we know it," added Bubba. "One time, I accidentally set my work boots on Vicki's dainty church shoes and I found out first hand that women's shoes are a precious commodity. I'm still paying back the loan."

Trey looked at the older, wiser men, then at Margie and Lindy who were nodding in agreement. Then at Chip, who smirked. And lastly at Carleigh.

Those big brown eyes, disappointment in their depths.

"Sir, not to intrude, but I have to respectfully agree with everyone else. Just fork over the sixty dollars."

Trey spied a customer standing behind the crowd.

And he knew that, while he had no problem owning up and paying for Jaxx's error, he was clearly outnumbered.

# Chapter Eighteen

THE DELIVERY DRIVER DELIVERED the pizza boxes to the conference room in time for the monthly pizza party. Carleigh slid into a chair next to Trey, her mind racing over last-minute articles due before the week ended. Across from her, Lindy snagged a chair and Chip sat beside her. Howard, Margie, and Bubba found places around the table.

After Howard blessed the meal, they chatted in their usual camaraderie. Carleigh couldn't help but notice that each time they had pizza parties or meetings, Chip sat by Lindy. She pulled out her phone and inconspicuously snapped a photo of the adoring look Chip gave Lindy as he hung on every word she said.

Carleigh leaned over toward Trey and whispered, "Did you notice how Chip always sits next to Lindy whenever we have pizza parties or meetings?"

"Kind of like you always sit next to me?"

She jabbed him in the rib. The guy was impossible. Annoying. Vexatious.

The phone rang, interrupting the chatter. Because Howard never wanted to miss an important news tip, he answered all calls, even during pizza parties.

"*The Oakville Daily*, Howard speaking."

Howard nodded as the caller spoke. "Really? I see. Yes, I will be sending *The Oakville Daily* Duo over to pen an article. I'm really sorry that happened, Kevin. Yes, we will be working in conjunction with Oakville PD to get this matter resolved. Absolutely. Once people read about it in *The Oakville Daily*, someone is sure to come forward with a tip or even a confession."

Their boss hung up the phone and wiped his brow. "This isn't good, folks."

Carleigh's heart sped up a few notches. What had happened?

As if reading her mind, Howard continued. "Sad as it is, crime has exploded a bit here in Oakville. Not serious stuff yet, but enough for us to wake up and take notice. Remember last week when we had the gas drive-off over at the Oakville Gas Mart? Well, that was Kevin from Buy it All. Early this morning at precisely eight-hundred hours, a man with curly red hair, which appeared to be a wig, stormed through the doors of Buy it All and stole a gallon of milk and a bag of dog food. Kevin asked if he could wait on him at checkstand number four, but the man ignored him and left the building without paying." Howard sat back in his chair and folded his hands across his wide girth.

Gasps filled the room. "How could this happen in Oakville?" Margie asked. "We usually don't have brazen robbers in the daylight hours."

"Exactly," added Bubba. "While a gallon of milk and a bag of dog food is no big deal in the scheme of things, what's the guy gonna steal next since he got away with this?"

"My thoughts exactly. Which is why I'm sending *The Oakville Daily* Duo over to get the news. Carleigh and Trey, this is our chance to help fellow Oakville residents. Kevin and Amy have done a lot for us through the years and have been a valuable asset to the community. We need to find out who did this and put a stop to it. Now then, you two finish your pizza, take the minivan, and make me proud. Oh, and Trey, take it easy with the van, understood?"

A half hour later, Trey hauled the camera equipment to the minivan. "Sure you don't want to drive?" he asked.

Carleigh shook her head. "No thank you. You couldn't pay me to drive this thing."

"Why? It's not that bad."

"It's not that. It's the fact I'm scared to death I'll hit something. Howard loves this vehicle."

"That's the truth." Trey paused. "You sure you're not trying to avoid the embarrassment of being seen behind the wheel?"

"Well, it does stand out since it's bright green."

"Ha ha, that it does. All right, just trying to be a gentleman and let you drive once in a while."

"I appreciate that, Trey. I really do. But you look like such a natural behind the wheel of this classic. Almost like it was made for you."

Trey scowled. "Can't say it's been my aspiration to own a vintage green minivan."

"You should make it an aspiration. Just think, after you're married, you can easily fit your wife, six kids, and Jaxx all comfortably with space to spare."

"Jaxx, yes. A wife and six kids. No."

"Not ever getting married, huh?"

"Maybe when I'm my parents' ages, but not in the near future."

They arrived at Buy it All a few minutes later. "Before I forget, would you remind me to tell you something about Chip?" Carleigh asked.

"Sure. I'll remind you if you remind me."

Typical Trey.

Buy it All was bustling with customers, and the aroma of fried chicken from the deli filled the air. "Let's go back to my office," suggested Kevin.

They followed him through a narrow hallway to the first door on the right. Carleigh removed a notepad from her bag, and Trey set up the camera equipment.

"Tell us what happened."

Kevin proceeded to tell them exactly what he'd told Howard. "I'm not naïve enough to think theft doesn't occur in this town. I've spoken to Officer Zemski before and he's mentioned we've had some flower pot thefts from yards in the past and that a few years ago there was a pickpocket who drove through and stole a few wallets and purses. Then there was the gas drive-off last week. But, although this is only a gallon of milk and a bag of dog food, it disturbs me that the guy just walked out and ignored me without a second thought as to what he was doing. You know me well enough to know that if someone was truly in need of milk or dog food or whatever else I have in the store, I'd gladly give them something, but stealing?"

"Absolutely, Kevin. I can't believe he was that brazen. I know the police have already been by and are working on the case, but we hope that by publishing an article, we can get some reader tips, or maybe even the perp will come forward and confess."

"That would be great, and if he did, all would be forgiven."

"Can you again describe the burglar's appearance?"

"He had on what I believe to be a wig. It was curly and reddish-orange."

Could this be the same guy who was sending flowers to Lindy? "Was he tall?"

"I wouldn't say tall, but tall is a relative term."

Carleigh considered Kevin's statement. He himself was around six foot, four, so tall to him would be different than what she considered tall.

"All right," said Trey. "Was he wearing a cowboy hat, a trench coat, or dark glasses?"

"Dark glasses, yes. The other things, no."

"Did you recognize him at all?"

Kevin stared at the ceiling. "There was something about his gait that seemed familiar. But otherwise, no, I didn't recognize him. And get this: when I called out to him, he stepped up the pace. I think if he wasn't lugging that heavy bag of dog food, he actually would have run."

"Did you see the type of vehicle he drove?" Trey asked.

"No, he turned the corner before I reached the front doors since I was in the middle of waiting on another customer."

"We'll make sure we publish all the details and hopefully someone will come forward or provide tips. If you think of anything else, please call us. We'll take a few photos on the way out."

"Thank you, Carleigh and Trey. I see why Howard calls you two *The Oakville Daily* Duo. You really work hard for paper and for the people of Oakville." He paused. "By the way, how are you liking that new grill?"

"I love it," said Carleigh. She tossed a self-satisfied grin Trey's way. She may not win in many of their competitions, but she *had* won that grill.

"That's awful about the burglar," Carleigh said when they reached the minivan.

Trey put the key in the ignition and started the vehicle. Thankfully, he hadn't run over any curbs, lost any hubcaps, had avoided all old dumpy cars driven by crabby elderly women, and made sure no tail lights were out during this trip. He put the van in gear and pressed on the gas pedal. He did have to admit the minivan had pep.

"Yeah. I feel sorry for Kevin and Amy. Hopefully we can find out who did this. Something weird, though, was that the same guy who bought Lindy flowers also had reddish-orange curly hair and could have been over six feet tall. Louella said he was tall, but Louella is barely five feet tall so anyone over five foot, two would seem tall to her."

"True. What if it is the same guy? Yikes. Lindy's secret admirer could be a criminal."

"They say you should always be careful about secret admirers."

"Who says that?"

Trey chuckled. "I don't know, the dating gurus."

"Since when do you listen to dating gurus?"

Great. Now he'd dug himself into a hole. "Since never. I'm just saying that dating can be a dangerous thing. One minute you're receiving flowers, the next minute you realize the guy who likes you is a milk and dog food burglar. You can't be too careful these days."

Like he would ever read dating advice. Who cared about dates anyway? His life was full enough with *The Oakville Daily*, Jaxx, church activities, and the full-time job of dealing with Quirky Carleigh. He dared a glance in her direction. She sat in the passenger side, thrumming her fingers on the console and biting her lip. Cute when she did that.

Cute, but definitely not dating material.

Dating material? *What?*

Trey shook his head. Arguing with himself could be a sign of some disorder and he really needed to stop. Carleigh may be cute and she may be funny and smart and kind, but she was not on his radar. And never would be. Ever.

"Why are you shaking your head? And why are your lips moving and no sound is coming out? Trey, are you all right?"

"I'm fine. Just rehashing all we know about the incident." *And reminding myself why you are not on my radar.*

"All right, so here's what we know: the thief could be Lindy's secret admirer. At least if this perp breaks her heart, there's always a backup."

Trey slid into *The Oakville Daily* parking lot. "What do you mean?"

"Well, that's what I wanted to talk to you about."

"Go on." Why did the woman talk in puzzles?

"So, remember how I asked you to remind me to tell you something about Chip?"

"Vaguely." Trey pulled into the reserved parking spot for the minivan and killed the engine. He faced Carleigh. "What are you getting at?"

"So, you noticed how he always sits by her."

"And how you always sit by me."

Carleigh jabbed him in the shoulder. "It's different. We sit by each other..."

"You sit by me."

"No, we sit by each other in case we have an article to discuss or need to brainstorm. You know, as *The Oakville Daily* Duo."

Her face glimmered a bright red and he almost felt sorry for her. Almost. "Okay, so people sit by each other."

"Yes, and today I noticed for the first time his adoring and uninterrupted gaze."

"Adoring and uninterrupted gaze? What are you, a romance novelist?"

"I would love to be an author someday. Anyway, I snapped a photo just because I knew you'd need proof." Carleigh swiped through her pictures and handed the phone to Trey.

Trey peered down at the phone. Sure enough, professionals on the matter could say that Chip's glance toward Lindy was, in fact, adoring. He did appear to be hanging on every word. "All right, so how does this play into anything?"

"So, if the secret admirer is a criminal, Lindy always has Chip."

"O…kay…but does she like him in that way?"

Trey watched as Carleigh pondered his question. She bit her lip again. "When we went out to lunch last week, she did bring up his name."

"In what way?"

"She said that Chip was late to work the other day."

He attempted to ponder how that meant Lindy liked him. "So, she was making a statement about his lack of punctuality? And for the record, Chip is hardly ever late, so it could be that she noticed he wasn't on time for once."

"True. But it's like she *really* noticed him. I told her Chip wasn't a bad catch."

Did Carleigh like Chip? And why did that matter to him?

It didn't.

"You're doing it again. Moving your mouth, but no sound is coming out. Trey, are you sure you are all right?"

"Yeah. I'm good. So, what did you mean when you said Chip was a good catch?"

"Well, he's smart, has a respectable work ethic, even to the point that he works two jobs, has a pleasing sense of humor, and isn't gross."

"Isn't gross?"

"You know, some guys are gross. He's not."

Trey attempted to wrap his mind around that one. Women were so bizarre. "Am I gross?" he asked, before he could stop the words from flying from his mouth.

"Why do you need to know?"

Why did he need to know? "I don't *need* to know. I'm just trying to figure out what you think gross is."

"You're not exactly gross."

"Exactly? Just kind of?"

"Right."

He was no closer to finding out the answer, and in truth, why did he even care if Carleigh thought he was gross? "Are you talking about appearances or personality?"

"Both."

A knock on the window caused both of them to jump. Howard motioned for Trey to open the door. "Look, you two. I pay you to write the news. Now then, come on in and do your job, pronto."

"Sorry, Howard."

Their boss shook his head. "Are you sure you two aren't dating? You sure like to spend time together."

Trey retreated to the back of the van to unload his equipment before Howard and Carleigh could see that his ears were not just a mild red, but a deep red.

Him like to spend time with Carleigh?

Not a chance.

Howard called an emergency meeting in the breakroom.

Carleigh slid next to Trey, and Chip sat next to Lindy, directly across from them. Howard plunked down in his usual spot at the head of the table, and Margie and Bubba entered last and filed into the remaining seats.

Howard reached for a stale donut from the donut box leftover from two meetings ago. "We need to stay on top of the theft from Buy it All and support Kevin and Amy through this challenging time. Now then, what did *The Oakville Daily* Duo uncover in their investigation?"

"Go ahead," Trey said, nudging Carleigh.

"If you insist."

"I do."

Chip snorted. "Hey, children. Let's not turn this meeting into an argument. Just tell us what you uncovered."

Howard reached for a second donut. "Well said, Chip. Now then, proceed."

Carleigh ignored Trey's smug glance and shared with her coworkers what she and Trey had learned. "Basically, it is a guy with a curly red wig, dark glasses, about six feet tall, and slim."

"Did Kevin say he was slim?" Trey asked.

"I took it to mean that he was slim. Kevin didn't say he was heavyset."

"Nor did he say he was slim."

Carleigh rolled her eyes. "I think he was slim. Besides, he moved quickly. A bigger guy might not be able to move that quickly."

"That is a common fallacy," added Bubba.

"We do know that he had a curly reddish-orange wig and was about six feet tall. His width and build are unknown at this time. How's that, Trey?"

"Much better. Thank you, Carleigh." He caught her eye, and mouthed something to her. She really could not understand his covert means of communication. He mouthed it again, and Carleigh was aware that everyone was staring at them.

"Care to share?" Howard asked.

"Yes, uh, Trey, I think we should share that."

"You do?"

"Yes, please do."

Trey narrowed his eyes, but proceeded to steeple his fingers in Howard-fashion. "Something did cause us concern about this whole situation."

"Really?" Margie asked. "Like what?"

"Well, the thief, as we mentioned, was seen wearing a curly reddish-orange wig."

"Yes, we've established that." Chip said.

"So, there was someone else who also was seen wearing a curly reddish-orange wig," Trey continued.

Carleigh nodded. Now she realized what Trey had been trying to communicate. "Yes, and wait until you hear this." She nodded toward Trey.

"We think that the thief might be the same man who is sending Lindy flowers."

Lindy paled. "No. Really?"

"Could be," said Carleigh. "We're not sure. It just seems like the physical descriptions are similar between what Kevin told us about the thief and what Louella said about the secret admirer."

Lindy gasped. "You asked Louella?"

"While we were in there on an unrelated assignment," said Trey, whose ears had turned red.

Chip frowned. "Now, back up the bus. Do you honestly think that a thief would be so thoughtful as to buy Lindy flowers? Doesn't make sense."

Margie, always the voice of reason added her thoughts. "There are some considerate thieves."

"The plot thickens." Howard took the last bite of his donut.

Chip stood and began pacing. "Well, I'm not so sure. Who saw the thief at Buy it All?"

"Kevin," chorused Carleigh and Trey.

"My cousin twice removed, who is an investigator in Iowa, told me once that eyewitness testimony can be unreliable. Perhaps Kevin or Louella are mistaken in the identity of the thief or the secret admirer. I doubt they are the same person."

"There is controversy on eyewitness testimony," Margie agreed. "But I seriously doubt neither Louella nor Kevin would be inaccurate in their testimony of what they saw."

Howard nodded. "This is all very interesting, and I have to say, good detective work, Carleigh and Trey. Wouldn't it be a feat and a half if our very own *Oakville Daily* staff solved this crime before Oakville PD did?"

"Do I detect a bit of competition, boss?" Bubba asked.

"No, not at all. Just saying that it would be a powerful testimony to the fact that our paper is truly number one in Oakville."

Carleigh heard Margie moan. "The *only* paper in Oakville."

"I am still grieved by the possibility that my secret admirer is living a double life as a thief." Lindy covered her mouth with her hand. "How could it be?"

"It's not," said Chip. "I don't believe it for a minute. What do you think he does? Steals items and sells them on the black market to afford the roses he sends you?"

"Oh, no. What if he does? I had him pegged as a nice guy."

Howard peered over his glasses. "You can't be too careful about folks these days. Hate to disappoint you, Lindy, but your secret admirer may not be the upstanding man you think he is."

# Chapter Nineteen

CARLEIGH ENDEAVORED TO FOCUS on the task at hand. But how could she concentrate on the Buy it All interview with the looming photo of she and Trey and their "engagement photo" staring up at her?

What were Trey's thoughts on the matter? He was flipping through the most recent edition of *The Oakville Daily*, one hand stroking his five-o-clock shadow of a beard. Had he intently perused the article and photos as well?

The interview with Kevin at Buy it All demanded her attention. But then, so did Margie's article. She unfolded the paper and re-read what Howard called "the history-making essay" and bit her lip.

"The Oakville Daily Duo Steps to the Forefront, Leaving no Story Unreported"

By Margie Siddons

Unparalleled excitement riveted through the streets of Oakville in recent days with the latest development at *The Oakville Daily*.

Carleigh Adams and Trey Montgomery, both reporters for *The Oakville Daily*, have joined forces to bring Oakville all the news. "They're a team now," said Howard, owner, CEO, editor, office manager, and opinion piece coordinator of the number one paper in Oakville. "It was a long time coming, and with their unique areas of expertise, I foresee it being a fruitful collaboration."

Oakville residents will recognize Carleigh from her Creative Corner articles that bring her artsy flair to life while encouraging readers to participate in innovative, crafty ideas. Carleigh has covered human-interest stories, the police blotter, and community and school sports.

Trey's weekly Trey's Sports Corner has been a subscriber favorite. He's also written a majority of the sports-related and court-coverage articles. Both reporters have blessed readers with their faith-related articles and have entertained subscribers with their late-breaking crime stories.

But they've never covered these major news stories together…until now.

Carleigh and Trey will now join forces as *The Oakville Daily* Duo, with Carleigh writing a majority of the stories and Trey taking a majority of the photos. They will now work in tandem and travel to assignments in the infamous Oakville Daily minivan, all the while ensuring that the folks of our town never miss a newsworthy item.

Co-workers weighed in on the recent memorable event. "They'll do great, they really will," said Chip, marketing extraordinaire, classified ads specialist, and subscriptions manager. "I have no doubt their sparring can be used in a way that will enhance *The Oakville Daily* and entertain readers at the same time."

"They don't always get along," noted Lindy, administrative assistant, receptionist, and payroll clerk. "But that's part of their charm. They'll definitely balance each other out."

Bubba, the printing press coordinator and janitor, agreed. "Carleigh and Trey ensure I have job security with all their articles. Howard made a wise choice in putting them together on the same team. Teamwork is what it's all about, and I think they'll be quick learners."

Readers will love this charismatic pair as they embark on their newest roles at *The Oakville Daily*.

Be sure to contact them if you have any news tips, and right now, there is a subscription special for new subscribers. When you call, just mention *"Oakville Daily Duo"* and you'll get a free month with a year's subscription.

Beneath the "engagement photo," Margie had written the caption, "Carleigh Adams and Trey Montgomery are thrilled to be joining forces as *The Oakville Daily* Duo."

Thrilled? Um, no. Try unenthused, lackadaisical, or tepid.

As if the photo wasn't enough, there had been commentary from their co-workers. Detailed commentary. She drummed her fingers on her desk. The photo of her and Trey really did resemble an engagement photo, and that very thought was enough to cause her severe insomnia until she was fifty.

She and Trey both smiled in the picture. Trey might have a glint of enthusiasm in his expression, but how had she managed to look so happy in such an aggravating moment?

Three words came to mind. Dismaying. Daunting. Appalling.

# Chapter Twenty

CARLEIGH JUST FINISHED TYPING her notes from the interview with Kevin at Buy it All when she noticed the afternoon had slipped away from her. The clock on the wall indicated it was five o'clock. Finally, this hectic and demanding workday had come to an end.

Chip jogged into the center of the work area and announced in his deep voice, "Hey, you guys up for a burger at the café?"

"I can't," said Margie. "Sorry, but I'm babysitting my grandbaby tonight. Have I showed you all the latest pictures?" She reached for her cell phone, but stopped short of swiping to her saved pictures. She must have seen everyone nodding that they were up-to-date on grandbaby photos.

"Sorry, I can't. I promised my grandma I'd take her grocery shopping tonight," Lindy said, pilfering through her purse, presumably for her keys.

Carleigh witnessed a flash of disappointment cross Chip's face. Poor guy. He wasn't able to get together often in the evenings with *The Oakville Daily* crew because of his second job. She was about to chime in and announce she could go when Trey beat her to it. "I'm up for a burger."

"Great!" Chip jogged in place, his oversized feet pounding the faded carpet. He simultaneously looked around the room, from Carleigh to Bubba, to Howard.

Carleigh nodded. "I can make it, Chip."

"Awesome. Well, that's three of us so far."

Bubba patted his rotund stomach. "I'd love to, but tonight's the wifey's birthday. I promised I'd make root beer floats, her favorite dessert. Can I take a raincheck?"

"I can't make it," said Howard. "I have choir practice at the church tonight."

"Well, that looks like just the three of us then," Chip nodded toward Carleigh and Trey.

Carleigh pondered the thought for a moment. She didn't want to be a tag along with Trey and Chip. Margie, Howard, Bubba, and Lindy waved their goodbyes and headed out the door. "If you and Chip just want to go…"

Trey shrugged. "Nah. You can come with us."

"Yeah, you can come with us, Carleigh."

Several minutes later, Carleigh pulled her car into The Oakville Greasy Spoon parking lot. The place, as usual, was packed. A diner with a wide variety of menu options, The Oakville Greasy Spoon was one of the most popular dining establishments in town. Trey arrived at nearly the same time and parked beside her.

"My stomach is already growling," said Trey, holding the restaurant door open for her.

Chip waved to them from a booth in the far corner. Red checkered curtains hung on the windows, matching the red barstools at the counter. Carleigh inhaled the aroma of hamburgers and French fries. One couldn't eat at the café often and maintain their figure or their healthy lifestyle, but a once-in-a-while venture was always welcomed.

The café was anything but quiet. Laughter, camaraderie, and deep conversation lingered throughout the pint-sized business. Chip had snagged one of the eight booths along the western side. Six or seven tables filled in the space between the booths and the counter area. Cramped, but homey, the Oakville Greasy Spoon had remained in the same family for four generations. And their décor had remained the same for nearly that long as well.

Doretta, one of the two waitresses and the co-owner with her husband, Cleveland, set glasses of water and three menus on the table. "Welcome! Let me know when you're ready to order." She rushed off to a table in the middle, flanked by more chairs than could fit and a family with two parents and six children of various ages.

"Ah, it's good to be here." Chip clasped his hands behind his head and reclined against the back of the booth cushion.

Carleigh attempted to ignore the fact that Trey slid right in beside her on the too-small, too-cozy bench seat. His shoulder touched hers, causing an immediate fluttering sensation in her stomach. A whiff of his aftershave floated toward her, mingling with the scents of the diner.

Time to focus her mind on something other than Trey.

Doretta interrupted her unwelcome thoughts about Trey when she brought them some complimentary homemade potato chips, something unique and well-loved by Oakville residents. "You all ready to order?" She tucked a stray graying hair behind her ear and offered a smile. Her friendly outgoing nature rivaled that of the often-serious and introverted, Cleveland.

"I'll have the crispy chicken sandwich and some French fries." One couldn't eat the calorie-laden meals at The Oakville Greasy Spoon too often and keep their waistline trim and their arteries clear. Carleigh made a note to put in more time on the elliptical at the rec center.

"I'll take the triple bacon burger with onion rings," said Trey.

"And I'll take the triple mushroom burger and tots," announced Chip, handing the unopened menus to Doretta.

Doretta finished writing their orders and placed the menus in her wide front apron pocket. "It'll be out soon."

Chip pointed toward the window that faced Oakville's Main Street. "There went Amy. Man, I sure feel sorry for her and Kevin."

Carleigh again recalled the entire incident with the clownish wig and how that could tie into Lindy's secret admirer. Poor Lindy. She'd been so thrilled to receive yet another bouquet. "The commonalities are truly bizarre," she muttered, more to herself than to Chip and Trey.

Chip angled his head toward her. "What do you mean the commonalities? And why are they bizarre?"

"Well, for one, the guy in the disguise with a reddish-orange wig. He is definitely making his face known around town."

"Yep," agreed Trey. "He's buying Lindy flowers and stealing milk and dog food. I'd say he's a busy guy."

221

An unreadable expression crossed Chip's face. "Back up the bus, folks. You have no proof that the guy buying Lindy flowers and the Buy it All thief are one and the same. We established this at the staff meeting."

"It's just absurd that this guy would have to disguise himself. I mean, I understand it will make him more difficult to identify, but a curly reddish-orange wig?" Carleigh shook her head.

"Hey, you do have to disguise yourself here in Oakville. Everyone seems to know everyone else and all the details of their life." Chip's peculiar expression returned for a brief moment. "Don't get me wrong. I've lived here since junior high and I have no desire to live anywhere else, but you can't have any secrets here. Nope, not even one."

Trey took a break from eating and stroked his imaginary beard. "Like what secrets would a person have, Chip?"

"Like none. I'm just saying that everyone in Oakville knows everyone else's business. You can't even perform a random act of kindness without someone knowing."

"Well, we are in the business of knowing everyone else's business," said Carleigh. She hadn't realized Chip lived in Oakville since junior high. He graduated a couple of years before she entered high school, so she never really knew him until she hired on at *The Oakville Daily*.

"And that's why Howard pays us the big bucks. Unfortunately, we may never know the identity of the thief or Lindy's secret admirer." Trey's hand brushed hers as he rested it on the table and she flinched as a tingling current zipped up her arm. It could only mean one

222

thing—that her arm had fallen asleep. There could be no other reason.

Why on earth was she so skittish around him today? Good grief.

"Howard mentioned someone in an old white van drove off without paying for gas at one of the gas stations again the other day," said Chip. "What is this town coming to? I know there's some petty crime every now and again and kids sometimes try some bratty things, but hopefully we won't end up with Carleigh having to provide pages and pages for the crime section."

Carleigh agreed. Right now, the crimes section and police blotter was a paragraph once a week and usually amounted to nothing serious or even newsworthy in any other newspaper.

"The weird thing, as Carleigh mentioned, is the disguise," said Trey. "A curly reddish-orange wig? Who knew that was the M.O. of criminals these days?"

The peculiar expression returned yet again to Chip's face. "Hey, wait a minute. Just because someone wears a curly reddish-orange wig doesn't mean they're a hardened criminal."

"Speaking from experience, Chip?"

Chip's hazel eyes enlarged behind his glasses. "No, not at all. I'm just saying that law-abiding people wear wigs too."

"Really?" asked Trey.

"Yes, and besides, someone mentioned the other day—might have been someone I chatted with at the coffee shop—that Oakville Party Supply had wigs on sale recently. They said you could pick up a wig at an insanely reasonable price. Something about it being in the weekly ad or something with an extra discount for having a 'favorite customer card.'"

Carleigh caught Trey's gaze. Was he thinking the same thing she was thinking? That they could interview the owner at Oakville Party Supply and find out who she'd sold wigs to in recent weeks? He nodded slightly, and she realized he was likely thinking the same thing.

Uncanny.

Frightening.

Unnerving.

Adversaries were not of the same mind.

They just weren't.

"You seem to know a lot about wigs." Should Carleigh probe deeper and see if perhaps Chip could assist them in discovering both Lindy's secret admirer and the Buy it All thief?

Chip flicked a potato chip crumb onto the floor. "Not really. It's not like I did my college thesis on wigs or anything. It's just that we can't necessarily lump all wig-wearers into one category. My second cousin twice removed is an investigator on the police force in Iowa and he would say that one has to examine all angles. Some criminals wear wigs, some who aren't criminals wear wigs too. Take clowns for example."

"That's true. Remember that clown at Stella's birthday party?" Trey asked.

Chip was still rambling about clowns and wigs and costumes when Doretta set the food on the table before them with a promise to check back and see if they wanted dessert later. The guy was obviously nervous about something.

"So, here's what I'm thinking," said Trey, biting into an onion ring. "If we find out who Lindy's secret admirer is, we find out who the thief is. Maybe we need to talk to Louella again and see if she remembers anything else about Lindy's secret admirer. Maybe her husband decided after all to install security cameras."

"What?" Chip coughed. Was he choking?

"Chip, are you all right?" Carleigh knew how to do the Heimlich. She proudly kept up her CPR and First Aid certifications just in case anyone should ever need help.

Chip held up a finger. "I'm fine." He cleared his throat and took a drink of his pop. "Now, what is this about security cameras?"

"Well, security cameras are all the rage now, what with the uptick in crime in more-populated areas, and apparently here in Oakville. They're fairly easy to install, too, from what I understand."

"Where did you hear this?" Chip asked, his voice still raspy from choking.

Carleigh leaned forward. "Are you sure you are all right, Chip? You seem shaken after your choking incident."

"I'm fine. I just want to know about Lew and the security cameras."

Trey shrugged. "Lew and my neighbor, Mr. Fortuna, were talking at our Bible study about Lew installing security cameras at the flower shop. Apparently, he's been wanting to install them for a while now, ever since someone stole a garden pinwheel spinner ornament from one of Louella's outdoor flower pots three summers ago. Once they find out about the Buy it All burglary, it'll probably be a done deal, if he hasn't installed them already. And if he has already installed them, voilà. We might be able to identify Lindy's S.A., and in the process identify the Buy it All thief."

Chip cocked his head to one side. "Is nothing sacred anymore? We have to have security cameras to identify someone's secret admirer?"

"If it helps solve another crime, it would be worth it."

"Not really," said Chip. "Because they are not one and the same guy. Can't be. A considerate guy who buys flowers is not a thief. We've already been over this."

Carleigh was amused at Chip's flustered responses. Maybe he wasn't the one to assist them on this matter. He was too easily rattled by the modern technology of security systems. "Even so, Lindy would probably want to know who's been buying those breathtaking bouquets of flowers for her."

"And if she doesn't want to know?" Chip asked.

"Studies show that most women would want to know," added Trey.

A glimpse at her adversary revealed his bright red ears. "I guess now we know what Trey does in his spare time. He reads studies and statistics about the behavior of women."

"What? Uh, no."

"Really?"

"So what if Lindy has a secret admirer?" chimed in Chip. "It's really no one's business except hers. I wouldn't want everyone knowing my business."

"But have you seen those stunning, colorful flowers all over her desk? That carnation bouquet with the baby's breath was exquisite."

Trey tossed her a dismissive blink. "Guys don't notice that stuff, Carleigh. We wouldn't know the difference between a dandelion and a rose."

"That's right. We don't notice that stuff. Besides, if someone has a crush on Lindy, that's her business, not ours." Chip avoided eye contact and kept his attention squarely on something to the right of his plate.

Suspicious.

"It's really weird. This guy who sends her these flowers has it all scheduled."

Chip's eyes magnified behind his glasses. "How do you know all this stuff?"

Carleigh shrugged. "Easy. From our conversation with Louella. She told us the S.A. has paid in advance and scheduled the deliveries thus far. In my humble opinion, the S.A. will be back to add to the deliveries. He must be a wealthy guy."

"Or is reselling the stuff he steals," added Trey.

A look of what could only be described as horror widened Chip's eyes once again. "Uh, no, I don't think so."

"Why not?" Carleigh noticed Chip had paused from eating his tater tots, one hand in midair, as if he'd been frozen in time.

"Isn't it obvious?"

Trey shook his head. "Not to us. Clue us in."

"See, a guy who sends flowers to a girl he likes isn't going to steal from the grocery store. Just isn't possible."

"And you know this, how?" Chip may be a pool of information, but in Carleigh's mind, he couldn't know about the motives of an S.A. and thief.

"Because my second cousin twice removed who is an investigator..."

"On the police force in Iowa, yes, you told us," retorted Trey.

"Yeah, him. Anyway, he has experience in profiling criminals and he would say criminals aren't secret admirers."

Carleigh took another sip of pop. "There are a lot of weirdos out there. Think about stalkers for instance."

"He's not a stalker and that they could be the same guy is impossible."

"We'll need to investigate further to know if that's the case or not. Maybe you can help us since you're such a wig expert." Trey quirked a smile at Carleigh. "Would you be all right if he joined the 'duo' and helped us solve this mystery? Maybe an *Oakville Daily* trio thing?"

"Sure, that would be fine."

"No, nada, absolutely not. I am not a detective and I don't care who is sending Lindy flowers, and as far as the thief from Buy it All, you can let the police handle that one. Why are you two so insistent that it's the same guy?"

"And why are you so insistent it's not?" Carleigh asked.

There was something super suspicious about Chip's behavior. What was he hiding?

They ate then, Carleigh bemoaning to herself the caloric intake of French fries. She wasn't a health food freak by any stretch of the imagination, but she was trying hard not to clog her arteries while still in her twenties.

The conversation resumed to other, more benign topics after a few minutes. Trey and Chip talked vehicles and the payment Chip would be making on his luxury vehicle until he was sixty-eight.

Two teens approached the table. "This is so awesome to see *The Oakville Daily* Duo here. Can we have your autographs?" the taller of the girls asked. They handed Carleigh and Trey two slightly soiled napkins.

"Uh, sure." Trey scribbled his name in illegible handwriting and passed the napkins to Carleigh.

She in turn, wrote in her best penmanship, "Best wishes, Carleigh Adams."

"Thank you!" the girls exclaimed and ran back to their table.

"Your writing is so big and loopy," said Trey.

"And yours is so small and sloppy."

"Small and sloppy?"

"Yes. You can't even read it."

"Children, children. Can we at least enjoy a meal without the two of you bickering?" Chip aimed what Carleigh presumed would be a future "dad look" at both of them. "You two know better than to cause a scene in public."

"Well, Dad, she does write big and loopy."

"And he does write small and sloppy. His writing makes a doctor's hieroglyphics look legible."

Trey looked askance at her and reached for his refill of pop that Doretta had brought.

Carleigh's spoon dropped to the floor. "Oops."

"I can get that for you."

"That's okay. I got it."

Carleigh wedged herself under the table to retrieve her spoon at the same time Trey did.

And their heads collided.

She pulled back quickly, bemoaning the tight quarters and the smarting from hitting her head against the most hard-headed person she'd ever met.

"You okay?" Trey asked.

For a minute, she thought she saw real concern in those green eyes.

Baffling. Perplexing. Curious.

"Yes. You?"

"Yeah." He held her gaze for a brief moment before the glint returned to his expression and then a chuckle.

"Now, after that brief break about how to determine if you have a concussion, we'll resume to our regularly scheduled program." Chip rolled his eyes. "You two."

Chip's phone rang. "I've got to take this." He excused himself from the table, leaving Carleigh and Trey crowded on their side of the booth.

Would it be rude to ask Trey to scoot over to Chip's side for a few minutes and give her some breathing space?

Yes, that would be rude, and Carleigh didn't need a book on etiquette to tell her so.

"Wow, did you hear how defensive he got over the wigs? Second time today. First the staff meeting and now tonight." Trey asked, turning toward her.

His face was literally three inches from hers. She could see up close a dimple in his chin. No wonder the guy was ultra-stubborn.

"I noticed that."

Trey's eyes widened and he leaned even closer and whispered. "And he was quite defensive about Lindy's secret admirer. You don't think he might know who's been sending her flowers, do you?"

"Maybe. He knows a lot people, having lived here for all these years. And he is a smart guy. We could use his help."

"Course, I think you have a crush on Chip."

Chip was nice, but definitely not her type and definitely not someone she would crush on. "Um, no."

"Are you sure?"

"Quite sure."

Trey's mouth quirked up on one side. "You told me he wasn't gross."

"And he isn't."

"It's all right if you like him, I mean, it doesn't bother me or anything."

"Doesn't bother you? Are you sure?"

Like she cared what bothered Trey. But still.

Trey's ears turned red. Interesting. "Doesn't bother me in the least. You can crush on whoever you want. You could do a lot worse than Chip."

"Look, let's get back to the topic at hand. Chip's wig knowledge."

"All right, but something really has him distracted tonight. I think we might be better off solving this mystery as the duo, rather than the trio."

"Good idea." Carleigh glanced around to be sure no one else in the café was listening, but everyone seemed to be content going about their own business.

Trey's face was so close to hers. His eyes traveled up and down her face, and he bridged the already-close gap between them.

And a revolting, repulsive, and abhorrent thought entered her mind.

Did he want to kiss her?

Only it wasn't *really* revolting, repulsive, and abhorrent. It might actually be... She blinked.

What on earth?

Wasn't she just lamenting earlier how she had the shoe incident fresh on her mind? Weren't she and Trey just arguing over her supposed crush on Chip and before that, his sloppy writing style? They couldn't get along to save their lives. They argued constantly, competed regularly, and irritated each other worse than a sticker weed stuck in the tongue of a tennis shoe.

Yet, Trey did have some admirable qualities. He loved the Lord, was funny, chivalrous, a dedicated and talented photographer, and a good-looking guy.

Huh? Um, no.

Why had her thoughts briefly meandered from reality to insanity? Either she was way too full from overly-greasy food or she was suffering from some sort of psychosis.

"Wow, this looks serious," said Chip, who slid back into his place across from them.

It was serious, all right. Carleigh needed to rein in any thoughts she might have that Trey the Irritating was anything but an annoying adversary.

# Chapter Twenty-One

JAXX GREETED TREY THE second he arrived home. Trey let him in through the glass door to the patio and his dog bounded toward him, his new squeaky chicken toy in his mouth.

"Hey, Jaxx." Trey patted his German shepherd behind the ears, then poured some dog food into his dish. He sat down at the table as Jaxx scarfed his kibble.

"You won't believe what a chaotic day it's been. First, we interview the owner of Buy it All about some guy in disguise stealing milk and dog food, and then Carleigh and I went with Chip to the café for dinner."

Jaxx finished his meal and sat in front of Trey, his ears perked up and his gaze intent, as if eagerly awaiting to hear all about Trey's day. "That's what I appreciate about you, old boy. You're a good listener. Anyway, I think I might be losing it or delirious or something. I can't believe I'm admitting this, but I was actually ruminating on how cute Carleigh is."

As if he suffered the horror of Trey's announcement right along with him, Jaxx tilted his head sideways and uttered a whine. "I know, Jaxx, I know. Sure, she's a Christian, is bubbly and fun to be around, is pretty, has a great sense of humor, and is thoughtful. She's a gifted writer too, but to think about her that way? What could be wrong with me?"

Jaxx barked.

"Sure. That could be it. I didn't sleep well last night and while the burger and onion rings at the café were amazing, it could be indigestion or something like that clouding my already feeble brain."

Trey scratched Jaxx behind the ears as he again rehashed the episode at the café. "We argued like we always do. She likes to squabble and then we were just sitting there super close... And you know something else? I think she may like Chip. She denies it, but I believe she may have a secret crush on him. Don't worry, though. I'm not jealous or anything."

Jaxx responded with a shake of his head.

"You believe me, right? Or are you shaking your head because you disagree with me? Oh, and then she is so stubborn she wouldn't even let me pick up her spoon that had fallen on the floor. Here I am, trying to be a gentleman. Trying to make Mom proud. But, no. She bent over to pick it up at the same time and we collided. She is the most hard-headed woman I've ever met. I probably have a goose egg on the side of my head." Trey reached up to the spot where Carleigh's head hit his. "We compete on everything and get on each other's nerves. How could I possibly like her in that way? I mean, come on. She's...this is Carleigh Adams we're talking about."

A car passed by outside on the street, lights flashing through the front window. "Good idea, Jaxx. I should close the curtain before anyone sees me carrying on an in-depth conversation with my dog."

Sometime later, Trey showered and headed to bed. Thoughts of Carleigh still flooded his mind. Something had changed regarding his feelings toward her. If he were a wise man, he'd do all he could to put this demented notion about liking her out of his mind.

He. Did. Not. Like. Carleigh Adams. Not in that way. Not now. Not ever.

Things got even more awkward at work the next day. Well, for Chip anyway, especially since the conversation once again veered toward wigs, criminals, and secret admirers.

Trey, Chip, and Lindy clustered around Carleigh's desk, drinking their first cups of coffee for the day. It wasn't uncommon for them to cluster around someone's desk while they discussed the plans for the day. Sometimes Margie, Howard, and Bubba would join them.

Carleigh clued Lindy in on the conversation at The Oakville Greasy Spoon the night before.

Lindy's dark eyebrows merged into her hairline. "Wow. I didn't know you were a detective, Chip."

"I'm not." Chip began jogging in place, apparently attempting to expel some of his nervous energy.

Trey nodded. "He's a wig expert."

"A wig expert?"

Chip shook his head. "No, I'm not. I just happened to know they were on sale at Oakville Party Supply the other day. The thief is probably a sinister villain, but the S.A. is probably just some ordinary guy wanting to impress an extraordinary gal."

"Ordinary guy wanting to impress an extraordinary gal? Ooh, sounds romantic," giggled Lindy.

"See what I mean?" Trey slapped Chip on the back. "Chip is a book of knowledge. I think you missed your calling."

Chip laugh-snorted. "Funny. I'd actually make a lousy detective, but I do have to say that maybe you should just focus on the thief." He paused. "And you two really need to let go of your presumption that there is a connection between the Buy it All thief and Lindy's secret admirer."

Carleigh, in her eye-blinding green dress-thing, smiled.

Trey noticed what a pretty smile she had.

No, he didn't. He didn't notice that at all. Trey chastised himself to stay on topic.

"I agree with Carleigh and Trey about finding out who the S.A. is. I mean, it would be beneficial for me to know who is spending all this money on me and being so thoughtful."

"What if he's ninety-four-years-old or a hardened criminal or something?" Trey asked.

"Yikes," shivered Lindy. "Maybe I don't want to know."

Chip glanced over at Lindy. "Don't worry, Lindy. It's highly unlikely, number one, that your secret admirer is ninety-four-years-old, and two, that he's a hardened criminal. My second cousin twice removed who serves on the police force in Iowa would say that the characteristics don't line up between the two. Carleigh and Trey are totally off base on this one."

"Maybe, maybe not," said Carleigh. "But I'm with you, Lindy. I would want to find out who is sending me those magnificent flowers. Look on the bright side. It could be this gorgeous hunk. Tall, athletic, good-looking..."

"Like me?" joked Trey.

Carleigh scrunched her nose at him. "No, Trey. Sorry."

"Look, folks, let's just focus on the thief." Chip shuffled his size fifteen feet from side to side. Something was making him awfully anxious. Trey wondered if Carleigh noticed the same thing. He'd have to ask her. Maybe they needed to add Chip's behavior to the list of mysteries they were trying to solve.

Since working at *The Oakville Daily,* Carleigh and Lindy had become close friends. They were close in age and with the commonality of the newspaper escapades, they never ran out of things to talk about.

They agreed to go to lunch at the Sandwich Mart. Perhaps having a wholesome sandwich with lettuce and tomato would make up for the greasy meal from last night. Besides, she burned plenty of calories constantly chasing Sullivan Theodore.

Carleigh slid into the booth and placed her purse beside her on the cushion. Lindy did the same. "So, I have a ginormous question to ask you," said Lindy.

"Sure."

Lindy picked at a chipped nail. "It's sort of awkward."

"We're friends. Ask away."

"All right. Promise you'll tell me the truth?"

"I always to try to be honest. And yes, I love your new skirt and flower-print blouse and I do think they go well with your sandals."

Lindy laughed. "Thank you. I couldn't wait for the weather to be warm enough to wear this outfit. But that's not my question."

What could have Lindy so apprehensive? "You can ask me anything, you know that."

A troubled expression clouded Lindy's face. "You're right. It's just awkward asking this, but here goes..."

The anticipation was nearly more than Carleigh could handle. "Yes?"

"Do you like Chip?"

"What?"

"Chip. Do you like him?"

Carleigh did her best to demonstrate a stoic expression so as not to appear appalled by the inquiry. But keeping a neutral countenance had always presented somewhat of a challenge for her. "He's a nice guy."

"Okay, I figured as much."

"What do you mean?"

Lindy's shoulders dropped, a departure from her usually straight posture. "I figured you might like him."

"Why would you figure that?"

238

"Because of what...oh, hello."

Carleigh followed Lindy's gaze toward the waitress, a woman they knew named Megan, who stood next to their table. "Sorry," said Megan, "but I was sorta waiting with anticipation to find out if it is true that you do like Chip and if so, how Lindy figured you did."

"Megan, this is a private conversation," said Lindy.

"Oh, I know. And you don't have to worry about a thing. Everyone in the restaurant is totally deep in conversation. It'll be just us who are privy to this discussion." Megan, a woman in her thirties, who spoke with the vernacular of a teenager from a beach town, waved her hand toward them. "I am totally, like, not going to tell anyone what you say. If you like Chip, great. I mean, he's a handsome guy and does such an awesome job on the classified ads in *The Oakville Daily*." Megan pulled a chair from a nearby table and plopped down beside Carleigh and Lindy's table. "So, do tell."

Carleigh wasn't sure what to do about Megan. The woman, attention fully engaged, rested her chin on her folded hands. She alternated her gaze between Carleigh and Lindy. How could Carleigh politely tell the woman that whether or not she liked Chip was none of her business? She didn't want to be unkind and Megan was a likeable person, just overly nosy. She offered a prayer heavenward for grace.

God answered immediately.

A balding man approached their table. "Excuse me, ma'am, we're ready to order."

"All right," Megan told the man. She whispered to Carleigh and Lindy, "You two hold that conversation until I help this man with his order, okay?"

Carleigh wasn't promising anything, much less to "hold the conversation" until Megan's return. "So where were we?"

"You were just about to tell me you are madly in love with Chip."

Carleigh shook her head so hard that she feared it would fly off her neck and land near the door. "No, absolutely not. I am not madly in love with Chip."

"It's totally okay if you are. I get that he's an amiable guy, super cute, and highly intelligent." Lindy's eyes took on a dreamy gaze that indicated she may have left the conversation and leapt headlong into dream-about-Chip-land.

"Why would you think I have a crush on Chip?"

"Don't get mad at him, but Trey mentioned to me this morning that you liked Chip."

"He what?"

"Carleigh, I know you two are adversaries, but don't be too harsh on him. It wasn't like he was gossiping or anything. He was just stating a fact. He actually seemed a little bothered by it."

"Okay, hold the phone. So, number one, I am not in love with Chip. He's nice, he's smart, and he's fun to work with, but he is not my type, and I don't think he's cute at all."

"Oh, he's cute all right. Have you seen the way his eyes light up when he's talking about something he's passionate about? It's adorable."

"Rest assured, I'm not interested in him."

"Really?"

"Really."

"Then why would Trey say that?"

Carleigh shrugged. "Who knows why Trey says the things he does. The guy is an oddity. Speaking of Trey, why was he bothered I might like Chip?"

"Truly?"

"Yes, truly."

"I think he likes you."

Carleigh choked on a sip of pop. Her eyes watered, her nose burned, and tears streamed down her face. After a few minutes of reassuring Lindy she would survive and reassuring Megan she needn't call an ambulance, Carleigh was able to again speak. "No way. He absolutely does not. We are adversaries, as you mentioned, and he irritates me and I irritate him. Have you heard us argue?"

"Well, he sounded bummed when he told me you have a crush on Chip. I tried to tell him that you and Chip don't really match, but he still seemed a bit dejected. And his ears were red. That was weird. But then, you know Trey, he just joked his way out of it and changed the subject."

"I've noticed his red ears before too, but I don't think he likes me in that way. We've come to a sort of understanding to get along for the sake of *The Oakville Daily*, but that's as far as it goes. I don't like him and I definitely don't like Chip."

Lindy settled back into the booth cushion. "You're sure you don't like Chip in that way?"

"I'm sure."

"That is such encouraging news."

"What's such encouraging news?" Megan asked, placing their order on the table. "What did I miss?"

"It's good news that our food is here," said Lindy, obviously hoping to avoid Megan's interrogation.

"So do you like Chip, Carleigh?"

"No, not in that way."

But Carleigh had a suspicion of who did like Chip in that way. Lindy placed a napkin in her lap and stared at her food with a dreamy expression.

Lindy's admirer may be a mystery, but Chip's was not.

# Chapter Twenty-Two

WHEN CARLEIGH RETURNED TO work a half hour later, she couldn't keep her mind off what Lindy said about Trey liking her. The thought amused and intrigued her. She glanced up and caught him looking over at her. Was it true what Lindy had said?

He gave her that lopsided smile. The one where only the left side of his mouth turned upwards and his eyes held a mischievous glint.

When had she noticed that?

All of the recent articles and the fact that she had to be his partner for *The Oakville Daily* Duo had caused her to mind to become scrambled and unreliable. Or too creative. Or in need of a serious reality check. Trey no more liked her than she liked him. And Trey's lopsided smile was no more appealing to her than wearing a pair of men's clunky work boots in lieu of her fashionable sandals.

Right?

Carleigh returned to her work post haste, knowing that in exactly twenty-three minutes and forty-nine seconds, she and Trey would be heading to Oakville Party Supply to inquire who purchased a reddish-orange clown wig during the past week.

Things would be uncomfortable for sure riding around in the minivan with Trey today.

She focused her energy into writing a follow-up article on how Oakville residents found their true love. Some had been high school sweethearts, others had met through a blind date, still others had been set up by family or friends. And some met at church or work. Carleigh allowed her mind to wander for a moment and ponder what it would be like to find true love. A love of a lifetime, as her mom would say. Her parents had a loving Christ-centered marriage, and Carleigh had seen many longtime married couples at church. Louella at the flower shop was still in love with her husband, Lew, after all those years, and Howard adored his wife. Bubba made his wife root beer floats as a sign of his undying devotion. And Margie and her husband went on frequent getaways, just the two of them.

But what if God didn't have a true love in mind for Carleigh? What if His plan included her being a single woman all her days, with no one but Sullivan Theodore IV to keep her company?

Whatever God's plan was for her life, she knew it would be a perfect and right plan, but a little niggle deep in her stomach prompted a wishful thought that maybe, just maybe, there was someone out there for her.

Of course, not for the next several years. The year she turned thirty would be a good year to get married.

"Daydreaming again?"

His voice caused her to jump. Trey lounged near her desk, hands in his pockets. "Swooning over the 'How I Met My One True Love, Part Two' article Howard assigned?"

"What? Swooning? No one uses that word anymore."

"And yet..."

"No, absolutely not. I was not swooning, as you say. I was trying to figure out how to combine a couple of sentences into something charming for our readers." Her face burned under his perusal and she turned her focus to her computer monitor.

"So, you say." He remained staring at her with a smug grin. "Maybe I can help."

"No offense, but what do you know about true love?"

"Not much, but I could help you string a few sentences together."

"If I need an editor, I'll let you know." Honestly. Could the guy just return to his desk? She'd never get finished in eighteen minutes and five seconds if she had to continually argue with her nemesis.

"Hey, there's a reason why I'm the top reporter for *The Oakville Daily*."

"Since there are only two reporters, three if you count Margie's part-time writing gig."

"Well, I'm further ahead than you are on this project. I already have the pictures of the couples profiled ready for the layout. I thought either this afternoon after we return from Oakville Party Supply or early tomorrow morning before deadline, we could get together and figure out if there's anything else we'd like to add to the article and photos. You know, to make it special since

Howard is all over this statistic about June being the most popular month to get married."

It was when Trey was rambling on about the layout that Carleigh realized somewhere along the way with this ludicrous interaction with Trey, she'd lost her gum. Had she swallowed it? Dropped it somewhere? Lost it on her keyboard? She scrutinized every nook and cranny in and around her desk. She picked up her coffee cup, but her gum was nowhere to be found.

"You are really scatterbrained today, Carleigh."

"Just have a lot on my mind."

"Like true love?" He chuckled. "So, what do you think about the layout? We should really get this ridiculous article behind us so we can focus on the thief and other more pressing things like finding out who Lindy's S.A. is."

She had to agree with him on the second part of his statement, not that she agreed with him on much. "Sure. Let's see if there's time after the Oakville Party Supply outing. I'd rather do it then instead of tomorrow morning. The hours before deadline are always stressful."

Carleigh half expected Trey to say it wasn't stressful for him, but he didn't. Instead, he tossed her a quizzical glance and pointed at the floor. "Hey, is that your gum squished into the carpet?"

Something was definitely up with Carleigh. She was always a featherbrain and somewhat distracted, but today she was even more so. Trey looked to his right where Chip sat at his desk, hard at work. Likely Carleigh was thinking of her true love, Chip. And Chip was likely thinking about Carleigh.

Did they have a date planned?

Did they know each other liked each other?

Would they break the news to *The Oakville Daily* crew in days to come?

Why were all these thoughts and questions bombarding him all at once? It wasn't like he was jealous or anything. Chip was a personable guy, and while Carleigh was annoying and thought she had to compete with him on everything, Trey did want what was best for her. He looked from Carleigh to Chip, then back to Carleigh. Thing was, they didn't make a suitable couple. Not at all. Carleigh should be matched with someone who was a little more fun-loving and someone who enjoyed solving offbeat mysteries. And a dog owner. Her true love would have to be a dog owner for sure. Chip had a parrot.

*Oh, so now you're some expert on matchmaking and have it all figured out who does and who doesn't make a suitable couple. Yeah, right.*

Thankfully, no one could read his mind. They would be shocked.

*He* was shocked.

It had to be the stress from putting together the photographs for this major feature article. Howard reiterated no less than four hundred times that he wanted it to coincide with the upcoming bridal preview at the local hotel convention complex. Not near enough time to meet that looming deadline.

That had to be the only explanation as to why he would even think of how Carleigh and Chip's relationship had gotten to him.

The *only* explanation.

The ride to Oakville Party Supply was mostly a quiet one, except for the squealing of the tires as Trey took the corners to their destination. "Did you miss your calling as a racecar driver?" Carleigh teased as he zoomed into the last available parking spot in front of the downtown store.

"It's the vehicle. Honestly, I'm an experienced driver." He winked at her.

Heat rushed up her face. What happened to the days when she would cringe at such an action on his part? She for sure needed more sleep.

Oakville Party Supply had been a staple in town for at least two decades. Everything from balloons to invitations, party gifts, wigs, costumes, wrapping paper, and bows lined the walls. An entire separate section hosted children's toys, and an enormous shelving unit in front of the store displayed an extensive variety of gag gifts.

Aubrey-Joan was the proprietor. A petite round woman of about five feet, two with short gray-streaked black hair, she loved her colorful ankle-length skirts and sensible cropped jackets. It didn't take much to tickle her funny bone, and oftentimes, she couldn't stop her contagious giggle, a tinkling laugh as small and as charming as she was.

"Well, hello there, *Oakville Daily* Duo." She waved at them while continuing to assist a customer at the counter. "I'll be right with you."

Carleigh had known Aubrey-Joan since the days of first grade Sunday school. The woman always brought the best craft supplies for the lesson. Carleigh wasn't sure Aubrey-Joan made any profits since she was constantly donating items to worthwhile causes.

She and Trey wandered around the store, Carleigh snagging a few items while they waited for Aubrey-Joan to finish with her customers.

"Did I tell you Lindy likes Chip?" Carleigh asked, adding a pack of thank you cards to her stack of intended purchases.

"Really?"

"Yes, she told me at lunch. She didn't make it sound like it was a secret."

"Wow. Is that okay with you, being her friend and all?"

"What do you mean?"

Trey raked a hand through his hair. "With you crushing on Chip, I just figured it might cause some conflict between the two of you. With both of you liking Chip and all."

"I..."

"There you two are. How are you?" Aubrey-Joan approached them, today wearing her ankle-length skirt with some colorful striped socks and taupe-colored leather sandals.

Carleigh *really* needed to set Trey straight. She did *not* have a crush on Chip. Never would.

But it would have to wait because Aubrey-Joan's tiny, perfectly round eyes hidden behind oversized, thin-rimmed glasses beckoned her attention.

"We're here to ask a few questions."

"Questions? You mean for an article?" Aubrey-Joan rubbed her hands together. "This is exciting. You haven't done an article on me or my store since we celebrated our twentieth anniversary last year."

Carleigh set down her items on the counter for later. "You could really help us, Miss Aubrey-Joan, if you can answer a few questions about some mysteries we are trying to solve."

"Mysteries? Ooh. I love mysteries. Are you two detectives now? I thought you were still at *The Oakville Daily*." She frowned, causing twin parallel lines to form on her forehead. "Officer Zemski didn't mention there were two new rookies on the force."

"Oh, we're not detectives," Trey assured her. "We are writing an article about the theft at Buy it All, and hopefully, in the process, we'll be able to assist the police with solving the crime."

Aubrey-Joan nodded. "Absolutely. That's what I love about this town. Everyone is just so willing to lend a hand. Now, Officer Zemski did ask me some questions already about wigs, but I can answer any that you might have."

"Thank you, Miss Aubrey-Joan. We appreciate that. And we absolutely must do another piece on Oakville Party Supply soon."

"Absolutely."

"So, the thief likely purchased his wig here. Do you remember who you've sold reddish-orange curly-haired wigs to in the last month or so?"

Aubrey-Joan closed her eyes and chewed on her lower lip. "Yes. This was one of the questions Brian—or rather Officer Zemski—asked me also. I have sold about eight such wigs in the last month and a half. They aren't really big sellers. The ones I sell the most of are the short black ones and the long blond ones. But I digress. About a month and a half ago, I sold one to a tall lanky man with huge feet."

Carleigh scribbled on her notepad and Trey repositioned his camera to his other arm. "A tall lanky man?"

"That doesn't completely fit the description of the thief," noted Trey.

"Right. That's what Officer Zemski said. But I feel like it's a wise idea to tell all the details. My daughter always says I share TMI—too much information—but I'd rather be TMI than NEI—not enough information."

Trey nodded. "Good point."

"So anyway, the tall lanky man had dark glasses and a cowboy hat. He had overly large feet and shuffled a

251

lot and was jittery with excessive energy. Maybe like he ate too much sugar or something. Then Mrs. Adair purchased four of them for a clown party they were having at the senior center. That makes five. Then the pastor's wife purchased one for a church function, and Mrs. Roper bought one for her grandson's birthday party. That makes seven. The last one was bought by a thin man with shifty eyes. I think he's the thief. Interesting thing was—and I forgot to mention this to Officer Zemski—but he had an overabundance of dog hairs, or at least I think it was dog hairs, maybe it was cat hairs, all over his black jacket. He himself had plentiful graying hair. Ugly and mean looking. Just like what you would suspect for someone stealing milk and dog food from Kevin and Amy." Aubrey-Jean took a deep breath from her long-winded dialogue.

"Very interesting. Did you recognize either he or the tall lanky man?"

"No. The tall lanky man seemed familiar like I should know him, but he had put on a fake Southern accent, and with those dark glasses that he never removed, I couldn't tell who he was. As for the presumed thief, I had never seen him a day in my life before he came into the store."

"Did he purchase anything else?"

"The thief? Yes. I made a list of the other items for Officer Zemski. They included a couple of leashes and some dog toys from aisle three. He also purchased two bean bag chairs. I attempted to carry on a conversation just to be friendly, but he would have none of it. He didn't speak a word. Rushed out of here super-fast."

"Did you see his vehicle?"

"Yes. An older model van. One of those kind with the rounded tops that looks like it could blow over in a windstorm. It had no windows. The typical type of vehicle they tell you to watch out for and not park next to in a parking lot. It had chipped white pain that was flaking off and the tires had seen better days. I saw all of this from the front window because I just had a feeling about him and it wasn't a good feeling."

"Can you remember anything else that stood out?" So cliché that it would be an old van, similar to what was often the vehicle of choice for the villians in the movies. Could it be the same van that drove off without paying for his gas recently?

Could the crimes be related?

# Chapter Twenty-Three

MAYBE TREY SHOULD HAVE been a detective instead of a reporter. Or maybe he should just emphasize the "investigative" in his job title.

*Investigative reporter.* He liked the sound of it.

Not only was he interested in finding out who the thief was and who Lindy's S.A. was, but he was also interested in finding out for sure if Carleigh liked Chip.

And vice versa.

Why he wanted to find that out, he had no idea. It wasn't like he liked Carleigh or anything. Well, not in that way at least.

She slid into the minivan and they drove back to *The Oakville Daily.* He wouldn't admit this to anyone, not even if it were his last dying breath, but he did enjoy riding around with her in the antique vehicle.

"So, what do you think about the thief?" He also valued her opinion.

Carleigh's recently-repaired oversized sunglasses took up half of her face. Women were so ridiculous when it came to fashions. But it did make her smile stand out, since that's about all he could see when she wore the hideous apparatus.

And he *might* like her smile.

Okay. He *did* like her smile.

Not that it mattered because her heart belonged to someone else.

Chip of all people. Who would have thought?

"I think the thief not only steals milk and dog food, but also gas. I'm sure Officer Zemski has made the same connection, but one thing I find interesting is that he had pet hair on his coat. He's obviously a pet owner. Probably a dog, according to Aubrey-Joan's list of his purchases and the potential theft of dog food. Oh, and he likes bean bag chairs."

"Also of note," said Trey, "is that she'd never seen him before. Oakville doesn't get many random visitors. They mainly come for our summer events during the tourist season, not just to buy arbitrary items at Oakville Party Supply and steal things from local businesses."

"Exactly. Look. There's Officer Zemski. Let's see if he has any additional information."

Trey drummed his fingers on the steering wheel. "You know he'll tell us we're not cops and to let him do his job without our interference."

"Probably. But we *are* reporters and it's our job to keep the public updated on the news. This is some of the biggest news to hit Oakville in years."

Trey drove into the coffee shop parking lot and parked next to Officer Zemki's patrol car.

Officer Zemski took a drink of his coffee. "What can I do for you two?"

"How are you today, Officer?"

"Good, Carleigh. Now what can I do for you?"

"We were wondering if you could shed some light on the recent theft from Buy it All. We were just at Oakville Party Supply..."

"I suppose you were interrogating poor Aubrey-Joan. You two really do need to let me do my job without interference."

"Sorry, sir," said Trey. "We didn't mean to intrude. We just asked her a few questions. As investigative reporters, we do like to stay on top of things."

"Investigative reporters. Is that the new title Howard gave you?"

Carleigh edged forward in her seat. "Any leads yet, sir?"

"No. But I can tell you that this person is not from Oakville. Unfortunately, we have not been able to locate his van yet."

"Ah, yes. Aubrey-Joan said he had one of those older model vans with no windows." Trey took out his notebook in case the officer threw them a nibble.

"Right. We have all of Oakville PD on the case, and have teamed up with the sheriff's department as well. I'm sure you realize I also double as a detective."

"Yes, sir. So, no idea who the perp is?" Trey asked, hoping he sounded in-the-know with his vernacular.

"Not yet.

Carleigh wrote something on her own notebook. "Will you please keep us posted, Officer? The residents of Oakville are concerned by this turn of events, and anything we can do to reassure them they still live in a safe community is paramount."

"We will be having a press conference next Wednesday at noon on the steps of city hall. We'll update the community at that time, but the residents are not in any immediate danger."

"Thank you, Officer." Trey prepared to put the van in drive.

"Yep. Stay safe out there."

They drove away from the officer's car. "Officer Zemski pretends to be harsh, but inside he's just a big soft teddy bear."

Trey chuckled at Carleigh's statement. "Guess that's a benefit of growing up here. You know everyone."

"I do, and I also know a lot of the history of this town. For instance, did you know that Officer Zemski and Aubrey-Joan dated in high school?"

"Really? I guess Officer Zemski is older than we think. He just always wears those dark glasses, but he does have gray in his beard."

"Good observation, Sherlock. And it's true about them dating. My mom went to school with them and they even went to prom together."

"Wonder what happened between them?"

"No idea. Mom didn't know either. They were a couple years behind her in school, so she wasn't up-to-date on all the particulars."

"Are they married to other people now?"

Carleigh shook her head. "Aubrey-Joan is widowed and I don't think Officer Zemski ever married. You've just given me an idea. Maybe we should ask Howard if we can do an article on true loves that should have been but never were."

Trey could feel his ears turning bright red. "What?"

"You know, as a follow-up to our true love series. We could write an article about the love that got away."

Would that be his case if he had actually liked Carleigh for more than a friend and lost her to Chip? Good thing he only liked her as a friend, although even that was negotiable on days when she won one of their competitions or arguments. "I don't think Howard wants to turn *The Oakville Daily* into a romantic happenings newspaper."

Carleigh laughed. "We wouldn't approach it that way, but it would be a newsworthy angle. Maybe we could wait a week or two until the true love articles have died down a bit. Wouldn't it be interesting, though, to find out why Officer Zemski and Aubrey-Joan broke-up?"

"Could be the height difference."

"That shouldn't matter if two people are in love."

Trey trained his focus on the road. There was a height difference between Carleigh and Chip of about a foot. Did his towering height bother her? "Spoken like someone in love with a tall person."

"What?"

"You and Chip."

"For the record..."

"Look, Carleigh. It's none of my business who you like. Chip's a Christian and he would treat you well."

"Trey..."

But they didn't have a chance to finish their conversation because just then Carleigh's phone rang.

And even though it was cliché, the awkward conversation had just been "saved by the bell."

A lead on some information for a future story captivated Carleigh's attention on the way back to *The Oakville Daily*. If she finalized all of these projects she was working on, it would be a miracle.

But she really needed to set Trey straight on the fact that she didn't like Chip in a boyfriend-girlfriend sort of way.

Why did it bother her that Trey thought she liked Chip?

And why did it bother Trey so much that he kept bringing it up? Could it be that Lindy was right? That Trey really did like her?

She plopped down at her desk and efficiently put all of her notes from Aubrey-Joan and Officer Zemski into her "Buy it All Thief" file. Then she opened up the true love article and printed it off so she and Trey could discuss the layout before the day ended.

Meeting with the officer had cut their time short, but his news would be helpful in an article to quell the residents' fears.

"Ready?" Trey asked, approaching her desk.

"Yes." She grabbed the article, slipped on her sandals, and followed Trey to the conference room. He held the door open for her and pulled out her chair before sitting next to her.

She really appreciated that he was a gentleman.

Carleigh had to admit he'd taken some phenomenal photos. The guy had a gift when it came to photography, and Howard had done *The Oakville Daily* an immense service by assigning him to be the primary photographer. Besides, it gave her more opportunity to write articles, and this particular series would definitely help with her first novel.

"Howard wants a variety of photos so I chose these because I thought they really captured the essence of Oakville with the diverse ages."

"The residents' personalities certainly shine through in these photos. Excellent job, Trey."

He grinned at her, and a tingling feeling took up residency in her stomach. She did her best to ignore it.

"Thanks." Trey scanned her article. "This is well-written. What did you have in mind for any other designs or photos?"

"What I think would be really romantic is to have a bunch of swirly red looping hearts outlining the entirety of the photographs."

"Swirly red looping hearts? No way. Too lovey-dovey."

Carleigh drew an example on a piece of scratch paper. She wound several hearts together across the page and down one side. "Like this. Don't you think it would be the perfect addition?"

"No. Only women would think that. How about we just do some straight black lines if we need some sort of border?"

"Because that would be ugly and plain. We need some pizazz."

Trey's brow furrowed. "Pizazz? Then how about stars or something like that?"

"Stars? Stars don't fit into the article. This is about true love being found and celebrated for a lifetime."

"Hmmf. Only women talk like that and only women would like swirly red looping hearts. I say leave it plain. Less is better."

"And I say only men would like the layout to be plain and boring. Of course, there are some men who are romantics and who would like to see the page pop with color and liveliness, and hearts *are* a testament to true love."

"Romantics, huh? Like Chip?"

She watched as his ears turned red simultaneously with his voice speaking the words. "Why are your ears so red?"

"They are?" He pinched his right ear. "No idea. Probably some condition. Don't try to change the subject. I was just saying that you probably are referring to Chip when you say that some men are romantics."

"Who knows if Chip is a romantic? All I know is that we need some panache, and this should do the trick. Besides it goes with the article."

"Nah. It's overboard."

Howard sauntered into the conference room, hands in his pockets. "Now then. Arguing again? What am I going to do with you two?"

"Sir, don't you think it would be advantageous to add a swirly red looping hearts border to the layout of the true love article?"

261

"And with all due respect, sir, this is a crazy idea. Who wants a bunch of messy hearts filling up perfectly-good white space and detracting from the photographs?"

Howard stared toward the opposite end of the conference room, seemingly at nothing, while he pondered what Carleigh had suggested and Trey had countered. She really hoped she'd win this battle. The hearts would really add to the article. "Yes, I think the looping heart border is a good idea. It will catch the eye of the reader." He paused and glanced down at the article and photos. "I really like how this is coming together. Trey, you need to be more open-minded when it comes to the creativity behind all of this. Swirly hearts are just the ticket. Women love that stuff, and statistics show half of our readers are women."

After Howard left the conference room a minute later, Carleigh smiled at Trey. While she should stuff her pride away, she just couldn't let this moment pass. "I love it when I win an argument."

Chalk up another point for Carleigh in the ongoing Carleigh versus Trey battle.

# Chapter Twenty-Four

AT CHURCH THAT SUNDAY, Trey sat next to Carleigh, as he usually did. Carleigh found that she minded much less than she once had. Or maybe it was just because she was becoming accustomed to his presence. At church. At work. In the neighborhood.

He wore a green short-sleeved crew neck that made his eyes more vibrant.

*Vibrant eyes?* She pondered the unwelcome observation.

Dad and Trey were getting along really well. Almost too well. Chummy, in fact. She had warned Dad last night at dinner not to even think about inviting Trey to lunch. Fortunately for Dad's sake, he had heeded Carleigh's admonition. After some arguing, of course.

She returned her focus to Pastor Gehrig, who had taken his place behind the podium for announcements. "We have just started a new discipleship ministry for unchurched teens in the community and are in need of several volunteers. There is no commitment at this time, but I'd just like to get a feel for how many might be interested in volunteering for this worthwhile project."

Before Carleigh could process what Pastor Gehrig was saying, Trey grabbed her right hand and raised both of their hands together. "I used to be a part of a ministry like this when I was a teen. I think we could do this," he whispered.

Her heart fluttered in her chest and she contemplated how natural it felt to have his hand holding hers.

Pastor Gehrig surveyed the congregants. "Thank you. I will be in the foyer after services to discuss this opportunity in further detail."

Trey brought down both of their hands, but continued to hold her hand. Had he forgotten their fingers were still intertwined? He squeezed her hand. Or maybe she just imagined it. Either way, his hand felt warm around hers. Comforting. Natural. Pleasant.

Carleigh wanted to pull away, but didn't. Not for a few seconds, anyway. As if Trey noticed his faux pas, he jerked his hand away. "Sorry. A colossal lapse in judgment," he muttered.

She missed the warmth of his hand, but wouldn't let on, so instead, she just nodded.

Carleigh powered up her laptop to begin working on her novel. Theodore Sullivan perched next to her on the extra dining room chair she'd pulled up beside her own. She appreciated the inspiration her treasured pet gave her, and he had inspired her choice for her main character's own dog. "Just one thousand words this evening, that's the goal."

Her laptop booted up and Carleigh gave Sullivan Theodore a pat on the head. "Today, the sheriff discovers Rufus is the criminal behind the bank robbery. You remember Rufus, right? He's the one who looks just like Howard. Same plump stature and crabby resting face. Oh, and his clothes are so early-1800s. Quite dated for the 1870s time period."

Sullivan Theodore wagged his tail and gave her a slobbery doggy kiss to show his interest and support. "Why, thank you, my dear pet. Just for that, I'll give the character inspired by you a second scene in the book."

The temptation to check her email before striving toward tonight's word count was too tempting, and Carleigh entered her password. Three new messages popped up. A spam, her church prayer chain requests for the day, and a message from Briar Salazar, editor at Heimisson Christian Publishing House with the subject line "Conference Pitch." Her heart pounded and her hands shook as she clicked on the message. She closed her eyes and prayed about the news she was about to read regarding her work-in-progress novel.

Sullivan Theodore yipped. "I know, I know. It's just so incredibly nerve-wracking," she said, eyes still closed. "What if Ms. Salazar didn't like my book? What if..."

Carleigh sighed. What-ifs never solved any problems and only compounded anxiety. Besides, last year she'd surrendered her writing to the Lord. And while she'd received several rejections for her writing thus far, a new one would still be devastating, even though she knew a positive response from such a well-known publishing company would be a minor miracle. "It's in the Lord's hands, but I'm a bundle of nerves, Sullivan Theodore. Jittery, keyed up, and a bit worried. But here goes nothing."

Carleigh opened one eye and squinted at the computer screen. Would the news only be half as bad if she could only see it with half of her vision? "Why is it I'm generally an optimistic person except when it comes to my novels?"

Sullivan Theodore placed his paw on her leg. "You're right. I need to open both eyes and read this email and quit being reluctant about it." She slowly opened the other eye, as her vision came into focus.

Dear Ms. Adams,

Thank you for providing me with the first three chapters of your work-in-progress titled "A Promise of Love." I am interested in reading the full manuscript. Please forward it to me as an attachment at your earliest convenience.

Sincerely,

Briar Salazar

Historical Romance Acquisitions Editor

Heimisson Christian Publishing House

Her jaw dropped, and Carleigh closed her eyes, then reopened them. Had she read the email correctly? Ms. Salazar wanted to see the entire manuscript? The editor, whom Carleigh had "met" during her online writer's conference a few months ago, wanted to read Carleigh's manuscript?

"Thank you, Lord!"

Her arms tingled and her heart pounded. Carleigh swallowed hard. "Can you believe it, Sullivan Theodore? I might just become a published author yet!" She squeezed her pet who let out three excited yips.

How could she even begin to write when she was so ecstatic? But write, she must. After she called Mom and Dad, of course, and shared the news.

"Meeting in the staff room, pronto," bellowed Howard. "I'm running across the street for donuts. I'll be right back."

Trey attempted to put his photo assignment for the Oakville Farm Supply's "Gardening Get-together" that was held last week on hold. Every winner would expect to be featured and he wished he'd taken more pictures of some of the entries.

Carleigh arrived at the conference room at the same time he did. The bounce in her step and her exuberant expression indicated she was especially chipper today. "You that excited Howard called a meeting?" he asked.

"Hardly. It's something else," she quipped, tossing him a smile. A smile that appeared genuine.

Strange. What was she up to?

They proceeded to walk into the conference room, and she offered a second smile. Two smiles in the course of three seconds. Not that he was complaining. But had he ever noticed she had a dimple in her left cheek? No, guys didn't notice things like that, or maybe they did. He frowned. His mind must be really muddled if he was giving any extra thought to Carleigh and her facial expressions. "Don't tell me. They had shoes on sale at the Oakville Shoe Mart and you got a pair in every color."

"Ooh, now that would be a girl's dream come true. Especially those super cute sandals with the flower ornament on the top."

Flower ornament? "Yeah, that would do it for me."

"No, it's actually something else." She tilted her chin up, as if to emphasize information only she was privy to.

When she gazed up at him like that, it did something to his insides. Kind of like when he took a bite of a juicy burger over at The Oakville Greasy Spoon loaded with lettuce, tomato, and extra mayo. Seriously bizarre considering she was still the same Quirky Carleigh he'd been forced to work with for the past two years. Yet, something had changed. He no longer found her quite as annoying. Maybe it was a coping mechanism.

Trey parked himself next to her, regretting it the instant he did so.

"So...seems like you're the one choosing to sit next to me now," she whispered.

He leaned toward her, inhaling a pleasant citrusy aroma. For a minute, it messed with him and he forgot all about the sarcastic remark he was intent on making. *Get it together, Montgomery*, he chided himself. Trey cleared his throat. "Habit, I guess," he mumbled.

"Uh huh. You say I always sit next to you, but you wasted no time taking this seat next to me, even though there are still several seats available."

"Would you rather sit by Chip?" There. His sarcasm had returned and he was back to normal once again after a brief hiatus.

"Well..."

Did she still like Chip? He hadn't forgotten all of the positives Carleigh had listed about their coworker. Chip entered just then and Trey sized him up. Chip jogged in place, checking his fitness tracker. "Man, I love this thing. Only one-hundred, thirty-three steps to go this hour."

Just what Chip needed for his hyper personality.

"Yesterday I got all my steps in for the twelve-hour day," beamed Chip. "It was definitely worth the price for this gadget. I can't believe I waited until last week to buy one."

"Wow, good job, Chip. Way to go to take steps to better health," said Carleigh.

Trey looked from Carleigh to Chip as they chatted about Chip's new fitness tracker. Carleigh's face still lit up with excitement, even more so while talking with Chip. Truly. What did she see in the guy? Sure, he was easy-going, intelligent, and had won some chess championships. He had an awesome vehicle. But sans the chess championships, Trey equaled him.

The niggling feeling of jealousy permeated through him.

Nope. Not jealousy. Just curiosity. Curiosity as to why Carleigh thought Chip was such a good catch.

Chip finally took a seat, fidgeting while he did so. Did he like Carleigh too? Lindy, Bubba, and Margie entered the room, followed by an out-of-breath Howard.

"I earned two donuts just for all that exercise." Howard plunked the brown donut box on the table. "Help yourselves, everyone. Karen made them fresh just minutes ago."

"I call dibs on a maple bar," said Bubba, rubbing his stomach in apparent anticipation.

The donut box made its rounds, and after pleasantries intended to give Howard a chance to down a sugar-sprinkled donut, he stood. "Now then, you are probably wondering why I called us here today. I know we're on deadline and the fine people of Oakville depend on us to deliver the news in a timely fashion. But, honestly, this could not wait."

Howard opened a manila envelope. "I have always been proud of *The Oakville Daily* team. You all work hard and wear many hats each day. I have to say, though, I am especially proud today. I received this in the mail and decided it was worthwhile to share sooner rather than later."

Howard took a bite of his second donut. "I am pleased to announce that Trey has won first place in the state Newspaper Writers and Photographers Contest."

Trey nearly choked on his donut. Had he heard correctly? "Say that again, Howard?"

"I most certainly will. You won first place in the prestigious Newspaper Writers and Photographers Contest.

It was for your outstanding photo coverage of Oakville's decorated war hero, Zander Velasquez's, return home from the Afghanistan."

A second round of applause filled the room. Suddenly Trey wished he hadn't eaten the donut so quickly. "Really?"

"Yes, really. Congratulations, Trey." Howard reached over and shook Trey's hand. "It doesn't surprise any of us, however, because your photography has always been stellar. I'm proud of you."

Carleigh offered him another smile. "Good job, Trey."

The rest of his coworkers offered their congratulations, pats on the back, and offers for a pizza celebration while Trey wondered if he would wake up any moment and realize his dream was just that—a dream. He couldn't wait to call Mom, Dad, and Austin and share the fantastic news. They'd for sure want to take him out to celebrate.

After the news sunk in and everyone had another donut, Lindy said to Carleigh, "I heard congratulations are in order for you too."

"Yes," Carleigh said, "but we can wait to talk about that."

"We absolutely cannot wait. This is super thrilling."

"What is super thrilling?" Margie asked. "Do tell."

"Carleigh received word last night that the editor from Heimisson Christian Publishing House wants to see Carleigh's full manuscript."

Margie clapped. "That is marvelous, Carleigh! Is that someone you chatted with during the editor appointments for your online writer's conference?"

"It is."

"Now then, it appears we have two things to celebrate today," said Howard. "This calls for another donut." He paused. "You're detail-oriented and have a way with words, Carleigh, and when you're a famous author someday, you can say you got your start at *The Oakville Daily*."

Everyone congratulated Carleigh. Trey flashed her a smile. "Good job, Quirky Carleigh. Can I have your autograph now?"

No wonder she had been smiling so much from the second he saw her today. They both had something to celebrate.

A fleeting thought entered his mind. What if he took her out for ice cream, just as a friendly gesture to commend her for being one step closer to publication?

*No, not happening. Why would you want to go anywhere with her? You have to spend every day with her and sometimes hours at a time covering stories. Not a cool idea.*

"Uh, Trey, why is your mouth moving and no words are coming out? You really freak me out when you do that."

"You imagine things, Carleigh."

"No, I saw it, really."

"Children, children. This is an extraordinary occasion. Must we quarrel?" Chip asked.

"Yeah, must *you* quarrel?"

"Now then," interrupted Howard, "congratulations to you both. You make *The Oakville Daily* proud. But now we must all get back to work. The day is slipping away."

More congratulatory responses followed before Chip, Lindy, Margie, Bubba, and Howard left the conference room. Carleigh and Trey stood to follow everyone else out of the room.

It was then that the words fell from his mouth before he could even put any thought to them. "Hey, Carleigh?"

"Yes?"

"Would you like to get some ice cream after work, you know, to celebrate?"

It only took him uttering fourteen words to discover his stupid error.

"What?" she asked.

"Nothing. Just mumbling to myself."

"Do you always invite yourself for ice cream?" She dipped her chin and raised her eyebrows. He noticed that dimple again.

"Yeah, something like that."

"Well, that's a stinker, because I would go out for ice cream to celebrate this momentous occasion for both of us."

"You would?"

"Maybe."

It was Trey's turn to raise his eyebrows. He could only imagine how red his ears were. "All righty then. How about six-thirty? And you can bring Theodore with you."

"Really? Sounds good. Oh, and his name is Sullivan Theodore, and you can bring Jumping Jacks with you."

"Jumping Jacks?"

But Carleigh was already heading back to her desk, leaving Trey to wonder when it was exactly that he'd lost his mind and decided to ask her out. And secondly, what would Chip think if he truly did like Carleigh?

273

# Chapter Twenty-Five

HAD SHE JUST FLIRTED with Trey the Irritating?

Say it wasn't so.

Brash. Impetuous. Foolhardy. And just plain ridiculous.

It had to be because she was so excited about her novel. Her common sense was clouded by her enthusiasm. Why else would Carleigh have accepted a date with Trey?

*Not a date. An outing. A field trip of sorts. A playdate for Sullivan Theodore and Jaxx.*

And where on earth had her witty "Jumping Jacks" quip come from?

Clearly, she was losing her mind.

Carleigh sat down in her chair and rolled it up to her desk. She glanced in Trey's direction, and he caught her eye. Her heart palpitated, which she attempted to ignore.

Two hours later, Carleigh pulled on a pair of jean shorts and a red floral flutter sleeve blouse. She stared at herself in the full-length mirror contemplating her choice of attire. She'd just purchased the breezy and stylish shirt to add to her fashion collection. Carleigh turned to one side, then the other, debating if this outfit, her sixth to try on, was the one to choose.

"Decisions, decisions," she muttered, noting the time on the pink clock on her wall. "Well, this will have to do. Trey will be here in fifteen minutes."

She reached for her red wedge sandals from her closet and a pair of dangly red teardrop earrings. If nothing else, she was color-coordinated.

With ten minutes to spare, Carleigh dressed Sullivan Theodore in his green camo t-shirt. "I have no idea why I'm so nervous, Sullivan Theodore. After all, this isn't a date. It's just an outing. An excursion. A picnic of sorts. Just a gathering amongst two coworkers and their pets to celebrate some career advancements. Not much different than the time we went to The Oakville Greasy Spoon, with the exception that Chip won't be with us."

Sullivan Theodore bobbed his head. She continued. "I spend so much time with Trey the Irritating working on news stories and during meetings at work and this is really no different."

Then why were her nerves frazzled?

Why had Trey asked her to go out for ice cream?

And why had she accepted?

If only Lindy hadn't shared about her email from Briar Salazar.

The doorbell rang as Carleigh stood lamenting her decision to spend even more time with her adversary than necessary.

Sullivan Theodore barked and raced toward the door. Trey stood on the porch, hands shoved in the pockets of his faded jeans. He wore a light blue t-shirt, a ball cap, and brown shoes. He almost looked attractive.

"Hey, Carleigh."

"Trey."

Seconds ticked by before Carleigh found her voice again. "Would you like to come in for a minute? I don't want Sullivan Theodore escaping."

Trey chuckled. "Yeah, no more criminal trespassing charges in his future." He walked into the house allowing the screen door to close behind him.

"Very funny. I am concerned since he'll be hanging around Jaxx this evening. I don't want him getting any nefarious ideas."

"No worries about that. But there is the concern that his mischievous behavior will rub off on Jaxx."

"No chance of that happening. Sullivan Theodore is very well behaved. I'm just going to grab my purse, then I'll be ready. Would you like to see the grill before we go?"

"Sure. Have you even used it yet?"

"Grilled some delicious burgers and hot dogs on it the other night for some friends from church." She didn't say she was more of a bystander while one of her friend's husbands did the grilling. The less details the better.

Trey walked through the sliding glass door and onto the deck. He ran his hand along the stainless steel of the grill's exterior. "Man. Wish I'd have won this. I'd be using it every night."

"Maybe next year when Buy it All has another customer appreciation celebration, you'll win one," she teased.

"I can always hope. Oh, well. The cookies were delicious. You ready to go?"

"Sure."

Trey followed her back into the house. He paused for a second in her living room. "You know, this is exactly the type of house someone like you would have."

"Someone like me? What do you mean?"

"All frou-frou girlie-like with pink everywhere and a blue-and-white plaid chair and matching couch. And way too many fluffy pillows." He shook his head.

Carleigh viewed her living room, nice and neat for the most part, with its cottage-like appearance. She'd found most of the items second-hand and Mom had helped her with the curtains and matching "fluffy" pillows, as Trey called them. "I'm rather proud of my decorating skills."

"Too feminine and dainty. Poor Theodore. How does he survive all the flower decorations? And what's with the old trunk? Planning on a vacation?" He pointed to her distressed white trunk she'd repurposed into a coffee table.

"It's actually not that old. My mom and I intentionally gave it a vintage look. It's the style these days."

Trey shook his head. "No thanks. I'll keep my modern man house."

"Modern man house is right. Along with a few smelly mismatched socks strewn on the floor, a dingy and ramshackle couch, and a table with only two chairs, one of which has a chewed-up leg. I'll take my feminine and dainty house, as you call it, over your masculine hovel any day."

"Well, if you ever decide you don't need the grill anymore, I will take that off your hands."

"As long as I throw in the pink fringed button pillow with it?"

Trey's eyes traveled to the round pillow on her plaid chair. It was one of her favorite finds from a garage sale several years ago. She'd sewn a button in the center to add to its unique character.

"Just the grill will do."

Sullivan Theodore perched his paws on the front window and began to bark. "He must see Jaxx," said Carleigh. "Are you ready for your playdate, Sullivan Theodore?"

"Playdate?"

"Yes, isn't that what this is? A playdate for our pets?"

"Uh, sure. Yes. Definitely." Trey held the door open for her and she followed him through it, Sullivan Theodore held firmly in her arms. She fumbled with her keys as she prepared to lock the front door.

"Need some help?"

"Sure." She surmised that one good thing about Trey was that he was gentlemanly. Carleigh handed Trey her keys. His fingers touched hers as he took the keys from her, and a peculiar fluttering took up residence in her stomach.

"There. All locked." He gave her one of his lopsided grins and for a minute she forgot who he was.

"Thanks."

"No problem."

They stood on the porch facing each other, Sullivan Theodore squirming to get down and be allowed to walk on his leash and Jaxx barking from Trey's truck. "Umm, shall we go?"

"No time like the present." Trey led her to his truck, which appeared to have been recently taken through the car wash. He opened the truck door and she climbed in. Sullivan Theodore greeted Jaxx, and Carleigh released the breath she had been holding.

Why she had a case of the nerves was far beyond her. She saw this guy more hours of her life each day than she'd care to admit. He was like an antagonist in a novel, always lurking about. Her rival and competitor.

Was it too late to feign illness and return home?

# Chapter Twenty-Six

TREY STARTED THE ENGINE. Intentionally spending time with Quirky Carleigh could be cause for having his brain examined. Why had he even suggested a trip to the ice cream stand? He should be home mowing the lawn and taking Jaxx for a walk around the block. Should he turn on the radio? Make small talk? Ask her what she thought of the weather?

He cleared his throat. "So. Do you like ice cream?"

Dumb. Dumb. Dumb. Of course, she liked ice cream or she wouldn't have accepted his suggestion to go to the ice cream stand. Why was he so skittish? This wasn't like some date. Carleigh herself had said it was for the dogs. And it was.

"Yes, I like ice cream. You?"

"Yeah."

Silence filled the cab, with the exception of Jaxx sneezing and the sound of a few vehicles passing by. He inhaled a citrusy scent that he had become accustomed to when around her. Was it too late to tell her they needed to cancel their plans because he had developed a bad case of indigestion from downing his microwaveable dinner too quickly?

For a town the size of Oakville, the Oakville Fun Park hosted a wide variety of activities—playground equipment, a walking path, a stage for outdoor concerts, an expansive grassy area, picnic tables, and the infamous ice cream stand. Several people milled about, enjoying the warm summer evening.

"Now, Jaxx," Trey said, turning toward his dog in the backseat. "Be careful of the company you keep while we're here."

"And, Sullivan Theodore, don't run around with any bad influences. You retain your exemplary reputation and make wise choices, even if those around you don't."

Trey chuckled. "Exemplary reputation? Jaxx, be sure you keep your distance from accomplished criminals."

"Accomplished criminals?" She raised an eyebrow.

They could sit here all evening and argue. Or they could get some ice cream. Trey preferred the latter. "Well, it's now or never, Jaxx. Let's go." He attached Jaxx's leash to his collar and opened the truck door. Carleigh did the same with Sullivan Theodore.

As they walked along the open grassy field toward their destination, Trey saw it coming. Fast, out-of-control, and aiming right toward Carleigh.

He took abrupt action.

Grasping Jaxx's leash in one hand, he used his other hand to pull Carleigh toward him and shield her head and face.

"What's going on?" she asked, her voice muffled against his chest.

Both dogs barked, warning of the oncoming danger.

Trey pivoted, swinging Carleigh around and putting his own body in the line of fire.

The football hit him hard in the shoulder, sounding with a thump, before a group of teenage boys ran toward them.

"Hey, guys, nice arm, but you might want to watch out for people walking through the park. What if it had been a kid?"

"Sorry, man. Total overthrow," said one of the boys. "Is everyone okay?"

"I think we'll be all right." Trey realized he still held Carleigh close, her hair tickling his nose. "Are you all right, Carleigh?"

"Yes. Is your shoulder okay?"

"Sorry again. We'll take it easier," another of the teens said before the group walked away.

"That was a white-knuckler," Trey said, his arm still around Carleigh, even though she had taken a step back. He drew in a deep breath. If the football had hit Carleigh in the head, she could have been hurt.

"Thank you for intercepting that so it wouldn't hit me."

"Hey, what can I say? I'm a regular knight in shining armor."

She laughed, her voice slightly jittery. "Well, thank you."

"What? No witty comeback to my 'knight-in-shining-armor' comment?"

"No, just thankful you kept the wayward football from giving me a concussion."

Trey kind of liked having her in the crook of his arm. "Just call me Trey the Protector."

"Instead of Trey the Irritating?"

"Ahh, there she is, my old Carleigh is back."

He realized only too late that he'd referred to her as his Carleigh.

His ears must be redder than Howard's favorite editing pen.

One minute, she and Sullivan Theodore were moseying through the park with her nemesis minding their own business, and the next minute, she was pulled into his muscled chest, inhaling the appealing scent of detergent mixed with aftershave.

Muscled chest? Carleigh inwardly gasped. Why should she notice if Trey was muscular or chubby? And why was she inhaling his aftershave?

Maybe the football *had* hit her in the head.

Trey's arm remained around her and she dared a peek at his hand resting casually on her shoulder. Oddly enough, it felt natural for his arm to be there. How could that be?

She met his gaze and held it for a few minutes, wondering how she had found herself in such a predicament. Awkward. Embarrassing. Troublesome.

When he'd mentioned being a knight in shining armor, she hadn't known what to say. For all of Trey's undesirable qualities, the fact that he had sheltered her from what would have been a painful experience gave him credence in her eyes. His show of chivalry impressed upon her. After all, a guy who sacrificed his own self to take a hit couldn't be that bad could he?

Trey removed his arm from around her shoulders. A niggle of disappointment clouded her better judgment. She averted her gaze and stared out across the park. "Are you all right?"

"Yeah, it'll leave a mark, but I'm happy to take one for the team. Or, should I say, take one for the duo?"

When his eyes lit up with humor, he was rather attractive.

Sullivan Theodore tugged on the leash. "Are you ready for some ice cream, Sullivan Theodore?"

He yanked again as if to confirm his answer.

Grateful for the welcome diversion from the embarrassing football incident and the mass of peculiar feelings that invaded her mind at seeing Trey in a slightly different light, Carleigh followed Sullivan Theodore's lead.

The ice cream stand was a haphazard shanty-like building with a brown and green exterior that had been built around the same time the park had been founded about a century ago. Minor updates, including a window air conditioner and updated wiring, combined with several instances of new paint jobs, lent charm to the aging building. Two separate lines of a dozen or so people stood waiting to place their orders at two open windows. The aroma of freshly-baked doughy pretzels, hot dogs, and cheesy nachos filled the air. Seven blue and white table-seat combos with red umbrellas and tiny American flags mounted to the umbrella poles surrounded the area in a patriotic theme with matching trashcans and an oversized chocolate ice cream statue. The business was consistently busy and donated a portion of its profits to the local veterans association.

"Has Jaxx ever had the ice cream here? When you order an ice cream cone or bowl for yourself, they give you a free mini cup of vanilla ice cream for your dog."

Trey shook his head. "No, Jaxx has some food allergies. If he ate ice cream, we'd be regretting it later."

"Oh, no. That stinks."

"Yeah. I found out the hard way one evening when I decided to gorge myself on a half-gallon of that Oakville Premium Ice Cream in vanilla flavor from Buy It All. Jaxx gave me those puppy-dog eyes that I couldn't resist and I gave in because I didn't realize he had allergies. Wasn't a pretty sight." He paused. "Although it's probably for the best, as Jaxx has no self-control when it comes to treats. He'd probably gulp it all up in one sitting."

Carleigh glanced down at Jaxx. He seemed so strong and invincible and like nothing would bother him. "Poor dog. I've heard canines can be sensitive to ice cream. And I know exactly what you mean by the puppy-dog eye look. On more than one occasion, Sullivan Theodore has talked me into a bite of water-based plain oatmeal or a piece of banana."

"Oatmeal and bananas? Who knew Theodore was such a health freak? He seems more like a junk food guy to me."

"Junk food guy? No, Sullivan Theodore is quite healthy." Their eyes connected and her pulse ramped up a few notches. What on earth was wrong with her today?

Usually, she couldn't get away from Trey fast enough. Today, she was actually enjoying his company.

Disturbing. Disconcerting. Distressing. And completely unsettling.

Best if she turned her focus elsewhere than on Trey, so she peered at the people waiting in line and decided some of them would make exemplary characters for her next chapter in *A Promise of Love*. One of her favorite authors once mentioned that characters were everywhere—you just had to know where to look. Oakville was clearly full of them.

The efficient workers caused the lines to move swiftly, and soon Carleigh and Trey were second in line. A mom reached for her toddler's ice cream on a waffle cone that outsized the little girl. She handed the cone to her daughter and grabbed a handful of napkins. Sullivan Theodore stood on his hindlegs, his forepaws batting at the air while he begged for a tasty bite. The little girl giggled, the ice cream teetering precariously atop the cone.

"Now, Sullivan Theodore, you'll have your own treat soon." Carleigh gently lifted her pet away from the toddler. Cones were not safe for dogs, and knowing Sullivan Theodore and his persuasiveness, he could easily coax the girl out of hers.

A teen girl with an orange topknot, oversized burgundy-framed eyeglasses, and a wad of bubblegum in her mouth greeted them. "Can I help you?"

Trey deferred to Carleigh, and she was reminded once again he was a gentleman. Proof that irritating guys *could* be attractive.

"I'd love a scoop of cotton candy ice cream on a waffle cone."

"And you?" the teen asked.

"I'll take a mint chocolate chip scoop on a waffle cone."

The teen snacked her gum and popped a big bubble. "And some mini cups for the dogs?"

"Just one, please," said Carleigh.

"He has food allergies," Trey offered about Jaxx.

Trey removed some cash from his wallet and Carleigh juggled her waffle cone and Sullivan Theodore's mini cup of vanilla ice cream while they wandered to one of the red, white, and blue tables.

"Here all right?" Trey asked, stopping at a table under a gigantic oak tree. He offered Jaxx a doggy treat the teen had given him in lieu of ice cream.

Jaxx inhaled the dog bone while Sullivan Theodore took his time eating the meager portion of vanilla ice cream, not minding that most of it gathered in his furry snout.

Carleigh did her best not to inhale her own pink, turquoise, and lemon cotton candy mix. Trey held his cone toward her. "Here's to the good news for our writing careers," he said, in a toast-like fashion.

Carleigh tipped her cone toward his, trying, but failing miserably, to ignore his close proximity.

# Chapter Twenty-Seven

TREY HADN'T EXPECTED TO have fun with Carleigh. Having spent so much of their time together arguing and competing, their venture to the ice cream stand was actually a welcome change.

"Well, what a pleasant surprise seeing you two here."

"Hello, Mrs. Bassanelli," he and Carleigh chorused. At the same time.

"My, but that is what we get when we put *The Oakville Daily* Duo together. They begin to speak the same words at the same time." Mrs. Bassanelli fiddled with her pearl necklace. "This reminds me so much of me and my beloved husband, God rest his soul. He said we were twins because we would finish each other's sentences on a routine basis. That's the sign of true love, I always say."

Trey knew his ears were bright red. He attempted to focus on Jaxx's and Sullivan Theodore's greeting of Stella in her puffy hat and pink bowtie. The shade matched Mrs. Bassanelli's shirt and scarf. Much better to focus on matching owners and their dogs than think about how he and Carleigh were like Mrs. Bassanelli and her late husband.

"My beloved and I shared the same birthday month as well. It's definitely meant to be if two lovebirds share the same birthday month. When is your birthday, Carleigh?"

"In November."

"And you, Trey?"

"Uh…" he wanted to lie, but his mom's wise words about lying never being right rang in his mind like an enormous clanging bell. "November."

"Oh, I just knew it. See, you two are meant to be." She placed her free hand against her heart. "You both remind me so much of Mr. Bassanelli and me."

"That's quite a compliment, Mrs. Bassanelli, but Trey and I aren't dating. We're coworkers only."

Carleigh's voice squeaked in response to the older woman's insinuation. A fleeting glance at her told Trey that her face was as red as the tips of his ears.

"Pshaw. Coworkers only? Well, you are a handsome couple. Now, enough of the pleasantries, how are you both doing?"

Trey and Carleigh spent the next few minutes catching up with Mrs. Bassanelli before she pointed toward the fenced-in dog park a short distance away. "Stella and I were just over at the dog park. Can you believe I saw that oddball clown I invited to Stella's birthday party over there? See? There he is, the man in the slacks and short-sleeved gray button-up shirt. He still hasn't delivered any of the pictures he took from Stella's party to the guests. Some clown he is. I'll think twice before hiring him for the next party."

The clown, sans the red curly wig, stood in the dog park, cell phone in hand. "Does he have a dog?" Trey asked.

"Oh, I'm sure he does. Probably a Doberman pinscher. No one tarries in the dog park if they don't have a pet."

"I'm sorry to hear about the pictures, Mrs. Bassanelli," Carleigh said, tucking a stray hair behind her ear. "Hopefully, he will get those to us soon. I was actually wondering about that very thing the other day."

"I paid a handsome sum for those, and if he values his reputation, he'll make good on the promise to deliver the photos to my guests, complete with 'Stella's Happy Day' cardboard photo frames. I should have known he may be a bit of a shyster."

"Did you ask him when the pictures would be ready?" Trey asked.

"No. I was too perturbed to say any words at all to him. I did glower at him, however."

Moments later, Trey and Carleigh wandered over to the dog park to allow Jaxx and Sullivan Theodore some time to run, play, and socialize.

Trey hadn't been all that concerned about the photo session with the clown. He'd done his best to forget about the entire birthday party episode for Stella. But it was fishy that the clown hadn't delivered on his promise.

Carleigh unclipped Sullivan Theodore's leash and he bounded toward the opposite end of the dog park. Jaxx raced after him, and Carleigh double-checked to be sure the dog park gate was closed and latched.

Although she wouldn't admit it to anyone, Sullivan Theodore did have a naughty side, and she didn't trust the little rascal not to attempt to escape and run back toward the ice cream stand.

The clown from Stella's party still hovered around the dog park, although there were no Doberman pinschers as far as Carleigh could tell. As a matter of fact, it didn't look like the clown had a pet at all. Yet he snapped photos of the other three dogs in the dog park and then aimed his cell phone toward Sullivan Theodore.

"Is your dog a Maltese shih tzu?" the clown asked Carleigh.

She sized up the man standing in front of them and pondered his inquiry. Had he remembered Sullivan Theodore from Stella's party? "Yes."

The man crossed his arms tight against his body and his eyes never left Carleigh's face. Something about him gave her the creeps. His bulging eyes, magnified by a pair of dirty wire-rimmed bifocal glasses, were far too close together, leaving minimal room for his beaked nose. Gray hair, plentiful for a man his age, was swooped to one side. He had prominent ears and bushy black eyebrows each in the shape of half-moons. She recalled his face from the party when he'd worn the clown wig, although she would not have recognized him if Mrs. Bassanelli hadn't pointed him out.

"Sir," she said, before she could stop herself. "You took photos of our dogs at a birthday party. Do you know when you might be delivering them?"

"I don't know what you're talking about. I don't take photos of dogs at birthday parties. You must have me confused with someone else."

"You sure look like the same guy," interjected Trey, "with the exception of a wig."

"Wrong guy." The man snarled. His right eye twitched, but he held Carleigh's gaze, as if to challenge her.

She shivered despite the warm summer weather.

The man stormed out the dog park gate then, not even bothering to close it. Carleigh rushed over to latch it. "Was that suspicious or what?" she asked Trey.

"Something is definitely up with that guy. I have a feeling no one is going to see those photos from Stella's party."

"I agree."

"And it's not a case of mistaken identity. He's the same guy."

Carleigh nodded. "Yes, he is."

Her mind could go to all sorts of places thinking about the unease she experienced in the clown's presence, but she instead attempted to focus on watching the dogs run around the dog park.

An hour later, Trey walked Carleigh to her front door. "Thanks for the ice cream."

"Sure. Congratulations on your book news."

"Congratulations to you on the photography award."

"Thanks." Trey stuffed his hands into his pockets. "All right, see you tomorrow at work, Carleigh."

"Good night."

They stood for a moment on Carleigh's porch, Sullivan Theodore tugging at the leash and barking at a passing squirrel. Trey took a step toward her and she held her breath. Would he kiss her?

And why would that thought even cross her mind?

Instead, Trey turned to leave. "Good night."

Disappointment lingered in her mind along with an alarming realization.

Maybe Trey the Irritating wasn't so irritating after all.

# Chapter Twenty-Eight

CARLEIGH ADDED THE FINISHING touches on *Building a Birdhouse on a Budget* for "Carleigh's Creative Corner" when she heard Chip's boisterous footsteps. The sound jolted her out of her muse as Chip moseyed by her desk, a yellow and blue box in his clutches.

"Hey, Chip."

"Carleigh, what brings you here so early? You're never here before everyone else."

"Truer words were never spoken. I'm actually trying to finish my article before Howard sends Trey and me on an assignment."

He lounged by her desk. "I heard something about you two covering a sixty-fifth wedding anniversary."

"Right. So I'm here at seven thirty, quite the rarity as you mentioned, to put the finishing touches on my DIY birdhouse on a budget article."

"Sounds intriguing."

"Hopefully our readers will love it. It helps they have some of the supplies on sale this week over at Thambert's Hardware." She paused, eyeing the yellow and blue box in Chip's right hand. "Is that what I think it is?"

"If you're thinking it's Rynsburger's Famous Chocolate Candies, you're right."

"Really? I love those things." At the thought of her favorite chocolates, Carleigh's mouth began to water.

"I've eaten far too many in the past week. Grandmother Bray sent me several boxes for my birthday and I've about made myself sick on them. I thought I'd bring them to work and see if anyone else wants any."

"Ooh, may I have one?" Carleigh reached for the box.

Chip set the box on Carleigh's desk. "You can have the entire box if you'd like. There are about six pieces left. I'm fine if I don't see any of Rynsburger's Famous Chocolate Candies until my next birthday."

"Thank you, Chip. This may be just what I need to sustain me through another *Oakville Daily* Duo assignment."

"No problem. Anything to help the cause. Say, aren't you and Trey getting along better these days?"

Carleigh thought back to the ice cream stand outing with Trey. Something about their relationship *had* changed. Or maybe it was her overactive imagination. Either way, she and Trey *were* getting along better. "For the moment, it seems," she said.

"That's good. I wrote an essay in college about why conflict resolution is integral to healthy relationships. Maybe I can dig it out sometime for you and Trey."

"I think we'll pass."

"Well, on that note, enjoy the chocolates."

"Thank you, and tell Grandmother Bray that her kindness has blessed more than one chocoholic in Oakville."

The door opened and Trey sauntered in.

"Chocoholics in Oakville. I like that. Sounds like an upcoming article." Chip chuckled. "Glad you like the gift."

"Specialty chocolates are one of my weaknesses. You know me well, Chip. I really appreciate your thoughtfulness. Thanks again." She reached for the decorated box and opened it, eyeing the delicatessens within.

"You're welcome. Have a good day, Carleigh."

Chip sprinted toward his desk as Trey passed by. "Want a piece of Rynsburger's Famous Chocolate Candies?" Carleigh asked.

"Those from Chip?"

"Yes. He's so thoughtful. These are my favorite chocolates of all time, but they're difficult to find. I have fond memories of eating them when I was a kid."

"Thoughtful, huh?"

"Here, try one." Carleigh wouldn't have sacrificed such an exceptional piece of candy for Trey on a normal day, but since he'd saved her from a rogue football during their ice cream outing...

"No thanks." Without another word, Trey stalked toward his desk.

Weird. Maybe he was having a bad day. But for anyone not to want a piece of Rynsburger's, it had to be something serious.

Trey plunked himself into his desk chair and simultaneously hit the power button on his desktop. He'd overheard Carleigh's and Chip's conversation about the chocolates.

At the ice cream stand, Trey thought things had changed for the better between Carleigh and him. For some strange reason, he was seeing her in a different light these past few days. While in his unusual stupor, he'd forgotten all about Carleigh's and Chip's feelings for each other.

Now the guy was bringing her chocolate? And not just any chocolate, but her favorite chocolate?

How could Trey compete with that?

A budding romance at *The Oakville Daily*. Who would have thought?

He leaned back in his chair and clasped his fingers behind his head. He had never really thought of himself as the jealous type. A basically-content guy with a lot of confidence, Trey figured envy was a waste of time. Yet, this whole ordeal with Carleigh and Chip hit him in the gut with the force of a poorly-thrown football.

Thankfully, he didn't have a crush on Carleigh so it failed to impact him in any meaningful way.

Today the bubbly and perky Quirky Carleigh wore a bright pink shirt. Her clothing tastes bordered on obnoxious. Good thing she wasn't an FBI agent attempting to covertly solve a crime. She'd never be able to hide or blend in with the crowd.

She was, however, supposed to be solving a couple of mysteries with him. Namely, who Lindy's secret admirer was, and more importantly, the Buy it All theft.

Howard rushed past their desks and bellowed, "Everyone, staff meeting. Pronto."

Bubba appeared out of nowhere, Margie had just arrived, and Lindy emerged from the supply room. Carleigh rushed toward the room, teetering on high-heeled shoes.

Trey followed and plopped next to Margie, leaving the seat by Carleigh open in case Chip wanted to sit there.

"Chip, that means you too!" Howard boomed.

Chip bounded toward the room in two easy steps. He halted in the doorway, then took the seat next to Carleigh.

Everyone in the room looked from Carleigh to Trey and back to each one once again.

"Now then. I received some disturbing news while at Karen's Bakery this morning. I will need my *Oakville Daily* Duo to do some investigating." Howard again glanced between Trey on one side of the table and Carleigh on the other. "I don't know what's going on between you two, but you both need to sit on the same side in your usual spots. Hop to it, pronto."

Trey stood and switched places with Chip. Did he notice a reluctance on Chip's part?

"Good. I have a crick in my neck as it is. I don't need to be bobbing my head back and forth making sure you two have all the necessary information to complete this investigation."

"Sir, not to interrupt," began Bubba, "But where are the donuts?"

"Worthwhile question, Bubba. I didn't bring any today. I ate a couple while at my wife's bakery and made haste here as quickly as possible. Which brings me to the subject at hand."

The room grew silent in anticipation for Howard's news. "Did the police solve the Buy it All mystery?" Lindy asked.

"No. But we have something alarming that threatens to destroy life as we know it in Oakville." Howard stood and began to pace. "Mrs. Gomez cornered me at Karen's just mere minutes ago. Her Chihuahua, Mighty, has been dognapped."

"Dognapped?" Carleigh gasped.

"You heard right."

"How do they know Mighty hasn't just wandered off?" Lindy asked.

"Because Mrs. Gomez received a ransom note."

"And just like that, Oakville became a crime-ridden city," Margie said, placed a hand to her heart. "What can we do?"

"We investigate and we solve this dognapping. It will take each and every one of us. I've already contacted Oakville PD and they are on the case. *Oakville Daily* Duo, as soon as your sixty-fifth wedding anniversary interview with the Ropers is completed, I want all of your energies focused on solving this crime and returning Mighty to Mrs. Gomez. Understood?"

"Understood," Trey and Carleigh uttered at the same time.

"Take the minivan, do what you need to do. Just solve this crime. See if Officer Zemski will give you the details of the ransom note, or even a copy of it so I can publish it in the paper and see if our readers can offer any insight. You're all excused."

The burden of worry seemed to overtake each *Oakville Daily* employee.

Who had kidnapped Mighty, and why?

# Chapter Twenty-Nine

IT STARTED LIKE ANY other day, except this day was turning out far from ordinary. Mighty was missing with no clues as to his whereabouts.

On a far less concerning note, Trey acted standoffish and distant from the second he arrived at work. Unconventional, considering the fact their ice cream outing had been such a memorable experience. Even during the wedding anniversary interview, Trey was distracted and had to have a few things repeated twice. Thankfully, he temporarily took a break from his aloof behavior while capturing several photos of the sweet couple.

Carleigh ate another of the Rynsburger's Famous Chocolate Candies. Only three candies left. If she kept up the nervous eating, she will have downed the box of six chocolates in less than four hours.

She tapped her fingers on her desk, causing a rhythmic tune. Nerves assailed her ever since the news of Mighty's disappearance. What if that had been Sullivan Theodore? Her lunch hour couldn't come soon enough so she could check on him.

Three hours later, Carleigh climbed into *The Oakville Daily* minivan. Trey loaded his camera equipment into the back in case they needed it, then slid into the front seat. "How about speaking with Officer Zemski first?" she suggested.

"Sure."

As usual Trey whizzed down the street as though a racecar driver on their way to Oakville PD. He kept his eyes on the road and his focus on anything but conversation.

"Trey? Are you all right?"

"Yep."

"I can't imagine if something happened to Sullivan Theodore. Are you worried about Jaxx?" Maybe that was it. Maybe he was as troubled about his pet as she was hers.

"It is concerning."

Officer Zemski was in the Chief's office when they arrived.

"All right, thank you, Chief. I'll get right on that." He motioned for Carleigh and Trey to have a seat in the adjoining conference room. He sat across from them.

They'd been in the conference room only one other time, and that was to discuss the Buy it All theft.

"Thanks for waiting. I know you two are eager to get involved and not just from a reporter standpoint. You two do need to allow the police to do their investigations without playing detective."

"Understood," responded Trey, but Carleigh thought he failed at being very convincing.

Officer Zemski must have honed in on that suspicion as well. "You two don't realize this could become a dangerous situation."

"We understand, Officer Zemski, and we appreciate all Oakville PD is doing to solve these crimes. Can you tell us if there have been any new developments?"

"We have had some, yes."

Carleigh pulled her notepad from her bag. "May we discuss those new developments for the paper?" She refused the urge to squirm. So maybe the developments weren't *only* for the paper.

"Some of them, yes. You may apprise your readers that we just received a call that several blankets were stolen from Oakville Thrift Store early this morning."

"Blankets?" Trey asked.

"Yes. Until recently, we've not had many thefts in Oakville, and now we've had several. The Buy it All incident, the gas drive-offs from Oakville Gas Mart, the blankets, and, of course, Mighty."

"So, you are considering the very real possibility Mighty was dognapped?" Carleigh scribbled the notes as rapidly as she could. She hoped Officer Zemski continued sharing what he knew.

"Normally, I would tone down the information I am about to share, but…" Officer Zemski sighed. "That this is happening on my watch is inexcusable."

Carleigh appreciated Officer Zemski's dedication. "Yes, it is."

"And so, knowing *The Oakville Daily* could prove beneficial in alerting residents, calming fears, and soliciting information, I, with the chief's permission, will give more details than I normally would in a matter such as this." He paused and took a drink from a quart-sized mug with the faded words, *Oakville Gas Mart* on the side of it.

"In answer to your inquiry, yes, I do believe Mighty was dognapped. My first question to Mrs. Gomez was whether her dog could have escaped into an alcove behind some furniture in Mrs. Gomez's condo. Or perhaps he'd slipped underneath her white vinyl fence in her postage-stamp-sized yard. This could have occurred when Mrs. Gomez opened her door to leave. Mighty is tiny at only three pounds, and she may not have seen him slip out." Officer Zemski paused. "But neither suggestion proved advantageous."

"From what I understand, Mighty is a compliant dog who has never caused any trouble," said Trey.

"Exactly. Mighty doesn't dig under fences, and he wasn't concealing himself behind Mrs. Gomez's antique furniture or her old cabinet-style tubed television set. Mrs. Gomez went for breakfast at the senior citizen center, as she does five days a week, and returned home to find him gone." Officer Zemski pinched the bridge of his nose. "Basically, Mighty the teacup Chihuahua was dognapped in the light of day from his home. Something unheard of in Oakville. However, I do have to say that Mrs. Gomez, like so many others in our town, failed to lock her door."

Trey reminded himself to make sure he locked his own door at home. "Howard mentioned a ransom note. Can you tell us anything more about that?"

"Yes. Mrs. Gomez found a ransom note on her porch, along with Mighty's miniature collar. This confirmed his abduction."

Carleigh gasped. "Poor Mrs. Gomez."

"Yes. She isn't taking this well, but I assured her we would do our best to find her pet."

"Are you at liberty to tell us what the ransom note said?"

"The original is in evidence, but I'll give you a copy."

"Can you tell us anything else about Mighty's disappearance?" Trey asked.

"Or the blanket theft?" Carleigh added.

"Nothing more on Mighty, but I can tell you that the blanket theft occurred before the thrift store opened this morning. Interesting that nothing else was stolen, and for collectors especially, the thrift store has some decent finds. No classic vinyl records, vintage dinnerware, or brand name used clothing was stolen. Only some blankets, and not just any blankets. These were the king and queen-sized blankets in the home décor section."

Carleigh flipped through her notebook to a clean page. "Did anyone see anything in either instance?"

"No one saw a thing. And, as you know, security cameras aren't that common in Oakville. A handful of residents have them, mainly to catch wildlife gnawing on their plants, and one or two businesses have them, but it's not typical here." Officer Zemski left the room and returned with a sheet of paper. "Here is a copy of the ransom note. Feel free to take it with you, and publish it in the paper. I've been in touch with Howard, and our best bet for a positive outcome with Mighty is if we at Oakville PD work in conjunction with *The Oakville Daily* and the public to solve this crime. However, we do need it stated that if anyone comes across any information, they need to relay it to the chief or myself, rather than taking matters into their own hands." Officer Zemski frowned. "Again, the public, *all* of the public, reporters included, need to relay any information to the chief, rather than taking matters into their own hands. This perp could be dangerous."

Trey nodded. "We understand. We'll print that critical reminder each time we provide an update. We're on our way to Mrs. Gomez's place next, so hopefully she can provide us with some photos of Mighty."

"Yes. Good idea. I have one of him as well. Here is a copy of the note."

```
Dear Pet Owner,
If you ever desire to see your beloved
pet again, start saving your pennies. I'll
be in touch with you about where and when
to place the thousand dollars I am seeking
for the return of your pet.
```

"Wow. A thousand dollars? Where will Mrs. Gomez get that kind of money?" Trey asked.

"Likely she won't be able to acquire that money on her own. But people in this town can rally around her and help her raise it or perhaps even donate funds. Regardless, this perp will be providing at least one more note." Officer Zemski pushed in his chair. "It would be advantageous to catch him or her in the act of stealing another pet."

"That would be ideal. Is there anything else you can tell us?" Carleigh asked, placing the note in her bag.

"Not on record."

"Off record?"

"If this stays off record, yes. I can tell you that we believe that all of these crimes are related."

The next stop was Mrs. Gomez's house. Trey zipped through the streets of town until they arrived at the Oakville Senior Village. Mrs. Gomez's condo was a pleasant orange-bricked home in the second row. A tasteful rose bush, a *Welcome All Friends* doormat, and a wind chime with an ornament featuring a dog and several bones, set Mrs. Gomez's condo off from the identical one next to hers.

Mrs. Gomez answered the door, a handkerchief in her left hand. Dark circles underlined her bloodshot and puffy eyes. "Do come in. I've been expecting you."

Carleigh and Trey stepped inside the condo. An open floor plan, elegantly-decorated with antique furniture and a tasteful painting of a fruit bowl with various fruits, the home reminded Carleigh of her grandmother's. She rested a hand on Mrs. Gomez's arm. "I'm so sorry about Mighty, Mrs. Gomez."

"Thank you, dear. Do have a seat." She waved a hand at the brown claw foot couch.

Several shelves lined the living room area, covered with framed pictures of smiling children, a black and white photo of a couple, presumably Mrs. Gomez and her late husband, and several photos of Mighty. Carleigh and

Trey took a seat on the couch, while Mrs. Gomez sat on the adjacent vintage recliner.

"I am fraught with nerves. I called and called to him and he didn't answer. This isn't like him." She dabbed at her nose with her handkerchief. "He's always been a well-behaved."

"Do you know anyone who would want to take Mighty?" Carleigh scribbled her notes of what Mrs. Gomez had said so far.

"No. I have no enemies and neither does Mighty. I have searched every nook and cranny with no success. He isn't anywhere. And then with the ransom note and his tiny collar..."

"We will do all we can to help Officer Zemski find Mighty and return him to you," Trey said. "I would like to put several photos of Mighty in the paper so that if any of our readers see him, they can contact the police department right away."

"Someone broke in and stole my dog while I was away. I'm so full of guilt for attending the senior citizen breakfast. If I hadn't, Mighty would still be here." Mrs. Gomez stifled a sob.

Carleigh's heart broke for the older woman and she placed an arm around the dear woman's shoulder. "I know Officer Zemski checked for prints and interviewed neighbors, but is there anything you can think of that might help us know who could have taken him?"

"No. I can't think of anything. We live a structured life and have a lot of friends, especially here in the Village."

They continued their conversation with Mrs. Gomez, Carleigh taking notes and Trey snapping photos of Mrs.

Gomez's pictures of her pet. "Have you thought about putting posters up?" Trey asked.

"As in missing-dog posters?"

"Yes. I'm sure the businesses in town would be happy to allow you to hang them up in the windows."

"That's a splendid idea. I bet my knitting club would help me in that endeavor. Thank you for suggesting that."

If only they could promise with one-hundred percent accuracy that Mighty would be returned safe and unharmed to his loving owner.

# Chapter Thirty

NEARLY EVERYONE ELSE HAD left for the day when Trey finished an assignment and logged off his computer. It had been a busy day, and he wasn't sad to see it coming to a conclusion.

"Want to grab a bite to eat at The Oakville Greasy Spoon?" Chip asked.

"Sure." A juicy burger was just the thing to take his mind off of the entire situation with Carleigh and Chip. He'd been processing the gift of the chocolates Chip had given to Carleigh all day.

An uninvited thought nagged at him after he and Carleigh had gone for ice cream.

He liked her. A lot. Trey supposed it shouldn't come as a surprise. They were always together on assignments, had joined the ministry outreach together at church, and he saw her six days a week. He'd somehow grown accustomed to their bantering camaraderie.

When it happened, he couldn't really say, other than the ice cream outing had cemented his feelings for her.

He wanted to get to know her better.

And then along came Chip. Or maybe Chip liked Carleigh before Trey even realized he himself liked her.

Whatever the situation between Carleigh and Chip, Trey wouldn't interfere if they liked each other.

A half hour later after letting Jaxx out, Trey arrived at The Oakville Greasy Spoon. As usual, the place was packed and the aroma of fried foods lingered far beyond the front door. Trey slipped inside and slid into a booth opposite of Chip.

"Glad it's Friday. It's been a week and half," Chip said, thumbing through the menu as if he hadn't seen it three thousand times before.

"Tell me about it. And then with the dognapping. Carleigh and I have been going nonstop to these interviews. Concerning how crime has erupted recently in Oakville."

Chip nodded. "I've lived here consecutively since junior high, with the exception of a stint in college, and I've never seen anything like it. Hope they get Mighty back and catch the perps causing all these problems."

"Off the record, Officer Zemski said that he believes the cases are connected."

"Could be."

"I think it has something to do with the guys seen wearing clown wigs. Carleigh and I are going to look into it further on Monday. Clowns are dangerous people, it seems."

A peculiar expression crossed Chip's face. "Like I mentioned before, not all clown-wig wearers are criminals."

"That according to your second cousin twice removed who works for the police force in Iowa?"

"Very funny."

Doretta came to take their order and deliver the home-made potato chips, which were devoured in a matter of minutes.

"Hey, just curious, do you like Carleigh?" Trey asked, savoring the taste of the iconic chips.

"Me? Why do you ask?"

Just as Trey suspected. Chip did like her. He pushed aside his disappointment. "Just seems like maybe you like her."

"Well, I do like her. She is nice and can be funny at times."

"Do you like her for more than, you know, a friend?"

"All right, I think I know why you're asking."

Did Chip know Trey's feelings for Carleigh? Sure, they hung out sometimes and Trey considered Chip a friend, but they'd never talked about Carleigh before today.

"No way," said Chip.

"No way, what?"

"I totally should have seen this coming." Chip jiggled his leg hard enough under the table that the entire booth shook. The guy was hyper, no doubt about it.

"Talk to me in something other than secret code, Chip."

"All right, so the first thing you talk about when we sit down is Carleigh. You and Carleigh have been doing interviews. You and Carleigh are investigating further into clown-wig wearers. Carleigh this, Carleigh that. I think *you* like her."

Was Trey that transparent? "Actually, I think you do. You're the one who brought her a box of chocolates. Her favorite, in fact, and she ingested them within minutes."

312

"Whoa. Back up the bus. Those chocolates were from my grandma for my birthday. She sent me, like, a dozen boxes, and I've already spent a significant amount of time bemoaning my lack of self-control. I brought the last half-eaten box to work hoping to unload it so I could avoid further temptation. Carleigh happened to be the first one I saw and the first one I asked about the chocolates. If I'd seen you first, I would have asked you if you wanted them. She mentioned she loved them, so I gave them to her."

Trey's stomach growled. A juicy hamburger would help him to be able to digest Chip's comments a little easier. "So, you didn't give the box of chocolates to her as a gift?"

"It was a gift, just not the kind of gift you're thinking."

"So, you don't like her as more than a friend?"

Chip shook his head. "I have my eye on someone else. I like Carleigh as a friend, but nothing more. But you on the other hand..."

"Is it really that obvious?"

"Totally obvious. Like I was saying, you lump you and her together in every sentence. Plus, I've seen you two. Sure, you act like you can't stand to be around each other, but you like each other. It's clear."

"And you're a relationship guru?"

"Something like that."

Trey took a deep breath. He didn't have to worry about Chip liking Carleigh after all. "Guess that's good news."

"Yep."

"Now, if she likes me, all will be well."

"Women are the most confusing of all Creation on this planet, so I'm no expert, but it seems like she likes you. Plus, you are *The Oakville Daily* Duo."

Monday arrived and Carleigh rushed to work. Today she and Trey would be more thoroughly investigating the dognapping. She couldn't say which she loved more—writing the articles or investigating them.

Perhaps she should write her next novel in the suspense genre.

Her phone rang, interrupting her thoughts of penning a novel. "This is Carleigh."

"Carleigh, this is Louella."

"Louella, hi. How are you?"

"I'm well, thanks. Say, I just wanted to let you know Lindy's secret admirer was recorded on our security camera. Lew finally got around to installing the cameras and we were eating popcorn last night and watching the footage. Thought *The Oakville Daily* Duo might want to come down and see the frame with the secret admirer."

Carleigh had been so focused on the dognapping that she'd nearly forgotten about solving the mystery of Lindy's secret admirer. She caught Trey's eye and motioned for him to come to her desk. Holding the phone in the crook of her neck, she penned, "Louella has security footage."

Trey snagged a pen and wrote, "Let's go."

He was close enough to her that she could smell his trademark aftershave. "We can come right now if that works for you, Louella."

"That works. See you soon."

Carleigh hung up the phone. Trey remained at her desk. He was in a much more pleasant mood today than on Friday. She was glad to have the "real" Trey back again.

"You ready?" he asked.

"Yes. Kind of exciting. We might actually solve this mystery."

Chip jogged over to her desk. "What's with the clandestine discussion over here?"

"Oh, Louella has some security footage for us."

"On the dognapping?"

"No. Another mystery we're working on." Carleigh grabbed her purse.

"What kind of mystery?"

Trey glanced at the receptionist desk and lowered his voice. "We think we may have solved the mystery of who Lindy's secret admirer is."

Chip's eyes bugged beneath his glasses. "Is that one of your job duties? I thought you two were focused on the dognapping."

"Oh, we are," said Carleigh, standing and nearly bumping into Trey. "But this mystery might just be solved first."

"I didn't even know it was a mystery. And really, what if the secret admirer wants to remain anonymous?"

Trey shrugged. "We aren't necessarily going to tell anyone or put it into print, it's just something we've been working on."

"I bet Howard would prefer you stay and work on the dognapping. I hear Mrs. Gomez is beside herself with worry."

"We've been working diligently on the dognapping and will continue to do so, but we have to talk to Louella anyway about the surprise ad she's placing for her upcoming wedding anniversary, so this will kill two birds with one stone, as they say. You ready, Trey? Louella is expecting us."

Chip jogged in place, his oversized feet taking up prime real estate in the area around Carleigh's desk. He'd indubitably log in enough steps for a week with all the nervous energy radiating off of him. "All I'm saying is that maybe this isn't a mystery to be solved. Maybe you should let it remain an enigma that reveals itself in proper time to the people involved. Does Lindy even know you're working on this?"

Lindy appeared then. "Working on what?"

"Louella has some security footage that may show us who your secret admirer is," Carleigh said.

"Ooh, that would be fantastic. I love the flowers he keeps sending me, but just between us, I've lost more than one night of sleep wondering if he's the same guy who stole the dog food and milk at Buy It All."

Chip shook his head. "I doubt he is."

"They both wear curly reddish-orange wigs," said Trey.

"See what I mean, Chip?" Lindy asked. She took a step toward him and Chip's face turned a deep crimson.

"There is a connection. I am so appreciative of the lovely bouquets, but if my S.A. is a criminal...I would be beside myself."

"You want to know who your secret admirer is?" asked Chip, his method of delivery sounding more like an auctioneer with his quick-paced words.

"I do. I basically hired Carleigh and Trey to find out, well not exactly hired them, but insinuated I'd like to know." Lindy smiled at Chip.

And Chip took a step backward and nearly tripped over his big feet.

Carleigh watched the interaction between Lindy and Chip. Chip was suddenly rendered speechless. Interesting. She'd have to process it all later. For now, she and Trey needed to get to Louella's post haste. Before Howard decided Chip's reasoning about priorities was correct.

Trey opened the minivan door for her. "I thought we'd never get out of there," he said.

"Me too. What was with Chip?"

"No clue. I figure this will be one mystery we can get out of the way and then we can focus one-hundred percent on Mighty's disappearance. Maybe this will even help us with that mystery."

They pulled into a parking spot at Louella's Flowers and Gifts. What should have taken seven minutes took three because of Trey's expedient driving skills.

"What would you do if you had an S.A.? Would you want to know who it was?" Trey asked.

"Probably so. I gravitate more toward spontaneity, but I'm with Lindy. I'd want to know, especially in light of the commonalities between her S.A. and the thief."

The aroma of dozens of blooms filled the air and Louella stood behind the counter, arranging an impressive bouquet. "So glad you two could come. The monitor is in the office." She led them to the humble closet-sized nook serving as her business office. "Lew paused it on the frame showing Lindy's secret admirer. It was the most recent time he came in to place some advance orders. The guy is always polite and seems genuinely interested in making Lindy's day better because of the flowers." The bell on the front door jingled. "Sounds like a customer. I'll be back in a few."

Trey motioned for Carleigh to sit in the office chair while he stood. The frame with the secret admirer showed a tall lanky man with a curly reddish-orange clown wig. Trey pressed the play button, and the man walked away from the florist shop. Then, as if he'd forgotten something, he pivoted and re-entered the business. In doing so, they caught a glimpse of his face.

Although he wore dark sunglasses, his face looked oddly familiar.

And something about his gait appeared recognizable.

"I think we know this guy," Carleigh said.

"There is something about him that reminds me of someone."

The secret admirer approached Louella. In a fake Southern accent, he said, "I almost forgot. Could you please include that little bird figurine in the next bouquet?"

"Absolutely," Louella replied. "The miniature blue one?"

"Yes."

Louella scribbled the notes on her notepad. "Excellent choice."

"Oh, excuse me. I only have fifty-six more steps." The secret admirer jogged in place while watching his fitness tracker.

Louella pressed buttons on her cash register. "That'll be $10.47."

The secret admirer finished jogging in place a few seconds more, paid for the item, and left. His hyper mannerisms and his ability to cover a considerable amount of space with only a few steps lent to his familiarity.

"Here, I'll back up the footage and replay it." Trey rewound the footage and they watched it again from the beginning.

"Someone else we know always makes sure to get all his steps in," Carleigh said.

Trey nodded. "Yep. And he always gives the number of how many more steps he has left."

They watched the footage three more times until Carleigh snapped her fingers. "That's it!"

"What?"

"Lindy's secret admirer is none other than Chip."

"Can you believe it?" Trey asked on the way back to *The Oakville Daily.*

"I can't. But it explains a lot, especially about how nervous he was next to Lindy today and how he didn't want us to go to Louella's."

"And how he always defended reddish-orange curly haired wig wearers."

Carleigh laughed. "Exactly."

Trey sailed into the minivan's parking spot and killed the engine. "I can't believe we didn't see it before."

"Well, at least Lindy doesn't have to worry about her secret admirer being a thief or a hardened criminal."

"True. I guess this also explains what Chip said the other day while we were eating at The Oakville Greasy Spoon."

"What did he say?"

Trey regretted making that statement out loud. "Oh, nothing."

"No, what did he say?"

When she gave him that inquisitive look with her head tilted to one side and her pretty eyes full of curiosity, he really couldn't deny her request. "Uh, not much. Just that he had his eye on someone else."

"Really? I didn't know guys talked about that kind of stuff."

Trey looked out the window, expecting Howard to appear at any moment. The guy seemed to have a sixth sense about where the minivan was at all times. "Yeah, they do sometimes."

"So, you two were talking about who you both liked, and he said he had his eye on someone else? Someone other than who?"

Trey knew his ears were bright red. He wished he had his cap so he could shove it over the tops of his ears and hide his telltale embarrassment. "Someone other than someone else."

"You are not making sense at all."

"Sometimes I don't."

"That's fine if you don't want to tell. I'm just curious."

"Yes, and that's one of the things I like about you—your curiosity and your willingness to solve mysteries too." The words tumbled from Trey's mouth, as if he had no control of his speech habits. "I mean, it's good to be curious and want to solve mysteries."

He dared a glance in her direction. Her eyes had widened and she strummed her fingers on the console. Her glasses had slipped down on her nose, and without a thought, Trey gently tapped them up to their rightful place. His hand lingered on her face, and his thumb, with a mind of its own, caressed her cheek. "Carleigh..."

If her eyes hadn't enlarged before, they did now. He looked from her eyes to her lips and back again to her eyes. If Howard showed up now, his ears wouldn't be the only thing bright red—his entire face would take on the hue. Trey inched forward slightly across the console and she did the same until they were mere centimeters from each other. She was even prettier this close.

Carleigh closed her eyes and Trey knew there was no going back now. His lips claimed hers in a yearning kiss—one which she returned, seemingly without hesitation.

Whoa. What just happened? Had he ever thought he'd kiss Quirky Carleigh? And that their first kiss would be in *The Oakville Daily* minivan?

The kiss ended all too soon, and Trey craned his neck to see if Howard was anywhere in the vicinity. They sat for several seconds, each staring out the windshield. What was she thinking? Was she all right with his choice to kiss her? He hoped so. He'd like to kiss her again if it weren't for the concern of Howard's sudden appearance at any time.

"Uh, Chip said he liked someone other than you."

"Other than me?"

"Yeah. I thought he liked you and you liked him."

She scrunched her nose. "Chip is nice, but I don't like him in that way."

"And he said he liked someone else, meaning Lindy."

"Were you concerned that I might like him and that he might like me?"

"I was."

Carleigh gaped at him. "But I thought..." she pointed at him, then back to herself. "I thought we were adversaries."

"Me too."

"Do adversaries kiss each other?"

322

Trey didn't have an answer for that. He didn't even have an answer as to why he kissed her, other than it was something he'd like to do again. "I kind of like you, Carleigh."

She smiled at him. "Me too."

He blew out the breath he'd been holding. "Well, we are *The Oakville Daily* Duo."

# Chapter Thirty-One

CARLEIGH INHALED HIS PLEASANT woodsy aftershave and noticed from this close proximity the vibrant sea green color of his eyes. She closed her eyes and met his kiss. Carleigh's pulse became erratic, shivers ran through her, and butterflies swirled in her belly. His kiss was warm and inviting and she wished it could have lasted much longer than it had.

In short, while Trey's kiss was somewhat unexpected, it was completely welcome.

Wait a minute. When had she thought she'd ever wanted Trey to kiss her? Well, besides on her porch after the ice cream date.

Her thoughts spun. She would have to admit undoubtably, unequivocally, and without question, that she was falling in love with Trey Montgomery.

When they finished their kiss, she sat for a moment staring out the windshield and contemplating if the unanticipated kiss really happened.

After a few minutes of conversation, Trey glimpsed in the rearview mirror. "Looks like we're about to have company."

"Howard?"

"No, Lindy."

Lindy tapped on Carleigh's window, and she opened the door. "Hi, Lindy."

"Did you two solve the mystery? I've been dying in there waiting to find out."

"We did."

"Oh, no. It's not the Buy it All thief, is it?"

Trey chimed in. "We don't know who that is yet, but no, it's not the same guy."

"Phew. I can sleep well tonight then. So, do tell. Is it some old toothless curmudgeon with bad body odor or a guy from the next county over? Don't keep me in suspense."

Carleigh caught Trey's eye. "We really didn't talk about whether or not to tell you who it was." No, there really hadn't been time to discuss that matter, not with...Carleigh recalled the kiss and the heat crept up her face. She hadn't minded one bit that Trey had kissed her, but would she come to her senses soon and realize he was still her adversary?

Likely not.

The kiss changed everything.

"Hello, anybody home?" Lindy asked, bringing Carleigh's thoughts from Trey to their predicament about exposing Chip's thoughtfulness.

"We have to discuss it first," Carleigh said, "and I better tell Howard about this ad Louella wants placed in *The Oakville Daily* for her and Lew's fortieth wedding anniversary. We have to be covert about it because Lew is placing an ad as well, and neither one can know about the other's ad."

Lindy's brows drew together. "All right, but can you tell me as soon as you discuss it?"

"We will," Trey promised. "Guess we better get inside before Howard wonders if we're having a staff meeting in the parking lot."

Carleigh pondered the irony. They'd discovered Chip's feelings for Lindy, and in the process, their feelings for each other.

When they arrived inside, Chip was pacing back and forth. "About time you two returned. Howard left for donuts and I've been fielding calls about updates regarding Mighty's disappearance."

"Looks like you wore a path into the carpet with your pacing," said Carleigh.

"You should have seen him while you two were away. I thought I was going to have to send him to the back room to help Bubba roll papers," Lindy laughed.

Chip stopped for a minute and checked his fitness tracker. "It's just that we need you two here working, not going on wild goose chases about inconsequential matters."

"Did you get all your steps in?" Trey asked.

Lindy hiked a thumb toward Chip. "He got all ten thousand steps in just in the first ten minutes after you two left."

Carleigh laughed at Lindy's exaggeration. "Well, we did discover who Lindy's secret admirer is."

"You did?" Chip's voice rose an octave.

Trey chuckled. "We did. Carleigh and I need to discuss whether or not we're going to divulge the information, and if so, when."

"I hope it's soon," said Lindy. "And I hope it's someone who's nice and kind."

Chip stopped in place. "It is."

"Oh, good, because I have been so worried it's some crazed weirdo."

"It's not."

Carleigh watched the interaction between Lindy and Chip and wondered when Lindy would catch on to the fact Chip seemed to know who the secret admirer was. She didn't have to wait long.

"Phew. Well, that's reassuring. Wait. How do you know it's a nice and kind person and not a weirdo?"

"I just know these things."

Carleigh met Trey's gaze and he shrugged.

Lindy smiled at Chip. "Do you know him?"

"I do."

"So, he's a friend of yours, then? Because that would make sense about how he knew my favorite color is yellow and sends me that color of flowers the most often and how the most recent bouquet had a little bluebird in it. I love bluebirds."

"I know."

"So, you told your friend?"

Carleigh stifled a giggle. Would Lindy be excited or disappointed when she discovered Chip and his "friend" were one and the same?

Chip took a deep breath. "Lindy, your secret admirer is me."

Not a sound filled the room except the ticking of the archaic black clock on the wall with the overly-frantic second hand. Carleigh prayed the phone would not ring.

"Oh."

Chip's face fell, and Carleigh wanted to tell him that it was all right, that there were other fish in the sea, as the saying went.

"Well," continued Lindy. "That's a good thing, then."

"It is?"

"Absolutely."

Chip's demeanor improved and the two of them began talking at exactly the same time.

It was at that very moment Howard burst through the door, a box of donuts in hand. "Meeting in the conference room pronto," he bellowed. "Mrs. Bassanelli's dog, Stella, is missing."

The calls and visits over the next several days were overwhelming. Trey could only imagine how busy the police station must be with reports of missing dogs.

Lil arrived mentioning Sunny, her Pomeranian, was missing after she left her sunning on the front porch. Lil had left for only a few minutes to water the rosebushes in her backyard.

Mrs. Moeller's bulldog, Wrinkles, was dognapped from her infamous vintage car while Mrs. Moeller made a pit stop into the craft store.

Tara Beth's Dalmatian, Lucy, disappeared from the library where she was waiting for Tara Beth to return from checking out the latest cookbook.

Blue, Gail's labradoodle, was dognapped at the Oakville outdoor antique show.

A yellow lab named Crabby and a Yorkshire terrier named Duke were also missing.

Each woman had a story to tell and each one had received a ransom note demanding a thousand dollars for the return of her pet. Their dogs' collars were left behind in the heist.

Trey, Carleigh, and Howard visited with each victim, collected photos and descriptions of the dogs, and offered to do what they could to assist in the recovery of the pets. Oakville Thrift Store was robbed of blankets again, and Buy it All discovered their dog food delivery never made it from the delivery truck into the store.

No one had seen much of anything regarding the dognapping, except for Louella, whose new video cameras recorded a man in a wig snatching Duke and stuffing him into an oversized duffle bag. The man was only seen from the back and was out of range after a few steps. Officer Zemski reviewed the footage and recognized the perp from the description Kevin at Buy it All had given, but could not identify the man as someone who resided in

Oakville. Nonstop coverage of the events filled the pages of *The Oakville Daily*, keeping its readers apprised.

After a busy day, Trey returned home, eager to take Jaxx on a walk and reassure himself that his own pet was safe. He parked his truck in the driveway, rolled up his window, and climbed out. The neighborhood was eerily quiet for a Friday evening. Mr. and Mrs. Fortuna were on vacation, as was Trey's neighbor to the right. The young couple across the street was likely still at work or had gone out for the evening. Trey had seen the family with a half dozen kids who lived kitty-corner to his house at the park during his drive home.

"Jaxx," Trey called, fiddling with his keys. He could usually hear Jaxx's deep-throated bark from the second he entered the driveway.

But not today.

Pulse escalating, Trey unlocked the door and called to his dog again. Still no answer. As he most often did on pleasant-weather days, Trey let Jaxx play in the backyard from the lunch hour until Trey returned home in the evening. He locked the gate, never worrying because Jaxx was a reasonable dog, rarely one to cause any trouble.

Trey dashed out the sliding door into his backyard, his eyes darting everywhere for a sign of Jaxx.

"Jaxx!" he called again.

As big as Jaxx was, he couldn't exactly play hide-and-seek. And the dog usually couldn't wait for Trey to arrive home so they could play fetch or go on a walk.

So where was he?

Jaxx's new favorite chew toy, the floppy chicken missing both legs, sat in the grass near the deck. Trey rounded the corner of his mid-sized backyard to the gate. It remained shut, but the lock was gone.

And that's when he knew.

Jaxx had become the latest dognapping victim.

# Chapter Thirty-Two

CARLEIGH PRAYED FOR EACH of the dog owners on her way home from *The Oakville Daily*. Most of the victims, with the exception of Mrs. Moeller and the dour-faced Gail, were sweet elderly women who had only their pets for companionship. That someone would intentionally attempt to hurt these women by stealing their beloved dogs was reprehensible.

She was thankful Sullivan Theodore IV was tucked away safely in her house. Officer Zemski reminded the residents of Oakville during his statement on the courthouse lawn yesterday to be sure to lock their doors.

"Oakville is not what it used to be," he remarked.

Carleigh had always locked her doors, but she was now even more diligent than ever in light of the dognappings.

The smell of freshly-cut lawn greeted her as she drove down the peaceful and quiet street to her house. She rolled her shoulders in an attempt to release some pent-up tension. For some reason she was a bit ramped up with anxiety. Could be because she'd dealt with so much second-hand pain and grief these past several days in addition to fretting about her own pet.

It would be a welcome reprieve to sit and snuggle Sullivan Theodore before she added some serious word count to her novel.

From the driveway, she spied her dog perched on the couch peering at her from the front window. She released the breath she was holding and offered up a prayer of gratitude that her pet was still safe.

When she opened the door, Sullivan Theodore bounded toward her, as he always did, eager for a hurried pat before he zipped outside for a bathroom break. Carleigh stopped him before he dashed out the front door due to his chronic habit of running off, and instead let him into the backyard.

She heard an unfamiliar whistling noise as she stood on the deck keeping a close eye on her pet. Carleigh glanced up, expecting to see a bird chirping in deep conversation in one of the trees in her backyard.

The whistling noise occurred again, and Sullivan Theodore raised his head and perked up his ears. She had two gates, one on either side of her chain-link-fenced yard. Upon noticing one was open, Carleigh hastily dashed toward it in an effort to stop her pet from escaping.

"I know I shut both gates," she muttered, wishing she hadn't worn her lime green high-heeled sandals.

But Sullivan Theodore reached the gate first and bounded through it.

Right into the arms of a waiting man with what appeared to be a doggy snack in his hand and a duffle bag slung over his shoulder.

Carleigh froze, unable to move.

The next hour was a blur. Officer Zemski arrived to ask questions regarding Sullivan Theodore's disappearance. Carleigh struggled to recall the description of the man who nabbed her pet. She held Sullivan Theodore's collar in her hand, which had been left just up the sidewalk from her house.

"I've seen the dognapper somewhere before," she admitted, the tears continuing to fall. She thought for a moment. "That's it! He's the clown who was at Stella's party."

Officer Zemski wrote the notes in a lined notepad. "Was he wearing a clown wig?"

"Not this time. He didn't have a wig at all, just gray hair, same as at the dog park that day. Oh, why didn't I run after him and rescue Sullivan Theodore?" She buried her face in her hands. If only she hadn't stalled when witnessing the man kidnapping her dog. If only she ran after him, or at the very least, called out to Sullivan Theodore. If only...

The officer placed a reassuring had on her shoulder. "You did the right thing by calling us. You have no way of knowing if he was armed or if he could have injured you or kidnapped you as well."

"I appreciate that, but if I'd reacted accordingly, I may have been able to prevent Sullivan Theodore's dognapping."

"Did you see his vehicle?"

Carleigh closed her eyes and massaged her temples where the beginnings of a headache was starting to form. Had she seen it? "Yes. It was a white van."

"Did you get a plate number?"

"No. I'm not sure it had a plate, or if it did, I didn't notice."

"Any other details about this guy's physical appearance?"

Carleigh recalled the man from the dog park. "He was skinny with thin-rimmed glasses over bulging eyes, bushy eyebrows, and prominent ears." She told Officer Zemski about meeting the man in the park. "He was creepy there, just as he was at Stella's party. Mrs. Bassanelli was actually the one who told us it was the clown, so she may have his contact information. I remember he was wearing blue jeans that day, just as he was today, and I think a red shirt."

Officer Zemski penned the information. "Anything else you can tell me?"

"Yes. He had bad teeth. Yellowed."

"All right. This helps. And there's Trey. Apparently, Jaxx is missing too, so I'll go talk with him now. If you think of anything else, let me know."

Carleigh nodded. Trey was there? Jaxx had been dognapped too? She saw him sprint down the sidewalk toward her and Officer Zemski. "Trey, I heard about Jaxx. Sullivan Theodore has been taken also."

"What?" He hurried toward her with a clear bag in his hand with Jaxx's collar and a piece of paper in it. "Was this just now?"

"Yes."

"Thank you for meeting me here, Trey," said Officer Zemski. "I wanted dispatch to let you know I was handling another dognapping case and I would speak with you right after I spoke with Carleigh. It seems as though the thief made his way through your neighborhood today. Did you see anything?"

"No. Jaxx was gone when I got home. The dognapper left behind Jaxx's collar and a ransom note."

Officer Zemski continued to question Trey before offering reassurance and climbing into his patrol car with Sullivan Theodore's dog collar and the bag from Trey. "I'll be in touch," he said. "In the meantime, if you think of anything else, let me know. Carleigh, do keep an eye open for any type of ransom note as well. He tends to leave those behind. In your case, you witnessed the dognapping, so he might be delivering a note to you after the fact."

Trey took her into his arms then, and she fell against his chest, the sobs returning. "What if we don't find them?"

"We will. We have to."

"It happened so fast, and I'm confident it was the clown from Stella's birthday party."

"Why does that not surprise me?"

"Wait a minute..." A thought rambled through her mind. "What do all the dognapped dogs have in common?"

"They're from Oakville?"

She appreciated his attempt to lighten the mood, and she gave him a weak smile. "True. And..."

"They are all purebreds?"

"Yes, likely because the perp can get a lot of money from selling a purebred dog."

He nodded, still holding her close. "Good observation."

"And I think we need to tell Officer Zemski this...all of the missing dogs were at Stella's birthday party."

Trey snapped his fingers. "That's why the dognapper was asking for addresses and taking photos, and probably notes too. Much easier to steal a pet when you know where they live."

"Even though not all pets were taken from their homes, several were, so that makes sense." Carleigh burrowed deeper into Trey's chest and closed her eyes. Had she ever believed she would find comfort in her former adversary's arms?

"It will be all right, Carleigh. We will find each of these dogs—each and every one—and have them returned to their rightful owners."

"And if we don't?" Pessimism wasn't typically in her nature, but when it came to her beloved pet, things changed.

"We will. We're *The Oakville Daily* Duo, right?"

He'd lost Jaxx, so he knew exactly what she was going through. "You're right. We solved the Chip and Lindy mystery, didn't we?"

"That's right. And with a lot of prayer and our investigative abilities, we can do this."

Carleigh hoped he was right because she wouldn't even contemplate the alternative.

"Meeting in the conference room!" Howard strode through the main area of *The Oakville Daily* with an over-sized box of donuts in hand.

Trey arched his back and stretched his arms overhead. He welcomed a break since he wasn't able to get his mind on work ever since Jaxx disappeared. He took his place beside Carleigh while Howard passed around the box of donuts. Trey helped himself to a maple bar and did his best to focus on his boss.

"Oakville PD hasn't had much luck in locating the person or persons stealing the canines. However, we did receive a handwritten note in a nondescript envelope today. I'd like to read to you what it says." Howard stole a bite of glazed donut, and when he was finished chewing, retrieved a letter from a file. "I've given the original to Officer Zemski, so this is a copy." He read:

To Whom it May Concern:
If you ever want to see your dogs again, you must pay the ransom. It is one thousand dollars per dog. Each owner needs to leave their money in a bag at Oakville Fun Park next Tuesday at midnight near the red curly slide with the breed of their dog, a photo of the dog, and their address written on a piece of paper. When I receive the money

for your dog, I will return it to your home within a week. If the police come with you, become involved in the money transaction, or try to locate me in the park, the deal is off and you will never see your dogs again.

Gasps filled the room. Where would Trey come up with a thousand dollars? He was confident none of the other victims would have that type of money either. Would the dognapper even keep his promise to return the dogs once he received the money?

"How are you holding up?" Trey asked Carleigh after the meeting.

"Not good. You?"

Trey shook his head. "It's been hard. I keep expecting Jaxx to greet me when I return home each evening."

"I know what you mean. I haven't slept at all the past several nights wondering if Sullivan Theodore is all right."

The worried expression in her eyes mirrored how he felt. "I wish there was more we could do."

Trey wanted to take her into his arms and reassure her that they would, in fact, locate their dogs—all of the dogs—healthy and safe. He wanted to promise her all would be all right.

But the doubt creeping into his mind warned of the possibility they may never see their pets again.

# Chapter Thirty-Three

THE DOGNAPPINGS CAUSED QUITE a stir in all of Oakville. Sightings of the dognapper's van added to the expounding trepidation, and Officer Zemski set up a dedicated phone line just to field calls with potential clues. Each clue was investigated, and Oakville PD made a public statement on the steps of City Hall to keep the residents apprised of the situation.

Howard published photos of each dog in *The Oakville Daily* and the handwritten note to *The Oakville Daily* in the hopes someone might offer a clue that would identify the thief.

Meanwhile, the residents feared the worst. Whose dog would be next? And who was the dognapper? Carleigh and Trey, determined to find their pets, became amateur detectives and integrated themselves into the investigation to uncover the culprit's identity.

Carleigh put the finishing touches on the most recent dognapping article and begged her eyes to focus on the wording one last time before turning it into Howard.

But it was a challenge to focus when tears were quick to arrive at just the thought of Sullivan Theodore in the clutches of such an abhorrent, odious, and heartless criminal. Was her pet hungry? Cold? Neglected?

She swallowed hard, struggling to stay focused on work. She scanned the article updating Oakville residents on the current situation.

"Oakville Continues the Search for the
Missing Pets"

Oakville PD, as well as the county sheriff's department and concerned citizens of Oakville, resumed searching for numerous missing dogs that have disappeared recently. Officer Zemski encourages residents to call the dedicated phone line at 555-7845 if they see an older model white van without a license plate or a thin man with gray hair, glasses, prominent ears, bulging eyes, and yellowed teeth. He might also be wearing a reddish-orange clown wig.

Officer Zemski reiterates residents should not approach the man, as it is unknown whether he is armed and dangerous. Be sure to lock your doors on your home and your vehicles at all times and never leave your pets unattended.

Lastly, law enforcement wants to reassure Oakville residents that, while this dognapper is relentless and continues to nab dogs, they are confident he will be located and justice will be served.

The dognapper was relentless, there was no doubt about that. His success as a canine thief soared every time he claimed another victim.

Carleigh retrieved the gold-framed photo of Sullivan Theodore she kept on her desk. He was dressed in his baseball jersey with *#1 Dog* printed on it. She recalled the day she purchased the jersey for Sullivan Theodore. It was the day he'd found and eaten all the doggy treats she'd accidentally left on the counter rather than in the cupboard. She still pondered how he managed to climb up there and reach them.

A regular Houdini if there was one.

When she attempted to reprimand her pet, he batted his puppy-dog eyes and hung his head. "I know you're sorry, Sullivan Theodore. I can see the remorse in your eyes, and I forgive you."

He climbed into her lap and snuggled while still sporting a doggy treat remnant in his furry canine mustache.

Even though he was ornery at times, Carleigh couldn't stay mad at Sullivan Theodore for any length of time.

Sadness washed over her anew.

Life without Sullivan Theodore would be lonely. Painful. Agonizing.

Would she ever see her pet again?

Her thoughts were interrupted when Lew stopped by to drop off his wedding anniversary announcement. His would appear on the same day as Louella's announcement to him. Neither knew the other was publishing an announcement on their anniversary. The thought brought a temporary smile to Carleigh's face.

"Hello, Lew."

Lew took a seat at her desk. "I think I finally figured out exactly what I want to say." He unfolded a piece of lined notebook paper that appeared to have been unfolded and refolded a dozen times. He focused on the announcement for a few seconds before relinquishing it to Carleigh. "I'd like to know what you think."

```
Happy Anniversary, my love.
Love,
Lew
```

Lew rubbed the back of his neck and his forehead puckered. If not for Lew's troubled expression, Carleigh might have giggled at his short announcement. It was clear the man only wanted the best for his wife, but couldn't put it into words. "Didn't you leave notes for Louella in high school as a secret admirer?"

"I did. But that was a really long time ago and I'm a bit rusty. I still write her notes from time to time, but I want this to be special. It's our big fortieth." Lew scratched his head. "I want to take her somewhere memorable, but it's all so nerve-wracking having this on the pages of *The Oakville Daily* for all to see."

"You could always just give her a private note."

Lew shook his head. "This needs to be public. I want the world to know how important she is to me."

"Is there somewhere she's always wanted to go?"

"Yes, South Carolina. She always wished we could have gotten married there. Unfortunately, I was poor when we married. The best I could do was a hotel stay in the next town."

Carleigh's heart lurched at the fondness this man felt for his wife. Lew and Louella were an inspiration. "Can you afford to take her to South Carolina now?"

"Might be a challenge to take time off from our businesses, but yes, I could manage that now."

"So..."

"But we're already married."

Carleigh smiled. "Yes, but have you heard of renewing one's vows?"

"Renewing vows? I've heard of it, but how does it work?"

"Well, from what I understand, you exchange your wedding vows once again, cementing the next decades of your life together as a married couple."

"I would marry her again."

Carleigh took a sheet of paper from the printer. "Here, let's write an announcement asking her to renew your vows in South Carolina on your anniversary."

Lew took a pen in his stubby fingers and began to write. After a few minutes, he passed the paper again to Carleigh. "Does this sound better?"

Carleigh read the words in Lew's nondescript small and messy handwriting.

Dear Louella,
You are the love of my life. Would you do me the honor of marrying me all over

again, this time in South Carolina on the beach?

Love,

Lew


"Perfect! I'll get it put on the same day as..." She barely caught herself before mentioning it would be the same day as Louella's announcement. "The same day as...when I put in another article." She paused, hoping Lew didn't notice her near-stumble. "Do you think you can make the arrangements with Oakville Travel Agency in time for your anniversary?"

"I think so. Louella usually handles this type of stuff, but since she's not supposed to know about it, yeah, I guess I could."

"This will work out well, Lew. Louella will be thrilled."

A smile lit Lew's face. "Thanks for all your help."

He paid Lindy for the ad space and left moments later. Carleigh placed his announcement next to Louella's.

Dear Lew,

I love you now more than ever. Thank you for being my husband. I know you've always wanted to take flying lessons. It's all been arranged and your lessons begin in a month.

Thank you for being the best husband ever.

Love,

Louella

Trey wandered through his quiet house, expecting at any moment for Jaxx to join him for a rehash of his day. But Jaxx wouldn't be listening to Trey's stories about his hectic day at the office. He wouldn't be begging for a doggy treat or hinting at wanting to go on a walk.

Jaxx's empty bed, surrounded by his plethora of chew toys was the exact way he'd left it the day he disappeared. Would Trey ever find him?

The stillness in the house bothered him, and he thought of Carleigh. He knew she was missing Theodore just as much as he was missing Jaxx. He removed his phone from his pocket and sent a text.

Hey, Carleigh, I'm in the neighborhood. Mind if I stop by?

Within a few minutes, she texted him back.

Hey, Trey, sure. Would you like to grill some burgers?

His mouth watered at the thought.

You bet! I'll get some hamburger at Buy it All and be at your house in a half hour.

He could almost hear her voice through her next text.

See you then!

Trey grabbed his keys and headed out the door. A visit with Carleigh and a hamburger on the new grill would be just the ticket to temporarily quelling the loneliness of missing Jaxx.

Twenty minutes later, he arrived at her house, a pack of ground beef, buns, chips, and strawberries in hand. He recalled the day she purchased strawberries at Buy it All and the whole mirror incident and chuckled.

Not long ago, he would not have wanted to spend his spare moments with Quirky Carleigh. But now? Now he realized he missed her when she wasn't around.

"Thought you'd like to do the honors of firing up the grill," she said, as he sauntered through the door.

"I'd love to do the honors." He placed the bag on her countertop. "Thought you might like some strawberries."

"Ooh, I love strawberries. Thank you."

The sadness in her eyes clouded her exuberance. "How are you holding up?"

"I miss him. I keep blaming myself for not doing something when he was in the process of being dognapped. And blaming myself for not keeping a better eye on him. It all happened so fast."

Trey took a step toward her, and she nearly fell into his arms. He wrapped her in an embrace, holding her gently. He closed his eyes and drew her closer, tenderly rubbing her back. "We'll find them, Carleigh."

"I keep praying," she said. "My mom really encouraged me the other day when she reminded me that it's in God's hands and that all throughout His Word, He tells us not to worry. To cast all our cares on Him. But sometimes it is a struggle."

"I agree. Our lesson in our men's Bible study last week was on Matthew 6:27, *'And which of you by being anxious can add a single hour to his span of life?'* I'm trying to give my concerns about Jaxx to the Lord. But you're right, it can be a struggle."

They remained in each other's arms for several minutes, the only noise their soft, synchronized breaths and the ticking of an oversized pink clock on the wall. Trey didn't consider himself a romantic guy, but he did have to admit he wouldn't mind if she remained in his arms for hours.

When Carleigh took a step back, his gaze found hers. When had he come to care so much about her? He inched forward and she did the same until their lips touched. He cupped her face and kissed her, not once, but twice, not wanting the moment to end.

Several minutes later, Trey flipped the burgers, then sat next to Carleigh at the two-person plastic table on her deck. The aroma of barbecue lingered in the air and Trey's stomach growled. "I could get used to this," he said.

"Grilling on the new grill I won at the Buy it All event?"

He chuckled at the sparkle lighting her eyes. "That and the company, of course."

Yes, he could easily grow accustomed to spending more time with Carleigh on a casual basis.

# Chapter Thirty-Four

AFTER THEY ATE THEIR hamburgers and vegged for a while on the deck, Trey left for home. Carleigh locked the doors, then settled into her nightly routine before bed. Trey coming over for a visit had been the perfect antidote to missing Sullivan Theodore, at least temporarily.

Curious how it wasn't that long ago she bemoaned the fact of having to spend more time with Trey. Now, she looked forward to those times they spent together, even if it involved the minivan, taking notes, or sitting next to each other in staff meetings.

While the weight of missing Sullivan Theodore never ventured far from her thoughts, Trey also claimed her attention.

The following day, Carleigh and Trey returned to Oakville Party Supply since Aubrey-Joan reported a man she thought was the dognapper had returned for some items. With the exception of *The Oakville Daily* minivan and Officer Zemski's patrol car, the parking lot was empty. "Maybe we can listen in on Officer Zemski's interview with Aubrey-Joan," Carleigh suggested.

"Good idea. I'm sure he wouldn't mind."

Trey held the door open for Carleigh and they strolled into the empty store. "I almost thought about how I needed to buy Jaxx another squeaky toy since Aubrey-Joan has some new inventory. But then I remembered..." His voice trailed, and Carleigh gave his hand a slight squeeze. She understood completely, since she missed Sullivan Theodore more than she could even express.

"Something happened to the bell. Usually, it rings every time someone enters the store," noted Trey.

She almost called to Aubrey-Joan as they continued toward the front registers, when Carleigh heard hushed voices from the backroom.

Trey held a finger to his lips. "Let's investigate," he whispered.

They crept toward the backroom, taking every precaution to step lightly on the wood floor.

Officer Zemski rested against the wall, presumably facing Aubrey-Joan, who was obstructed from their view. "I've always wondered what happened to us, Aubrey-Joan."

"I don't know. I think it was a misunderstanding."

Carleigh's eyes connected with Trey's. Were they hearing what they thought they were hearing? A serious conversation between Officer Zemski and Aubrey-Joan about their long-ago relationship? She wanted to tell Trey they really shouldn't be eavesdropping, but thought better of it. She'd always wanted to know the answer to Officer Zemski's question.

"I loved you, Aubrey-Joan."

"We were so young back then."

"Young, but in love."

Carleigh's heart warmed at hearing the sentiments between the two and she really hoped she and Trey would not get caught. Should they make some sort of noise to alert Officer Zemski and Aubrey-Joan of their presence?

"Do you think we could pick up where we left off?" Aubrey-Joan asked in a hushed voice.

"I don't see why not. It's worth a try at least."

Seconds ticked by before Aubrey-Joan spoke again. "Thank you for the potted plant. It's beautiful and means a lot to me that you remembered how much I love African violets."

"Some things are hard to forget. Like you. Let's give it another chance, Aubrey-Joan. See where things lead. We're older and wiser now."

Carleigh knew her eyes bugged out of her head and a quick perusal of Trey confirmed the tips of his ears shone like a beacon. Who knew Officer Zemski was such a romantic?

Guilt washed over her for meddling into such a private conversation. She tapped Trey on the shoulder and inched backwards. Hopefully, he would get her implied meaning about pretending they had just arrived.

He did, and he also took several giant steps back. They waited for a few minutes, then Trey called out, "Aubrey-Joan?"

A rustle of something and then Aubrey-Joan's shaky voice. "Uh, just a minute. I'm in the back room."

Trey tossed Carleigh a knowing glance and she smiled. Seemed as though love was certainly in the air these days.

Trey parked the minivan in its usual spot at *The Oakville Daily*. "Wow. What a day. First, Officer Zemski and Aubrey-Joan and their discussion about renewing their romance. Then the issue of the purported dognapper showing back up to purchase more items. I think it's really a matter of time before the police nab him."

"We can only hope so and that the dogs are all healthy and safe. What if he's sold them already?"

"I hope not. He's made some money already from the ransoms, even though the dogs were never returned as promised." Trey really hoped Jaxx and the rest of the dogs were being cared for. He sighed, not wanting to dwell on Jaxx's predicament. "On another note, what do you think about what we overheard?"

"Well, people have always wanted to know what happened between Officer Zemski and Aubrey-Joan. As the saying goes, there's no time like the present to rekindle that romance."

"True," said Trey. "And they're not getting any younger."

Carleigh tapped her chin with her finger. "Maybe we should write an article about love rekindled."

"Yeah…no. Too many lovey-dovey stories. We'll lose the male readership of *The Oakville Daily* if we keep publishing articles like that."

"But look at Officer Zemski. He's quite the romantic. Bringing her African violets, professing his love for her."

"Speaking of professing one's love, we should probably get back to our desks before Howard comes out here and finds us lollygagging in his classic vehicle."

Carleigh groaned. "Nothing could come between him and this old minivan."

"Except maybe donuts."

They shared a laugh, and Trey envisioned Howard eating box after box of donuts in the minivan. Thoughts of Carleigh flooded his mind. He liked her laugh, liked her smile, liked her. A lot. Hurriedly, before Howard could stroll outside to find them, his lips found hers. When they parted, he reminded himself that kissing Carleigh in the minivan couldn't last forever. "Well, should we go resume our duties as *The Oakville Daily* Duo before Howard finds us and demotes us to the obituaries?"

# Chapter Thirty-Five

TREY CROSSED FIFTH ONTO Main Street.

And that's when he saw it.

An older model white van. He squinted, trying to see if there was a license plate. "Wait. Is that who I think it is?"

Carleigh directed her full attention toward the vehicle, the only other one on the street, but a block away. "Yes, I think it is!"

Trey's heart pounded. "Should we follow him?"

"Let's do."

That's what he appreciated about Carleigh. She shared his adventurous spirit. "I'll hang back a bit so he doesn't know he has a tail."

"Listen to you. Sounding like you're an FBI agent or something."

He chuckled. "We'll see where he goes and try to figure out if it truly is the dognapper, milk and dog food thief, and gas thief. If so, we'll call Officer Zemski."

"Sounds good." Carleigh remained perched forward in her seat.

"Maybe you could avoid being so obvious."

"Says the one who is hunched over the steering wheel with his face pressed against the windshield."

Trey settled back in his seat just enough to avoid inviting suspicion.

"What if this is the guy who has stolen all the dogs? What if...oh, no. What if...I hope the dogs are all right. I really miss Sullivan Theodore." Her voice wavered.

The thought had crossed Trey's mind as well on more than one occasion. Life wasn't the same without Jaxx. Carleigh's usual over-the-top bubbly personality had been more subdued, and rightfully so in the days since Sullivan Theodore disappeared. He would do just about anything to reunite the dog with his owner.

"I miss Jaxx too. In the books and movies the dogs find their way back to their owner through blizzards, hurricanes, rough terrain, and hundred-mile distances. I keep thinking one day Jaxx will appear on the porch, his tail wagging, and life will be back to normal again."

"My heart breaks for all of the Oakville residents who've lost dogs in the past couple of weeks. I can't fathom someone causing such pain, especially to elderly people whose dogs are their only companions."

"I agree. The guy can't hide out forever, and we do have the ransom notes."

"But what good are ransom notes when he doesn't keep his end of the bargain? If our calculations are accurate, so far this guy has walked away with several thousand dollars and no one has received their dog in exchange for the ransom money."

Trey sighed. "Officer Zemski seems to think they're closing in on him. That's why we need to make sure this is him, and if so, alert Zemski so he can arrest this guy."

He followed the white van from a comfortable distance. They continued down Main Street, past the gas station and used car lot, past Oakville Real Estate agency, and past the golf course. The white van increased its speed, and Trey increased his speed as well, doing his best to stay somewhat hidden behind a blue sportscar with out-of-state plates.

"It won't do for this guy to see that *The Oakville Daily* van is following him. I sure wish Howard would have been a little wiser in choosing the color for the newspaper's primary mode of transportation."

"Hopefully the dognapper isn't especially alert. I mean, who drives down Main Street in a town where you're a wanted criminal?"

"Unless it's not him." The thought struck Trey more than once in the past few minutes. They drove by several houses as they entered a two-lane highway. The sportscar exited onto the first road to the right, leaving Trey directly behind the white van.

If this was the dognapper, how would they be able to follow him unnoticed to the place where he kept the dogs, rescue each one of the pets, and return them to their owners?

Yet, if they succeeded, Carleigh would be reunited with Sullivan Theodore and Trey would have Jaxx back.

And all would be right with the world once again.

Trey was doing an impressive job following the van, seemingly unnoticed. Carleigh did her best not to let the anxiety get the best of her, but even so, she bit her lip, picked at her chipped purple fingernail polish, proceeded to tap her fingers on the console, and resisted the urge to suggest Trey follow the van more closely. She didn't want to lose this one chance to rescue Sullivan Theodore and the other dogs.

She couldn't let her mind go there. *Lord, please let this be the dognapper and please let the dogs be safe. Please don't let him have sold them yet.* Tears blistered her eyes, as she recalled the first time she'd ever met Sullivan Theodore. She'd adopted him from a friend's litter of pups three years ago. There had been a choice of five puppies, but she knew Sullivan Theodore was the one for her when he perched at her feet, his furry face looking up at her in expectation. He'd tilted his head from one side to the other, as if to ask what the holdup was in taking him home. He won her heart that day.

A warm hand touched her arm. "Carleigh? You okay?"

"Yes. No." Her shoulders fell. "I just want Sullivan Theodore, Jaxx, and the other dogs to be all right."

"They will be. We'll get to the bottom of this."

The tenderness in the depths of his eyes as he tore them briefly away from the road to look at her, combined with the comfort in his touch reassured her. God was in control of the situation. She would have faith He would help them retrieve all the stolen dogs and return them to their owners, safe and uninjured.

With minimal warning, the white van took a sharp right turn onto a side road. Trey inadvertently drove past the road, stopped, did a quick u-turn, then again tagged along behind the white van. "I think he's trying to lose us."

"Don't let him."

"I'll do my best."

Dust rose from the white van's abrupt speed on the dirt road. Hopefully it obscured the clown's vision of the bright green van behind him.

"Hang on, Carleigh."

The minivan sped along, skidding on loose gravel as it passed acres of lush green farmland on both sides. Trey took a sharp turn and the front of the minivan went one way while the back end went the other, the tires almost seeming to peel away from the vehicle. Carleigh clutched the door handle.

"Sorry about that." Trey righted the minivan and resumed driving, following the puff of dust from the vehicle in front of them. He made the ascent up a hill and Carleigh gasped.

A red pickup was making a left turn onto Appleton Road.

They'd been following the wrong vehicle.

Trey slammed his hand against the wheel. "What? How did that happen?"

Carleigh closed her eyes and offered a prayer for guidance. How could it be that they were so close to victory, only to have it slip through their fingers? She scanned, first to the right, then to the left. There was no way they would ever find the white van in such a vast expanse. There was literally no one for miles, save the red pickup disappearing into the horizon and a tractor in the far distance.

Trey veered the minivan to the side of the road. "Now what?"

Carleigh caught a plume of dust in her peripheral vision. "Trey, look!" The white van skittered off in the opposite direction. Had the driver known they were behind him and purposely attempted to lose them by taking a covert turn somewhere along the way, unbeknownst to Carleigh and Trey?

With the expertise of a race car driver, Trey whipped the minivan around and stepped on the gas pedal. The vehicle lurched forward, as if to argue with the speed Trey demanded of it.

Trey crept slowly down the dirt road, attempting to keep his distance. The white van's dust dared to cloud his vision, but he kept urging the minivan forward. "Try calling Officer Zemski," he suggested. Adrenaline kicked in full force, and Trey knew if he had to, he could apprehend the dognapper. Confidence and reality warred in his mind, and he knew wisdom dictated they ensure the police were on their way.

"Hello, Officer Zemski? This is Carleigh Adams. Trey and I have located the dognap..." she sighed. "I lost the signal."

"Keep trying." Trey maneuvered the minivan around a pothole. The white van was still in his sights, and he squinted against the mid-day sun.

Carleigh dialed again. "Hello, Officer Zemski? Yes. We have located the dognapper. We're behind him now, traveling west on..."

"Let me guess. It cut out again?"

"Yes."

"The signal is spotty around here." Had the dognapper noticed them? Trey wished the minivan wasn't bright green. A camo green would have been more conducive to their pursuit.

"We're still on Hawthorne Road, right?" Carleigh asked, as she hit speed dial.

Trey nodded. "Yes. The dognapper is headed off Hawthorne onto..." He paused to catch his bearings on his location. He'd only been this way once. "West Road."

"Officer Zemski, we are on Hawthorne heading onto West Road. No, we won't. Yes, we will. Yes, we still see him. All right." She clicked off.

Trey accelerated on the straight road. "Is Officer Zemski on his way?"

"Yes, he called in the sheriff's office because we're in county jurisdiction. I promised we wouldn't approach the dognapper and that we'll be cautious. He's concerned we'll meddle too much and get injured or worse."

"He has a point. There's no telling what this guy will do. He's ruthless."

"Barbarous. Callous. Malevolent."

"What?"

"Nothing. Just describing the dognapper."

"Spoken like a true writer." He paused as a million thoughts rammed through his mind. "Hopefully Officer Zemski and the sheriff will arrive soon. There's no telling what this guy will do. He could flip out if he thinks we're threatening his plans."

Fifteen minutes later, they came upon what they assumed to be the dognapper's hideout. Tucked within a grove of trees, a rundown brown house stood adjacent to a dilapidated cinder block garage. They swerved to one side of the road behind some trees and killed the engine. "Let's update Zemski on our location."

Carleigh punched in the numbers. Hopefully, there was a signal. "Officer Zemski? Yes, this is Carleigh. We have located the dognapper's hideout. It's at the end of West Road, a brown house in a grove of trees. No, we won't. Yes, we will. All right."

"More warnings not to take matters into our own hands?"

"Yes, he made sure to remind me that we aren't to approach the dognapper, that we are to be cautious and aware of our surroundings, and that we sit tight because they are about fifteen to twenty minutes out."

"Could be awhile then since that fifteen-to-twenty minutes is going to feel like an eternity." Trey plopped back against the minivan driver's seat and blew out a pent-up breath. "We can't just do nothing," he muttered to himself, more than to Carleigh.

"From what we know, the dognapper is a vindictive person with a motive and strong desire to accomplish his nefarious intentions. He won't appreciate our interference."

"Appreciate it or not, I'm going to check on the dogs. I won't apprehend or even go near him, especially since we made a promise to Officer Zemski, but I do want to see where he's keeping the dogs and ensure they are all right." He squeezed Carleigh's hand. "We will get Jaxx and Theodore back."

"Are we even sure they're here?"

"That's what I hope to find out." He returned his focus to the dognapper's residence and rolled down his window with the hand crank. A mixture of barks and howls filled the air.

"I wonder where they are?"

"Not sure. Could be in the house or the garage or another location on the property."

Carleigh spied the villain. "Look! It's the dognapper!"

The thief obviously hadn't noticed them, but he did bellow a harsh "Shut up!" presumably to the dogs. He withdrew a cigarette from his shirt pocket and lit up, then proceeded to walk toward the white van.

"Is he leaving?" Carleigh asked.

Trey shrugged. "If he does, he'll know we're here because it appears there's only one way out."

The man instead popped the hood of the van and began to tinker with the engine.

Trey peered at his fitness tracker. Only a minute had passed since his last silent inquiry of the time.

The dognapper slammed the hood and kicked a tire on the van. He then stormed into the house.

"I think the dogs are in the garage," said Trey. "I'll take a peek while we wait."

"I'm coming with you."

"Carleigh, you know Officer Zemski would want you to stay in the van." Even as he said it, Trey knew he'd not win this argument.

"We're *The Oakville Daily* Duo, not *The Oakville Daily* Individual. I'm coming with you."

He chuckled. "All right. I guess I wouldn't want it any other way." He sobered. "Glad I have the right partner to undertake this mission, but we need to be quiet so we don't draw the dognapper's attention. There's a possibility he may have seen us, but if not, let's not make our presence known." He took both of her hands in his and began to pray. "Lord, please guide and protect us in this endeavor. Please go before us. In Jesus' Name, Amen."

Trey planted a kiss on the tip of Carleigh's nose. "Ready?"

"Ready as I'll ever be."

Carleigh savored Christian suspense novels. Not as much as the historical and contemporary ones, but close. What she did not savor was feeling like she was trapped in the middle of one.

Trey motioned Carleigh to follow him. *Lord, please keep us safe and please don't let me trip over anything.* She bemoaned the fact that she'd worn her sandals rather than tennis shoes.

Choruses of multiple dogs barking echoed through the air. Trey paused and tucked her behind him. His head on a swivel, he gazed to the right, then to the left, ahead of them, and behind them, then motioned for her to again follow him. "The garage," he mouthed, pointing to the block building hosting plentiful mold growing on its exterior.

Weathered barrels, piles of dog feces, a rusted piece of a derelict vehicle, and mounds of garbage encompassed their route. To the side, a heap of leashes, dog bowls, and a filthy bean-bag chair rested against a tree stump. Finally, they reached the garage. Trey peered into a broken window, its shards of glass creating a star-like design. "Take a look."

Carleigh stood on tiptoe and saw numerous dogs, several of whom she recognized, crammed inside the crowded garage. She searched for Sullivan Theodore and Jaxx. "I hope he's feeding and watering the dogs," Carleigh whispered. She again peered into the dismal environment. When she zoned in on their pets, tears misted her eyes. *Thank You, Lord,* she breathed, before taking a step back. When Sullivan Theodore's eyes connected with hers, she couldn't ascertain over the rowdy noises of the other dogs, but it sounded like her pet voiced a cheerful yip. "I see our dogs," she said.

Trey wrapped his arms around her, and Carleigh allowed herself to rest in his embrace. "It's going to be all right," he whispered in her ear.

But the peaceful reassurance was not to last. The reflection of the dognapper in the intact part of the window advancing toward them with a hammer in his hand captured her attention. "Trey, look out!"

# Chapter Thirty-Six

IN A MOMENT THAT would impress even Officer Zemski, Trey whipped around and placed himself between Carleigh and the dognapper. The dognapper continued toward them.

"I'll not have anyone ruin my plans," the dognapper bellowed, flinging the hammer toward Trey and Carleigh. They both dodged the tool, and it collided with the exterior garage wall.

The dognapper advanced, and the two wrestled in an all-out skirmish. Trey was clearly the stronger opponent, but in an unanticipated moment, the dognapper gained the upper hand. Trey struggled beneath him. They tussled again, Trey gaining the upper hand, and it continued on for what seemed like hours.

That's when an idea occurred to Carleigh.

She dashed toward the pile of dog supplies and grabbed a stainless-steel dog dish. Wielding it with all her might, she whacked the dognapper. He moaned and fell over, clutching his head. Trey assisted in the dognapper's descent to the ground. "Are you okay?" she asked, rushing toward him.

"Never been better," Trey teased, a glint in his eye despite a minor bloody nose. "Where did you learn to swing like that?"

"I might have played softball a time or two in grade school."

"Well, it came in handy. I'm impressed." He tossed her a crooked smile, and her pulse slid up another notch, if that were possible due to all of the excitement.

"How's the nose?" Carleigh offered a prayer of gratitude that Trey wasn't hurt worse in the altercation.

"Nothing a little time won't heal. Come on, let's tie this guy up and check on the dogs while we wait for Officer Zemski."

Besides having to dwell amongst numerous piles of feces, the dogs appeared to be fine. The reunion with Sullivan Theodore couldn't come soon enough. She snuggled her favorite pet—well, her only pet—and promised him all the doggy treats he could eat once they returned home.

"This has been a long time coming," said Trey, as he scratched behind Jaxx's ears.

Officer Zemski, followed by two county sheriff vehicles and an ambulance, arrived a short time later. "While I should lecture you two, I'll refrain. It could have been highly dangerous..." Officer Zemski paused. "Like I said, I'll refrain from the lecture. Dr. Hill from Oakville Veterinary Clinic will arrive shortly to transport all of the dogs and give them a look-over before we return them to their owners. I'll need to get a statement from both of you, and Trey, I'd like you to talk to an EMT about the nose before you two leave."

"Yes, sir," they chorused.

Trey wrapped an arm around Carleigh's shoulder. "Thanks for the dog dish clobbering. I wasn't concerned, but it did help."

Wasn't concerned? And she thought coveralls were a fantastic fashion statement. She stood on tip-toe and planted a kiss on his cheek. "You really had me scared for a minute. I'm just thankful you're all right. We can't be *The Oakville Daily* Duo if there's only one of us."

Carleigh proofread the article one final time before emailing it to Howard.

### "Serial Dognapper Captured and Dogs Freed"

After a harrowing time of disappearing pets, the mystery of missing dogs has been solved and the perp has been captured.

Delmer Addlesperger, fifty-eight, of Clarkton, was arrested Thursday on charges of grand theft and burglary. Other charges are pending, including theft charges at Buy it All, Oakville Thrift Store, and Oakville Gas Mart.

Thankfully, all dogs were accounted for and in reasonable health.

"He dognapped my beloved Sunny from my own front porch while I watered the rosebushes in my backyard," lamented Lil. "If a front porch isn't safe anymore, what is?" Sunny apparently had been dognapped and hidden in a shoebox to avoid suspicion. Addlesperger used a variety of methods, including shoeboxes, totes, duffle bags, toys, and treats.

Our very own Trey, who is one half of *The Oakville Daily* Duo was disturbed to discover his German shepherd, Jaxx, was enticed by a chew toy laced with a sleep aid. "Jaxx would have never gone with someone otherwise. He's a friendly dog, but he has discernment," Trey said. Fortunately, Jaxx did not suffer any permanent damage from the sleep aid.

"As for Stella, she is very choosy who she would go with," commented Mrs. Bassanelli, whose poodle was also stolen. "How that nasty man captured her is still a mystery to me. All I know is that Stella is in therapy for the trauma she suffered due to the conditions she was forced to endure."

Mrs. Moeller left her bulldog, Wrinkles, in her car while she made a pitstop into the craft store. "I went into the store to buy some yarn for my yarn ball bookmarks. I'm selling them during the outdoor farmer's market later this month in case

371

anyone is interested. When I returned, Wrinkles was gone. I knew he couldn't have gone far. He's just not that fast on his feet because he's rather portly."

Addlesperger apparently had experience with canines. According to a source at Clarkton Veterinary Clinic, Addlesperger was a former employee. "He worked for me for nearly a year as an assistant," said Dr. Nichols, Clarkton's only vet. "I discovered he was practicing veterinary medicine without a license and I had to fire him. Needless to say, he was not happy about the job termination. I received threatening phone calls and he also egged, toilet papered, and vandalized my clinic soon after. He served some jail time for those offenses."

Indeed, it appears from preliminary investigations that Addlesperger was seeking revenge by stealing dogs in Oakville, forty-five miles away. "He was also seeking an easy way to make money," said Officer Zemski, "by asking for a thousand dollars in ransom money and subsequently planning to sell the dogs to new owners, rather than returning them in exchange for the ransom money. Addlesperger evaded law enforcement a couple of times, including once at the Oakville Fun Park. He had it all planned out, and it was a rather clever plan."

However, not clever enough to keep this purported criminal from being discovered.

Addlesperger was found in an abandoned house near the county line with nearly two dozen dogs. Officer Zemski, who was called to the scene after *The Oakville Daily* Duo discovered the covert location, was appalled at what he discovered. "The location was filthy, but thankfully, the dogs were fed and given water. Addlesperger had a motive in keeping the dogs healthy for the buyers and had scheduled to sell several of the dogs in the next two days, contingent upon him accepting offers from interested buyers. He never had any plans to return the dogs, despite his letter to *The Oakville Daily* indicating otherwise. I am thankful we found the dogs when we did. Had the sales gone through, we may not have been able to locate the dogs, as many of the buyers were from out of state."

Interestingly enough, all but eight of the dogs who were dognapped had attended Stella's birthday party a few months ago. Addlesperger dressed as a clown and offered his photography services. "I thought he was just the most despicable man," said Mrs. Bassanelli, who hired him for the party. "He went by the name 'No Name' and lacked any sort of jovial behavior. I knew I would never hire him again based on his unpleasant disposition, but I never imagined he could be corrupt." Addlesperger recorded names and addresses of the dogs from their owners so he could supposedly mail the photos of the dogs. "He had a motive, for sure," continued Mrs. Bassanelli. "What a horrid man."

The remaining eight dogs were dognapped from Clarkton and were owned by customers of the Clarkton Veterinary Clinic.

Oakville residents can now rest easy thanks to some savvy investigative techniques from Oakville PD and *The Oakville Daily* Duo. "We're fortunate here in town that we all look out for each other," said Officer Zemski, who is up for awards for Police Officer and Detective of the Year the fourth year running. "Hopefully we'll never have to face such an atrocity again."

For indeed, residents are hopeful that things will return to normal now that Delmer Addlesperger has been arrested.

# Epilogue

## One Year Later

CARLEIGH COMPLETED THE ARTICLE and perused it one last time.

"Oakville Returns to Normal"

By Carleigh Montgomery

Things are much calmer in Oakville these days. Yesterday, a jury found Delmer Addlesperger of Clarkton guilty on multiple counts. The dogs involved in the dognapping scheme have all recovered and are doing well with their owners.

"I'm so thankful Stella was found safe," said Mrs. Bassanelli. She recently threw a doggy carnival for Stella and all of her friends and their people. It was an astounding success.

In other news, as *Oakville Daily* readers are aware, love is in the air at *The Oakville Daily*. Carleigh and Trey, otherwise known as *The Oakville Daily* Duo, recently married in a ceremony at Oakville Community Church with Pastor Gehrig officiating. Nearly all of Oakville's residents attended the ceremony. Karen's Bakery provided the wedding cake and Louella's Flowers and Gifts provided the floral arrangements. Sullivan Theodore and Jaxx, happy to be brothers now, wore matching blue plaid shirts and coordinating bow-ties.

Speaking of Louella—she and Lew renewed their vows on the beach in Hilton Head, South Carolina. This is the second marriage for both of them. "I really am quite fond of this guy," Louella said of both her first and second husband.

Last week, Chip at *The Oakville Daily* popped the question to his coworker, Lindy, and they have set a wedding date for next July. Officer Zemski, in a covert operation with the assistance of area residents, presented Aubrey-Joan with a sparkling engagement ring in honor of their upcoming nuptials.

Other *Oakville Daily* staff happenings include Howard's recent award for Best Small Town USA Newspaper Editor. He won a weeklong vacation for he and his wife, Karen, to the Annual Newspaper Owner's Convention in Florida. In addition, the town rallied around him and presented him with a gift box of goodies from Oakville merchants. Howard's employees and subscribers alike agree there is no one more deserving of this prestigious award.

Margie announced she and her husband were soon to be grandparents again. "I'm ecstatic," she commented.

Bubba and his intern, Justin, recently attended a printing press seminar in a neighboring county, where they learned all of the new press techniques for the changing times. They will use their knowledge to print even more papers, given that *The Oakville Daily's* subscriber base has grown in recent months.

We at *The Oakville Daily* are humbled by our readers and subscribers. Thank you for your support.

Carleigh hit the "send" button and emailed the article to Howard. Normally, they didn't write articles highlighting the staff's private lives, but with all that occurred recently, Howard felt the town of Oakville deserved an update.

She studied the three framed photos on her desk. One was of just her and Trey on their wedding day. Another of their wedding included her and Trey, Mom and Dad, and Trey's parents and brother. The last photo was of her, Trey, Sullivan Theodore, and Jaxx. She smiled at how her relationship with her one true love all started with the naughty Sullivan Theodore escaping and venturing into Trey's house via the doggy door.

Carleigh surveyed the office, casting a glance at each of her coworkers. She enjoyed her job working for Howard, and it gave her valuable writing experience. Especially in light of the fact Briar Salazar at Heimisson Christian Publishing House offered her a three-book contract, securing her dream to become a novelist.

Her eyes connected then with Trey's, and he came over and brushed her cheek with a kiss. "How is the article coming, Mrs. Montgomery?"

"It's finished and sent to Howard. It's a different article than we usually write, but I think I covered everything in updating Oakville residents. How are the photos coming along?"

He pulled a chair beside her and wrapped an arm around her shoulder. "Just about finished." He paused. "What do you say we go out for ice cream at the park after work with the dogs?"

"Sounds like a date and the perfect ending to a perfect day for *The Oakville Daily* Duo."

Trey scanned the office then. He hastily placed a kiss on her waiting lips. "More kisses later," he winked.

Carleigh smiled and leaned in to his embrace. Who knew she and the former inspiration for the antagonist in her book would find love in the headlines?

# Author's Note

It was a stressful time in our world when I set out to write *Love in the Headlines* in the latter part of 2021. I wanted to create a lighthearted and fun book that could temporarily take the reader's mind off all the negative news we are bombarded with on a daily basis. I endeavored to write a tender romance with plentiful humor where the reader would solve the mysteries and know immediately who the "culprits" were while watching the characters attempt to figure it out.

Those who are familiar with my writing know I spend a lot of time in the late 1800s penning Christian historical romances, but I also manage to meander into the present from time to time. *Love in the Headlines* is my third Christian contemporary romance and joins the ranks of another full-length novel and a novella. There is another contemporary on the horizon. Stay tuned.

An author's life is never dull and we really should double as investigators no matter what genre we write. Over the years, I've been fortunate to interview people for all sorts of scenes in my contemporary and historical books. For *Love in the Headlines*, I had to make a phone call to a nearby town about the same size as Oakville to discuss police procedure.

The woman who answered the phone was very gracious. I explained I was an author writing a story about dogs being dognapped and asked the process of investigating such a matter. She answered, "Dognapped? Wow. This is a really weird call." I told her I thought about emailing instead, but she reassured me the phone call was the best route. I wondered if after we hung up she announced to her coworkers, "You will never believe the call I just received!"

Long story short, among other items, she confirmed that Officer Zemski could easily double as both a patrol officer and an investigator and that if it was a serious enough crime, other agencies could be brought in. It would be treated as a theft, just as I suspected.

We shared several good laughs during the duration of my call. I'm always super appreciative of those who take the time to answer the sometimes-bizarre questions of writers.

Another hilarious moment was when in final proof-reads it was discovered I had referred to "Chip" as

"Chirp." Oops! I'm thankful for dedicated editors who find these errors before the book goes to publication.

The newspaper, town, and awards and achievements in the book are fictional. But what if...what if there were a town like Oakville—a small, close-knit, American town where everyone knows everyone else. A place where faith and church are important. A slow-paced town where the newspaper's main goal is to provide a family-friendly news outlet and everyone is excited when their photos or stories are featured. As Howard, the owner, mentioned, "We should have an entire cache of great photos and well-written articles that will cause parents, grandparents, aunts, uncles, and everyone twice removed to purchase copies of *The Oakville Daily*."

I hope you enjoyed reading this book with its tender romance, faith, and abundant humor as much as I enjoyed writing it. I'll be honest when I say that Carleigh, Trey, Sullivan Theodore, Jaxx, Howard, Chip, Lindy, Mrs. Bassanelli, and the rest of the gang were some of my favorite characters to write. Thank you for sharing them with me.

# The Inspiration Behind Love in the Headlines

When the idea for *Love in the Headlines* popped into my head, I knew I wouldn't have to go far to find the inspiration for Sullivan Theodore IV, the spunky and mischievous shih tzu in the story.

For, once upon a time, a little white puppy needed a home.

From the second my niece and nephews walked through the door with him, Sulley Jaxx became more than just a pet. He became a member of the family.

It's definitely not uncommon for dogs to become members of families. However, Sulley's adoption became even more special because of his new family.

Years ago, my mom suffered a serious accident and she subsequently became wheelchair-bound. Unable to live the active life she once did, she and my dad were blessed to be able to move into the "mother-in-law apartment" of my sister and brother-in-law's house.

My niece, Ally, has been diagnosed with the autoimmune disorder, POTS, which can, at times, seriously interfere with her daily activities.

Enter Sulley.

My mom and Ally have what could only be considered as a "joint custody" arrangement. While Sulley's favorite person is Ally, he is also quite partial to snuggling with my mom in her chair, and truly, my mom spoils him and lets Sulley get away with *everything*.

Sulley begs treats off a big softie known as my dad, aka Poppy to his grandchildren, and Sulley runs like the wind with my nephew, Kolten. He recently gained a new admirer when my nephew, Seth, and his wife, Autumn, had their baby daughter.

And the inspiration behind the newspaper reporters? Back when video cameras were big, clunky, and oversized, my sister, cousin, friends, and I pretended to be reporters. We'd report and record the news, including some fun and very fabricated stories. Sometime I'll have to do an archeological dig and locate those old VHS tapes.

I also wrote "articles" with friends and co-workers at my after-school job as the main characters of those articles. On numerous occasions, we would sit in the breakroom with its slanted floor and laugh at new "article" ideas. I wanted to be a reporter for a time and was blessed to be a photojournalist when my daughters were little. That launched my career as an author, my dream since I was in second grade.

# Acknowledgments

To my family. I can never thank you enough for your encouragement, support, and patience as I put words to paper. I'm so grateful for you. An especially huge thank you as I straddled present day and the 1800s to develop two stories at once.

To my husband. Thank you for your confidence in me as I pursue this dream.

To my daughters. Thank you for taking the time to read my rough drafts (sometimes *very* rough) and offering feedback. Your insight is invaluable.

To my Penny's Peeps Street Team. Thank you for spreading the word about my books. I appreciate you all so much!

To my readers. May God bless and guide you as you grow in your walk with Him.

And, most importantly, thank you to my Lord and Savior, Jesus Christ. It is my deepest desire to glorify You with my writing and help bring others to a knowledge of Your saving grace.

*Let the words of my mouth and the meditation of my heart be acceptable in your sight, O Lord, my rock and my redeemer. – Psalm 19:14*

If you enjoyed this glimpse into the lives of Carleigh and Trey, please consider leaving a review on your social media, Amazon, Goodreads, Barnes and Noble, or Book-Bub. Reviews are critical to authors, and those stars you give us are such an encouragement.

Sign up for Penny's newsletter and receive book and writing updates, encouragement, notification of current giveaways, occasional freebies, and special offers. Newsletter frequency is twice a month.

Coming soon exclusively for newsletter subscribers—the free short story starring Frederick Morton from *Love's New Beginnings* in the Wyoming Sunrise Series. You can sign up now and I'll let you know when it's available. Stay tuned!

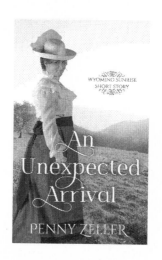

**Read a sneak peek from**

# Love Under Construction

**Chokecherry Heights**

*Book One*

**She builds websites.**

**He builds houses.**

**Together, can they build a family for two orphans?**

# Love Under Construction

## A Sneak Peak

TEARS PRICKED IRELYNN BRADY'S eyes. "Please help me," she whispered. Not her first prayer for this situation, and likely far from being her last.

Because God's help was the only way she had any hope of handling the insurmountable task set before her.

Irelynn gripped the steering wheel and glanced in the rearview mirror. The children in the back seat had fallen asleep, exhausted from their hectic day. Their sweet round faces weren't the only thing that reminded her she must succeed.

It was also the promise she'd made to their mother, Nicole.

Raindrops splattered on the windshield, and Irelynn flipped on the switch for the windshield wipers. If only the noise of the wipers, combined with the pattering rain, could drown out the emotions that warred within her.

The death of her best friend.

Suddenly becoming a single mom to twin three-year-olds.

A house too small for the unanticipated addition to her family.

And that pesky nemesis, Quinton Gregory, thrown into the mix for good measure.

A woman's voice on the radio interrupted her thoughts. "The scripture verse of the day is from Philippians 4:13. *'I can do all things through Him who strengthens me.'*"

The comfort from God's Word seeped deep into her heart, and she shoved aside a momentary niggle of apprehension at the stack of burdens that had landed in her lap. The past days had been challenging and turbulent and had left Irelynn wondering how she'd ever succeed at the new role in her life. But succeed, she must.

For the young innocent lives now in her care depended on it.

Moments later, Irelynn inhaled the scent of rain as she hoisted the children, one at a time, into the house. She tucked in one, then the other, into their toddler beds that she'd moved from Nicole's house and into her own room. The two remained sleeping, although Max stirred and mumbled "Mama" in his sleep.

Irelynn's heart broke. She had no right to complain when these children had lost so much.

She was about to dash to her car to retrieve her purse and the kids' overnight bags when her phone rang. She recognized the number and grabbed it before the ring tone could awaken the twins.

"Hello?"

"Irelynn?"

"Hi, Jamie."

"Do you have a minute?"

"Sure." Irelynn stepped back onto the porch and watched the torrential downpour. Better to be out here in the weather beneath the protective porch roof than inside fearing she'd awaken the twins.

"As you know, business has slowed as of late."

Irelynn held her breath and braced herself for Jamie's next comment.

"As such," her boss continued, "I'll have to cut your hours to part-time for the foreseeable future. Dan is doing some marketing in the hopes of drumming up business, but it'll probably be a while before we see the fruits of his labor."

Irelynn swallowed hard. She needed this job, especially now that she was partially responsible for Mia and Max.

"Irelynn, are you still there?"

She took a deep breath. "I'm still here."

"Good. Look. I know this comes at a bad time, but we are hopeful it's only temporary. I would completely understand if you needed to find a different job with more hours."

"Thank you, I appreciate that." What else could she say? Yes, she needed a job with more hours. A new mortgage and family didn't afford her many options when it came to finances.

The conversation ended, and Irelynn clicked off. Could things get any worse?

Tears flowed freely then, and Irelynn lifted another prayer heavenward. How could she support the twins on her now meager income? She couldn't...wouldn't let Nicole down.

Doing her best to shove the concerning thoughts aside, Irelynn dodged out to the car for the items she'd sought to retrieve before the phone rang. The sound of a vehicle driving down the road captured her attention. Squinting, she realized it was just who she did not want to see.

*I have to see him twice in one day?*

The newer model pickup truck pulled into her driveway behind her car, and Mr. Arrogance himself stepped out of the truck and into the rain. Irelynn took cover on the porch. What could the man possibly want?

Then her eyes settled on something held loosely in his grasp. Mia's baby doll.

Quinton Gregory stepped onto the porch and shook the rain from his blond hair. "Mia forgot this."

"They're sleeping, so I'll give it to her."

He looked as though he didn't believe her. "All right."

Quinton seemed to see right through her. Could he tell that she'd been crying? More like sobbing. She absolutely, positively, would not let him know that there had been times in the past few days when she'd felt as though she was on the brink of failure.

"Thank you," Irelynn said, taking the doll from him.

Quinton nodded, but said nothing. Instead, he sprinted back to his truck through the downpour of rain without so much as a backward glance in her direction.

What were the odds that the man who had stood her up on their first and only date would be the one with whom she'd have to share custody of two children?

# About the Author

Penny Zeller is known for her heartfelt stories of faith and her passion to impact lives for Christ through fiction. While she has had a love for writing since childhood, she began her adult writing career penning articles for national and regional publications on a wide variety of topics. Today, Penny is the author of over a dozen books. She is also a fitness instructor.

When Penny is not dreaming up new characters, she enjoys spending time with her husband and two daughters, camping, hiking, canoeing, reading, running, cycling, gardening, and playing volleyball.

She is represented by Tamela Hancock Murray of the Steve Laube Agency and loves to hear from her readers at her website, www.pennyzeller.com, and her blog, www.pennyzeller.wordpress.com.

Social Media Links: https://linktr.ee/pennyzeller

If you love Penny's contemporary romance
novels, travel back in time and check out
her Christian historical romances.

*Some memories are best forgotten...*

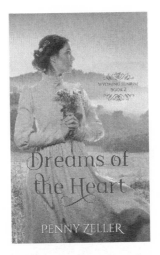

*Sometimes the hardest battles take place in the heart.*

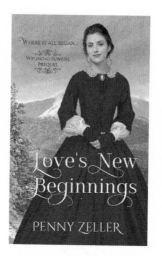

*Where it all began...*

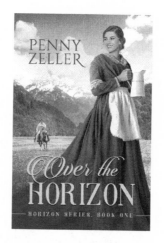

*A most unusual proposal...*

Made in the USA
Columbia, SC
07 April 2023

15014476R00245